P9-EJJ-336

BOOKS BY ILAN STAVANS IN ENGLISH

Fiction:
The One-Handed Pianist and Other Stories

Non-Fiction:
Art & Anger: Essays on Politics and the Imagination

Bandido: Oscar 'Zeta' Acosta & the Chicano Experience

The Hispanic Condition:
Reflections on Culture and Identity in America

Imagining Columbus: The Literary Voyage

Editor:
Tropical Synagogues:
Short Stories by Jewish Latin American Writers

Growing Up Latino: Memoirs and Stories
(co-edited with Harold Augenbraum)

The Oxford Book of Latin American Essays

Translation:
Sentimental Songs, by Felipe Alfau

PROSPERO'S MIRROR

A TRANSLATORS' PORTFOLIO OF LATIN AMERICAN SHORT FICTION

EDITED
BY
ILAN STAVANS

CURBSTONE PRESS

Printed in the United States on acid-free paper by Royal Book Manufacturing
Cover design: Les Kanturek

This book was published with the support of the Connecticut
Commission on the Arts, the National Endowment for the Arts,
and donations from many individuals. We are very grateful for
this support.

Library of Congress Cataloging-in-Publication Data

   Prospero's mirror : a translators' portfolio of Latin American short fiction /
   edited and with an introduction by Ilan Stavans. — Bilingual ed.
        p.   cm.
     ISBN 1-880684-49-7 (alk. paper)
     1. Short stories, Spanish American. 2. Short stories, Spanish American—
   Translations into English. 3. Spanish American fiction—20th century.
   4. Spanish American fiction—20th century— Translations into English.
   I. Stavans, Ilan.
   PQ7087.E5P76   1997
   863'.01089868—dc21   97-16443

published by
CURBSTONE PRESS   321 Jackson Street   Willimantic, CT 06226
          phone: (860) 423-5110   e-mail: curbston@connix.com
               http://www.connix.com/~curbston/

TABLE OF CONTENTS

TRANSLATION AND IDENTITY
by Ilan Stavans

The original is unfaithful to the translation.
— Jorge Luis Borges,
"Sobre el *Vathek*, de William Beckford" (1943)

I.

Translation, its delicious traps, its labyrinthine losses, was at the birth
of the Americas, and I am often struck by the fact that to this day, the
role language played during their conquest is often minimized, if not
simply overlooked. There's little doubt that without the "interpreters,"
as Hernán Cortés referred to them, an enterprise of such magnitude
would have been utterly impossible. Although *la conquista* was a
military endeavor encompassing social, political, and historical
consequences, it was also, and primarily, a verbal occupation, an
unbalanced polyglotic encounter. More than a hundred different
dialects spoken from the Yucatán peninsula to modern-day California
were reduced to silence and Spanish became the ubiquitous vehicle of
communication, the language of business, government, and credo.
Through persistence and persuasion, Cortés and Pizarro, to name only
the most representative warriors, took control of the powerful Aztec
and Inca empires. Cortés, for one, was astute enough to convince their
unprepared, naive monarchs, Moctezuma II and Cuauthémoc, that
he indeed was Quetzalcóatl, the Plumed Serpent, a bearded god the
Aztec calendar had been prophesying as a triumphant sign for the
coming of a new age. But to make themselves understood, he and his
Spaniard knights were constantly looking for a very special type of
soldier: the translator, capable of using words as weapons, reading
not only the enemy's messages but its mind as well, someone who, in
modern terms, would be not only perfectly multilingual but, more
importantly, a cultural analyst able to explain one culture, one
weltanshauung to another. Only by enlisting a "word wizard" were

they able to achieve their goals; translators needed to be true loyalists, part of the invader's army, at once supporters and promoters who would eventually have a share of the gain and make victory their own.

These reflections recently came to mind during a pleasant afternoon reading of sacred Nahuatl poetry. Indeed, although I don't purport to be a specialist in pre-Columbian literature, my interest in the ancient cultures of the Americas has produced ongoing readings and book-collecting, and I was happily wandering through the work of Daniel G. Brinton, the first American ever to translate from the Nahuatl into English, when I was overcome by the obvious: the difficulty of making the pre-Columbian people accessible to modern readers. Their poems, an expression of their vision of time, their dreams and frustrations, have changed countless times in front of our very eyes; they are what we want them to be; and what one commentator believed they were is light-years away from the views of others. In spite of the many generous scientific discoveries, dating back to the early nineteenth century, about Macchu Picchu, Tenochtitlán, and other ruined population centers, the pre-Columbians are nothing but our own image reflected in a distorted mirror: the observer observing himself in others. From the moment it clashed with European culture to our fin de siècle Nahuatl civilization was betrayed and misrepresented, then renewed and reinvented by innumerable interpreters. More than five hundred years after their tragic subjugation, their world view remains a puzzle—alien, exotic, unclear to us—the product of adventurous scholars (mostly Mexicans) unmasking a certain facet, contradicting a predecessor, searching for lost sources. And although since World War II the new discoveries have been nothing but outstanding, the added collective efforts are still incomplete; it certainly doesn't manage to present a fair, comprehensive view of their complexity simply because the Nahuatl civilization was almost erased by the European invaders and finding clues to its identity is a challenge worthy of a superhuman detective.

All this signals the insurmountable impotence of translation, the act of bridging out by means of language. Obviously, finding such useful "bridges," such vital entities, proved to be an incredibly difficult task. For purposes of argumentation, let me focus on Cortés's conquest of Mexico. Bernal Díaz del Castillo, in his chronicle of the conquest of Tenochtitlán, recounts how, around 1517, two Mayans, Melchorejo and Julianillo, were captured in the Yucatán peninsula by Captain

Francisco Hernández de Cordoba. In spite of their shyness and introversion, which we would probably interpret today as simply a lack of desire to cooperate, they were forced to become interpreters. Translators in spite of themselves. To fit into their new role, they were treated better that other prisoners of war: after traveling to Cuba to answer questions by a governor anxious to know if their land had any gold mines, and thus passing the crucial test of a tete-a-tete with the highest authority, Melchorejo and Julianillo were asked to dress up and behave like Europeans; they were given their own hamlet in Santiago; they were required to attend mass and were indoctrinated in the ways of the Church; and, also, they taught as much oral Spanish as they could digest. But in spite of the intense training, their patrons remained suspicious of the Indians' ultimate motives and service, mainly because, as Díaz del Castillo puts it, Melchorejo and Julianillo were incapable of looking at you in the eyes. They had an obnoxious way of looking down, to the floor, not a sign of respect but to evade contact. And just as expected, when the interpreters traveled to Cozumel with the expedition of Juan de Grijalba, it was clear to many that the Spanish message was only partially being conveyed to the natives, if nothing because, after a friendly exchange, the enemy didn't show up for the next agreed meeting. The Spaniards, regardless to say, were very worried.

We know very little about Melchorejo and Julianillo. Unlike the military heroes of the time, these translators are but a passing footnote in history, their words overshadowed by the weaponry of those interested in action, in wealth, in fame, not in communication and understanding. Even if their skills were indeed questionable, they deserve some sort of remembrance; instead, their fate, I'm afraid, is the one commonly granted to translators: oblivion. While their death is actually recorded by Díaz del Castillo, it is done only in passing, without much fanfare; they have no monuments and their memory is never celebrated. Julianillo apparently died either of nostalgia or as victim of one of the many epidemics decimating the native population at the time. Melchorejo, on the other hand, had a more heroic, if also more tragic death: he changed sides around 1519, when he understood that Cortés's real intentions were disastrous. Rather than delivering his translation in a cold, straightforward, objective manner, after the crucial battle in Tabasco he took off his European costume, regained his Indian identity, and ran to his people to explain what he knew. But

his was not a happy welcome: after listening to what he had to say, the Tabascans killed him in revenge for his many lies, his betrayal, and his hypocrisy.

No doubt the most distinguished bridge between languages and cultures during the conquest of Mexico, at least the one mythologized since early on, was a woman whose name is as evasive as her biography but who, we know for sure, acted as an interpreter wholeheartedly and with very few reservations. Known as Marina, Malina, Malinalli, Malintzin, and Malinche, she was at once a translator, Cortés's concubine, an endeared presence among the Spanish army and Latin America's counterpart to Pocahontas in West Virginia. Some historians believe she was born in a small town some 40 kilometers from Coatzacoalcos, was sold as merchandise after her father's death, was a smoking matron, and became Cortés's mistress (she mothered one of his sons: Martín Cortés) after he stole her from a high-ranking official. Cortés himself mentions her often in his *Cartas de Relación*, and so does Díaz del Castillo in his chronicle. Whereas Melchorejo and Julianilo remain in shadow, Malinche is famous: her stature inspires and infuriates, so much so that Mexicans call *malinchista* a person who sells his country to foreign forces for his own sake. Malinche knew the value of sleeping with the powerful commander of the Spanish army: she was fluent in many native dialects and quickly picked up the rules of Spanish; but more than anything, she understood the role of translator as loyalist and charlatan: aside from interpreting, her function was to advance her lover's military purposes; her words were intimately linked to her body: one couldn't function without the other; the message and her personal beliefs were deeply intertwined. In short, Malinche personifies the translator as concubine. Scorned for years, Mexicans today perceive her as the true mother of the nation, the woman who used her body to betray her people, who incorporated European manners into her repertoire to incubate the mestizo race.

Malinche, of course, was never an impartial, objective interpreter; far from our modern view of what literary translators are called to do, she wasn't looking for aesthetic beauty, for honest communication across cultures. Her role was purely strategic: she misled and deceived her peers, and ultimately helped dismantle the Aztec empire; she used words as artillery to unveil the secrets of the Aztec mind and thus helped Cortés and his men appreciate the real strength of their enemy. But it would be a mistake to assume that her role as word wizard was

something new and alien to the Nahuatl and other autochthonous people. Interpreters such as her must have prevailed in Mexico between the late fourteenth and the early sixteen centuries. In order to interact, to do business, the many pre-Columbian cultures that populated Mesoamerica before 1492 were surely in need of interpreters. While a true *lingua franca* did not exist, dialects were considered more or less important depending on the force its speakers excerpted. Which means that the Nahuatls, the Mayans, the Otomis, and other groups, were somehow acquainted with the role of adapting their words for those unknowledgeable of their tongue. Yet all this can be an understatement if one fails to realize that, once aligned with the Spaniards, translators such as Malinche were involved in a sophisticated form of deception. They could see the military advantage the invaders had over the natives; they were witnesses to a catastrophe of immense proportions; and yet, more often than not their personal interests had more weight than the suffering of their people. It's the classical portrait of the scoundrel: once in power, the Spaniards would grant them high esteem and would celebrate them as heroes. And while these translators (mostly aborigines) are obviously not to be blame for the dynamite the Europeans fired against the native population, they certainly played a crucial role in their tragic eclipse. Since the idea of preserving one's past among the Nahuatl, where oral tradition was fundamental and an advance alphabet was still in the making, wasn't like Europe's, chroniclers, liberal friars and priests devoted to saving what was being demolished could not do enough to record the past and fully describe the present. Their own capacity to understand native culture was limited, linguistically and psychologically. Consequently, what we have left today is but a minuscule slice of ancient native Mexican civilization. Add the fact that since 1523 other so-called interpreters of Nahuatl civilization have contributed to tarnishing the scope through which we could begin to appreciate them: proselytes finding Christian imagery in ancient manuscripts, destroying and revamping old texts. To understand the implications of the conquest in Mexico, imagine who would we be today if only a twelfth of the *Divine Comedy* was all that was available from ancient and medieval Europe—and not in Italian but in a language totally forbidden to us.

II.

As a result, the corpuses of pre-Columbian literature available today are quite small. For argument sake, take Nahuatl poetry again as an example: what we have are no more than twenty sacred hymns, collected by Fray Bernardino de Sahagún; songs scattered in several annals and testimonies; the manuscript of *Cantares mexicanos y otros opúsculos*, collected by an anonymous priest, kept at Universidad Nacional Autónoma de México; and the manuscript of *Romances de los señores de la Nueva España*, at the University of Texas at Austin. Most of what we know about the Nahuatl people is a result of the intense scholarly studies of Angel María Garibay and Miguel León Portilla. The lack of familiarity with the original culture makes the translation process unfair and problematic: translations are first done into Spanish, and then to other European languages. A few exceptions occur: Eduard Seler, for example, has worked directly in German; and Daniel G. Brinton, the first ever to bring Nahuatl poetry out from its closure in his books *Rig Ved Americanus* and *Ancient Nahuatl Poetry*, both published in Philadelphia at the end of the nineteenth century. His work was based on the manuscript of *Cantares de los mexicanos*, which, as he stated from the outset, was an incomplete transcription by one Abbé de Bourbourg, signaling, once again, the innumerable hands under which this type of material has been exposed to. How much was a product of Brinton's own making and how much wasn't has been the subject of speculation. León Portilla, Seler, and Garibay have found his translations loyal if extravagant. And his anthropological obsession to compare the Nahuatl people to ancient India also puts him in trouble. But more than anything else, his erratic English makes for an interesting if questionable work. Still, Brinton's work is amazing in that it needed no intermediary language: from Nahuatl he went to English. Although León Portilla himself has recently published a collection of his own, *Fifteen Poets of the Aztec World*, where he translates to English material he collected in book form in 1967 and subsequently expanded at least on five occasions, which is immensely more reliable that Brinton's, his technique, yet again, had Spanish as the bridge language.

Correlating Brinton's work to León Portilla's can be a frustrating act. More than a hundred years of research and analysis run from the pages of one into the other. Brinton only had a segment of the Nahuatl

legacy in front of him; he had no predecessors to map his route; and more importantly, he was unable to individualize poets because other historical sources were still unknown. And yet, in spite of his many shortcomings, his Victorian English translations ought to be acknowledged because he happily inaugurated a tradition that is slowly expanding. His task as interpreter, perhaps unconsciously, was an attempt to undo what Julianillo, Melchorejo, and Malinche had helped achieve: the closing of the Nahuatl mind. But one should approach them cautiously: once we overcome the initial sense of joy from coming for the first time face to face with a universe long outshined, I cannot but encourage the reader to reach out for *Fifteen Poets of the Aztec World*, which identifies individual poets and comments historically and literally on themes and motifs: flowers, life as a dream, the cravings of the heart, the death of a monarch, the passing of time, etc. The effort to establish a link between the two translations will not be meaningless and will somehow help reduce the endless chain of misinterpretations Nahuatl literature has been victimized by. The work of Garibay and León Portilla has done much to uncover, to disclose what translators and interpreters during the colonial period and afterwards had actively misinterpreted.

Nowadays we thankfully have volumes such as J. Richard Andrews's *Introduction to Classical Nahuatl*, which begin to unveil the Nahuatl language and worldview for us. We are beginning to learn, for example, to what extent the Nahuatl people were people devoted to contemplation and the role poetry played in society. We have also been able to penetrate the oeuvre of a handful of Nahuatl poets, most importantly King Netzahualcóytotl (1401-1472) and Aquiauhtzin de Ayapanco (circa 1430-1490). Diego Durán, in his *Historia de las Indias*, described the Nahuatl poet as playing a crucial role among the elite: rulers were constantly surrounded by singers and dancers, and rhymes were taught to children in school. Concerts, sometimes from early morning to nightfall, were performed in front of a large audience and beloved poets, accompanied by melodious instruments, were asked to perform in public. If the importance of music, lyrics, and dance in modern Mexican villages is any sign, Durán's words must be true: people rejoice in fiestas and use poetry to recount individual or collective anecdotes and happenings. Sahagún, Clavigero, and Torquemada explained that Nahuatl poetry was divided into historical and fictitious plots. But Garibay and León Portilla have taken us much

farther: they explored the fiesta as ritual, analyzed the sacred hymns known as *Teocuícatl*, and made available what León Portilla calls *la visión de los vencidos*, the Indian accounts and eye-witness testimony of the conquest. After Brinton opened the door, they expanded our horizon.

But Brinton and his successors are as much interpreters, bridges in the tradition of Melchorejo, Julianillo, and Malinche. Brinton's language of reception, English, allowed him to open up, in his own terms, the pre-Columbian mind to Western civilization. Similarly, Cortés's and Pizarro's translators, albeit reluctantly, had made accessible to Europeans their own personal interpretation of the Americas by means of explaining in a rudimentary Spanish their non-Western linguistic codes. The overall result is nothing but a global misapprehension, one could even say delusion. This verbal maze can only be captured in full the moment one realizes that Hispanics and Brazilians today communicate in a language that is theirs only by imposition. The fact that they talk, the fact that they read and write in Spanish and Portuguese already carries along a degree of falsification. In order to insert themselves into Western culture, they have appropriated, or have been appropriated by, a communication vehicle that wasn't theirs in the first place. In short, as a result of its colonial history, Latin America, paraphrasing Robert Frost, is what is lost in translation. It is also what is lost in interpretation.

Literature, more specifically the art of fiction, is the magnifying glass which more clearly exposes the abyss between reality and language, world and word. Why have the region's artists and writers been so imaginative and its politicians so unimaginative? The answer, perhaps, is that in the eyes of foreigners the colorful, exotic, or to use the fashionable term, "magical," reality south of the Rio Grande has always been a field of dreams. We might not know much about the pre-Columbian civilizations but what is clear from the historical artifacts we have inherited from them (hieroglyphics, codices, vessels and architectural wonders), is that they had a florid fantasy life. André Breton once described Latin America as "a Surrealist Continent," a land were chaos and the unknown, where the instinctual and the unconscious, prevail—a land, clearly, essential unWestern. Others have added layers to his concept, describing it as "marvelous." But the Cuban musicologist and *homme de lettres* Alejo Carpentier, ins his famous 1949 prologue to *The Kingdom of This World*, tried to reverse Breton's

concept. After a trip to Haiti, he argued that Latin America was the perfect stage of *lo real maravilloso*, where the triteness of Europe was left behind, where the search for an imaginary utopia is mixed with astonishing surprises, where the world is always in a stage of unfinishedness. He realized during his journey "that the presence and authority of the real marvelous was not a privilege to Haiti but the patrimony of all the Americas, where, for example, a census of cosmogonies is still to be established. The real marvelous is found at each step in the lives of the men who inscribed dates on the history of the Continent and who left behind names still borne by the living: from the seekers after the Fountain of Youth or the golden city of Manoa to certain rebels of the early times or certain modern heroes of our wars of independence, those of such mythological stature as Colonel Juana Azurduy." And yet, to make the real marvelous accessible to internal and external observers, it is a requisite for it to be translated to a "standard" code of communication. When the Mexican thinker José Joaquín Fernández de Lizardi plots *The Itching Parrot*, when the Chilean poet Pablo Neruda shapes his masterpiece *Canto general*, when the Guatemalan Miguel Angel Asturias delivers *El Señor Presidente*, when the Brazilian mulatto Joaquim María Machado de Assis writes his *Epitaph for a Small Winner*, when Isabel Allende gives the final touches to *The House of the Spirits*, the appropriation of a non-native language has been completed to deliver a view of this side of the Atlantic to international readers, the very same readers educated by Ovid, Dante, Cervantes, and Shakespeare. The images might be original, but not so the verbal code used. In fact, we can even talk about a form of linguistic cannibalism: in order to be members of Western civilization, Latin Americans need to be initiated in, and then are forced to perfect, the language of the invader. Cannibalism, as a metaphor of the struggle to at once define and translate oneself to the rest of the world, is certainly not a new idea. It runs throughout the chronology of the whole hemisphere, acquiring different masks, being called by different names, depending on the context. In Brazil, for instance, Oswald de Andrade, while stationed in Paris in the twenties with his wife, painter Tarsila do Amaral, awoke to the possibilities of the so-called primitive art of his own country as a source of inspiration. And some years after returning home in 1923, he published the *Manifesto Antropófago*. Its central message, in the words of critic Edward Lucie-Smith, was that "Brazilian artists most devour outside

influences, digest them thoroughly and turn them into something new." In other words, to use the verbs and punctuation, the manners and excesses of Europeans ad nauseam until a refreshing view, a distinctive Brazilian approach to the universe, can be recognized. Translation as anthropophagy.

All this makes any translation from Spanish into English, or for that matter any other European language, an attempt at removing what was already once removed. If what Malinche conveyed to Cortés is already a falsification, a deformation, and interpretation, her words, or what she purportedly said, once they are translated from Spanish into another tongue, take the listener even farther away from the original source. By this I'm not suggesting, at least not in concrete terms, that whenever he writes, García Márquez, or any other Latin American literati before or after him, is, in essence, translating himself. His native vocabulary is his by subject of inheritance: he was born into, and raised in, Quevedo's language; and for that simple reason it's his as much as it's Quevedo's. One cannot forget, obviously, that, as a product of endless transformations, Spanish itself is a hybrid, a sum of part, an addition: its roots can be found in vulgar Latin, in Arabic, in Castilian and other Romance tongues of the middle ages and renaissance. Besides, as all other languages, Spanish is the property and product of its speakers, no matter who they have been and where they have lived. Which means that García Márquez, by virtue of history, is as much its owner as any Spaniard today. And yet, Aracataca, where the Colombian was born in 1928, was a landscape where pre-Columbian languages and dialects were used. That is, its usage necessarily implies the eclipse of other grammatical structures, subdued by external forces.

Furthermore, when the Spanish knights and Catholic proselytes arrived, they didn't only bring forth their physical presence but, also and more importantly, a whole set of values and traditions, which include, among a vast array of offerings, the novel and verse poem as we know them. In order for *One Hundred Years of Solitude* to be written in the mid sixties, its author needed to be immersed, in one form or other, in the European novelistic tradition: he had to know what the novel as cultural artifact is about, its purposes and limitations. He obviously had to be acquainted with at least a small number of early practitioners. For García Márquez to revolutionize the genre, he first

was required to be familiar with it—he was first required to impregnate himself in its European style and language. When writing it, he unconsciously, one could even say inadvertently, cannibalized a foreign artistic vessel and, even if it was his from his very birth on, he also appropriated an outside tongue.

What kind of collective identity emerges from this act of losing and regaining oneself in translation? A complex question. Since Cortés and Pizarro, the continent has been inhabited by a conflicted view of itself. Where does it belong, to the Iberian peninsula or to the native Aztec, Inca, Quechua, Olmec, Mayan, and other pre-Columbian world views? Spanish, no doubt, is spoken without the discomfort of knowing it is a borrowed language. And yet, the whole region lives in a permanent state of nostalgia, of longing for a past that is long gone but could perhaps be rescued, relived, renourished. Identity, then, as a schism, a division, a wound—a sense that, in the translation process, the original and the copy will never match.

III.

I should say at this advanced point that, while the two previous sections were devoted to the amazement and trifles of translation, my original intention in this introduction was to talk about something altogether different: the discovery of Latin American letters by United States readers. But as I began to write, I realized the topic was really of marginal importance when compared to a number of subdivisions: first and foremost, translation as a concept in the southern hemisphere; and second, the idea of discovering another culture by means of language. I was therefore forced to take a step back to reflect on the role played by translators during the early stages of the conquest, and then link their product—what they do—to collective identity. My argument can be summarized as follows: the birth of Latin America is also the overshadowing of many aboriginal tongues; in order to enter Western history, the continent has been forced to appropriate a foreign, non-native vehicle of communication; consequently, its collective identity is shaped as a hybrid (Cortázar used the image of the axólotl and Octavio Paz the salamander—a fish in permanent mutation). Obviously, this hybrid is not only cultural but linguistic, a sum of alien words, of apparently unrelated masks, used to define something emerging in a different verbal dimension. That's why it is incredibly

ironic that Hispanics and Anglo-Saxons share a common border: their intermingled histories are a succession of misunderstandings and abuse, a chronology of miscommunication and, like the 1523 conquest of Tenochtitlán, a loss in translation.

It has been repeated to exhaustion that the United States and the rest of the Americas are divided by a bleeding injury: the Rio Grande, an innavigable 1,880-mile-long river that keeps them apart. This isn't only a physical border but a mental and verbal one: to the north, a methodical, puritan culture, perfectly suited for its mathematical English; to the south, a culture of confusion using Spanish and Portuguese, ill-conceived Romance languages designed for romance, remorse, and melancholy.[1] Identity as a maze for Hispanics and as a progressive line for Anglo-Saxons. When the British puritans settled in the Thirteen Colonies, they didn't face a challenging power like the Aztec or Inca empires. Their encounter with the natives was largely a matter of reaching out to distant frontiers. Their enemy wasn't as well-equipped militarily, as philosophically sophisticated, as the populations found by the Spanish and Portuguese knights. Also, miscegenation, both genetic and verbal, was never a real issue, not in a scale comparable to Hispanic culture. The results are worldviews drastically opposed, visions hardly compatible with one another. As a result, the two have shared a *diálogo de sordos*, a conversation made of laws and treaties designed to ease the tension, to make more manageable the illegal immigration waves, the unfair economic pacts that constantly threaten to push these neighbors to a flagrant confrontation. Let's not forget that the United States, while calling itself, presumptuously no doubt, America, is also part of the Americas; but a very different one at that—forcing others to see her as different, superior, a class of its own.

And where are the Melchjorejos and Julianillos of the border, writers and translators attempting a concurrence? Shrieking on both sides. The literature produced in *el norte* has always been popular down the border, thanks to innumerable, often anonymous translators. Shortly after Washington Irving's 1828 biography of Christopher Columbus was issued in Great Britain, it was already available in Spanish, first in Madrid and Barcelona, immediately after across the

---

1. See my book *The Hispanic Condition: Reflections on Culture and Identity in America* (New York: HarperCollins, 1995).

Atlantic, in large urban capitals of the southern hemisphere. Along the same vein, Domingo Faustino Sarmiento's masterful *Life of Facundo: Civilization and Barbarism* evidences the impact of James Fenimore Cooper's fictional frontier dwellers in Argentina and Chile. José Martí and Rubén Darío, to name only two of the most distinguished *modernistas*, were not only well acquainted with, but strongly influenced by, Walt Whitman, Ralph Waldo Emerson and the New England Transcendentalists. Edgar Allan Poe was a decisive force behind the naturalist stories of Uruguayan Horacio Quiroga. All this proves that, by means of translation, Latin America has been well-equipped in following the intellectual and artistic trends of its neighbor up north. But by the early sixties, when John Dos Passos, Ernest Hemingway, and William Faulkner were ubiquitous names among readers in Bogota, Mexico City, and Montevideo, few if any in the United States knew anything about the literature of their southern neighbors. While a couple of bibliographies are available, no reflective census of what has been done in terms of Latin American literature in translation is yet available, a much needed enterprise that would help us understand the awakening of Anglo-Saxons to Hispanic and Brazilian cultures. Among the early enthusiasts was Daniel G. Brinton, whose translations of the Nahuatl into English, as I stated earlier, helped introduce, anthropologically and poetically, a forgotten civilization. Until the late twenties, Darío was probably the region's most distinguished man of letters, but he was far better known in Spain (thanks to his friend, Juan Ramón Jiménez) and only rarely was mentioned north of the Rio Grande. Quiroga's *Stories of the Jungle* appeared in London by Methuen in 1923, translated by Arthur Livingstone, but they failed to be reprinted in the United States. Few translators were active, and those that were had tremendous difficulty convincing editors to embark on south-of-the-border projects. An exception was Harriet de Onís, born in 1899 and wife of the Columbia University professor Federico de Onís. A folklorist fluent in both Spanish and Portuguese, de Onís was a crucial innovator in that she brought attention in English translation in 1935 to Ricardo Güiraldes' *Don Segundo Sombra*, and was also responsible for disseminating the works of Cuban ethnographer Fernando Ortíz, Colombian essayist Germán Arciniegas, Bolivian feminist Argentina Díaz Lozano, and the early novels of Brazilian Jorge Amado. Hers was a slow revolution: a colleague of hers, Earle K. James, brought out a translation of José

Eustasio Rivera's *The Vortex* in 1935, but it wasn't until the forties when her translations and those of other enthusiasts would begin reaching a less minuscule audience, often thanks to anthologies, which have served the role of offering an assortment of styles. (Very few and scattered ones were published from the twenties and forties, including Isaac Golberg's *Brazilian Tales* and Waldo Frank's *Tales from Argentina*, and Angel Flores's *Fiesta in November*.)

Mexico's vecinity to the United States, the interest by writers like Graham Greene, Mike Gold, and Katherine Anne Porter in the 1910 revolution of Pancho Villa and Emiliano Zapata and its aftermath, as well as the late thirties expropriation of the oil industry, brought particular attention to its native writers. The inventory, while not vast, is intriguing: Enrique Munguía's now dated translation of Mariano Azuela's classic *The Underdogs*, appeared in 1929, was followed by de Onís's 1930 translation of Martín Luis Guzmán's *The Eagle and the Serpent*; and then Katherine Anne Porter, whose own stories in *Flowering Judas* were set in Mexico, published in 1942 a translation, with preface, of Fernández de Lizardi's *The Itching Parrot*.[2] But not only Mexicans were in vogue: De Onís translated the Peruvian Ciro Alegría, a now forgotten novelist very popular before and during World War II. And in the forties Chilean María Luisa Bombal performed her own outstanding translations of *The House of Mist* and *The Shrouded Woman* in the late forties, a decade that also saw Mexican José Ruvueltas's talents appreciated north of the border. Bombal, perceived today as a forerunner of "magical realism," is the first renown Latin American writer to "refurnish" herself, to perform an act of self-translation. The practice would gain recognition several decades later, in part as a strategy by authors to escape being misunderstood and as an attempt to establish direct contact with editors. Among those who wrote originally in English, or "adapted" their own oeuvre, were Borges, with his "Autobiographical Essay," first published in *The New Yorker*; Manuel Puig, with his novel *Eternal Course to the Reader of These Pages*; Guillermo Cabrera Infante, with *Holy Smoke*; João Ubaldo Ribeiro, with *Sargent Getulio* and *An Invisible Memory*; as well as with Carlos Fuentes's essays in *Myself with Others*.

---

2. Actually, Porter cheated: it wasn't her translation but Eugene Pressly's, begun in Mixcoac and finished in Paris; she originally wanted to promote Pressly's work, but when, after polishing a bit, she showed it to some agents and was rejected, she decided to give her name to it.

It wasn't until the late sixties, as a result of Borges being awarded the Formentor Prize (he shared it with Samuel Beckett), Asturias receiving the Nobel Prize for Literature in 1967, and almost simultaneous to the explosive literary boom that brought international attention to García Márquez, Cortázar, Mario Vargas Llosa, Cabrera Infante, Donoso, and Fuentes, that things began to change, thanks in large part to the translators like Gregory Rabassa and Helen Lane, many of whom have been my teachers, mentors and friends. This volume is designed as a tribute to their mammoth effort. My purpose was to anthologize their extraordinary work, accompanying it by brief comments on their style and method. I invited them, the veterans and their pupils, the celebrated and the upcoming, to submit a short story from Hispanic or Portuguese America that, in their eyes, deserves attention but for one reason or another had failed to receive it in the Anglo-Saxon world. I also asked them to answer the following questions: Why and when did you become a translator? What's your approach to the craft: for instance, do you read the text a few times first and then write? At what time do you work; and what kind of relationship do you need to have with the author and her/his text to produce a satisfactory product (in your eyes, at least)? Why did you select this story when I first approached you about the project? The selection, then, had little to do with a single individual—it constitutes the preferences of each of the contributors, and thus, has an aggregated, companionship feeling to it. Although some of the writers included are familiar names, many are known to only a small elite of specialists. What is clear is that each translator has chosen a favorite author, and used them to display the best of their talent. Collating the original and its translation is a rewarding enterprise: it serves as a voyage through the mind of a translator struggling to go beyond literalness and encompass, through words, an entire culture. Also of note is the fact that Rabassa was alone in submitting a Brazilian writer. He delivered Trevisan's tale "to get recognition for Brazil in the Latin American context, and to bring some attention to Dalton, who has gone almost unrecognized...." Perhaps as a result of strong marketing forces controlling their craft, but also because of personal preferences and verbal fluency, the translators invited to participate in this project, almost mechanically, have once again isolated Brazil as a cultural zone, stressing the relevance of the Spanish-speaking nations surrounding it to a level that diminishes its stature.

In order to succeed in their task, many often strike relationships with the writers they translate. Rabassa, once again, believes "it often depends on a writer's knowledge of English and on political circumstances." Cortázar, he claims, was very helpful. "Most of the changes he made in *Hopscotch* were his own doing. García Márquez also gives you a free reign. He has an open mind, a sort of Joycean attitude. He accepts any kind of interpretation of his works, sometimes one way out in left field. When I would show him my work, he would say: 'That's right! that's right!' Which means that he is a real writer in the sense that he is unconscious about the moves he makes in his work and can see something he didn't know existed before. I had a beautifully dangerous triangular situation with José Lezama Lima in Havana. Because of the Communist regime, direct communication wasn't good. Also, he was difficult about his work. He was put in touch with me through Cortázar, a great admirer of his. I would send pages to Cortázar in Paris, and he would give them to a courier he knew in the Cuban embassy in Paris, who would go to Havana, give them to Lezama Lima, and then back to Paris and New York. We got going pretty well until about halfway through, when Cortázar become persona non grata. Communication stopped. By then I was enough into it, so I finished the job trying to stay as close to the author's intentions as possible. All this is to say that I do like to send manuscripts to the author. I would send to Vargas Llosa, for instance, and it would come back with a little note: 'No, I meant this instead of that.' He would give me a synonym, but it wouldn't work." But other translators prefer dealing with what Baudelaire once described as "dead literary corpses." That is the case of Toby Talbot, responsible for bringing to English Jacobo Timerman's *Prisoner Without A Name, Cell Without a Number*. Although, as she argues, working with living writers like Humberto Constantini and Luisa Valenzuela has helped Talbot resolve issues that fall in the gray-area gap between English and Spanish, the relationship can also become a bilingual tug-of-war. "Constantini fought over every epical y and we negotiated fiercely for inclusion or deletion," she recalls. Dead authors, on the other hand, "seem to be the ones looking most fixedly over my shoulder."

I hardly ought to say that it has been a rewarding privilege reading, talking to, and corresponding with them for a number of years—an apprenticeship that has taught me the harmony and discord between Cervantes's and Shakespeare's tongues. They are all inspired, passionate

professionals with the insurmountable conviction that through works of the imagination (theirs and others) they can bring very distant neighbors back together, at least temporarily. Rabassa, for instance, got into translation through serendipity. "When I was an Associate Editor of *Odyssey*," he claims, "my mission was to scout out good literary stuff from Latin America. As we also needed the items translated, I tried my hand at it and did quite a few of the entries. Then Sarah Blackburn from Pantheon Books asked me if I would consider translating *Hopscotch*, by Cortázar. I did some samples: I liked them, she liked them, and Julio liked them too. Happily, I went on to win a National Book Award in 1967. I have been translating ever since." He finds that translation "is little more than the closest possible reading of a text." Alberto Manguel, on the other hand, himself a novelist and anthology editor, believes that "translation is one of the most careful reading methods I know, and forces you to disentangle the text as you proceed. The translator sees the text in all its imperfections, all its faults of logic, all its mistakes and botched-up passages. The translator's eye is relentless. I believe that polishing the translated text requires more attention than reading the original. When the stars are kind, the translated text should read as if it had been written by a twin soul of the author in another language. A few times you succeed: Roy Campbell's translation of St. John of the Cross, for instance." Rick Francis thinks that "translations are the antidotes for provinciality and stultifying insularity. One can appropriate while translating, but to do so is to miss the marvelous opportunity to alter our language towards the foreign," whereas Suzanne Jill Levine, whose close collaborations with Cabrera Infante and Puig have brought her critical esteem, thinks that "it isn't surprising that many translators and writers are also musicians or music fans."

If, as Ezra Pound once stated in *ABC of Reading*, literature is news that stays news, translators have the capacity for renewing the news, for refreshing it time and again. Original works of art, once they enter the canon, cannot be touched; but translations often prove obsolete by virtue of their antiquated language.[3] Fresh new translations are required to satisfy new reading appetites. Which means that in the

---

3. I discuss the topic in "The Verbal Quest," *Art and Anger: Essays on Politics and the Imagination* (Albuquerque, NM: University of New Mexico Press, 1996). The piece is reprinted in *The Oxford Book of Latin American Essays* (New York and Oxford: Oxford University Press, 1997).

near future it is foreseeable that Rabassa's translation of *One Hundred Years of Solitude* or Donald Yates's faithful rendition of Borges's short stories, will be replaced by others, more akin to their time. The future Angel María Garibays and the Miguel León Portillas, with their useful academic tools, will unravel misunderstandings we are probably unaware of today. They will take us much farther, exploring rituals, analyzing attitudes, and making available a sort of visión de los vencidos for the next millenium. The energy and passion of this extraordinary group of contemporary translators, almost all of which are gathered in this book, will be seen as inaugural yet replaceable. But it won't matter. Guilty as they might be of distortion, the original opening up of a secluded universe, the championing of the Americas in the eyes of foreigners, exotic or otherwise, has already been achieved, thanks no doubt to their effort. They are the modern Melchorejo and Julianillo, direct descendants of Daniel G. Brinton. Reluctance has been left behind. They don't have to escape their patrons; on the contrary, they are wise, active participants in the translation encounter. There's little doubt that the region lives today in far less isolation, in far more dialogue, than say a century ago. Silence has been replaced by words, and words in one language have traveled to another. In that sense, Harriet de Onís and her successors are yet another crew of courageous explorers in the tradition of Sir Walter Raleigh and, why not, Alvar Nuñez Cabeza de Vaca: they reach out to the geography of the imagination; they penetrate latitudes forbidden to most people, they interpret, they make accessible the inaccessible—they help us be better by expanding our horizon. While the old saying, traduttore, traditore, applies in that their effort entails a degree of treason (in order to make an imaginary reality available, they have to falsify, to personalize, to adapt its message to their own language and culture, and adaptation necessarily carries along a degree of distortion), in spite of that, their vision has also been crucial to breach an abysmal gap: they reinvent, they enter an already furnished house and redecorate it, and their craft has particular significance precisely because it applies to a region whose birth has been perceived as a colossal misunderstanding, a chaotic melange of words, facts and acts. Ironically, what was once lost in translation during the conquista of the Americas can now be reconquered by the exact same means.

ACKNOWLEDGMENTS

This volume began when Steve Moore, senior editor at Dalkey Archive Press, invited me to edit a special issue of the *Review of Contemporary Fiction* devoted to translations from Latin America. The idea was tempting and it quickly evolved into a full-length book. I am grateful to him for his friendship and intellectual spark. Many other people also have been involved along the way. Wholehearted thanks to my student, Jennifer A. Mattson, for helping in the preparation of the manuscript; Bruce Wilcox at the University of Massachusetts Press, for editing the manuscript and offering insightful comments; Judy Doyle and Sandy Taylor, for embracing the idea the moment it reached their ears; and Margaret Sayers Peden, for offering guidance and writing an endearing epilogue. Thanks to each of the authors and their estates for granting permission to use their work. And of course, my unconditional gratitude to each and every one of the translators and authors, whose work serves me as model and map.

All royalties for this book will be donated to a fund administered by PEN-American Center to enhance and promote new translations from Latin America.

My introduction first appeared in *Michigan Quarterly Review* and was reprinted in my collection *Art and Anger: Essays on Politics and the Imagination,* Albuquerque, University of New Mexico Press, 1996. All translations are published with the permission of the translator. The Spanish and Portuguese originals appeared as follows: "La cena," *El plano oblicuo,* vol. III of *Obras Completas* by Alfonso Reyes, Mexico, Fondo de Cultura Económica, 1956; "El lugar de su quietud," *The Censors,* by Luisa Valenzuela, Willimantic, Connecticut, Curbstone Press, 1992; "Carta a Gianfranco," *Hierba del cielo,* by Marco Denevi, Buenos Aires, Corregidor, 1973; "Como una buena madre," *Viajando se conoce gente,* by Ana María Shúa, Buenos Aires, Editorial Sudamericana, 1988, translation first published in *Massachusetts Review;* "Oculten la luna," *Polaroids,* by Jorge Lanata, Planeta, 1991; "La música de la lluvia," *Las reglas del secreto: antología,* by Silvina Ocampo, edited by Matilde Sánchez, Mexico, Fondo de Cultura Económica, 1991; "Coto de caza," *Coto de caza y otros cuentos,* by Rubén Loza Aguerreberre, Montevideo, Ediciones de la Banda Oriental, 1993; "Incidente en la cordillera," *A View from the Mangrove,* by Antonio

Benítez-Rojo, London, Faber and Faber, 1998, translation first published in *Review: Latin American Literature and Arts;* "Movimiento perpetuo," *Complete Works and Other Stories,* by Augusto Monterroso, Austin, University of Texas Press, 1995; "La noche clara de los coroneles," *Pudimos haber llegado más lejos,* by Jorge Medina García, Tegucigalpa, Honduras, Editorial Guaymuras, 1989; "Three Nightmares," *The One-Handed Pianist and Other Stories,* by Ilan Stavans, Albuquerque, University of New Mexico Press, 1996, translation first published in *The Literary Review;* "Tres tiros na tarde," *The Vampire of Curitiba and Other Stories,* by Dalton Trevisan, New York, Alfred A. Knopf, 1972; "Mangos de enero," *Viento de agua,* by Jorge Turner, Mexico, 1977; "Con Jimmy en Parcas," *Cuentos completos,* Alfredo Bryce Echenique, Madrid, Alianza Editorial, 1985; "El cocodrilo," *Las hortensias y otros relatos,* by Felisberto Hernández, Montevideo, Editorial Arca, 1966; "Los camalotes," *El reencuentro: cuentos,* by José Carmona Blanco, Montevideo, Ediciones de la Banda Oriental, 1978.

PROSPERO'S MIRROR

La cena

The Dinner

Rick Francis, translator of Alfonso Reyes

Rick Francis taught at Washington University in St. Louis and now lives in Toledo, Ohio. He translated Julián Ríos's *Larva: Midsummer Night's Babel* and Severo Sarduy's *Colibrí*, among other Iberian and Latin American works. His interest in Alfonso Reyes, one of Mexico's most-respected intellectuals and foremost twentieth century *homme de lettres* (1889-1959), was aroused when, as a student, he read Reyes's story "La cena," written in 1912. He had known Reyes had been a poet, essayist, and classics scholar, as well as a career diplomat; that his translation of the *Iliad* was still considered the best available in Spanish; and that he was the author of *Visión de Anáhuac* and thirty other books on Greek mythology, Latin American history, poetry and criticism. But not until reading "La cena" did Francis become aware of Reyes's scattered attempts at short story writing. "I was first attracted to the story as an early example of Mexican dreamlike fiction," he said during a conversation. "As I read the story, it evoked in me the dreamy tone of Juan Rulfo's *Pedro Páramo,* and of Carlos Fuente's *Aura*, with which it shares a number of similarities of plot and structure. In the experimental fervor of the second decade of this century, a young Reyes reset a Gothic-style nightmare of reincarnation, loss of will, and encroaching enclosures in that distinctly modernist version we know as fantastic literature. The result is an open-ended constellation of fears that are no less disturbing when you tell yourself it's just a dream. No need for a crumbling mansion; with a twist on time and identity, electric streetlights are as unsettling as any fog-choked London gas lamps."

And what compelled Francis to translate it? He wanted to show his discovery, to let others see what he had seen in Reyes's work. And since no English version was available to teach "The Dinner" in the classroom—"a search yielded only one reference, to a 1917 publication more shadowy than the story itself, which proved impossible to track down"—he proceeded to translate it in the early nineties. Also, as a native of the United States, Francis had another reason to embark on the project. "Only a tiny trickle of non-U.S. works are published in this country, despite the astounding ubiquity of U.S. fiction and film abroad. This trade imbalance, ostensibly to our credit, is in fact a cultural liability. I believe the literary capacity of this language can be enriched by translating into it, and in fact the language needs it, as Madame de Stael thought Italian literature needed translations in the early nineteenth century. Translations are the antidotes for provinciality and stultifying insularity. One can appropriate while translating, but to do so is to miss the marvelous opportunity to alter our language towards the foreign."

Alfonso Reyes
LA CENA

La cena, que recrea y enamora.
—San Juan de la Cruz

Tuve que correr a través de calles desconocidas. El término de mi marcha parecía correr delante de mis pasos, y la hora de la cita palpitaba ya en los relojes públicos. Las calles estaban solas. Serpientes de focos eléctricos bailaban delante de mis ojos. A cada instante surgían glorietas circulares, sembrados arriates, cuya verdura, a la luz artificial de la noche, cobraba una elegancia irreal. Creo haber visto multitud de torres—no sé si en las casas, si en las glorietas—que ostentaban a los cuatro vientos, por una iluminación interior, cuatro redondas esferas de reloj.

Yo corría, azuzado por un sentimiento supersticioso de la hora. Si las nueve campanadas, me dije, me sorprenden sin tener la mano sobre la aldaba de la puerta, algo funesto acontecerá. Y corría frenéticamente, mientras recordaba haber corrido a igual hora por aquel sitio y con un anhelo semejante. ¿Cuándo?

Al fin los deleites de aquella falsa recordación me absorbieron de manera que volví a mi paso normal sin darme cuenta. De cuando en cuando, desde las intermitencias de mi meditación, veía que me hallaba en otro sitio, y que se desarrollaban ante mí nuevas perspectivas de focos, de placetas sembradas, de relojes iluminados... No sé cuánto tiempo transcurrió, en tanto que yo dormía en el mareo de mi respiración agitada.

De pronto, nueve campanadas sonoras resbalaron con metálico frío sobre mi epidermis. Mis ojos, en la última esperanza, cayeron sobre la puerta más cercana: aquél era el término.

Entonces, para disponer mi ánimo, retrocedí hacia los motivos de mi presencia en aquel lugar. Por la mañana, el correo me había llevado una esquela breve y sugestiva. En el ángulo del papel se leían, manuscritas, las señas de una casa. La fecha era del día anterior. La carta decía solamente:

Alfonso Reyes
THE DINNER

Translated by Rick Francis

The supper, that delights and enchants.
—St. John of the Cross

I had to run through unknown streets. My journey's end seemed to roll just ahead of my steps, and the appointed hour was already throbbing on the public clocks. The streets were desolate. Snakes of spotlight beams danced before my eyes. At every moment circular brick flower beds sprang up, and in the artificial light of night their greenness took on a surreal elegance. I think I had seen a multitude of towers—I don't know whether in the houses or in the flower beds—displaying to the four winds, four round spheres of clock faces illuminated from within.

I was running, spurred on by a superstitious feeling about the hour. If the clocks strike nine, I said to myself, before my hand is on the door knocker, something awful will happen. And as I ran frantically I remembered having run through that place at the same hour and with a similar yearning. When?

Finally the pleasure of that false memory so absorbed me that I resumed my normal pace without realizing it. From time to time, from pauses in my musings, I saw I was in another place, and new views unfolded before me: glowing spotlights, little plazas with flowers, illuminated clock faces... I don't know how much time elapsed while I slept in the dizziness of my anxious breathing.

Suddenly, nine resounding peals trickled over my skin with metallic chill. As a last hope my eyes fell upon the closest door: that was my destination.

Then to put myself in the right frame of mind, I went back over the reasons for my being there. In the morning the mail had brought me a brief and suggestive invitation. A street address was handwritten in the corner of the piece of paper. The date was yesterday's. The letter merely said:

"Doña Magdalena y su hija Amelia esperan a usted a cenar mañana, a las nueve de la noche. ¡Ah, si no faltara!..."

Ni una letra más.

Yo siempre consiento en las experiencias de lo imprevisto. El caso, además, ofrecía singular atractivo; el tono, familiar y respetuoso a la vez, con que el anónimo designaba a aquellas señoras desconocidas; la ponderación: "¡Ah, si no faltara!..." tan vaga y tan sentimental, que parecía suspendida sobre un abismo de confesiones, todo contribuyó a decidirme. Y acudí, con el ansia de una emoción informulable. Cuando, a veces, en mis pesadillas, evoco aquella noche fantástica (cuya fantasía está hecha de cosas cotidianas y cuyo equívoco misterio crece sobre la humilde raíz de lo posible), paréceme jadear a través de avenidas de relojes y torreones, solemnes como esfinges en la calzada de algún templo egipcio.

La puerta se abrió. Yo estaba vuelto a la calle y vi, de súbito, caer sobre el suelo un cuadro de luz que arrojaba, junto a mi sombra, la sombra de una mujer desconocida.

Volvíme: con la luz por la espalda y sobre mis ojos deslumbrados, aquella mujer no era para mí más que una silueta, donde mi imaginación pudo pintar varios ensayos de fisonomía, sin que ninguno correspondiera al contorno, en tanto que balbuceaba yo algunos saludos y explicaciones.

—Pase usted, Alfonso.

Y pasé, asombrado de oírme llamar como en mi casa. Fue una decepción el vestíbulo. Sobre las palabras románticas de la esquela (a mí, al menos, me parecían románticas), había yo fundado la esperanza de encontrarme con una antigua casa, llena de tapices, de viejos retratos y de grandes sillones; una antigua casa sin estilo, pero llena de respetabilidad. A cambio de esto, me encontré con un vestíbulo diminuto y con una escalerilla frágil, sin elegancia; lo cual más bien prometía dimensiones modernas y estrechas en el resto de la casa. El piso era de madera encerada; los raros muebles tenían aquel lujo frío de las cosas de Nueva York, y en el muro, tapizado de verde claro, gesticulaban, como imperdonable signo de trivialidad, dos o tres máscaras japonesas. Hasta llegué a dudar... Pero alcé la vista y quedé tranquilo: ante mí, vestida de negro, esbelta, digna, la mujer que acudió a introducirme me señalaba la puerta del salón. Su silueta se había colorado ya de facciones; su cara me habría resultado insignificante, a no ser por una expresión marcada de

6

"Doña Magdalena and her daughter Amalia await your presence to dine, tomorrow at nine p.m. Ah, if you could come!..."

Not one word more.

I always consent to experiences of the unexpected. Moreover, the situation offered a unique attraction: the invitation's tone, both familiar and respectful, with those unknown ladies remaining unnamed; its deliberation: "Ah, if you could come!..." so vague and so sentimental it seemed suspended over an abyss of confessions, all helped make up my mind. And I arrived with the anxiety of an ineffable emotion. Sometimes in my nightmares, when I recall that fantastic night (with its fantasy made of daily things and its ambiguous mystery growing from the humble root of the possible), it seems to gasp for breath through boulevards of clocks and tall towers solemn as sphinxes pointing toward some Egyptian temple.

The door opened. I was facing the street and suddenly saw a rectangle of light fall on the ground, throwing the shadow of an unknown woman next to mine.

I turned around: with the light behind her blinding my eyes, the woman was only a silhouette to me, on which my imagination could paint various sets of physiognomy, none corresponding to the outline, till I spluttered some greetings and explanations.

"Come in, Alfonso."

Then I stepped in, surprised to hear myself greeted as at home. The entrance hall was deceptive. The romantic words of the invitation (at least they seemed romantic to me) had given me the hope of coming across an ancient house, full of tapestries, old portraits and throne-like chairs; an old house without style, but full of respectability. Instead I found myself in a tiny hall with a fragile, graceless staircase, which in turn promised tight modern proportions in the rest of the house. The floor was of polished wood; the few pieces of furniture had that cold luxury of things from New York, and on the wall, papered in light green, as an unpardonable sign of triviality, two or three Japanese masks grimaced. I even began to doubt... But I raised my eyes and calmed down: before me, dressed in black, svelte, dignified, the woman who had appeared to greet me showed me to the door of the salon. By now her silhouette had colored in with features; her face would have been insignificant

piedad; sus cabellos castaños, algo flojos en el peinado, acabaron de precipitar una extraña convicción a mi mente: todo aquel ser me pareció plegarse y formarse a las sugestiones de un nombre.

—¿Amalia?—pregunté.

—Sí—. Y me pareció que yo mismo me contestaba.

El salón, como lo había imaginado, era pequeño. Mas el decorado, respondiendo a mis anhelos, chocaba notoriamente con el del vestíbulo. Allí estaban los tapices y las grandes sillas respetables, la piel de oso al suelo, el espejo, la chimenea, los jarrones; el piano de candeleros lleno de fotografías y estatuillas— el piano en que nadie toca—, y, junto al estrado principal, el caballete con un retrato amplificado y manifiestamente alterado: el de un señor de barba partida y boca grosera.

Doña Magdalena, que ya me esperaba instalada en un sillón rojo, vestía también de negro y llevaba al pecho una de aquellas joyas gruesísimas de nuestros padres: una bola de vidrio con un retrato interior, ceñida por un anillo de oro. El misterio del parecido familiar se apoderó de mí. Mis ojos iban, inconscientemente, de doña Magdalena a Amalia, y del retrato a Amalia. Doña Magdalena, que lo notó, ayudó mis investigaciones con alguna exégesis oportuna.

Lo más adecuado hubiera sido sentirme incómodo, manifestarme sorprendido, provocar una explicación. Pero doña Magdalena y su hija Amalia me hipnotizaron, desde los primeros instantes, con sus miradas paralelas. Doña Magdalena era una mujer de sesenta años; así es que consintió en dejar a su hija los cuidados de la iniciación. Amalia charlaba; doña Magdalena me miraba; yo estaba entregado a mi ventura.

A la madre tocó—es de rigor—recordarnos que era ya tiempo de cenar. En el comedor la charla se hizo más general y corriente. Yo acabé por convencerme de que aquellas señoras no habían querido más que convidarme a cenar, y a la segunda copa de Chablis me sentí sumido en un perfecto egoísmo del cuerpo lleno de generosidades espirituales. Charlé, reí, y desarrollé todo mi ingenio, tratando interiormente de disimularme la irregularidad de mi situación. Hasta aquel instante las señoras habían procurado parecerme simpáticas; desde entonces sentí que había comenzado yo mismo a serles agradable.

to me, if not for a marked expression of piety..; her brown hair, brushed somewhat carelessly, just then caused a strange conviction in my mind: that entire being seemed to unfold and form itself on the suggestion of a name.

"Amalia?" I asked

"Yes." And it seemed to me that I myself had answered.

The living room, as I had imagined, was small. But the furnishings, in answer to my wishes, clashed terribly with the entrance hall. There were the tapestries and great respectable chairs, the bearskin on the floor, the mirror, the fireplace, the decorative vases; the piano full of photographs and tiny statues—the piano played by no one—and, next to the main drawing room, the easel with a larger-than-life portrait (obviously altered) of a gentleman with thick, slack lips and a forked beard.

Doña Magdalena, who was already waiting for me in an enormous red chair, was also dressed in black and wore on her breast those hideously large jewels of our parents: a glass ball with a portrait inside, encircled with a gold ring. The mystery of family likeness suddenly absorbed me. My eyes went, unconsciously, from Doña Magdalena to Amalia, and from the portrait to Amalia. Doña Magdalena, who noticed it, aided my study with some timely explanation.

The most appropriate thing would have been to feel uncomfortable, show my surprise, bring about some explanation. But Doña Magdalena and her daughter Amalia hypnotized me, from the first moment, with their parallel glances. Doña Magdalena was a woman of about seventy; thus she consented to leave to her daughter the details of the introduction. Amalia chatted; Doña Magdalena watched me; I was resigned to my fate.

It was up to the mother—according to social custom—to announce the dinner hour. In the dining room the conversation became more general and topical. Eventually I convinced myself that these ladies hadn't wanted anything more than to invite me to dinner, and by the second glass of Chablis I felt immersed in the perfect self-centeredness of a body filled with spiritual generosity. I talked, I laughed, I extolled with all my ingenuity, trying inside to fool myself about the strangeness of my situation. Till that moment the ladies had managed to seem friendly toward me; from then on I felt it was I who was good company to them.

El aire piadoso de la cara de Amalia se propagaba, por momentos, a la cara de la madre. La satisfacción, enteramente fisiológica, del rostro de doña Magdalena descendía, a veces, al de su hija. Parecía que estos dos motivos flotasen en el ambiente, volando de una cara a la otra.

Nunca sospeché los agrados de aquella conversación. Aunque ella sugería, vagamente, no sé qué evocaciones de Sudermann, con frecuentes rondas al difícil campo de las responsabilidades domésticas y—como era natural en mujeres de espíritu fuerte— súbitos relámpagos ibsenianos, yo me sentía tan a mi gusto como en casa de alguna tía viuda y junto a alguna prima, amiga de la infancia, que ha comenzado a ser solterona.

Al principio, la conversación giró toda sobre cuestiones comerciales, económicas, en que las dos mujeres parecían complacerse. No hay asunto mejor que éste cuando se nos invita a la mesa en alguna casa donde no somos de confianza.

Después, las cosas siguieron de otro modo. Todas las frases comenzaron a volar como en redor de alguna lejana petición. Todas tendían a un término que yo mismo no sospechaba. En el rostro de Amalia apareció, al fin, una sonrisa aguda, inquietante. Comenzó visiblemente a combatir contra alguna interna tentación. Su boca palpitaba, a veces, con el ansia de las palabras, y acababa siempre por suspirar. Sus ojos se dilataban de pronto, fijándose con tal expresión de espanto o abandono en la pared que quedaba a mis espaldas, que más de una vez, asombrado, volví el rostro yo mismo. Pero Amalia no parecía consciente del daño que me ocasionaba. Continuaba con sus sonrisas, sus asombros y sus suspiros, en tanto que yo me estremecía cada vez que sus ojos miraban por sobre mi cabeza.

Al fin, se entabló, entre Amalia y doña Magdalena, un verdadero coloquio de suspiros. Yo estaba tan desazonado. Hacia el centro de la mesa, y, por cierto, tan baja que era una constante incomodidad, colgaba la lámpara de dos luces. Y sobre los muros se proyectaban las sombras desteñidas de las dos mujeres, en tan forma que no era posible fijar la correspondencia de las sombras con las personas. Me invadió una intensa depresión, y un principio de aburrimiento se fue apoderando de mí. De lo que vino a sacarme esta invitación insospechada:

—Vamos al jardín.

At times the pious air of Amalia's face repeated her mother's face. And the satisfaction, utterly physiological, of Doña Magdalena's face occasionally reverted to her daughter's. It seemed that these two motifs floated in the ambiance, flitting from one face to the other.

I could never have anticipated the pleasures of that conversation. Although she vaguely suggested I don't know what recollections of Sudermann, with frequent recourses to the problematic area of domestic responsibilities and—as was natural in spirited women—sudden Ibsenesque lightning bolts, still I felt as at ease as in the house of some widowed aunt, next to some cousin, a childhood friend now in early stages of spinsterhood.

At first, the conversation centered entirely on matters of trade and economics, with which the two women seemed pleased. There is no better topic when we are invited to dine in some house in which we are not comfortable old friends.

Later, things took another turn. Every phrase began to flit away as if accompanied by some distant request. Each led to an end which even I did not suspect. Eventually there appeared on Amalia's face a sharp, disturbing smile. She began to combat visibly against some internal temptation. Her mouth trembled, at times, with the anxiety of her words, and she always finished with a sigh. Her eyes suddenly dilated, staring with such an expression of fear or abandon on the wall behind me, that more than once, surprised, I even turned around myself. But Amalia seemed unaware of the discomfort that it caused me. She continued with her smiles, her starts and her sighs, so that I shuddered each time her eyes looked over my head.

Finally a real dialogue of sighs began between Amalia and Doña Magdalena. By now I was growing uneasy. Toward the center of the table, and incidentally so low that it was a constant annoyance, hung a lamp with two lights. And on the walls it projected the colorless shadows of the two women, in such a way that it was not possible to determine the correspondence between shadows and people. An intense depression came over me, from which I was saved by this unexpected invitation:

"Let's go into the garden."

Esta nueva perspectiva me hizo recobrar mis espíritus. Condujéronme a través de un cuarto cuyo aseo y sobriedad hacía pensar en los hospitales. En la oscuridad de la noche pude adivinar un jardincillo breve y artificial como el de un camposanto.

Nos sentamos bajo el emparrado. Las señoras comenzaron a decirme los nombres de las flores que yo no veía, dándose el cruel deleite de interrogarme después sobre sus recientes enseñanzas. Mi imaginación, destemplada por una experiencia tan larga de excentricidades, no hallaba reposo. Apenas me dejaba escuchar y casi no me permitía contestar. Las señoras sonreían ya (yo lo adivinaba) con pleno conocimiento de mi estado. Comencé a confundir sus palabras con mi fantasía. Sus explicaciones botánicas, hoy que las recuerdo, me parecen monstruosas como un delirio: creo haberles oído hablar de flores que muerden y de flores que besan; de tallos que se arrancan a su raíz y os trepan, como serpientes, hasta el cuello.

La oscuridad, el cansancio, la cena, el Chablis, la conversación misteriosa sobre flores que yo no veía (y aun creo que no las había en aquel raquítico jardín), todo me fue convidando al sueño; y me quedé dormido sobre el banco, bajo el emparrado.

—¡Pobre capitán!—oí decir cuando abrí los ojos—. Lleno de ilusiones marchó a Europa. Para él se apagó la luz.

En mi alrededor reinaba la misma oscuridad. Un vientecillo tibio hacía vibrar el emparrado. Doña Magdalena y Amalia conversaban junto a mí, resignadas a tolerar mi mutismo. Me pareció que habían trocado los asientos durante mi breve sueño; eso me pareció...

—Era capitán de Artillería—me dijo Amalia—; joven y apuesto si los hay.

Su voz temblaba.

Y en aquel punto sucedió algo que en otras circunstancias me habría parecido natural, pero que entonces me sobresaltó y trajo a mis labios mi corazón. Las señoras, hasta entonces, sólo me habían sido perceptibles por el rumor de su charla y de su presencia. En aquel instante alguien abrió una ventana en la casa, y la luz vino a caer, inesperada, sobre los rostros de las mujeres. Y—¡oh cielos!— los vi iluminarse de pronto, autonómicos, suspensos en el aire— perdidas las ropas negras en la oscuridad del jardín—y con la expresión de piedad grabada hasta la dureza en los rasgos. Eran

This new perspective made me regain my spirit. They led me through a room whose spare cleanliness made me think of hospitals. In the dark of the night I could make out a small artificial garden, like that of a church cemetery.

We sat under the trellis. The ladies began to tell me the names of the flowers that I didn't see, relishing the cruel delight of quizzing me afterwards on their recent instruction. My imagination, unsettled by such a long session of eccentricities, found no rest. It scarcely let me listen and almost didn't let me answer. The ladies were now smiling (I guessed as much) in full awareness of my state. I began to mix up their words with my fantasy. Their botanical explanations, when I recall them today, seem as monstrous as delirium: I think I heard them talk of flowers that kiss; of stalks that tear themselves from their roots and climb up your body, like snakes, up to your neck.

The darkness, the weariness, the supper, the Chablis, the mysterious conversation about flowers I couldn't see (and I still don't believe there were any in that stunted garden), were all conducive to sleep; and I fell asleep on the bench, under the trellis.

"Poor captain!" I heard when I opened my eyes. "He left for Europe all full of illusions. For him the lights are extinguished."

In my vicinity the same darkness reigned. A warm breeze made the trellis tremble. Doña Magdalena and Amalia were talking next to me, resigned to my silence. It seemed to me they had exchanged places during my brief sleep; so it seemed to me...

"He was an artillery captain," Amalia told me. "Young and handsome as any."

Her voice wavered.

And at that point something happened that in other circumstances would have seemed natural, but that startled me then and sent my heart to my throat. Until then the ladies had only been perceptible to me by the sensation of their voices and their presence. At that moment someone opened a window in the house, and the light fell unexpectedly on the faces of the women. And—good God!—I saw the faces suddenly lit up, suspended in the air—the black clothing absent in the darkness of the garden—with the expression of piety recorded even in the hardness of their faces.

como las caras iluminadas en los cuadros de Echave el Viejo, astros enormes y fantásticos.

Salté sobre mis pies sin poder dominarme ya.

—Espere usted—gritó entonces doña Magdalena—; aún falta lo más terrible.

Y luego, dirigiéndose a Amalia:

—Hija mía, continúa; este caballero no puede dejarnos ahora y marcharse sin oírlo todo.

—Y bien—dijo Amalia—: el capitán se fue a Europa. Pasó de noche por París, por la mucha urgencia de llegar a Berlín. Pero todo su anhelo era conocer París. En Alemania tenía que hacer no sé qué estudios en cierta fábrica de cañones... Al día siguiente de llegado, perdió la vista en la explosión de una caldera.

Yo estaba loco. Quise preguntar; ¿qué preguntaría? Quise hablar; ¿qué diría? ¿Qué había sucedido junto a mí? ¿Para qué me habían convidado?

La ventana volvió a cerrarse, y los rostros de las mujeres volvieron a desaparecer. La voz de la hija resonó:

—¡Ay! Entonces, y sólo entonces, fue llevado a París. ¡A París, que había sido todo su anhelo! Figúrese usted que pasó bajo el Arco de la Estrella: pasó ciego junto al Arco de la Estrella, adivinándolo todo a su alrededor... Pero usted le hablará de París, ¿verdad? Le hablará del París que él no pudo ver. ¡Le hará tanto bien!

("¡Ah, si no fallara!"... "¡Le hará tanto bien!")

Y entonces me arrastraron a la sala, llevándome por los brazos como un inválido. A mis pies se habían enredado las guía vegétale del jardín; había hojas sobre mi cabeza.

—Helo aquí—me dijeron mostrándome un retrato. Era un militar. Llevaba un casco guerrero, una capa blanca, y los galones plateados en las mangas y en las presillas como tres toques de clarín. Sus hermosos ojos, bajo las alas perfectas de las cejas, tenían un imperio singular. Miré a las señoras: las dos sonreían como en el desahogo de la misión cumplida. Contemplé de nuevo el retrato; me vi yo mismo en el espejo; verifiqué la semejanza: yo era como una caricatura de aquel retrato. El retrato tenía una dedicatoria y una firma. La letra era la misma de la esquela anónima recibida por la mañana.

El retrato había caído de mis manos, y las dos señoras me miraban con una cómica piedad. Algo sonó en mis oídos como una

They were like the illuminated faces in the paintings of Echave the Elder, huge and fantastic celestial bodies.

I leaped to my feet before getting control of myself.

"Wait," shouted Doña Magdalena, "the worst is yet to come."

And then, to Amalia:

"My daughter, go on; this gentleman cannot leave us now and go off without hearing it all."

"So then," said Amalia, "the captain left for Europe. He went through Paris at night, he was in such a hurry to get to Berlin. But his greatest wish was to know Paris. In Germany he had to do I don't know what studies in some cannon factory... The day after arriving, he lost his sight in a boiler explosion."

I was going crazy. I tried to ask; what would I ask? I tried to talk; what would I say? What had happened there next to me? Why had they invited me?

The window closed again, and the faces of the women disappeared again. The daughter's voice rang out:

"Oh! Then, and only then, he was taken to Paris. To Paris, which had been his greatest desire. Imagine him going under the Arc d'Etoile, guessing at everything around him... But you will speak to him of Paris, won't you? You will talk to him about the Paris he couldn't see. It will do him such good!"

("Ah, if you could make it!..." "It will do him such good!")

And then they hauled me to the living room, carrying me by the arms like an invalid. Around my feet the vegetable tendrils had entwined; there were leaves around my head.

"Here he is," they said, showing me a portrait. He was a military man. He was wearing a soldier's helmet, a white cape, with silver stripes on the sleeves like three bugle calls. His beautiful eyes, under the perfect arched eyebrows, had a singular authority. I looked at the women: the two smiled as if relieved after completing a mission. I contemplated the portrait again; I saw myself in the mirror; I verified the similarity: I was like a caricature of that portrait. The portrait had a dedication and a signature. The handwriting was the same as on the unsigned invitation received that morning.

The portrait had fallen from my hands, and the two women looked at me with comic piety. Something resounded in my ears

araña de cristal que se estrellara contra el suelo.

Y corrí, a través de calles desconocidas. Bailaban los focos delante de mis ojos. Los relojes de los torreones me espiaban, congestionados de luz... ¡Oh, cielos! Cuando alcancé, jadeante, la tabla familiar de mi puerta, nueve sonoras campanadas estremecían la noche.

Sobre mi cabeza había hojas; en mi ojal, una florecilla modesta que yo no corté.

like a crystal chandelier smashed against the floor.

And I ran, through unknown streets. Electric beams danced before my eyes. The clocks on the towers, clogged up with light, were spying on me... My God! When I reached the familiar panel of my door, out of breath, the night was shuddering with nine resounding clangs.

On my head were leaves; in my lapel, a modest little flower I had not cut.

EL LUGAR DE SU QUIETUD

THE PLACE OF ITS SOLITUDE

Helen R. Lane, translator of Luisa Valenzuela

Helen R. Lane lives in Albuquerque, New Mexico. Always eager to introduce new experimental material to American readers, she has translated works from French and Spanish, including Mario Vargas Llosa'a *A Fish in the Water* and Octavio Paz's *The Double Flame: Love and Eroticism*, as well as stories and novels by Juan Goytisolo. Lane received a degree in Romance Languages in 1953 from the University of California at Los Angeles. Her husband's career as an automobile and aircraft designer required almost yearly moves to Latin America, Europe, and Asia. "Since such mobility is hardly compatible with a serious academic career," she writes in her personal correspondence, "I decided that translation was a good option; after all, I had training in four languages. Luckily, it has proved to be precisely that—for the last forty years."

Responding to the question of how she works, Lane writes: "Since one of my consuming interests in literature is the development of motifs and symbolic schemata in a work, I read through the work once or twice to acquire some idea of the narrative organization, and then at least twice more to have an idea of the principal themes with which the author is working. Before beginning the first draft, I make a list of these, which I continually annotate while I am working. My first draft is always almost an interlinear, word-for-word translation, and only in later drafts do I take up for myself the problems of the relationship between the original text in the source language and the effect of the final text in the target language. Since my time at university, when my days were taken up with studying, teaching, and library research, translation has always been a decidedly nocturnal activity for me."

In latter days, Lane always has a choice of the translation she cares to take on. "I insist on the author's being willing to collaborate with me," she adds, "and choose only writers who have at least a working knowledge of English. I always submit to them the list of queries, which vary from questions of quite literal meanings of words or expressions to questions regarding the author's own interpretation of passages that I find puzzling."

She chose this story by Luisa Valenzuela, an Argentine born in 1938, and author of *The Lizard's Tail, Bedside Manners*, and other novels and short story collections, because "it's a great example of my early translation style, when I did not as yet collaborate with the author; and because I feel that it evidences the author's preoccupation with the atmosphere in Argentina in the years of dictatorship and her deliberately ironic, sidelong representation of this preoccupation." Valenzuela began her career writing for newspapers and magazines in Buenos Aires, but soon was awarded a fellowship at the University of Iowa's Writing Program, which inaugurated a period of long absences from her native country. She was awarded a Guggenheim Fellowship in 1982, and returned to Argentina when democracy was reinstated. Critics agree that her style is clearly influenced by the art of Julio Cortázar.

Luisa Valenzuela
EL LUGAR DE SU QUIETUD

"Toda luna, todo año,
todo día, todo viento
camina y pasa también.
También toda sangre llega
al lugar de su quietud"
(Libros del Chilam-Balam)

Los altares han sido erigidos en el interior del país pero hasta nosotros (los de la ciudad, la periferia, los que creemos poder salvarnos) llegan los efluvios. Los del interior se han resignado y rezan. Sin embargo no hay motivo aparente de pánico, sólo los consabidos tiroteos, alguna que otra razzia policial los patrullajes de siempre. Pero oscuramente ellos deben saber que el fin está próximo. Es que tantas cosas empiezan a confundirse que ahora lo anormal imita a lo natural y viceversa. Las sirenas y el viento, por ejemplo: ya las sirenas de los coches policiales parecen el ulular del viento, con idéntico sonido e idéntico poder de destrucción.

Para vigilar mejor desde los helicópteros a los habitantes de las casas se está utilizando un tipo de sirena de nota tan aguda y estridente que hace volar los techos. Por suerte el Gobierno no ha encontrado todavía la fórmula para mantener bajo control a quienes no viven en casas bajas o en los últimos pisos de propiedad horizontal. Pero éstos son contadísimos: desde que se ha cortado el suministro de energía ya nadie se aventura más allá de un tercer piso por el peligro que significa transitar las escaleras a oscuras, reducto de maleantes.

Como consuelo anotaremos que muchos destechados han adoptado el techo de plexiglass, obsequio del Gobierno. Sobre todo en zonas rurales, donde los techos de paja no sólo se vuelan a menudo por la acción de las sirenas sino también por causa de algún simple vendaval. Los del interior son así: se conforman con cualquier cosa, hasta con quedarse en su lugar armando altares y organizando rogativas cuando el tiempo—tanto meteoro como

Luisa Valenzuela
THE PLACE OF ITS SOLITUDE
Translated by Helen R. Lane

All moon all year
all day all wind
comes by and passes on.
All blood arrives
at the place of its quietude.
(Books of Chilam-Balam)

The altars have been erected in the country but the vapors reach us
(those of us who live in the city, in the suburbs, those among us
who believe that we can save ourselves). Those from the countryside
have accepted their fate and are praying. Yet there's no visible motive
for panic, only the usual shootings, police raids, customary patrols.
But they must be dimly aware that the end is at hand. So many
things are so confused now that the abnormal is imitating the
natural and vice versa. The sirens and the wind, for example: the
police car sirens are like the howling of the wind, with an identical
sound and an identical power of destruction.

To keep a better watch on the inhabitants of the houses, a type
of siren is being used in the helicopters that is so highpitched and
strident that it makes the roofs fly off. Luckily the government has
not yet found the formula for controlling those who don't live in
single houses or on the top floors of high buildings. And there are
very few of these: since the electricity has been cut off nobody
ventures beyond the third floor because of the danger of stairways,
the hideout of malefactors.

We must add that as consolation many who lost their roofs
have had them replaced with Plexiglas skylights, gifts of the
government. Above all in rural areas, where the straw roofs
frequently fall off not only because of the sirens but also because of
windstorms. That's what they're like in the country: they put up
with anything, even with remaining where they are and setting up
altars and organizing prayer meetings when time and weather

cronológico—se lo permite. Tienen poco tiempo para rezar, y mal tiempo. La sudestada les apaga las llamas votivas y las inundaciones les exigen una atención constante para evitar que se ahogue el ganado (caprino, ovino, porcino, un poquito vacuno y bastante gallináceo). Por fortuna no han tenido la osadía de venirse a la ciudad como aquella vez siete años atrás, durante la histórica sequía, cuando los hombres sedientos avanzaron en tropel en busca de la ciudad y del agua pisoteando los cadáveres apergaminados de los que morían en la marcha. Pero la ciudad tampoco fue una solución porque la gente de allí no los quería y los atacó a palos como a perros aullantes y tuvieron que refugiarse en el mar con el agua hasta la cintura, donde no los alcanzaban las piedras arrojadas por los que desde la orilla defendían su pan, su agua potable y su enferma dignidad.

Es decir que ellos no van a cometer el mismo error aunque esto no ocurrió aquí, ocurrió en otro país cercano y es lo mismo porque la memoria individual de ellos es muy frágil pero la memoria de la raza es envidiable y suele aflorar para sacarlos de apuros. Sin embargo no creemos que el renacido sentimiento religioso los salve ahora de la que se nos viene; a ellos no, pero quizá sí a nosotros, nosotros los citadinos que sabemos husmear el aire en procura de algún efluvio de incienso de copal que llega de tierra adentro. Ellos pasan grandes penurias para importar el incienso de copal y según parece somos nosotros quienes recibiremos los beneficios. Al menos—cuando los gases de escape nos lo permiten—cazamos a pleno pulmón bocanadas de incienso que sabemos inútil, por si acaso. Todo es así, ahora: no tenemos nada que temer pero tememos; éste es el mejor de los mundos posibles como suelen decirnos por la radio y cómo serán los otros; el país camina hacia el futuro y personeros embozados de ideologías aberrantes nada podrán hacer para detener su marcha, dice el Gobierno, y nosotros para sobrevivir hacemos como si creyéramos. Dejando de lado a los que trabajan en la clandestinidad—y son pocos—nuestro único atisbo de rebeldía es este husmear subrepticiamente el aire en procura de algo que nos llega desde el interior del país y que denuncia nuestra falta de fe. Creo—no puedo estar seguro, de eso se habla en voz muy baja—que en ciertas zonas periféricas de la ciudad se van armando grupos de peregrinación al interior para tratar de comprender—y de justificar—esta nueva tendencia mística. Nunca fuimos un

permit. They have little time for prayer, and bad weather. The southeast wind blows out their votive candles, and floods demand their constant attention to keep the livestock (goats, sheep, pigs, a very few cows, and a fair number of chickens) from drowning. Fortunately they haven't had the nerve to come to the city as they did seven years ago, during that historic drought, when thirsty men flocked to the cities in search of water, trampling the parched bodies of those who had died along the way. But the city was not a solution either because the city-dwellers didn't want them and drove them off with sticks like howling dogs, and they had to take refuge in the sea in water up to their waists, safe from the rocks hurled from the shore by those defending their bread, their drinking water, and their feeble dignity.

They aren't going to make the same mistake; even though this didn't happen here but in a neighboring country, it amounts to the same thing because while their individual memory is fragile their collective memory is enviable and comes to the surface to get them out of difficulties. Nonetheless we don't believe that the rebirth of religious sentiment will save them from what's happening now; it won't save them, but perhaps it will save us city-dwellers who know how to sniff the air for a breath of copal incense that reaches us from the interior. They have great difficulty importing copal incense and we may be the ones to reap the benefits. Exhaust gases permitting, we do our best to breathe great lungfuls of incense—we know it's useless—just in case. That's the way everything is now: we have nothing to fear yet we're afraid. This is the best of all possible worlds, as they keep reminding us over the radio, and the way other worlds will be; the country is on its way to the future, and secret agents of aberrant ideologies can do nothing to halt its march, the government says, so in order to survive we pretend that we believe it. Leaving aside those who are working in the underground—there are few of them—our one hint of rebellion is the surreptitious sniffing of the air in search of something that comes to us from the countryside and shows up our lack of faith. I believe—I can't be sure, the subject is discussed furtively—that in certain suburban districts of the city groups of pilgrims are being formed to go to the interior to try to understand—and to justify—this new mythical tendency. We were never fervent believers and suddenly now we

pueblo demasiado creyente y ahora nos surge la necesidad de armar altares, algo debe de haber detrás de todo esto. Hoy en el café con los amigos (porque no vayan a creer que las cosas están tan mal, todavía puede reunirse uno en el café con los amigos) tocamos con suma prudencia el tema (siempre hay que estar muy atento a las muchas orejas erizadas): ¿qué estará pasando en el interior? ¿será el exceso de miedo que los devuelve a una búsqueda primitiva de esperanza o será que están planeando algo? Jorge sospecha que el copal debe de tener poderes alucinógenos y por eso se privan de tantas cosas para conseguirlo. Parece que el copal no puede ser transportado por ningún medio mecánico y es así como debe venir de América Central a lomo de mula o a lomo de hombre; ya se han organizado postas para su traslado y podríamos sospechar que dentro de las bolsas de corteza de copal llegan armas o por lo menos drogas o algunas instrucciones si no fuera porque nuestras aduanas son tan severas y tan lúcidas. Las aduanas internas, eso sí, no permiten el acceso del copal a las ciudades. Tampoco lo queremos; aunque ciertos intelectuales disconformes hayan declarado a nuestra ciudad área de catástrofe psicológica. Pero tenemos problemas mucho más candentes y no podemos perder el tiempo en oraciones o en disquisiciones de las llamadas metafísicas. Jorge dice que no se trata de eso sino de algo más profundo. Jorge dice, Jorge dice...ahora en los cafés no se hace más que decir porque en muchos ya se prohíbe escribir aunque se consuma bastante. Alegan que así las mesas se desocupan más rápido, pero sospecho que estos dueños de cafés donde se reprime la palabra escrita son en realidad agentes de provocación. La idea nació, creo, en el de la esquina de Paraguay y Pueyrredón, y corrió como reguero de pólvora por toda la ciudad. Ahora tampoco dejan escribir en los cafés aledaños al Palacio de la Moneda ni en algunos de la Avenida de Río Branco. En Pocitos sí, todos los cafés son de escritura permitida y los intelectuales se reúnen allí a las seis de la tarde. Con tal de que no sea una encerrona como dice Jorge, provocada por los extremistas, claro, porque el Gobierno está por encima de estas maquinaciones, por encima de todos, volando en helicópteros y velando por la paz de la Nación.

Nada hay que temer. La escalada de violencia sólo alcanza a los que la buscan, no a nosotros humildes ciudadanos que no nos permitimos ni una mueca de disgusto ni la menor señal de descontento. (Desconcierto sí, no es para menos cuando nos vuelan

feel the need to set up altars. There must be something behind all this. In the cafe today with my friends—so you won't think we're in really bad straits, I might mention that friends can still get together in a cafe—very cautiously we touched upon the subject (we must always be careful, since the walls have ears) of what's going on in the interior. Has excessive fear brought them back to a primitive search for hope, or are they plotting something? Jorge suspects that the copal has hallucinogenic powers and they deprive themselves of many things in order to get it. It appears that copal cannot be transported by mechanical means, so it must come from Central America on the back of a mule or a man. Relays to transport it have already been organized and we might suspect that ammunition or at least drugs or instructions arrive inside the bags of copal bark, if it weren't for the fact that our customs officials are so alert and clear-thinking. The local customs, of course, don't permit copal to enter the cities. We don't want it here either, although certain dissident intellectuals have declared our city an area of psychological catastrophe. But we have much more burning questions confronting us and we can't waste time on speeches and lectures on so-called metaphysics. Jorge says it's something much more profound. Jorge says, Jorge says... All we can do in cafes nowadays is talk, because in many of them we're no longer allowed to write, even though we keep ordering food and drink. They claim that they need the tables, but I suspect that those cafe owners who suppress the written word are really agents provocateurs. The idea started, I think, in the cafe at the corner of Paraguay and Pueyrredón, and spread through the city like a trail of lighted gunpowder. Now no writing is permitted in the cafes near the Mint, nor in some along the Avenida de Rio Branco. In Pocitos yes, all the cafes allow writing and intellectuals gather there around 6:00 p.m. So long as it isn't a trap, as Jorge says, set up by the extremists, of course, since the government is above such machinations—in fact, above everyone in their helicopters, safeguarding the peace of the nation.

Nothing to fear. The escalation of violence only touches those who are looking for it, not us humble citizens who don't allow ourselves so much as a wry face or the least sign of discontent. (Of consternation yes, and there's good reason when they blow the roof

el techo de la casa y a veces la tapa de los sesos, cuando nos palpan de armas por la calle o cuando el olor a copal se hace demasiado intenso y nos da ganas de correr a ver de qué se trata. De correr y correr; disparar no siempre es cobardía).

Acabamos por acostumbrarnos al incienso que más de una vez compite con el olor a pólvora, y ahora nos llega lo otro: una distante nota de flauta que perfora los ruidos ciudadanos. Al principio pensamos en la onda ultrasónica para dispersar manifestaciones, pero no. La nota de flauta es sostenida y los distraídos pueden pensar que se trata de un lamento; es en realidad un cántico que persiste y a veces se interrumpe y retoma para obligarnos a levantar la cabeza como en las viejas épocas cuando el rugido de los helicópteros nos llamaba la atención. Ya hemos perdido nuestra capacidad de asombro pero el sonido de la flauta nos conmueve más que ciertas manifestaciones relámpago los sábados por la noche a la salida de los cines cuando despiertan viejos motivos de queja adormecidos. No estamos para esos trotes, tampoco estamos como para salir corriendo cuando llegan los patrulleros desde los cuatro puntos de la ciudad y convergen encima de nosotros.

Sirenas como el viento, flautas como notas ultrasónicas para dispersar motines. Parecería que los del interior han decidido retrucar ciertas iniciativas de poder central. Al menos así se dice en la calle pero no se especifica quiénes son los del interior: gente del montón, provincianos cualquiera, agentes a sueldo de potencias extranjeras, grupos de guerrilla armada, anarquistas, sabios. Después del olor a incienso que llegue este sonido de flauta ya es demasiado. Podríamos hablar de penetración sensorial e ideológica si en algún remoto rincón de nuestro ser nacional no sintiéramos que es para nuestro bien, que alguna forma de redención nos ha de llegar de ellos. Y esta vaguísima esperanza nos devuelve el lujo de tener miedo. Bueno, no miedo comentado en voz alta como en otros tiempos. Este de ahora es un miedo a puertas cerradas, silencioso, estéril, de vibración muy baja que se traduce en iras callejeras o en arranques de violencia conyugal. Tenemos nuestras pesadillas y son siempre de torturas aunque los tiempos no estén para estas sutilezas. Antes sí podían demorarse en aplicar los más refinados métodos para obtener confesiones, ahora las confesiones ya han sido relegadas al olvido: todos son culpables y a otra cosa. Con sueños anacrónicos seguimos aferrados a las torturas pero los del interior

off the house and sometimes the top of one's head as well, when they frisk us for arms in the street, or when the smell of copal becomes too intense and makes us feel like running to see what's up. Like running and running; acting absurdly is not always cowardice.)

We've finally become used to the smell of incense, which often competes with the smell of gunpowder, and now something else is coming our way: the distant sound of a flute. In the beginning we thought it was ultrasonic waves to break up demonstrations, but that wasn't it. The flute note is sustained, and to those not paying much attention it may sound like a lament; in reality it's a persistent melody that makes us lift our heads as in the old days when the roar of helicopters drew our attention. We have lost our capacity for amazement. We don't dance to that tune, nor do we break into a run when the patrols arrive from all directions and converge on top of us.

Sirens like the wind, flutes like ultrasonic notes to break up riots. It would appear that those in the interior have decided to borrow certain devices from the central power. At least that's what they're saying on the street, but it's never specified who those in the interior are: riffraff, provincials, foreign agents, groups of armed guerrillas, anarchists, researchers. That flute sound coming on top of the smell of incense is just too much. We might speak of sensorial and ideological infiltration, if in some remote corner of our national being we didn't feel that it's for our own good—a form of redemption. And this vague sensation restores to us the luxury of being afraid. Well no, not fear expressed aloud as in other times. The fear now is behind closed doors, silent, barren, with a low vibration that emerges in fits of temper on the streets or conjugal violence at home.

We have our nightmares and they are always of torture even though the times are not right for these subtleties. In the past they could spend time applying the most refined methods to extract confessions, but now confessions have been consigned to oblivion: everyone is guilty now, so on to something else. In our anachronistic dreams we city people still cling to tortures, but those in the interior

del país no sueñan ni tienen pesadillas: se dice que han logrado eliminar esas horas de entrega absoluta cuando el hombre dormido está a total merced de su adversario. Ellos caen en meditación profunda durante breves períodos de tiempo y mantienen las pesadillas a distancia; y las pesadillas, que no son sonsas, se limitan al ejido urbano donde encuentran un terreno más propicio. Pero no, no se debe hablar de esto ni siquiera hablar del miedo. Tan poco se sabe—se sabe la ventaja del silencio—y hay tanto que se ignora. ¿Qué hacen, por ejemplo, los del interior frente a sus altares? No creemos que eleven preces al dios tantas veces invocado por el Gobierno ni que hayan descubierto nuevos dioses o sacado a relucir dioses arcaicos. Debe tratarse de algo menos obvio. Bah. Esas cosas no tienen por qué preocuparnos a nosotros, hombres de cuatro paredes (muchas veces sin techo o con techo transparente), hombres adictos al asfalto. Si ellos quieren quemarse con incienso, que se quemen; si ellos quieren perder el aliento soplando en la quena, que lo pierdan. Nada de todo esto nos interesa: nada de todo esto podrá salvarnos. Quizá tan sólo el miedo, un poco de miedo que nos haga ver claro a nosotros los hombres de la ciudad pero qué, si no nos lo permitimos porque con un soplo de miedo llegan tantas otras cosas: el cuestionamiento, el horror, la duda, el disconformismo, el disgusto. Que ellos allá lejos en el campo o en la montaña se desvivan con las prácticas inútiles. Nosotros podemos tomar un barco e irnos, ellos están anclados y por eso entonan salmos.

Nuestra vida es tranquila. De vez en cuando desaparece un amigo, sí, o matan a los vecinos o un compañero de colegio de nuestros hijos o hasta nuestros propios hijos caen en una ratonera, pero la cosa no es tan apocalíptica como parece, es más bien rítmica y orgánica. La escalada de violencia: un muerto cada 24 horas, cada 21, cada 18, cada 15, cada 12, no debe inquietar a nadie. Más mueren en otras partes del mundo, como bien señaló aquel diputado minutos antes de que le descerrajaran el balazo. Más, quizá, pero en ninguna parte tan cercanos.

Cuando la radio habla de la paz reinante (la televisión ha sido suprimida, nadie quiere dar la cara) sabemos que se trata de una expresión de deseo o de un pedido de auxilio, porque los mismos locutores no ignoran que en cada rincón los espera una bomba, y llegan embozados a las emisoras para que nadie pueda reconocerlos

don't dream or have nightmares: they've managed, we are told, to eliminate those hours of total surrender when the sleeper is at the mercy of his adversary. They fall into profound meditation for brief periods and keep nightmares at a distance; and the nightmares are limited to the urban community. But we shouldn't talk of fear. So little is known—we know the advantage of silence. What do those in the interior do, for example, in front of their altars? We don't believe that they pray to the god invoked so often by the government, or that they've discovered new gods or resurrected the old ones. It must be something less obvious. Bah. These things shouldn't worry us, we live within four walls (often without a roof or with a skylight)—men addicted to asphalt. If they want to burn themselves on incense, let them; if they want to lose their breath blowing into an Indian flute, let them. None of that interests us. None of that can save us. Perhaps only fear, a little fear that makes us see our urban selves clearly. But we should not allow ourselves to experience fear because with a breath of fear so many other things come our way: questioning, horror, doubt, dissent, disgust. Let those far away in the fields or in the mountains show a great interest in useless practices if they like. We can always take a boat and go away; they are anchored in one spot and that's why they sing psalms.

Our life is quiet enough. Every once in a while a friend disappears, or a neighbor is killed, or one of our children's schoolmates—or even our own children—falls into a trap, but that isn't as apocalyptic as it seems; on the contrary, it's rhythmic and organic. The escalation of violence—one dead every twenty-four hours, every twenty-one, every eighteen, every fifteen, every twelve—ought not to worry us. More people die in other parts of the world, as that deputy said moments before he was shot. More, perhaps, but nowhere so close at hand as here.

When the radio speaks of the peace that reigns (television has disappeared—no one wants to show his face), we know it's a plea for help. The speakers are aware that bombs await them at every corner; they arrive at the station with their faces concealed, so when they walk the streets as respectable citizens, no one will recognize

después cuando andan sueltos por las calles como respetables ciudadanos. No se sabe quiénes atentan contra los locutores, al fin y al cabo ellos sólo leen lo que otros escriben y la segunda incógnita es ¿dónde lo escriben? Debe ser en los ministerios bajo vigilancia policial y también bajo custodia porque ya no está permitido escribir en ninguna otra parte. Es lógico, los escritores de ciencia ficción habían previsto hace años el actual estado de cosas y ahora se trata de evitar que las nuevas profecías proliferen (aunque ciertos miembros del Gobierno—los menos imaginativos—han propuesto dejarles libertad de acción a los escritores para apoderarse luego de ciertas ideas interesantes, del tipo nuevos métodos de coacción que siempre pueden deducirse de cualquier literatura). Yo no me presto a tales manejos y por eso he desarrollado y puesto en práctica un ingenioso sistema para escribir a oscuras. Después guardo los manuscritos en un lugar que sólo yo me sé y veremos qué pasa. Mientras tanto el Gobierno nos bombardea con slogans optimistas que no repito por demasiado archisabidos y ésta es nuestra única fuente de cultura. A pesar de lo cual sigo escribiendo y trato de ser respetuoso y de no

La noche anterior escuché un ruido extraño y de inmediato escondí el manuscrito. No me acuerdo qué iba a anotar; sospecho que ya no tiene importancia. Me alegro eso sí de mis rápidos reflejos porque de golpe se encendieron las luces accionadas por la llave maestra y entró una patrulla a registrar la casa. La pobre Betsy tiene ahora para una semana de trabajo si quiere volver a poner todo en orden, sin contar lo que rompieron y lo que se deben de haber llevado. Gaspar no logra consolarla pero al menos no ocurrió nada más grave que el allanamiento en sí. Insistieron en averiguar por qué me tenían de pensionista, pero ellos dieron las explicaciones adecuadas y por suerte, por milagro casi, no encontraron mi tableta con pintura fosforescente y demás parafernalia para escribir en la oscuridad. No sé qué habría sido de mí, de Betsy y de Gaspar si la hubieran encontrado, pero mi escondite es ingeniosísimo y ahora pienso si no sería preferible ocultar allí algo más útil. Bueno, ya es tarde para cambiar; debo seguir avanzando por este camino de tinta, y creo que hasta sería necesario contar la historia del portero. Yo estuve en la reunión de consorcio y vi cómo se relamían interiormente las mujeres solas cuando se habló del nuevo encargado: 34 años, soltero. Yo lo vi los días siguientes esmerándose

them. No one knows who attacks the speakers—after all, they only read what others write. But where do they write it? Under police surveillance and in custody? That makes sense. Science fiction writers foresaw the present state of affairs years ago and the government is now trying to keep new prophecies from proliferating (although certain members of the government—the less imaginative among them—have suggested permitting freedom of action for the writers so as to lift interesting ideas from them). I don't go along with such maneuvers, which is why I've devised an ingenious system for writing in the dark. I keep my manuscripts in a place that only I know about; we'll see what happens. Meanwhile the government bombards us with optimistic slogans that I don't repeat because they're all so familiar, and this is our only source of culture. Despite which I continue to write and try to be law-abiding and not

Last night I heard a strange noise and immediately hid my manuscript. I don't remember what I was going to jot down; I suspect it's not important anymore. I'm glad I have quick reflexes because suddenly someone turned the master switch, all the lights came on, and a squad of police entered to search the house. It'll take poor Betsy a week to put everything back in order, to say nothing of what they broke or what they must have taken away. Gaspar can't console her, but at least nothing more serious has happened than the search. The police questioned them as to why they had taken me in as a boarder, but they gave an adequate explanation and luckily, as if by a miracle, they didn't find my little board painted in phosphorescent colors so that I can write in the dark. I don't know what would have happened to me, Betsy, and Gaspar if they'd found it all; my hiding place is ingenious and I wonder whether it might not be better to hide something more useful in it. Well, it's too late to change now; I have to keep walking along this path of ink and tell the story of the doorman. I was at a tenants' meeting and saw the single women mentally licking their chops when the new doorman was described: thirty-four years old and a bachelor. In the days that followed I saw him lavishing a lot of

por demás con los bronces de la entrada y también leyendo algún libro en sus horas de guardia. Pero no estuve presente cuando se lo llevó la policía. Se murmura que era un infiltrado del interior. Ahora sé que debí haber hablado un poco más con él, quizá ahora deshilachando sus palabras podría por fin entender algo, entrever un trozo de la trama. ¿Qué hacen en el interior, qué buscan? Ahora apenas puedo tratar de descubrir cuál de las mujeres solas del edificio fue la que hizo la denuncia. Despechadas parecen todas y no es para menos ¿pero son todas capaces de correr al teléfono y condenar a alguien por despecho? Puede que sí, tantas veces la radio invita gentilmente a la delación que quizá hasta se sintieron buenas ciudadanas. Ahora no sólo me da asco saludarlas, puedo también anotarlo con cierta impunidad, sé que mi escondite es seguro. Por eso me voy a dar el lujo de escribir unos cuentitos. Ya tengo las ideas y hasta los títulos: Los mejor calzados, Aquí pasan cosas raras, Amor por los animales, El don de la palabra. Total, son sólo para mí y, si alguna vez tenemos la suerte de salir de ésta, quizá hasta Puedan servir de testimonio. O no, pero a mí me consuelan y con mi sistema no temo estar haciéndoles el juego ni dándoles ideas. Hasta puedo dejar de lado el subterfugio de hablar de mí en plural o en masculino. Puedo ser yo. Sólo quisiera que se sepa que no por ser un poco cándida y proclive al engaño todo lo que he anotado es falso. Ciertos son el sonido de la flauta, el olor a incienso, las sirenas. Cierto que algo está pasando en el interior del país y quisiera unirme a ellos. Cierto que tenemos—tengo—miedo.

Escribo a escondidas, y con alivio acabo de enterarme que los del interior también están escribiendo. Aprovechan la claridad de las llamas votivas para escribir sin descanso lo que suponemos es el libro de la raza. Esto es para nosotros una forma de ilusión y también una condena: cuando la raza se escribe a sí misma, la raza se acaba y no hay nada que hacerle.

Hay quienes menosprecian esta información: dicen que los de la ciudad no tenemos relación alguna con la raza ésa, qué relación podemos tener nosotros, todos hijos de inmigrantes. Por mi parte no veo de dónde el desplazamiento geográfico puede ser motivo de orgullo cuando el aire que respiramos, el cielo y el paisaje cuando queda una gota de cielo o de paisaje, están impregnados de ellos, los que vivieron aquí desde siempre y nutrieron la tierra con sus cuerpos por escasos que fueran. Y ahora se dice que están

extra care on the bronze fittings at the main entrance and also reading a book while on duty. But I wasn't there when the police took him away. Rumor has it that he was an infiltrator from the interior. I know now that I should have talked with him, perhaps I would finally have understood something, untangled some of the threads of the plot. What are they doing in the interior, what are they after? I'd be hard put to say which of the single women in the building turned him in. They all look spiteful and perhaps have reason to, but are they all capable of running to the telephone and condemning someone out of spite? The radio gently urges us so often to inform, that they may even have felt they were doing their duty. I can now write all this down with a certain impunity, since I know I'm safe in my hiding place. That's why I can afford the luxury of writing a few stories. I even have the titles "The Best Shod," "Strange Things Happen Here," "Love of Animals," "The Gift of Words." They're only for me, but if we're lucky enough to survive all this, perhaps they'll bear witness to the truth. Anyway they console me. And with the way I've worked it out, I have no fear of playing their game or giving them ideas. I can even do away with the subterfuge of referring to myself in the plural or in the masculine. I can be myself. Only I want it known that even though I'm a little naive and sometimes given to fantasy, not everything I've recorded is false. Certain things are true: the sound of the flute, the smell of incense, the sirens. It's also true that strange things are happening in the interior of the country and that I'd like to make common cause with them. It's true that we are—I am—afraid.

I'm writing secretly, and to my relief I've just learned that those in the interior are also writing. By the light of the votive candles they're writing the book of our people. This is a form of illusion for us and also a condemnation: when a people writes for itself, it is dying out and nothing can be done about it.

Some make light of this bit of information: they say we city dwellers have no connection with people of the interior, that we all descend from immigrants. I don't see how coming from somewhere else can be a reason to be proud when the very air we breathe, the sky and the landscape when there's a drop of sky or landscape left, are impregnated with them—those who have always lived here and have nourished the earth with their bodies. And it's said that they're now writing the book and it's hoped that this task will take many

escribiendo el libro y existe la esperanza de que esta tarea lleve largos años. Su memoria es inmemorial y van a tener que remontarse tan profundamente en el tiempo para llegar hasta la base del mito y quitarle las telarañas y demitificarlo (para devolverle a esa verdad su esencia, quitarle su disfraz) que nos quedará aún tiempo para seguir viviendo, es decir para crearles nuevos mitos. Porque en la ciudad están los pragmáticos, allá lejos los idealistas y el encuentro ¿dónde?

Mientras tanto las persecuciones se vuelven cada vez más insidiosas. No se puede estar en la calle sin ver a los uniformados cometiendo todo tipo de infracciones por el solo placer de reírse de quienes deben acatar las leyes. Y pobre del que se ofenda o se retobe o simplemente critique: se trata de una trampa y por eso hay muchos que en la desesperación prefieren enrolarse en las filas con la excusa de buscar la tranquilidad espiritual, pero poco a poco van entrando en el juego porque grande es la tentación de embromar a los otros.

Yo, cada vez más calladita, sigo anotando todo esto aún a grandes rasgos (¡grandes riesgos!) porque es la única forma de libertad que nos queda. Los otros todavía hacen ingentes esfuerzos por creer mientras la radio (que se ha vuelto obligatoria) transmite una información opuesta a los acontecimientos que son del dominio público. Este hábil sistema de mensajes contradictorios ha sido montado para enloquecer a la población a corto plazo y por eso, en resguardo de mi salud mental, escribo y escribo siempre a oscuras y sin poder releer lo que he escrito. Al menos me siento apoyada por los del interior. Yo no estoy como ellos entregada a la confección del libro pero algo es algo. El mío es un aporte muy modesto y además espero que nunca llegue a manos de lector alguno: significaría que he sido descubierta. A veces vuelvo a casa tan impresionada por los golpeados, mutilados, ensangrentados y tullidos que deambulan ciegos por las calles que ni escribir puedo y eso no importa. Si dejo de escribir, no pasa nada. En cambio si detuvieran a los del interior sería el gran cataclismo (se detendría la historia). Deben de haber empezado a narrar desde las épocas más remotas y hay que tener paciencia. Escribiendo sin descanso puede que algún día alcancen el presente y lo superen, en todos los sentidos del verbo superar: que lo dejen atrás, lo modifiquen y hasta con un poco de suerte lo mejoren. Es cuestión de lenguaje.

long years. Their memory is eternal and they have to go a long way back in time to arrive at the origin of the myth, dust the cobwebs off it, and demythicize it (in order to restore to the truth its essence, to take off its disguise). They say that we'll still have time to go on living, to create new myths for them. The pragmatists are in the city, the idealists are far away. Where will they meet?

Meanwhile the persecutions grow more insidious. One can't go out in the street without seeing men in uniform breaking the law for the mere pleasure of laughing at those who must obey it.

Though I'm quiet these days, I go on jotting it all down in bold strokes (and at great risk) because it's the only form of freedom left. Others still make enormous efforts to believe the radio, which transmits information quite different from what is already public knowledge. This clever system of contradictory messages is designed to drive the population mad; to preserve my sanity, I write in the dark without being able to reread what I've written. At least I feel that I'm supported by my fellow countrymen in the interior. I'm not writing a book like them, but it's something. Mine is a modest contribution and I hope it never gets into the hands of readers: I don't want to be discovered. Sometimes I return home so impressed by people who wander blindly in the streets—people who have been beaten, mutilated, bloodied, or crippled—that I can't even write. But that doesn't matter. Nothing would happen if I stopped writing. If the people in the interior stopped writing—history would stop for us, disaster overcome us. They must have begun their story with the earliest times; one has to be patient. If they go on writing they may someday reach the present and overcome it, in all the meanings of the verb to *overcome:* leave it behind them, modify it, and with a little luck even improve it. It's a question of language.

CARTA A GIANFRANCO

LETTER TO GIANFRANCO

Alberto Manguel, translator of Marco Denevi

Alberto Manguel was born in Buenos Aires in 1938 and for years lived and taught in Toronto, Canada. He is the author of *A History of Reading* and editor of *Black Water* and *Other Fires*, among numerous other anthologies. "I started translating from English into Spanish," Manguel writes from Paris, where he once lived, "when I was in high school in Buenos Aires, because I wanted my friends to read certain texts I liked and which were only available in the original. Then I began translating for publication: works by Sylvia Plath, Mark Twain, Katherine Mansfield, Arnold Wesker, John Hawkes. My first published translation from Spanish into English was Borges's novella, *The Congress*, for Ricci in Milan. I have also brought German, Italian and French authors into English, like Marguerite Yourcenar and Philippe Sollers. Years after I left Argentina, I no longer translated into Spanish, only into English." He adds: "My method—to give it a grand name—varies. Sometimes I read the whole thing several times; more often, I try to translate at a first or second reading and then work at length on the translation. I believe translation is one of the most careful reading methods I know, and forces you to disentangle the text as you proceed. The translator sees...all its faults of logic, all its mistakes and botched-up passages. The translator's eye is relentless. I believe that polishing the translated text requires more attention than reading the original. When the stars are kind, the translated text should read as if it had been written by a twin soul of the author in another language. A few times you succeed: Roy Campbell's translation of *St. John of the Cross*, for instance."

Manguel's view of the liaison between author and translator is fascinating. "The less you know about a writer, the better. By and large, writers are the worst readers for their own texts and lie like fiends about the meaning of their work. If possible, I like my writers to be dead and, if that cannot be easily accomplished, I prefer them not have the slightest knowledge of English. There's nothing worse than a writer who thinks he or she knows 'some English' and insists on telling you how they would say it 'en inglés'."

He is an inexhaustible supporter of Denevi's prose, which, in his eyes, is essential to understanding contemporary Argentine letters. Born in 1922 in Sáenz Peña, a suburb of Buenos Aires, and still living in Argentina, Denevi is the author of *Rosaura at Ten*, which won the Kraft Prize, as well as a dozen other published and unpublished titles. In 1955 his story "Secret Ceremony," included in Alberto Manguel's anthology *Evening Games,* was awarded the *Life in Spanish Prize* for the best Latin American short story. Denevi is a member of the Academia Argentina de Letras and an accomplished playwright. He has also written for television and has been a newspaper columnist for *La Nación*. He is a fervent lover of the short story genre. "Of all the forms literature manifests itself in," he once claimed, "short fiction is the one that interests me the most." His story collections in Spanish include *Falsificaciones, El emperador de China y otros cuentos, Parque de diversiones, Hierba del dielo, Salón de lectura, Robotobor,* and *Arminta o el poder.*

Marco Denevi

CARTA A GIANFRANCO

Querido Gianfranco: me voy a París el lunes. Así como suena: a París y en avión. Debe ser el lunes porque acabo de leer en el diario que todos los lunes parte a las once de la noche un avión para París, y yo a las aviones subo sólo de noche y a las once. ¿Y por qué justamente a París? Por qué no justamente a París, diga más bien. A París se termina por ir como a una boda o a un entierro, con ganas o sin ganas, fatalmente. Apenas llegue le mandaré una tarjeta postal con la Torre Eiffel y una frase cursi: Querido Gianfranco, me vine a París el lunes, y en París mi primer recuerdo es para usted.

Me alojaré en un hotelito que hay en una novela de Francis Carco. El hotelito está situado en un barrio de mala fama, en una calle tortuosa pavimentada con adoquines rosados y ásperos, a la vuelta de un bistró donde se reúnen prostitutas, apaches y bohemios. La propietaria del hotelito es una señora que chapurrea el portugués, se llama madame Pomargue y en su juventud fue artista de varieté, así dice ella. Esa señora no se opondrá a que yo lleve a mi habitación a los hombres que me persigan por los bulevares o en el bistró me conviden con un coñac barato. Al contrario, me dará un dormitorio con espejos estratégicos y cortinados rojos de casa equívoca, me prestará su escandalosa ropa interior de cuando trabajaba en el circo y me enseñará el argot de los arrabales. A la mañana me traerá el desayuno en la cama y querrá que le cuente mis aventuras de la noche anterior. Según Francis Carco es una señora muy simpática pero la enloquecen los enanos. Trataré de que ninguno de mis amantes sea enano porque madame Pomargue se pondría celosa y buscaría la manera de quitármelo. La creo capaz de asesinarme por un lindo liliputiense.

Todavía no sé de dónde sacaré el dinero para el pasaje. Casi seguro que subiré al avión sin pasaje aunque con cara de sentirme

Marco Denevi
LETTER TO GIANFRANCO

Translated by Alberto Manguel

Dear Gianfranco, on Monday I'm leaving for Paris. Just like that: for Paris and in a plane. It has to be Monday because I've just read in the paper that every Monday at 11 P.M. there's a plane leaving for Paris, and I never get on a plane except at night, at 11 P.M. And why Paris of all places? Why not Paris of all places, is what I say. One ends up going to Paris as if one were going to a wedding or a funeral, whether one is in the mood for it or not, through a quirk of fate. As soon as I arrive, I'll send you a postcard with the Eiffel Tower and a kitsch message: *Dear Gianfranco, I left for Paris on Monday and in Paris my first thoughts are of you.*

I'll stop at a small hotel that appears in a novel by Francis Carco. The hotel is situated in a neighborhood of ill repute, on a tortuous street paved with rough pink cobblestones, around the corner from a bistro where whores, *apaches* and bohemians meet. The owner of the hotel is a lady who speaks a little Portuguese, her name is Madame Pomargue and in her youth she was a show girl, at least that's what she says. This lady won't object to my bringing up to my room the men who will pursue me along the boulevards or offer me a cheap cognac in the bistro. On the contrary, she'll give me a room with strategic mirrors and the red drapes of a bawdy house, she'll lend me her scandalous underwear from the days when she worked at the circus, and she'll teach me the argot of the underworld. In the morning, she'll bring me breakfast in bed and she'll want me to tell her my adventures of the previous night. According to Francis Carco, she's a very agreeable lady but she has a maddening weakness for dwarves. I'll see to it that none of my lovers is a dwarf, otherwise Madame Pomargue might become jealous and look for a way to steal him away from me. I believe her capable of murdering me for the sake of a handsome Lilliputian.

I still don't know where I'll find the money for the fare. I'm almost certain I'll climb onto the plane without a ticket, but looking

ya un poco harta de tanto viajar a París todos los lunes por la noche. Cuando allá arriba aparezca el inspector y pida los boletos y yo le conteste que olvidé el mío en casa, ¿usted cree que me arrojarán al espacio por el ojo de buey? ¿Serán tan groseros con una mujer que va sola a París y al hotelito de madame Pomargue? Yo en cambio pienso que me considerarán una invitada de honor, me servirán caviar y champán y cuando lleguemos al aeropuerto pondrán para mí una escalerilla alfombrada de rojo. Ya habrán cablegrafiado desde el avión y en el aeropuerto estará esperándome una multitud de muchachos jóvenes y buenos mozos, especialistas todos en sudamericanas y en poetisas solteras, todos con nombres de galanes de cine y sobrenombres de gígolos y de macros. Pero yo me iré del brazo de uno que sea rubio como usted, alto como usted, tenga los ojos como usted, por dentro verdes y por fuera dorados, y le gusten como a usted las mujeres como yo.

Me siento muy feliz ahora. De golpe me entró la loca de escribirle una carta y se la escribo. Por la radio oí que decían que había dejado de llover y que había sol. Mentira, Gianfranco. Es una trampa para que usted y yo salgamos a la calle y nos ahoguemos en alguna alcantarilla. Quieren hacernos morir antes de que nos encontremos como siempre en el bar de Paraguay y Maipú, para que después los basureros nos levanten como a dos montones de hojas secas, como a dos ratas. Sigue lloviendo, Gianfranco. La lluvia se repite, es siempre la misma, como una comparsa de ópera. Baja por un lado, sube por el otro lado, vuelve a bajar y así seguirá hasta que el agua se le gaste. No vale la pena mirarla. Usted quédese en su habitación y yo me quedaré en la mía. En la mía yo le escribo esta carta y en la suya usted la lee.

En la suya hay una estufa de leña y en la estufa un gran fuego encendido. Usted tiene puesto un pijama de seda cruda y sobre el pijama una bata rameada color malva. No sé cómo es el color malva, pero muchas veces leí "un cielo color malva", "el vestido malva de Valentina", y me imaginé un color tan hermoso que no he podido atribuirle nunca ningún color en particular. Gianfranco, usted está un poco despeinado pero le queda bien, le da un aire de adolescente situado entre la angustia y el ardor, entre la indiferencia y el capricho. Desde aquí huelo su perfume, ese perfume que usa, ese aroma de tabaco rubio, frutas cítricas y maderas nobles que lo

like someone rather fed up with traveling to Paris every Monday night. When up there the inspector comes round asking to see our tickets and I tell him that I've forgotten mine at home, do you think they'll hurl me into the air through one of those little round windows? Will they be as brutish as that to a woman traveling all on her own to Paris, to Madame Pomargue's hotel? I think that instead they'll consider me their guest of honor, offer me champagne and caviar, and when we reach the airport they'll call for the red-carpeted stairway. They will have wired ahead from the plane and at the airport a crowd of handsome young men will be waiting for me, all specialists in South American women and single female poets, all bearing the names of film stars and the nicknames of pimps and gigolos. But I'll leave on the arm of one as blond as you, tall as you, someone with your eyes, green in the middle and golden around the edge, someone who, like you, loves women like me.

Now I feel very happy. Suddenly I was overcome by this crazy urge to write you a letter, and now I'm writing it. On the radio I heard them say that it had stopped raining and that the sun was shining. All lies, Gianfranco. It's a trap, so that you and I go out into the streets and drown in some godforsaken gutter. They want us to die before we meet at our usual place, in the cafe at the corner of Paraguay and Maipu, so that afterwards the street-sweepers sweep us up like a couple of piles of dry leaves, like a couple of dead rats. It's still raining, Gianfranco. Rain repeats itself, it is always the same rain, like the chorus in an opera. Comes down on one side, rises on the other, comes down again and will continue like this until the rainwater is all worn out. It's not worth watching it. You just stay in your room and I'll stay in mine. In my room I am writing you this letter, in your room you are reading it.

In your room is a wood stove and in the stove a big blazing fire. You are wearing raw silk pajamas and over the pajamas a cerulean-colored dressing-gown. I have no idea what a cerulean color looks like, but many times I've read of "a cerulean-colored sky," "Valentina's cerulean-colored dress," and I imagine a color so beautiful that I have never been able to give it any particular tone. Gianfranco, you're a little disheveled but it suits you, it lends you an air of adolescence midway between anguish and ardor, indifference and caprice. From where I am I can smell your perfume, that cologne you wear, that scent of blond tobacco, citrus fruit and fine

envuelve como si usted mismo lo exhalase, como si usted estuviese hecho no de carne y hueso sino de algún otro material que despide esa fragancia. Es que usted no es un hombre como los demás, Gianfranco. No tiene sus vulgaridades, sus libidinosidades. Usted no es el fétido jabalí que son ellos. Usted está todo formado de espíritu.

No salga, testarudo. No ha llegado el mediodía. Llueve y cuando llueve todas las horas del día son horas sin citas ni compromisos, son horas para escribir una carta o para leerla. Tampoco hoy es martes ni ninguno de los días de la semana. Cuando llueve es un día filtrado entre dos días como un amante entre el marido y la mujer. De modo que siéntese en su poltrona junto al fuego, cruce las piernas, no, las piernas las cruzan las mujeres y algunos hombres muy flacos y muy tristes, usted coloque el tobillo derecho sobre la rodilla izquierda, échese hacia atrás, apoye la nuca en el filo del respaldo y así, en esa postura que lo exhibe como un arreglo floral, sostenga con una mano el cigarrillo y con la otra mi carta y léame, Gianfranco, léame.

Aquí no hay calefacción. Luego de cinco días de lluvia mi cuarto ha empezado a derretirse y a chorrear como una vela de sebo. Las paredes se han puesto esponjosas y como miga de pan, los muebles están blandos y del techo caen lentos goterones. Cinco días que no abandono casi la cama. Se me terminaron las galletitas, el queso y el café, pero no importa porque con la humedad las galletitas ya eran de felpa vieja, el queso sabía a jabón de tocador, y el café a purgante.

En estos días sólo he leído los diarios. Son todos diarios atrasados pero tampoco me importa. Al contrario, me hace bien leer diarios atrasados. Me siento a salvo de los crímenes, las muertes y las catástrofes que a los demás los han ido alcanzando y en cambio yo los leo en los diarios que dicen hoy sucedió, hoy se cayó tal avión, hoy hubo un incendio, hoy estalló una bomba, hoy, hoy, hoy, y para mí es ayer o antes de ayer, y aquí estoy, salvada, al margen de ese hoy que se come a los vivos. Leyendo diarios viejos me siento casi eterna.

Leí hasta los avisos clasificados. Qué alivio leerlos y pensar que esas vacantes ya están ocupadas y que no debo levantarme temprano para conseguir empleo. Antes yo los leía en el riesgoso hoy y siempre caía en la trampa. "Señorita culta con redacción propia se necesita",

wood, which envelops you as if you yourself were its source, as if you were made not of flesh and bones but of some other substance giving off this fragrance. Because you're not a man like other men, Gianfranco. You don't possess their vulgarity, their libidinous lust. You are not a fetid boar like the rest of them. You are made entirely out of spirit.

Don't go out, you stubborn man. It is not yet midday. It's raining and when it rains all the hours of the day are hours without rendez-vous or engagements, they're hours in which to write letters or read them. Neither is it Tuesday today, nor any other day in the week. When it rains it's a day wedged in between two days like a lover between a husband and a wife. Therefore, sit in your armchair by the fire, cross your legs, no, women cross their legs and certain very thin melancholic men, you place your right heel over the left knee, lean back, rest your neck against the top edge of the armchair, and in this position which shows you off as in a floral arrangement, hold in one hand a cigarette and in the other my letter, and read me, Gianfranco, read me.

There's no heating here. After five days of rain my room has begun to melt and drip like a wax candle. The walls have turned into sponges or moist bread dough, the furniture is soft and from the ceiling fall slow and cumbersome drops. For five whole days I have barely left the bed. My cookies are all gone, as well as the cheese and the coffee, but it doesn't matter because with the dampness the cookies had turned to old felt, the cheese tasted of beauty soap and the coffee of laxative.

These past days I've read nothing but the newspapers. They're all old newspapers, but I don't care. On the contrary, it does me good to read old newspapers. I feel safe from crime, from death and from catastrophes that have reached other people, and I instead read about them in the papers that say that it all happened today, that today a plane crashed, today a fire broke out, today a bomb exploded, today, today, today, and for me it's yesterday or the day before yesterday, and here I am, saved, away from that today that gobbles up the living. Reading old newspapers I feel almost eternal.

I read even the classified ads. What a relief to read them and know that those vacancies are already filled and that I don't need to get up early in order to find a job. Before, I used to read them in the perilous today and would always fall into their trap. "Well educated

e iba. Pero ahí me las encontraba a ellas, tan altas, tan educadas, y tan despiadadas, vestidas a la última moda, con sus párpados ocres y sus uñas de mandarín. Lo primero que hacían era preguntarme la edad. Yo les decía a veces treinta y ocho y a veces cuarenta y dos. Algunas enarcaban las cejas finas de coré griega y rezongaban: "Pero el aviso pedía secretarias menores de veinticinco años". Otras, sin mirarme, pero con una expresión de disgusto como si yo las importunase con mi sola presencia, me daban un papel. El papel era la solicitud de empleo. Estudios cursados, idiomas que domina, cuáles son sus pretensiones en materia de sueldo. Y referencias. Yo nunca sabía que poner en las referencias y lo ponía a usted. Después ellas me tomaban la solicitud sin leerla, sin mirarme, y mirando por la ventana o descifrándose las uñas de Lingunchang me decían: "Nosotros la llamaremos, buenas tardes". Pero nunca me llamaron para darme el empleo. ¿Comprende por qué, Gianfranco? Porque esperaban que yo leyese el próximo aviso, volviese a ir y ellas pudieran preguntarme otra vez la edad. Era una emboscada. Felizmente he abierto los ojos. Y lo que ellas no saben es que las engañé. Porque jamás en la solicitud de empleo dije que en 1961 me dieron un premio de poesía y que César Tiempo escribió en *Davar* que mi libro parecía una colección de estampas (no sé si estampas o miniaturas) coloreadas e iluminadas por los Limbourg. Pero ellas no lo saben ni saben quiénes son los Limbourg.

Los diarios traen también la lista de las conferencias y de las exposiciones de pintura. Yo antes iba a las conferencias. Por fin he comprendido que todas las conferencias son una broma estúpida que nos hacen los conferenciantes. Simulan hablar de Ortega y Gasset o de la problemática de la novelística latinoamericana y en realidad repiten durante una hora frases sin sentido, mezclan párrafos tomados al tuntún de los manuales de literatura. Todas las conferencias son la misma conferencia, sólo que los conferenciantes cambian el orden de las palabras y las pronuncian como si estuviesen convencidos de lo que dicen y hasta hacen ademanes. Y el público tan tonto ahí sentado los escucha y no entiende nada pero pone cara de entender y al final aplaude y piensa qué hombre tan inteligente ése que yo no pesqué casi nada de lo que dijo y mientras tanto aquel farsante corre a otra sala de conferencias a

young lady able to type properly," and I'd be off. But there I'd meet them, the women, so tall, so well brought up, so heartless, dressed in the latest fashion, with ochre eyelids and mandarin nails. The first thing they'd do was ask me my age. Sometimes I'd say thirty-eight and sometimes forty-two. A few would arch their thin Greek kore eyebrows and protest: "But the ad specified secretaries under twenty-five." Others, without looking at me, but with a grimace of disgust as if I were importuning them merely with my presence, would hand me a piece of paper. The paper was a job application. Academic degrees, languages spoken, salary expectations. And references. I would never know what to put under "references," so I'd always put your name. Then they'd take the application without reading it, without even looking at me, and staring out of the window or deciphering their Ling Yung-Chang nails, they'd say: "We'll give you a call, good afternoon." But they never called to offer me the job. Do you know why, Gianfranco? Because they expected me to read the ads on the next day, and go and apply once again, and once again they'd be able to ask me my age. The whole thing was a trap. Happily I've since opened my eyes. And what they don't know is that I've deceived them. Because nowhere on the application did I say that in 1961 I received a poetry prize, and that the poet César Tiempo wrote in the magazine *Davar* that my book was like a collection of block-prints (I don't know if he said block-prints or miniatures), illuminated by the hand of the Limbourgs. But they don't know, nor do they know who the Limbourgs were.

The newspapers also print the list of conferences and art exhibits. I used to attend the conferences. But now, at last, I've come to realize that all conferences are a stupid joke played on us by the lecturers. They pretend to be speaking about Ortega y Gasset, or about the problem of the Latin-American novel, but in fact they repeat for a full hour nonsensical phrases, mingling without rhyme or reason paragraphs taken from literary textbooks. All conferences are the same conference, but the lecturers change the order of the words and pronounce them as if they were convinced of what they were saying, and they even accompany the whole thing with gestures. And the foolish public sits there listening and understands nothing but looks as if it understood and finally breaks into applause and thinks, *what an intelligent man, I wasn't able to make out a single word of what he said* and all the while the con-artist

repetir el mismo galimatías y a recibir los mismos aplausos. No iré más.

Para colmo yo me sentaba en la última fila, al fondo del salón que era siempre muy largo y muy estrecho, y hasta donde yo estaba la voz del conferenciante llegaba lo mismo que un hilo de orín que corriese por debajo de los pies de la concurrencia. Yo al rato me aburría y miraba a mi alrededor con mis ojos por dentro malvas y por fuera violetas, y rogaba a Dios que aquel discurso terminase y cuando terminaba me ponía de pie y salía a los apurones como si corriera a una cita y se me hubiese hecho tardísimo, pero una vez en la calle me iba caminando sola y despacio hasta mi casa, mirando las vidrieras de los negocios para demorar el momento de llegar y tener que prepararme la comida para mí sola. Además, Gianfranco, le advierto: a las conferencias concurren ciertos hombres con el único propósito de relacionarse con mujeres solitarias. Se les sientan al lado, las rozan con el codo y con la pierna, les buscan conversación, les sirven una pastilla de anís y después pretenden invitarlas a tomar juntos un café pero es otra emboscada. Las enamoran, les dan una cita y luego no aparecen más, no las llaman más por teléfono, las dejan morirse de angustia y de bochorno en una esquina céntrica.

Tampoco iré a las exposiciones. Los días de inauguración están copadas por una gente siniestra que se coloca de espaldas contra la pared y contra los cuadros, hablan y hablan y fuman y a los cuadros ni los miran, los ocultan con sus cuerpos y la humareda, y al fin cuando la inauguración termina se van todos al mismo tiempo y los cuadros aparecen arañados, cuarteados, borroneados, despintados, hechos un desastre. No me explico cómo los pintores permiten que el público de las inauguraciones les sabotee así la pintura. Y después no va nadie más a las galerías, porque quién quiere ver esos mamarrachos todos descoloridos y viejos. Algún jubilado que no tiene a dónde ir, solteronas, ancianos que entran para guarecerse de la lluvia o del frío y desfilan delante de los cuadros como delante de una rueda de presos entre los que deben identificar al que les asesinó a la hija. Los miran de reojo, con desconfianza, con susto y con apuro, y al fin huyen antes de ser víctimas de un ataque de esos cuadros siniestros.

Yo en un mismo día he ido a cinco y a seis de esas muestras de pintura póstuma. He mirado cada cuadro hasta odiarlo y hasta no

runs off to another conference hall to repeat the same gobbledy-gook and receive the same ovation. I'll never go again.

To make matters worse, I used to sit in the last row, at the end of the hall that was always very long and very narrow, and the voice of the lecturer would reach me like a rivulet of urine running under the feet of the public. After a while I'd be bored and would cast my eyes around (my eyes that are cerulean in the center and violet around the edges), and prayed to God that the conference should come to an end, and when it finally came to an end I'd stand up and leave in a hurry as if I were terribly late for an appointment. But once in the street I'd walk home slowly, all on my own, peering into shop-windows to delay the moment of coming home and having to prepare a meal for myself alone. And let me tell you something else, Gianfranco, let me warn you: conferences are attended by a certain kind of men whose only purpose is to approach solitary women. They sit next to them, rub against them an elbow or a knee, start a conversation, offer them a mint and then pretend to invite them to have a coffee together. But it's just another trap. They charm them, suggest a rendezvous and then never reappear, never phone them again, leave them to die of anguish and shame at a downtown street corner.

Nor will I attend any more art exhibits. The openings are taken over by sinister people standing with their backs to the wall and to the paintings, talking and talking and smoking and not even glancing at the paintings; they hide the paintings with their bodies and their smoke, and when the opening is over at last, they all leave at once and the paintings appear scratched, cracked, smudged, chipped, ruined. I can't understand how painters allow the public at these exhibits to sabotage their work in this way. And after that opening, no one goes to the galleries, because who wants to see those atrocities, all old and discolored? A solitary pensioner with nowhere to go, spinsters, old men who come in to seek refuge from the rain or the cold and who totter past the paintings like past a row of prisoners amongst whom they must identify the murderer of their daughter. They glance at them sideways, hurriedly, with distrust and fear, and finally they escape into the street rather than become the victims of these ghastly works of art.

I, in a single day, have been to five or six of these exhibits of posthumous paintings. I've observed each canvas to the point of

verlo, lo miré de cerca y desde lejos, lo miré sentada y de pie, lo miré como si sospechase una falsificación o tratase de descubrir, bajo esas groseras pinceladas, alguna perdida Madonna del Renacimiento, y todo porque cuando terminase de mirarlos y de levantarme y sentarme y consultar el catálogo tendría que volverme a casa caminando sola y detenerme frente a las vidrieras para no preparar una triste compota de manzana. Alguna vez, en un rincón de la galería, estaba el pintor, el autor de los cuadros, casi siempre con una mujer muy fea y antipática y muy varonil. El pintor me vigilaba, me espiaba para ver que cara ponía yo. Dios mío, qué impudicia la de esas pintores que quieren descubrirnos la boca abierta de la admiración o los ojos del arrobo mientras miramos sus cuadros. Yo, cada vez que los veía ahí, acechando como rufianes mis idas y venidas frente a las pinturas, me sentía furiosa y adrede ponía una expresión de contrariedad y a él no lo miraba hasta que de golpe, al tercer o cuarto cuadro, daba una violenta media vuelta y entonces sí le clavaba la vista y salía rabiosa de la exposición como de un urinario de hombres donde hubiese entrado por error.

En la calle paso de largo frente a las vidrieras donde hay maniquíes femeninos. Detesto a esas jovencitas altas, rubias, de párpados ocres. Podría mirarlas un día entero con mirada de serpiente y ellas seguirán sondriéndose con todo su desdén, seguirán mofándose de mí porque visten a la última moda y yo ando todavía con mi ropa de hace cinco años. Tampoco me detengo frente a los maniquíes masculinos. Me dan miedo esos jóvenes de pelo rubio y largo, cara color sepia, pupilas encendidas por un fulgor de droga y el cuerpo tan duro y tan esbelto. Están ahí, altos, temibles, listos para saltar sobre mí. Yo camino delante de ellos con la cabeza gacha, trato de que no me descubran. En cambio me atraen las vidrieras de los almacenes, todas esas botellas, esos frascos, las cajas de fruta abrillantuda, los cajones de ciruelas negras y de pasas de uva, las latas de caramelos. Ultramarinos. Qué hermosa palabra, Gianfranco. Almacén de ultramarinos.

Pero las vidrieras que prefiero son esas que nadie mira, mal iluminadas, tristes como habitaciones cuyo ocupante murió y nadie tocó desde entonces, esas donde hay aparatos ortopédicos, jeringas o piedras esmeriles. Las veo tan solas y tan despreciadas que me paro a mirarlas y así me hago la ilusión de que son sitios hechos

hatred, to the point of no longer seeing it, I observed it from near and from far, I observed it sitting down and standing up, I scrutinized it as if I suspected it of being a fake or as if I were trying to discover, under the coarse brushstrokes, a lost Renaissance Madonna, and all because when I'm done with looking at them and with standing up and sitting down and consulting the catalogue, I have to walk back all alone, and I stop in front of the shop-windows so as not to have to go home and prepare a sad apple compote. Sometimes, in a comer of the gallery, I'd see the artist, the author of those paintings, almost always accompanied by an ugly, disagreeable, very masculine woman. The artist would watch me, would spy on me to see my reaction. My God, the impudence of these artists who want to discover us with our mouths open in admiration or with our eyes enthralled as we admire their paintings! Every time I'd see one of them there, preying like a ruffian on my comings and goings in front of their work, I'd become furious and on purpose I'd pull a consternated face and avoid looking back at him, until suddenly, after the third or fourth painting, I'd turn violently around and fix my eyes on him, and leave the exhibition fuming as if I'd gone into the men's room by mistake.

On the street I never stop at the shop-windows with female mannequins. I detest these tall, blond young women with golden eyelids. I could stare at them for days with a serpent's eye, and they'd still be smiling scornfully, mocking me because they dress in the latest fashion and I walk about in my five-year-old clothes. Neither do I stop in front of the male mannequins. I'm afraid of those young men with their long, blond hair, light brown faces, pupils lit up by a drug-induced brilliance and the bodies so hard and so trim. There they are: tall, frightening, ready to jump on me. I walk past them with my head lowered, trying not to be seen. Instead, I'm attracted to the windows of grocery stores: all those bottles, all those jars, those boxes of candied fruit, of black prunes and raisins, the tins of sweets. *Ultramarine.* What a beautiful word, Gianfranco. Ultramarine shops.

But the windows I prefer are those which nobody looks at, badly lit, as sad as rooms whose occupant has died and that no one has touched since, windows with orthopedic contraptions, syringes or pumice stones. I see them so lonely and despised that I always stop to look at them, and imagine that these are places created on

adrede para que nos juntemos los solitarios. A veces algún hombre se detiene y mira, él también, lo que yo miro. ¿Sabe, Gianfranco? Entre ese hombre y yo se establece un vínculo sutil, una simpatía, una comunión. No necesitamos hablar. A los dos nos gusta sentirnos al margen de la muchedumbre que contempla las vidrieras de los maniquíes. No nos interesan, en realidad, los aparatos ortopédicos ni los abrasivos ni esos insecticidas, pero los miramos con dolor porque nadie los mira sino nosotros. Nuestra misión es ésa: asumir el desprecio de la gente.

Necesito irme, Gianfranco. Irme a una ciudad donde los poetas seamos como prostitutas: que caminemos por la calle y los hombres nos sigan y nos ofrezcan dinero en voz baja, pero no para hacer el amor sino para que les recitemos una poesía. ¿Cuánto cuesta un pasaje a París? ¿Cien mil pesos? ¿Cómo los conseguiré? ¿Quién me los prestará o me los regalará? ¿De dónde los robaré? Venderé mis alhajas, mi piano de Leipzig, mis porcelanas inglesas y me iré a alguna parte muy lejos. O viajaré como polizón. Buenos Aires no es una ciudad para poetas. Aquí todo el mundo tiene la vista fija en un punto a mi derecha o a mi izquierda, nadie en mí. Avanzo entre esas miradas como entre las paredes de un túnel abierto sólo para mí. Qué risa, soy la mujer invisible. Gianfranco, entre yo y el extremo del túnel espero que esté Dios porque si no me volveré loca.

Por fin sé a quién se parece usted. Se parece a Le Clézio, ese novelista tan joven y tan buen mozo que vi fotografiado en el suplemento de La Nación. Pero Le Clézio tiene los ojos por fuera azules y por dentro grises, unos ojos fríos, irónicos y creo que también crueles. Los suyos son ardientes y apasionados y al mismo tiempo castos como los de un niño. Cuando nos conocimos en la librería L'Amateur usted se me acercó y me pidió que le firmase un ejemplar de "Los rostros de la muerte" que acababa de comprarle a aquel vendedor que seguramente le dijo ésa es la autora y me señaló con el dedo, usted añadió en voz baja como si me confiase un secreto me llamo Gianfranco, y entonces yo lo miré en los ojos y le puse aquella dedicatoria "A Gianfranco que tiene los ojos por dentro verdes y por fuera dorados" que a usted tanto le gustó. Después salimos juntos de la librería y caminamos hasta que todas las calles cambiaron repentinamente de nombre.

purpose for us solitary beings to meet. Sometimes a man will stop and stare too, at my same window. And you know what, Gianfranco? Between that man and myself there establishes itself a subtle link, a sympathy, a communion. We don't need to speak. We both enjoy feeling that we are set aside from the crowds that stare at the mannequin windows. The truth is that we're not interested in the orthopedic contraptions nor in the abrasives nor in the insecticides, but we look at them with deep-felt sorrow because no one except us looks at them. That is our mission: to take upon ourselves that which the others despise.

I need to leave, Gianfranco. Leave and go to a city where we poets are like prostitutes: where we can walk down the street and men will follow us and, in a low voice, offer us money, not to make love to them but to recite poetry. How much does a ticket to Paris cost? A hundred thousand pesos? How will I find that kind of money? Who will lend it to me or give it to me as a gift? Where will I steal it from? I'll sell my jewels, my Leipzig piano, my English china and go somewhere far, far away. Or I'll become a stowaway. Buenos Aires is not a poet's city. Here every man fixes his eyes on a point to my right or to my left, never on me. I advance among those looks as through a tunnel opened for myself alone. How funny, I'm the invisible woman! Gianfranco: I hope God is somewhere between myself and the end of the tunnel, otherwise I think I'll go crazy.

At last I know who you remind me of. You remind me of Le Clézio, that French novelist so young and so handsome whose photograph I saw in the literary supplement of *La Nación*. But Le Clézio has eyes that are blue around the edges and grey in the center: cold, ironic eyes—even cruel, I believe. Yours are ardent and passionate, and at the same time as chaste as those of a child. When we met at the bookstore L'Amateur, you approached me and asked me to sign a copy of *The Faces of Death* which you had just bought from the salesman who had no doubt told you that there was the author, and pointed at me with his finger. You added in a low voice, as if you were confiding a secret, *my name is Gianfranco,* and then I looked you in the eyes and wrote "To Gianfranco whose eyes are green in the center and golden around the edges," and you liked that very much. Then we left the bookstore together and walked until all the streets suddenly changed names.

Yo tenía puesto todavía me acuerdo mi tapado de piel de nutria y usted un pantalón de franela gris, tricota blanca de cuello alto, saco sport color miel, mocasines borravinos y medias azules con una cuchilla roja. Las mujeres lo miraban con rencor, parecía que le hacían mudos y terribles reproches. Pero usted no se fijaba en ellas. Usted iba como abriéndome paso, como quitando del medio todos los estorbos. Los demás se apartaban y usted y yo caminábamos como por una alfombra tendida sólo para nosotros dos. Yo le llegaba al mentón y sin embargo era una mujer alta, con el pelo color sangre y la voz profunda de Lauren Bacall. Cuando las calles cambiaron de nombre nos dimos cuenta de que estábamos muertos de cansancio y entramos en un café, y ahí usted siguió abriéndome paso hasta una mesita ubicada en un rincón entre mamparas de madera y plantas artificiales.

Un café de la belle epoque, dijo usted. Al mozo le pidió dos cafés pero el mozo se equivocó o no se equivocó y nos trajo dos coñac como si estuviésemos en el bistró a la vuelta del hotelito de madame Pomargue. Nos reímos mucho y después tomamos el coñac lentamente, mirándonos para ajustar nuestros movimientos. Después una orquesta en un palco empezó a tocar Brahms. Después usted tomó el libro y leyó en voz baja todos mis poemas. Después lo cerró con un ademán de sacerdote que manipula un objeto sagrado, lo colocó sobre la mesa, se puso de codos, apoyó la barbilla en las manos y me miró. Y en ese momento nos dimos cuenta de que nos amábamos porque amábamos la poesía. Pero usted no me pidió un beso como los hombres que van a las conferencias, ni me dejó sola como los que miran conmigo las piernas ortopédicas y los herrajes. Usted se quedó junto a mi hasta que todas las luces se apagaron.

¿Y si me fuese a Nueva York? Aunque en Nueva York me disolvería como un terrón de azúcar en agua caliente. Mejor París. París o Roma o Londres. No, Londres no, Londres jamás. O quelle ville de la Bible. En Londres moriría estrangulada por un Jack el Destripador de rostro color sepia y pelo largo. No se preocupe, viajaré. Necesito no seguir siendo una mujer que en la sala de espera de una estación simula aguardar la llegada o la partida de un tren y entre tanto está ahí sentada lo mismo que una pordiosera o una prostituta.

Los hombres que me amaron hace ocho o diez años ya no existen para mí. Aunque quisieran casarse conmigo les contestaría

I was wearing, I still remember, my fur coat, and you were wearing grey flannel trousers, a white turtleneck, a honey-colored sports jacket, oxblood moccasins and blue socks with a red stripe. In the street, the women glared at us; they seemed to be hurling at you wordless and terrible accusations. But you paid no attention to them. You walked on as if making way for me, as if removing obstacles from my path. The others would step aside and you and I would walk as if along a carpet unrolled exclusively for the both of us. I reached your chin and yet I'm a tall woman, hair the color of blood and a deep voice like Lauren Bacall's. When the streets changed names we realized we were dead tired and we entered a cafe, and you continued to make way for me until we reached a little table set in a corner among wooden flowerboxes and artificial plants.

A *belle epoque* cafe, you said. You asked the waiter for two coffees but the waiter made a mistake or didn't make a mistake and brought us two cognacs just as if we'd been at the bistro round the corner from Madame Pomargue's hotel. We laughed and then slowly sipped our drinks, watching one another in order to adjust our movements. Then an orchestra, up in one of the balconies, started playing Brahms. You took the book and read in a low voice all my poems. Then you closed it with the gestures of a priest manipulating a sacred object, laid it down, put your elbows on the table, leaned your chin on your hands and looked at me. And at that very moment we realized we loved one another because we both loved poetry. But you didn't ask me to kiss you, like the men at the conferences, nor did you leave me on my own like those who stare with me at the orthopedic legs and the bits of metal. You stayed by my side until all the lights were extinguished.

And if I flew to New York? Even if I know that in New York I'd melt like a lump of sugar in hot water. Better Paris. Paris or Rome or London. No, not London, never London. *O quelle ville de la Bible.* In London I'd die strangled by a Jack the Ripper with a light brown face and long hair. Don't worry, I'll travel. I must never again be a woman who in the waitingroom of a train station pretends to wait for the arrival or departure of a train, while she sits there like a beggar or a prostitute.

The men who loved me eight or ten years ago no longer exist for me. Even if they wished to marry me I'd tell them that I don't

que no los desprecio pero que no los amo. Juan Carlos Birelli desapareció la última vez cuando en la confitería Jockey Club me pidió que fuésemos a un hotel de parejas y yo no quise ir y no lo vi más, ni él me vio más, ni me escribió ni me llamó por teléfono desde esa tarde en que yo bebí un jugo de pomelo y él un café. No puedo amarlo. Además ni sé si lo quiero o me dejé besar dos o tres veces para romper mi soledad.

Es terrible, Gianfranco. Es terrible hacer como que no se ven los defectos del hombre que nos toma una mano. Hasta que un día una no puede más y entonces se sienten ganas de vomitar.

¿Le hablé alguna vez de Julio Wialicki? Era muy joven, muy alto, muy rubio, muy pálido pero con labios rojos de mujer. Tuvimos seis encuentros en el bar de Paraguay y Maipú. Tres los olvidé y los otros tres quisiera haberlos olvidado. Tenía los ojos de cenizas por fuera y por dentro y cuando yo lo acariciaba en la ceniza aparecía como un remolino. Al verme entrar se levantaba, me besaba en la mejilla con sus labios de goma húmeda, me ayudaba a quitarme el abrigo y me decía que elegante estás y qué bien te queda el pelo color Tiziano. Pero no me miraba, miraba siempre las otras mesas como si buscase o temiese la presencia de alguien, y al rato ya se ponía malhumorado y yo sentía que me detestaba. Hasta que descubrí que sus miradas en redondo pasaban muchas veces por encima de algún muchachito de esos de blue jeans. Entonces me despedí de él para siempre sin explicarle por qué me despedía ni él me lo preguntó, y desde hace años me despierto pensado en él o me duermo pensado en él, pero no lo desprecio aunque no lo amo.

Usted no me besa en la mejilla ni en la boca, no me invita a ir a un hotel, nunca me ha dicho qué elegante estás y cuando me dejé el flequillo y lo corté un poco desparejo tampoco me dijo nada. Pero usted me toma la mano derecha con su mano derecha, la lleva hasta su brazo izquierdo, la hace descansar allí y la aprieta fuerte con el brazo contra su cuerpo y yo siento el calor de su cuerpo, siento sus músculos de felino joven. Pero ¿y las exposiciones que visito sola? ¿Y las conferencias que oigo sola sin entenderlas y sin querer oírlas? ¿Y las vidrieras donde los maniquíes lucen los vestidos que yo nunca

think badly of them but that I simply don't love them. Juan Carlos Birelli disappeared for the last time after asking me in the Jockey Club Tea-Room to go with him to a hotel where rooms are rented by the hour, and I wouldn't go, and I never saw him again, and he never wrote or phoned since that afternoon when I drank a grapefruit juice and he a coffee. I can't love him. I don't even know if I like him or if I let myself be kissed two or three times just to interrupt my loneliness.

It's terrible, Gianfranco. It's terrible to pretend not to see the defects of the man who is holding your hand. Until one day you can't take it any longer and then you feel like throwing up.

Have I ever told you about Julio Wialicki? He was very young, very tall, very blond, very pale but with the red lips of a woman. We met six times in the cafe of Paraguay and Maipu. Three of the times I've forgotten; the other three, I wish I could forget. He had ashen eyes in the center and also around the edges, and when I caressed him a sort of whirlpool would appear in the ashes. When he saw me come in, he'd rise to his feet, kiss my cheek with his damp rubber lips, he'd help me take off my coat and tell me how elegant I looked, and how well the Titian-colored hair suited me. But he never looked at me; he would always be looking towards the other tables as if he were searching for or fearing someone else's presence, and after a while he'd become cross and I could tell then that he hated me. Until I discovered that his searching looks would be directed more than once at certain young boys in jeans. For that reason I said goodbye to him forever without telling him why I was saying goodbye, nor did he ask me, and for many years now I wake thinking about him or I fall asleep thinking about him, but I don't despise him—even if I don't love him.

You don't kiss me on the cheek nor on the mouth, you don't ask me to go with you to a hotel, you've never said *how elegant you look,* and when I grew a fringe and cut it off unevenly, you said nothing either. But you hold my right hand in your right hand, carry it to your left arm, allow it to rest there and press it hard with your arm against your body, and then I can feel the heat of your body, your young feline muscles. But what about the exhibitions I attend all alone? And the conferences I listen to alone without understanding them and without even wanting to hear them? And the shop-windows where the mannequins display dresses that I will

podré comprarme? Y mis amigos, ¿dónde están mis amigos, callados todos como olas dormidas? ¿Por qué ya no me publican mis poemas en los suplementos literarios? ¿Por qué, cada vez que les llevo un poema, me hacen esperar horas y horas en esas antesalas de piso de baldosas frías y en lugar de recibirme mandan a empleados para que pasen delante de mí y me vigilen con disimulo? Ya no publico más Ahora escribo para mí y para los que me leerán dentro de cien años. De "Los rostros de la muerte" se vendieron noventa y tres ejemplares, y uno lo encontré en una librería de viejo de la calle Corrientes, todavía con mi dedicatoria. El nombre de la persona a la que se lo había dedicado estaba borrado pero yo sé quién es. Es Julio Wialicki o es Juan Carlos Birelli. Compré el ejemplar y me lo traje a casa, y donde estaba el nombre borrado puse el suyo, Gianfranco.

Ahora los editores me piden no sé cuántos miles de pesos para publicar "Los juegos de la locura". Dicen que los libros de poesía no se venden. Tienen razón. Pero la poesía para mí es como para otros hablar: no puedo quedarme todo el tiempo callada. Veo pasar los objetos de mi amor o de mi miedo y necesito gritarles, necesito llamarlos o ahuyentarlos, y los editores vienen a decirme que no, que me quede muda porque ellos no ganan dinero con mis voces, con mi voz, con la única voz que tengo para entenderme con los demás y conmigo misma. Me condenan al soliloquio, Gianfranco. Pero el soliloquio continuo es como el continuo diálogo: los dos conducen a la locura. No importa. Yo sé que de aquí cien años mi poesía será el idioma de los hombres. No es vanidad, Gianfranco. Sin la ilusión de la gloria nadie escribiría nada. Y a veces, ya lo ve, no conformamos con la ilusión de esa ilusión, con la gloria póstuma. Qué heroicos o qué estúpidos somos los poetas, es verdad. Mi letra cambia de color porque cambio de bolígrafo. El anterior se me gastó.

Oí que cuando una persona se pone de luto le parece que hay más gente de luto que nunca. A mí me pasa al revés. Cuando vivía papá y yo no tenía problemas de dinero veía pobres por todas partes. Ahora los pobres han desaparecido, las mujeres que antes caminaban con un recién nacido a cuestas y no tenían qué comer ni dónde dormir son respetables amas de casa. Y yo la única que

never be able to afford? And my friends, where are my friends, silent as sleeping waves? Why don't they publish my poems anymore in the literary supplements? Why, every time I take them a poem, they make me wait for hours in those cold, tiled waiting-rooms, and instead of seeing me they send clerks to walk by me and keep an unobtrusive eye on me? I no longer publish. Now I write only for myself and for those who will read me a hundred years from now. Of *The Faces of Death,* ninety-three copies were sold, and one of those I found in a secondhand bookstore on Avenida Corrientes, still carrying my inscription. The name of the person to whom I had inscribed it had been effaced, but I know who it was. It was either Julio Wialicki or Juan Carlos Birelli. I bought the book and brought it home with me, and there where the name had been effaced I wrote in yours, Gianfranco.

Now publishers want me to put up I don't know how many thousands of pesos to publish *The Games of Madness.* They say that books of poetry don't sell. They're right. But poetry is for me like speech is for others; I can't remain silent forever. I see the objects of my love or fear go by, and I need to yell out to them, I need to call them to me or shoo them away, and the publishers come and tell me I'm wrong, that I should remain silent because they don't earn money with my voices, with my voice, with the only voice I have to speak to others and to myself. They condemn me to a soliloquy, Gianfranco. But a continuous soliloquy is like a continuous dialogue: in both directions lies madness. No matter. I know that a hundred years hence my poetry will be the language of humankind. This isn't vanity, Gianfranco. Without the illusion of glory no one would write anything. And sometimes, as you see, we are satisfied with the illusion of that illusion, with posthumous glory. How heroic or how stupid we poets are! True enough. My writing changes color here because I'm changing pens. The previous ballpoint ran out.

I've heard that when someone wears mourning it seems to that someone that there are more people wearing mourning than ever before. With me it's the other way round. When Daddy was alive and I had no money problems, I used to see poor people all over the place. Now the poor have vanished, the women who used to walk the streets with tiny babies in arms and had nothing to eat and nowhere to sleep have become respectable housewives. And I'm the

camina sola por la calle y da vueltas y vueltas. Para mí no hay empleos, ni invitaciones, ni maridos, ni novios, ni amigos, ni automóviles, ni alhajas, ni cartas, ni llamados telefónicos. Me pregunto cómo hace toda esa gente para construirse cada uno su lugarcito en el mundo, su alvéolo, y en cambio yo soy la suelta, la mostrenca. A veces se me figura que Dios me trazó este destino. Dios no ha querido que me distrajera de la poesía. Y entonces creo que sí es así, es porque mi poesía vale tanto como la de Baudelaire o la de Pavese. Pero qué precio debo pagar por ello, Gianfranco. Escribir "Los rostros de la muerte", escribir "Los juegos de la locura" y después enloquecer y morir.

Cuando me dieron el premio de poesía tuve mi cuarto hora de invitaciones, de amistades, hasta de citas por teléfono. Todos querían conocerme. Yo creí que venían a mí como yo iba a ellos, para vivir lo que escribíamos. Gianfranco, sé que no me diferencio de los que no son poetas sólo por lo que escribo. Sé que la diferencia se propaga a mi rostro, a mis gestos, hasta a mi vestimenta, y mis gustos, y mis ideas, a toda yo. Por eso al rato ya estaba yo callada y las mujeres, con la expresión de haber oído en el cuarto al lado los gritos de una enferma y querer disimular, hablando todas juntas de sus viajes a Europa, del escándalo de un premio literario mal concedido o de los amores seniles de algún escritor célebre. Los hombres las miraban como si ellas repitiesen una lección que ellos les habían enseñado, cada tanto les corregían algún nombre, alguna fecha, pero también se miraban entre ellos como para ponerse de acuerdo o para recordarse mutuamente algo, y entonces uno de los dos o los dos que se habían mirado me lanzaban una ojeada de refilón como para comprobar que yo seguía ahí y que no se habían equivocado. Y yo, muda, me sonreía sin deseos de sonreír y dejaba de entender la conversación de aquellas mujeres que se quitaban unas a otras la palabra de la boca como si quisieran impedir que los gritos de la enferma de la habitación de al lado volvieran a oírse. Hasta que todos se despedían con la promesa de llamarse por teléfono y de verse otro día en otra parte, y a mí en la calle me daban la mano y me felicitaban por mis poemas y por mi premio y después subían a sus automóviles y yo me volvía caminando sola a mi casa.

only one who walks the streets, round and round again. For me there are no jobs, no invitations, no husbands, no fiancés, no friends, no cars, no jewels, no letters, no phone calls. I ask myself how all those people manage to make for themselves a little corner in this world, their nest, and I instead am like a stray, a lost sheep. Sometimes I believe that God forged this destiny for me. God hasn't wanted anything to distract me from poetry. And that leads me to believe that, if that is so, then my poetry is as good as Baudelaire's or Pavese's. But at what cost, Gianfranco! To write *The Faces of Death,* to write *The Games of Madness,* and then to go crazy and die.

When I received the poetry prize I had my fifteen minutes of invitations, friendships, even rendezvous over the phone. Everyone wanted to know me. I thought they were coming to me just as I was going to them, to live out what we were writing. Gianfranco, I know that I don't distinguish myself from those who are not poets, merely because of what I write. I know that the difference spreads to my face, to my gestures, even to my clothes, and to my tastes, and to my ideas, to my whole self. That is why in no time at all I had plunged myself into silence, and the women, with the expression of having heard next door the cries of a sick person and wishing to pretend that nothing had happened, would talk all at the same time of their trips to Europe, of the scandal of an ill-conceived literary prize or of the senile love affairs of a celebrated writer. The men stared at them as if they, the women, were repeating a lesson that they, the men, had taught them; every so often they, the men, would correct a name, a date, but they'd also exchange glances among themselves to agree about something or to remind each other of something, and then one of the two men, or both the men who had exchanged glances would look in my direction, discreetly, as if to check that I was still there and that they hadn't made a mistake. And I, silent, smiling without wanting to smile, stopped understanding the conversation of those women who kept interrupting one another as if to prevent the cries of the sick person next door from being heard. And then they'd all say goodbye with the promise of phoning one another and of seeing one another in some other place, and in the street they'd shake my hand and congratulate me on my poems and my prize, and then they'd climb into their cars and I'd find myself walking home all on my own once again.

Suelo encontrarlos en las conferencias y en las antesalas de los diarios. Fingimos no reconocernos. Cuando las conferencias terminan y yo me levanto y salgo, oigo a mis espaldas que se invitan a ir a las comidas de las embajadas y a los cócteles del Cinzano Club, pero yo sigo saliendo sola, sigo caminando sola por la calle y me detengo frente a la vidriera de los aparatos ortopédicos y a veces me compro un chocolate y me lo voy comiendo despacio y con lágrimas en los ojos. En las antesalas de los diarios miro fijo una pared mientras ellas me mandan sus perfumes de Christian Dior y ellos su olor a tabaco rubio, a frutas cítricas y a maderas nobles. Los empleados los saludan y a mí me vigilan con hostilidad. Alguien abre una puerta, los llaman por sus nombres de pila o por sus sobrenombres, se abrazan, se besan, se dan la mano, se ríen y al fin desaparecen dentro de los hondos despachos alfombrados y yo me pongo de pie y salgo con mi último poema en la cartera.

Tampoco quiero reunirme con esas viejas y esos viejos que se juntan en algún fúnebre café de la avenida de Mayo. Los odio. Una vez me arrastraron con ellos, me preguntaron si me gustaba Bartrina o Lorenzo Stechetti, me recitaron sus nidos de cóndores. Otra vez me pidieron que les recitase yo mis versos, y yo harta les recité la balada de Florentino Prunier de Duhamel y ellos me miraron consternados o se sonrieron con indulgencia y un viejo, ondulando como una sopa espesa, me aseguró que yo le hacía recordar a Guido Spano. Entonces me levanté y me fui y no volví más. Pero tengo miedo de que me persigan. Tengo miedo de que se apoderen de mis poemas inéditos y los transformen en acrósticos o en romances de García Lorca. Los odio todavía más que los otros. Porque los otros me rechazan y al menos así rechazada me mantengo intacta, pero éstos me aceptan sólo para cubrirme de sus gelatinas.

Gianfranco, ¿estoy condenada a escribir a solas, a leer a solas, a vivir a solas, a ser a solas la hermana de Aloysius Bertrand y de Lautréamont y de todos los grandes espíritus, la hermana que comprende cada una de sus palabras secretas, que comparte cada uno de sus estremecimientos y, apenas salgo a la calle, a convertirme en una mujer extraña y solitaria que no puede esperar no ya el amor pero ni siquiera la simpatía o el interés de nadie? ¿Ser un gran artista para la posteridad exige el costo de ser una criatura chocante

I often meet them at the conferences and in the waitingrooms of the periodicals. We pretend not to recognize one another. When the conference is over and I get up and leave, I hear them behind my back inviting each other to dinners at embassies and cocktails at the Cinzano Club, but I continue to go out on my own, continue to walk on my own down the street and stop at a shop-window of orthopedic contraptions, and sometimes buy myself a chocolate bar and eat it slowly with tears in my eyes. In the waitingrooms of the periodicals I stare fixedly at a wall while they, the women, shower me with their Christian Dior perfumes and they, the men, with their scent of blond tobacco, citrus fruit and precious woods. The clerks greet them and watch me with hostility. Someone opens a door, calls them by their first names or nicknames, they hug, they kiss, they shake hands, they laugh and finally they disappear within the deep recesses of the carpeted offices, and I stand up and leave with my latest poem in my handbag.

Nor do I wish to join those old men and women who meet in some funereal cafe on Avenida de Mayo. I hate them. Once they dragged me along, they asked me if I liked the verses of Batrina or Lorenzo Stechetti, they recited for me their hosts of daffodils. On another occasion, they asked me to read my poems, and I, fed up, recited for them Duhamel's "Ballad of Florentin Prunier," and they looked at me with consternation or smiled indulgently, and one old man, undulating like a thick soup, assured me that I reminded him of that ancient Argentine classic, Guido Spano. Then I stood up and left and never returned. But I'm afraid they'll come after me. I'm afraid they'll grab hold of my unpublished poems and turn them into acrostics or into ballads *a la* García Lorca. I hate them even more than I hate the others. Because the others simply reject me and at least rejected I keep myself intact, but these old people take me in only to smother me in their jellies.

Gianfranco, am I condemned to write all on my own, to read all on my own, to live all on my own, to be the sister of Aloysius Bernard and the Count of Lautréamont, and all those great spirits, the sister who understands every single one of their secret words, who shares each of their tremors? Am I condemned to become a strange and solitary woman who can't expect—I don't say love—but even sympathy or concern from anyone? Does being a great artist in the eyes of posterity require being something repulsive in

para sus contemporáneos? No me cite, por favor, los casos que me desmienten. Déjeme con la idea de que mi rostro, mis gestos y mis ridiculeces hacen méritos frente al dios de la poesía. ¿O ese dios no permite que lo extorsionen? ¿Es indiferente a nuestro dolor, Gianfranco? ¿Indiferente como el Universo? ¿Somos nosotros los que creemos que el dolor nos asegura una compensación, y nos equivocamos?

Enoch Soames. ¿Leyó el cuento horrible de Max Beerbohm? ¿Seré otro Enoch Soames, un Enoch Soames que vendió su vida al dolor con la esperanza de las monografías, los ensayos y las antologías para cien años después, y cien años después yo no tendré ni siquiera el consuelo de verme transformada en la heroína de un cuento? Pero yo lo tengo a usted, Gianfranco. Y usted, que ama a Aloysius Bertrand y a Lautréamont y lloró cuando le recité la Balada de Florentino Prunier, usted también ama mis poemas y no lo alarman mis ojos alucinados, mis vestidos y mi pelo de gorgona. Gracias, Gianfranco. Usted, que es mi contemporáneo, es también mi posteridad. Usted es mi joven secreto que se dejaría matar por mis libros.

Estoy escribiéndole esta carta en un cuaderno. Son las tres de la tarde. Dormí un rato. Hace una semana viajé a Mar del Plata. ¿Sabía que en estos últimos años he viajado cada tres meses a Mar del Plata pero nunca en verano? Viajo sola en ómnibus, me alojo sola en un hotel miserable de La Perla, paseo sola por la rambla, miro sola el mar, almuerzo sola en un restaurante de la calle Belgrano (no ponen manteles sino papel de estraza y a menudo debo compartir la mesa con matrimonios de ancianos o con hombres solos que me miran una vez y no me miran más), a la tarde vuelvo a pasear sola por las calles céntricas y desoladas, me compro un alfajor de dulce de leche y a las cuatro o a las cinco voy al Casino. Juego a la ruleta. Gano, pierdo, vuelvo a ganar y a perder. Salgo del Casino sola, me compro otro alfajor, regreso caminando sola al hotel de La Perla, me acuesto sola, escucho sola el mugido del mar y me duermo sola.

Pero la semana pasada me fui con cien mil pesos. El empleado del Banco me decía no cancele la cuenta, deje por lo menos mil pesos, pero yo no le hice caso y retiré todo el dinero que tenía. Estaba harta de ir todos los meses y sacar una pequeña suma y

the eyes of one's contemporaries? And please don't list the cases to the contrary. Leave me with the idea that my face, my gestures, my ridiculous behavior win me points in the court of the god of poetry. Or does that god not allow himself to be bribed? Is he indifferent to our suffering, Gianfranco? As indifferent as the universe? Is it we who believe that suffering guarantees compensation? And are we wrong?

Enoch Soames. Have you read that terrifying story by Max Beerbohm? Am I to be another Enoch Soames, an Enoch Soames who sold her life to suffering in the hope of being the subject of studies, essays, anthologies, a hundred years hence, and a hundred years hence I won't even have the consolation of seeing myself transformed into the heroine of a short story? But I have you, Gianfranco. And you, you who love Aloysius Bertrand and the Count of Lautréamont, and wept when I recited for you the "Ballad of Florentin Prunier," you also love my poems and are not alarmed by my hallucinated eyes, by my dress and my Gorgon hair. Thank you, Gianfranco. You, who are my contemporary, are also my posterity. You are that secret young man who would allow himself to be killed for the sake of my books.

I'm writing this letter to you in an exercise book. It's three o'clock in the afternoon. A week ago I traveled to Mar del Plata. Did you know that in these past few years I've traveled to that seaside resort every three months, but never in the summer? I travel alone by bus, I stay alone in a miserable hotel on La Perla beach, I walk alone down the promenade, alone I look at the sea, alone I eat in a restaurant on Calle Belgrano (where they don't lay out tablecloths but use paper coverings, and I often have to share my table with elderly couples or single men who look up at me only once and then never again), in the afternoon I walk alone along the desolate downtown streets, I buy myself a small sweet pastry, and at four or five I go to the Casino. I play roulette. I win, I lose, I win and lose again. I leave the Casino alone, I buy myself another pastry, I walk back alone to the hotel on La Perla, I go to bed alone, alone I listen to the bellowing of the sea and alone I fall asleep.

But last week I went to Mar del Plata with a hundred thousand pesos. The bank clerk told me not to close the account, to leave at least a thousand to my credit, but I paid no attention to him and withdrew all the money I had. I was fed up with going every month

después pasar de largo frente a todas las vidrieras. Yo veía disminuir el saldo en la libreta. Primero, cuando murió papá, me pareció una suma enorme que me alcanzaría para toda la vida. Después todos los meses había menos, menos, menos. Entonces empecé a leer los avisos clasificados. Hasta que la semana pasada me harté, como le dije, y fui al Banco y saqué todo lo que me quedaba en la cuenta de ahorro. Eran cerca de cien mil pesos. Pensé que iba a ganar en el Casino y con lo que ganaría iba a pagar la edición de "Los juegos de la locura", y todavía me sobraría dinero para sostenerme unos años más, hasta que me diesen el Premio Nacional y la pensión, y quizá "Los juegos de la locura" sería un best seller, se vendería más que Papillon y que Love Story y yo cobraría sumas fabulosas. No se ría, Gianfranco. Todos los autores pensamos lo mismo.

Tomé el ómnibus que sale de Constitución a las 2 y 25. Felizmente nadie se me sentó al lado. Durante todo el viaje mire por la ventanilla. En una partida comí un chocolate y en otra bebí un jugo de pomelo. Llegamos a Mar del Plata de noche y a las 9 ya estaba en el Casino. No fui al hotel de La Perla. No llevaba valija ni nada, sólo la cartera con los 96.300 pesos. A las 11 lo había perdido todo menos el dinero para el boleto de vuelta. A las 11 y 15 estaba en la estación terminal. El ómnibus salía a las 12 y 55. Esperé ahí sola como si en vez de la mujer que soy fuese una mujer sin alma y sin nombre. No sé como hice para estar tan silenciosa, tan sola y tan hambrienta. Desde el chocolate que había comido a las 4 de la tarde y el jugo de pomelo a las 7 no volví a probar bocado hasta que llegué a casa a la mañana siguiente. Debo de ser una puta (perdón, Gianfranco) o un ángel humano porque en la estación terminal medio a oscuras y barrida por el viento me sentí casi dichosa pensando que soy buena, que todo cambiaría algún día o alguna noche y con mi mundo íntimo intocado por quienes no tengo interés en que lo manoseen. Al mar no lo vi ni de cerca ni de lejos pero lo oí gritar como una ballena herida. Viajé a Buenos Aires durmiendo dulcemente. Sin felicidad pero sin pedir nada a nadie. Estaba como en una cápsula de vidrio viajando sola por el espacio.

and withdrawing a small sum and then walking by all those shop-windows. I could see in my bankbook the balance of my account quickly diminishing. First, when Daddy died, it seemed like an enormous sum that would last me for as long as I lived. Then every month there was less, less, less. That was when I started reading the classified ads. Until last week I'd had enough (as I just said) and went to the bank and took out all my savings. It was almost a hundred thousand pesos. I thought I'd win at the Casino and with my winnings I'd pay for the printing of *The Games of Madness,* and I'd still have enough to keep me for another few years, until they decided to give the National Literary Prize and my pension. And perhaps *The Games of Madness* would become a bestseller, would sell more copies than *Papillon* and *Love Story,* and I'd earn fabulous amounts of money. Don't laugh, Gianfranco. All us authors think the same.

I took the bus that leaves Constitución at 2:25 p.m. Fortunately, no one sat next to me. Throughout the whole trip I looked out of the window. At one of the stops I ate a chocolate bar and at another I drank a grapefruit juice. We arrived in Mar del Plata after dark; at 9 o'clock that night I was already at the Casino. I didn't go to the hotel on La Perla. I had no suitcase, no luggage at all, only my handbag with 96,300 pesos. By 11 o'clock I'd lost everything except the money for the return fare. At 11:15 I was at the terminal. The bus was scheduled to leave at 12:55. I waited there alone, as if instead of being the woman I am I were a woman without a soul and without a name. I don't know how I managed to remain so silent, so very alone and so very hungry. Since eating that chocolate bar at 4 and drinking that grapefruit juice at 7, no food or drink passed my lips until I got home next morning. I must be a whore (excuse my language, Gianfranco) or a human angel, because in the half-dark windswept terminal I felt almost contented thinking that I'm good, that everything would change some day or night, and that my intimate world was still untouched by those whom I don't want groping at it. I didn't catch a glimpse of the sea, neither from near nor from afar, but I heard it cry out like a wounded whale. I traveled back to Buenos Aires sleeping softly. Without happiness, but without asking anything from anyone. I felt I was in a glass bell traveling alone through space.

De nuevo me dormí y ahora me desperté y no sé qué hora es. Olvidé darle cuerda a mi relojito y el relojito marca una hora que no entiendo, las agujas están abiertas en un ángulo absurdo. Marqué en el teléfono el número de la hora oficial y tampoco entiendo lo que me farfulla entre dientes esa estúpida mujer. Las radios o están mudas o transmiten siempre la misma música. No oigo ningún ruido en la calle ni en el resto de la casa. Quizá duerman todos porque es de noche. quizá sea de día y se hayan muerto o se hayan ido. Las persianas de mi habitación permanecen cerradas. Escribo a la luz del velador. Pero usted no salió de su cuarto, ¿verdad? Usted sigue leyendo mi carta y en cuanto terminemos yo de escribirla y usted de leerla me llamará por teléfono, me dirá querida voy para ahí y vendrá cargado de paquetes y de flores.

El silencio es hondo como un pozo donde todo cae desde muy arriba. No quiero salirme de mi cama ni levantar las persianas y mirar hacia afuera. Prefiero imaginarme sola en la ciudad. Hace mucho tiempo que todos se han ido a otra parte y me han dejado sola, jugando con mis poemas como con monedas en desuso. Una vez me dieron el premio de poesía para conformarme y para que no me moviese de mi rincón. Después todos se fueron de parranda por todas las costas azules del mundo y yo como una niña enferma me quedé aquí escribiendo sola mis poemas. Sé que cuando me haya muerto volverán y se apoderarán de mi poesía como de un tesoro recién descubierto. ¡Pero entre tanto yo estoy viva, Gianfranco, estoy viva y sola! Y desde mi soledad oigo el rumor del mundo como el de una fiesta a la que no he sido invitada. Dios mío, esto parece un plagio de don Arturo Capdevila. Perdóneme, Gianfranco. Cambiemos de tema. Cuando llegue toque el timbre tres veces, así sabré que es usted. Tráigame una caja de frutas abrillantadas. Tengo el antojo de las frutas abrillantadas. Y bombones. Y una botella de vino blanco. Siento sed.

Quizá mientras dormía sonó el teléfono y no lo oí, y era Julio Wialicki. A Julio Wialicki (o a Juan Carlos Birelli, ya no me acuerdo o no quiero acordarme) lo conocí en una librería. Un vendedor le dijo que yo era la autora de "Los rostros de la muerte", acababan de darme el premio, y el lo compró y me lo trajo para que yo le pusiera una dedicatoria. Pero nunca me recitó mis poemas y a la cuarta o a

I've fallen asleep again and now I've woken up and I don't know what the time is. I forgot to wind up my watch and the watch shows a time I don't understand, the hands open at an absurd angle. I rang up the operator to ask for the time, and I couldn't make out what the stupid woman was mumbling between her teeth. The radio stations are either silent or are broadcasting identical music. I can hear no sounds on the street nor in the rest of the house. Maybe everyone is asleep because it's nighttime, maybe it's daytime and everyone is dead or gone. The shutters of my room are closed. I write by the light of the nightlamp. But you haven't left your room, isn't that right? You carry on reading my letter and as soon as I finish writing it and you finish reading it, you'll give me a call, you'll say *My dear, I'm on my way,* and you'll arrive laden with parcels and flowers.

The silence is as deep as a well into which everything falls from very high above. I don't want to leave my bed and open the shutters and look outside. I prefer to imagine myself alone in the city. Everyone has departed a long time ago, leaving me on my own, playing with my poems as if they were coins no longer in circulation. Once upon a time they gave me the poetry prize to satisfy me and to keep me in my place. Then they all went off to enjoy themselves on all the cotes d'azur in the world, and I, like a sick little girl, stayed home writing my poetry, all alone. I know that when I'm dead they'll return and grab hold of my poems as if they were a newly discovered treasure. But in the meantime I'm alive, Gianfranco, I'm alive and I'm alone! And from my loneliness I hear the commotion of the world like that of a party to which I haven't been invited. My God, this seems like a poor imitation of a lachrymose and didactic poem! Forgive me, Gianfranco. Let's change the subject. When you arrive, ring three times, that way I'll know it's you. Bring me a box of candied fruit. I have a yearning for candied fruit. And chocolates. And a bottle of white wine. I'm thirsty.

Maybe while I was sleeping the phone rang and I didn't hear it, and it was Julio Wialicki. I met Julio Wialicki (or was it Juan Carlos Birelli? I no longer remember or care to remember) in a bookstore. A salesman told him that I was the author of *The Faces of Death,* they had just given me the prize, and he bought it and brought it over to me for an inscription. But he never read my poems out loud

la quinta vez que nos encontramos ya empecé yo a hacer ver que no veía y a quedarme ahí sentada al lado de un hombre como se está al lado de un enfermo incurable fingiéndole que rebosa de salud. No los amo a ninguno de los dos y aunque me propusieran casamiento les contestaría que no.

Como me dolía la mano de tanto escribir descansé un rato. El techo sigue escupiéndome sus salivazos coléricos o distraídos. Es el inconveniente de vivir en el ultimo piso de una casa de departamentos. Por la radio han empezado a hablar locutores sonámbulos y a decir que son las dos y son las tres de la mañana. Apenas llegué de vuelta de Mar del Plata revisé todos los cajones, todos los bolsillos de mis vestidos y las carteras viejas y los monederos y los floreros y los costureros, pero no encontré un centavo, lo único que encontré fue la libreta de ahorro con el sello en la tapa y en todas las páginas, el sello rojo que grita cancelada cancelada cancelada. Los últimos trescientos pesos me los gasté en un taxi desde Constitución y todavía le dejé al chofer veinte pesos de propina, porque era un muchacho rubio aunque no pude verle los ojos porque no se dio vuelta ni una sola vez a mirarme. Le pregunté si le gustaba la poesía y me contestó que sí. Le pregunté si había leido "Los rostros de la muerte" y me contestó que lo único que había leído eran los versos de Homero Manzi. No me ofendí como con los carcamanes de aquel café mortuorio de la avenida de Mayo, Manzi era todo un señor poeta y qué lindo que hasta los choferes de taxis lo lean. Le pregunté cómo se llamaba y me contestó que Gianfranco.

Estoy muy cansada ahora y sin sueño. Siento que amanece. Sé que amanece porque las cosas han empezado a adelgazar y a estirarse como gatos hambrientos. Desde la calle me viene un ruido de automóviles que huyen en todas direcciones. Usted sigue sentado junto al fuego, leyéndome. Pero ya no es rubio. Ni rubio ni joven. De pronto he descubierto que todos los hombres jóvenes y rubios me desvían la vista. Usted es moreno y tiene cincuenta años. El nombre no se lo cambio porque me gustan esos nombres italianos que terminan en o y tienen una ere en el medio. Tampoco lo conocí en una librería, que disparate. Lo conocí junto a la mesa 38 del Casino. Mis fichas eran malvas como mis ojos por dentro y las suyas eran verdes como sus ojos por dentro. Donde yo ponía una ficha malva usted ponía una ficha verde, y así estuvimos mirándonos sin

to me, and the fourth or fifth time we met I began to realize that he didn't understand, and felt as if I were sitting next to an incurable invalid, letting him think he was in full health. I love neither of them, and if they asked me to marry them, I'd say no.

As my hand started aching from so much writing, I stopped for a while. The ceiling continues to shower me with its angry or distracted spittle. That is the inconvenience of living on the top floor of an apartment building. On the radio, insomniac broadcasters have started to babble and are saying that it's two o'clock, three o'clock in the morning. As soon as I got back from Mar del Plata I rummaged through all the drawers, through all the pockets of my dresses, through all the handbags and purses and vases and sewing-baskets, but I couldn't find a single cent; all I found was the savings account booklet with the official stamp on the cover, and on every page the red seal that cried out *canceled, canceled, canceled*. The last three hundred pesos I spent on a taxi from Constitución and even gave the driver twenty pesos as a tip, because he was a young man, blond, even though I couldn't see his eyes because he didn't turn round once to look at me. I asked him if he liked poetry and he said yes. I asked him if he had read *The Faces of Death* and he answered that all he had ever read were the tango lyrics of Homero Manzi. I wasn't offended as I was with the fossils in that mortuary cafe on Avenida de Mayo. Manzi was a real poet, and how nice that even taxi drivers read him. I asked him what his name was and he said Gianfranco.

Now I'm very tired but not sleepy. I sense that dawn is breaking. I know that it's dawn because all things have begun to slim down and stretch like hungry cats. From the street comes the sound of cars fleeing in all directions. You are still sitting by the fire, reading me. But you're no longer blond. Neither blond nor young. Suddenly I've discovered that all blond young men turn their eyes away when they see me. You have dark hair and you're about fifty. Your name I won't change because I like those Italian names that end in o and have an r in the middle. Neither did I meet you in a bookstore, what nonsense! I met you next to table 38 at the Casino. My chips were cerulean like the center of my eyes and yours were green like the center of yours. There where I placed a cerulean chip you placed a green one, and that is how we watched one another without

mirarnos un rato largo. Los dos ganábamos, los dos perdíamos, los dos volvíamos a ganar y a perder, y siempre, sobre el paño, su ojo verde miraba a mi ojo malva. Hasta que su ojo dorado miró a mi ojo violeta y nos sonreímos. Desde entonces usted es Gianfranco.

Sé que no vendrá a visitarme mientras yo no termine de escribir esta carta. Pero no quiero terminar de escribirla porque cuando termine tendré que empezar a pensar en lo que haré mañana para seguir viviendo. Me pararé en el atrio de San Nicolás de Bari, y cuando pase alguna de esas matronas que entran como escabulléndose bajo sus mantillas, atiborradas de rosarios y misales, la enfrentaré con mis ojos por dentro de hambre y por fuera de locura y la matrona, asustada, me dará dinero sin yo pedírselo. O estaré todo el día de pie en una esquina de Corrientes hasta que, al anochecer, un hombre vestido con sobretodo negro de auriga, maloliente de seborrea y vetustos alcanfores, se detendrá cerca de mí, pondrá cara de sufrimiento y de ganas de orinar, simulará que mira pasar los automóviles y al fin se dará vuelta y me colgará los ganchos oxidados de sus ojos. Entonces le sonreiré, empezaré a caminar y el hombre se vendrá detrás de mí. O voy a llamar por teléfono a Juan Carlos Birelli, voy a decirle que acepto acompañarlo hasta el hotel para parejas y una vez en la habitación del hotel lo mataré y le robaré la cartera. No tengo cosas que empeñar. El piano no es de Leipzig, no vale nada, está apolillado y le faltan varias cuerdas. Mis joyas son fantasías de dos por cinco. Y mis porcelanas, ninguna porcelana, loza barata. De mis libros no me desprenderé aunque me muera de hambre. Y aún sentada en una estación de ferrocarril seguiré escribiendo mis poemas en hojas de diarios viejos. ¿Se da cuenta, Gianfranco? Me resigno a todos los martirios con tal de poder jugar a la posibilidad, ni siquiera segura, de que hombres a los que jamás conoceré hereden lo que ahora amaso con lágrimas y con sangre.

Pero también, para qué mentirle, también pienso en ese Le Clézio tan rubio, tan joven y tan buen mozo. Entonces me digo que mis rarezas de mujer tal vez no sean, como a menudo me jacto para consolarme, ninguna garantía de nada. Que creer que he canjeado mis verdugos de hoy por mis futuros feligreses es la más triste de mis fantasías, quizá un despecho rencoroso y estéril. Sin embargo, si ahora mismo se me presentase el Diablo y me propusiera convertirme, a cambio de mi alma, en una muchacha joven y

watching one another for a very long time. We both would win, we both would lose, we both would win and lose again, and all the time, on the felt, your green eye would watch my cerulean eye. Until your golden eye looked at my violet eye and we smiled. Since that moment, you're Gianfranco.

I know you won't come visit me until I finish writing this letter. But I don't want to finish writing it because when I finish it I'll have to start thinking about what I'll do tomorrow to go on living. I'll stand in the atrium of the church of San Nicolas de Bari, and when a matron walks by, one of those matrons who enter as if hiding under their mantillas, cluttered with rosaries and missals, I'll confront her with my eyes of deep hunger and madness on the surface, and the matron, frightened, will give me money without my asking for it. Or I'll stand all day long at a corner of Avenida Corrientes until, at nightfall, a man dressed in a charioteer's black overcoat, smelling foully of scoriasis and of ancient mothballs, will stop by my side, will make a pained face as if wishing to relieve himself, will pretend to watch the cars pass and finally will turn and hang on to me with the rusty hooks of his eyes. Then I'll smile at him, I'll start walking away and the man will come following at my heels. Or I'll phone Juan Carlos Birelli, I'll tell him I agree to accompany him to the hotel, and once in the room I'll murder him and steal his wallet. I have nothing to pawn. The piano isn't from Leipzig, it's worth nothing, it's mothridden and several of its strings are missing. My jewels are cheap paste. And my china isn't china, just vulgar crockery. I won't let go of my books even if I starve. And even sitting in a train station I'll continue to write my poems on old newspaper pages. Don't you understand, Gianfranco? I'll resign myself to all sorts of martyrdoms just to be able to bet on the possibility, faint at best, that people whom I'll never know inherit what I now collect with blood and tears.

But also, why deny it, I think of that Le Clézio so blond, so young and so handsome. And then I tell myself that my oddness is not, as I often boast to console myself, guarantee of anything. That to believe that I've exchanged today's executioners for tomorrow's devotees is the saddest of my fantasies, perhaps a sterile and resentful boast. And yet, if even now the Devil were to appear and suggest transforming me, in exchange for my soul, into a young and beautiful young woman, the first thing I'd ask him is if I'd still

hermosa, lo primero que le preguntaría es si seguiría siendo la hermana secreta de Aloysius Bertrand y de Pavese, y si el Diablo me contestase que no, yo rechazaría el pacto. Ya ve, soy como esos homosexuales que sufren los puntapiés de la sociedad y, si volvieran a nacer, querrían ser otra vez homosexuales.

Ya no se qué escribirle, Gianfranco. Tengo los dedos agarrotados. No me iré a Europa. Me iré a un pequeño país centroamericano donde la gente sea muy dulce, muy pobre y muy buena. Vestiré trajes de hilo, calzaré sandalias y me peinaré con una trance larga hasta los pies. Adoptaré un nombre de mujer morena, carnosa y sensual. Me llamaré Aglonga Gonuyaz. Seré la Meme Albaquime. Por las mañanas enseñaré a los niños a leer y escribir, y los padres me pagarán con cestos llenos de frutas y de confituras. Pasearé todas las tardes por playas tatuadas por las olas, a las orillas de un mar de zafiro. Y a la noche, tendida en una hamaca bajo las casas palmeras de cuello de jirafa, compondré himnos panteístas. Mulatos adolescentes y muy hermosos, de piel color de nervadura, me seguirán a todas partes, como tigres hipnotizados. Custodiarán mi sueño como perros insomnes. Mi belleza será un sol que los tostará más que el sol de la canícula. De día sus ojos parecerán guijarros calcinados. De noche brillarán como luciérnagas de fiebre. Pero yo de día pasaré entre ellos sin mirarlos, alta, airosa, inmaculada, lo mismo que una Virgen llevada en procesión sobre angarillas. Y a la noche, envuelta en el mosquitero como en una nube de incienso, me dormiré más casta que las palmeras.

La tinta del bolígrafo empieza a palidecer. Antes de que se gaste del todo y yo no pueda seguir escribiendo quiero decirle, Gianfranco, que esta carta no es una carta. Ni usted existe ni existe esta mujer tan loca y tan infeliz. Dentro de quince o de veinte días, en alguna revista, en algún suplemento literario saldrá publicado un cuento y el cuento se llamará "Carta a Gianfranco". Incluirá este mismo párrafo que ahora escribo para desconcertar a los lectores.

O quizá la mujer sí existió, pero la encontraron muerta en su cuarto, muerta de hambre, literalmente, o envenenada con pastillas somníferas. Entre sus manos, no, es demasiado cursi, sobre la mesita de luz estaba el cuaderno donde había escrito este fatigoso monólogo. Alguien, digamos alguno de sus amigos, uno de aquellos hombres que la llamaron una vez por teléfono y no la llamaron más, acudió citado por la policía (ella tenía su número anotado en

be the secret sister of Aloysius Bertrand and of Pavese, and if the Devil were to say no, I'd turn him down. You see, I'm like those homosexuals who suffer the kicks of society, and if they were to be born again, they'd still choose to be homosexuals.

I no longer know what to write to you, Gianfranco. My fingers are all stiff. I won't go to Europe. I'll go to a small country in Central America where the people are very sweet, very poor, very kindhearted. I'll wear linen dresses and sandals, and will plait my hair into one long braid down to my feet. I'll take on the name of a dark woman, fleshy and sensual. I'll call myself Aglonga Gonuyaz. I'll be Meme Albaquime. In the mornings I'll teach the children to read and write, and the parents will pay me with baskets of fruit and preserves. I'll take walks every afternoon along beaches tattooed by the waves, at the edge of a sapphire sea. And at night, lying in a hammock beneath the chaste giraffe-necked palm trees, I'll compose pantheistic hymns. Handsome and adolescent mulattoes, with skin the color of rich veins, will follow me everywhere like mesmerized tigers. They'll watch over my sleep like insomniac guard dogs. My beauty will be a sun that will bronze them deeper than the sun in the sky. During the day their eyes will seem like charred pebbles. At night they'll shine like feverish fireflies. But during the day I'll walk among them without looking at them, tall, haughty, immaculate, like a Virgin carried in procession on a platform. And at night, wrapped up in a mosquito net as if in a cloud of incense, I'll fall asleep even chaster than the palm trees.

The ink of the ballpoint pen is beginning to pale. Before it runs out completely I want to tell you, Gianfranco, that this letter isn't a letter. Neither do you exist nor does this woman, so crazy and so unhappy. In fifteen or twenty days, in some magazine, in some literary supplement, a story will be published, a story called "Letter to Gianfranco". It will include this same paragraph which I now include to disconcert the readers.

Or perhaps the woman did exist, but they found her dead in her room, dead of hunger, literally, or poisoned with sleeping pills. In her hands—no, that's too purple—on the night table was the exercise book in which she had written this laborious monologue. Someone, let's say one of her friends, one of those men who called her once on the phone and then never again, arrived, summoned by the police—she had his phone number written down

una libreta), se apoderó del cuaderno, vio en seguida la oportunidad de aprovecharlo para un cuento, alteró nombres y lugares, modificó algunas frases y al fin publicó esta "Carta a Gianfranco" como una invención suya.

O admitamos que no fue tan miserable. Pensemos, mejor, que sintió la punzada de la culpa, lo invadieron los remordimientos, quiso abofetearse y abofetear a todos los que como él no habían sabido ser el imaginario Gianfranco y publicó la carta, claro que corregida para que su autora no fuese individualizada, inútil precaución, como cantan en el Barbero, porque son muchos los poetas que podrían suscribirla.

Hay otra posibilidad, Gianfranco. Que esta carta sea realmente una carta y usted su destinatario. La ha recibido, la leyó, y después de reelaborarla, de eliminar los datos comprometedores, de sustituir mis adjetivos por los suyos y de cambiar su nombre por el de ese Gianfranco al que se empeña en presentar como un personaje de ficción, la publica con todo desparpajo, sin saber que cayó en la celada que yo le tendí: usted será mi Max Beerbohm.

¿Y quién habrá escrito, entonces, esta última página que pretende poner al descubierto o un robo o un recurso literario, y en la que son evidentes ciertas modificaciones en el sentido? ¿Yo, la mujer de carne y hueso, o usted? ¿Yo, para vengarme por anticipado de usted, y usted no la elimina porque, como escritor que es, no sabe resistir la tentación de hacerles creer a los lectores que Eugenia Grandet existe? ¿O usted, por esa misma razón, por ese gusto por la ambigüedad que, apuntando simultáneamente a la realidad y a la imaginación, está en el origen de toda literatura?

Basta, Gianfranco. Por fascinantes que le resulten a usted, estos juegos (estas piruetas, dirán sus detractores) no interesan a nadie más que a usted mismo. Mujer de sangre y de dolor o fantasma de humo de palabras, tanto da. Lo único que exigen sus lectores es que no los engañe con lágrimas de estearina. Y usted y yo sabemos que mis lágrimas contienen toda la amargura del mar.

Y ahora adiós, Gianfranco. Ya puede salir de la habitación donde lo tuve prisionero un día y una noche. Es la mañana, hay sol, hace buen tiempo. Ojalá la tinta me alcance para poner, al pie de esta carta, mi nombre.

somewhere—picked up the exercise book, immediately saw the opportunity of using it as a story, changed names and places, altered a few sentences and finally published this "Letter to Gianfranco" as his own invention.

Or let's admit that he wasn't a crook. Let's imagine that instead he felt the pinprick of guilt, was invaded by remorse, wanted to slap himself and slap all those who like himself had not known how to be the imaginary Gianfranco, and published the letter—corrected of course, so that the author would not be recognized, a useless precaution because, as the song has it, many are the poets who could put their name to these words.

There's another possibility, Gianfranco. That this letter is indeed a letter and that you are indeed its recipient. You've received it, you've read it, and after rewriting it, after eliminating the compromising details, after substituting my adjectives for yours and changing your name for that of Gianfranco, whom you insist in presenting as a fictional character, you shamelessly publish it, without knowing that you've fallen in the trap I've sprung for you: you'll be my Max Beerbohm.

And who then has written this last page that apparently reveals either a theft or a literary device, and in which certain changes of meaning are so evident? I, the woman of flesh and blood, or you? I, to have my anticipated revenge on you, and you don't destroy the page because, being a writer, you cannot resist the temptation of making the readers believe that fictional characters exist? Or you, for that very same reason, because you enjoy that ambiguity which, pointing at the same time at both reality and the imagination, lies at the root of all literature?

Enough, Gianfranco. However fascinating you find these games (these sleights-of-hand, your detractors will say), they interest no one but yourself. A woman of blood and suffering, or a phantom of words and smoke: it makes no difference. The only thing your readers demand is that you don't deceive them with tears of wax. And both you and I know that my tears contain all the bitterness of the sea.

And now farewell, Gianfranco. You can now leave that room where I held you prisoner for one day and one night. It's morning, the sun is shining, the weather's fine. I hope that I'll have enough ink in the pen to sign, at the bottom of this last page, my name.

Como una buena madre

A Good Mother

Dick Gerdes, translator of Ana María Shúa

Dick Gerdes taught at the University of New Mexico in Albuquerque and is now on the faculty of George Mason University. He translated Alfredo Bryce Echenique's *A World for Julius* and a novel by Chilean Diamel Eltit; and authored a study on the life and art of Mario Vargas Llosa. Gerdes had dismissed translation as a career path when his early efforts to obtain the rights to translate Alfredo Bryce Echenique's *Un mundo para Julius* failed, but Echenique himself approached the Latin American literature professor twenty years later to discuss putting the novel into English. That serendipitous introduction turned out to be a "baptism of fire," as Gerdes himself terms it, due to Bryce Echenique's post modernist style. The challenge of creating *A World for Julius* did not prevent Gerdes, however, from embarking on a range of other projects, and he is now editor-in-chief of the International Translation Center at the University of New Mexico.

Gerdes believes that translators must be both literary critics and intimates of the milieu of each piece. "In-depth knowledge of the culture that one translates stands out as one of the basic requirements for success," he maintained during a telephone conversation. He is committed to enabling wider audiences to discover a new generation of "exhilarating writers" from Latin America, among whom he considers Argentine Ana María Shúa, a one-time Guggenheim Fellow born in 1951 in Buenos Aires, on of the foremost. Shua, who has worked as a publicity agent, now teaches literature at the Universidad de Buenos Aires. She is the author of *Los días de pesca, Viajando se conoce gente,* and *Soy paciente.* Having translated "A Good Mother," Gerdes has embarked on a book-long manuscript by Shúa, hoping to bring her talents to the attention of an audience in the United States.

Ana María Shúa
COMO UNA BUENA MADRE

A mi tió Lucho, a cambio de Caperucita

Tom gritó. Mamá estaba en la cocina, amasando. Tom tenía cuatro anos, era sano y bastante grande para su edad. Podía gritar muy fuerte durante mucho tiempo. Mamá siempre leía libros acerca del cuidado y la educación de los niños. En esos libros, y también en las novelas, las madres (las buenas madres, las que realmente quieren a sus hijos) eran capaces de adivinar las causas del llanto de un chico con sólo prestar atención a sus características.

Pero Tom gritaba y lloraba muy fuerte cuando estaba lastimado, cuando tenía sueño, cuando no encontraba la manga del saco, cuando su hermana Soledad lo golpeaba y cuando se le caía una torre de cubos. Todos los gritos parecían similares en volumen, en pasión, en intensidad. Sólo cuando se trataba de atacar al bebé Tom se volvía asombrosamente silencioso, esperando el momento justo para saltar callado, felino, sobre su presa. El silencio era, entonces, más peligroso que los gritos: ese silencio en el que mamá había encontrado una vez a Tom acostado sobre el bebé, presionando con su vientre la cara (la boca y la nariz) del bebé casi azul.

Tom gritó, gritó, gritó. Mamá sacó las manos de la masa de la tarta, se enjuagó con cuidado, con urgencia, bajo el chorro de la canilla, y secándose todavía con el repasador corrió por el pasillo hasta la pieza de los chicos. Tom estaba tirado en el suelo, gritando. Soledad le pateaba rítmicamente la cabeza. Por suerte Soledad tenía puestas las pantuflas con forma de conejo, peludas y suaves, y no los zapatos de ir a la escuela.

Mamá tomó a Soledad de los brazos y la zamarreó con fuerza, tratando de demostrarle, con calma y con firmeza, que le estaba dando el justo castigo por su comportamiento. Tratando de no demostrarle que tenía ganas de vengarse, de hacerle daño. Tratando

Ana María Shúa

A GOOD MOTHER

Translated by Dick Gerdes

To my Uncle Lucho, in exchange for Little Red Riding Hood

Tom screamed. Mommy was kneading dough in the kitchen. Tom was four years old, robust and pretty big for his age. He could scream really loud for the longest time. Mommy would always read books on how to take care of children and how to best educate them. In those books, and also in novels, mothers (the good mothers, the ones who really care about their children) were capable of determining why a child would be crying just by the way he or she was behaving.

But Tom would scream at the top of his lungs and cry out loud when he was hurt, when he was sleepy, when he couldn't get his arm into his sleeve, when his sister Soledad would beat on him and when his tower of blocks would come tumbling down. His screaming always seemed the same in terms of volume, passion, intensity. Only when it was a matter of attacking the baby, Tom would grow astonishingly quiet, just waiting for the right moment to jump—catlike—on top of his prey. That silence, hence, was even more dangerous than the screaming: the kind of silence like the time when Mommy had found Tom lying on top of the baby, applying pressure with his stomach over the baby's face (mouth and nose) that, by then, was turning blue.

Tom screamed, screamed, and screamed some more. Mommy removed her hands from the dough, carefully but quickly washed them under the faucet and, continuing to dry her hands on a dishrag, ran down the hallway to the children's room. Tom was spread out on the floor, screaming. Soledad was kicking at his head repeatedly. Fortunately, Soledad had her slippers on, the ones shaped like little bunny rabbits, all soft and furry, and not her school shoes.

Mommy took Soledad into her arms and gave her a good shaking, trying to demonstrate to her that, while remaining calm yet firm, she was giving her the punishment she deserved. And she was trying not to show her that she wanted revenge, to really hurt

de portarse como una buena madre, una madre que realmente quiere a sus hijos.

Después levantó a Tom y quiso acunarlo para que dejara de gritar, pero era demasiado pesado. Se sentó con él en el borde de la cama acariciándole el pelo. Tom seguía gritando. Era un hermoso milagro que no hubiera despertado al bebé. Cuando mamá sacó un caramelo del bolsillo del delantal, Tom dejó de gritar, lo peló y se lo comió.

—Quiero más caramelos—dijo Tom.

—Yo también quiero caramelos—dijo Soledad—. Si le diste a Tom me tenés que dar a mí.

—No hay más caramelos. Vos Sole, más bien que no te merecés ningún premio. Y a vos parece que no te dolía tanto que con un caramelo te callaste—como una buena madre, equitativa, dueña y divisora de la Justicia. Pero una buena madre no consuela a sus hijos con caramelos, una madre que realmente quiere a sus hijos protege sus dientes y sus mentes.

—Queremos más caramelos—dijo Soledad.

Y ahora Tom estaba de su lado. Entre los dos trataron de atrapar a mamá, que quería volver a la cocina. Tom le abrazó las piernas mientras Soledad le metía la mano en el bolsillo del delantal. Mamá sacó la mano de Soledad del bolsillo con cierta brusquedad. Calma. Firmeza. Autoridad. Amor.

—¡No! Los bolsillos de mamá no se tocan.

—Tenés más, tenés más, sos una mentirosa, ¡nos engañaste!—gritaba Soledad.

—Mamá mala, mamá mentirosa, ¡mamá culo!—gritaba Tom.

—Empezaron los dibujitos animados—dijo mamá. Autoridad. Firmeza. Culo.

Tom y Soledad la soltaron y corrieron hacia el televisor. Soledad lo encendió. Levantaron el volumen hasta un nivel intolerable y se sentaron a medio metro de la pantalla. Una buena madre, una madre que realmente quiere a sus hijos no lo hubiera permitido. Mamá pensó que se iban a quedar ciegos y sordos y que se lo tenían merecido. Cerró la puerta de la cocina para defender sus timpanos y volvió a la masa de tarta. Masa para pascualina La Salteña es más fresca porque se vende más. Una buena madre, una madre que realmente quiere a sus hijos, ¿compraría masa para pascualina La Salteña?

her; she was trying to behave like a good mother, like a mother who really cares about her children.

Then she lifted up Tom and wanted to cuddle him so he would stop crying, but he was too heavy. She sat down with him on the edge of the bed and stroked his hair. Tom continued screaming. It was a prodigious miracle that he hadn't wakened the baby. When Mommy took a candy from her apron pocket, Tom stopped yelling, removed the wrapper, and ate it.

"I want some more," said Tom.

"I want some too," said Soledad. "If you give some to him you have to give some to me."

"There isn't any more. Soledad, you really don't deserve any prize. And you, sir, don't seem to be that hurt if a candy will shut you up just like that," she said, like a good mother, always fair, the guardian of Justice. But a good mother doesn't comfort her children with candy; a mother who really cares about her children would protect their teeth, and their brains.

"We want more," said Soledad.

And now Tom was on her sister's side. Between the two of them, they tried to trap Mommy, who wanted to return to the kitchen. Tom grasped her legs while Soledad stuck her hand into the apron pocket. Mommy yanked her hand out of her pocket. Composure. Firmness. Authority. Love.

"No! No one gets into Mother's apron pockets."

"You have more, you do, you're a liar, you've cheated us," yelled Soledad.

"Bad Mommy, Mommy liar, Mommy asshole!" screamed Tom.

"The cartoons are on," said Mommy. Authority. Firmness. Asshole.

Tom and Soledad let her go and ran to the TV. Soledad turned it on. They turned up the volume full blast and sat down 18 inches from the screen. A good mother, a mother who really cares about her children, wouldn't allow it. Mommy thought they would probably go deaf and blind...but they deserved it. Trying to protect her ear drums, she closed the kitchen door and got back to kneading the dough for the crust. This dough for quiche Lorraine is fresher because they sell more of it. A good mother, a mother who really cares about her children, would she buy this brand of dough for quiche Lorraine?

Acomodó la masa en la tartera, incorporó el relleno, que ya tenía preparado, cerró la tarta con un torpe repulgue y la puso en el horno. A través de la masa infernal de sonido que despedía el televisor, se filtraba ahora el llanto del bebé. Como una respuesta automática de su cuerpo, empezó a manar leche de su pecho izquierdo empapándole el corpiño y la parte delantera de la blusa. Sonó el timbre.

—¡Un momento!—gritó mamá hacia la puerta.

Fue al cuarto de los chicos y volvió con el bebé en brazos. Abrió la puerta. Era el pedido de la verdulería. El repartidor era un hombre mayor, orgulloso de estar todavía en condiciones de hacer un trabajo como ése, demasiado pesado para su edad. Mamá lo había visto alguna vez, en un corte de luz, subiendo las escaleras con el canasto al hombro, jadeante y jactancioso.

—Los chicos están demasiado cerca del televisor—dijo el hombre, pasando a la cocina.

—Tiene razón—dijo mamá. Ahora había un testigo, alguien más se había dado cuenta, sabía qué clase de madre era ella.

El olor a leche enloquecía al bebé, que lloraba y picoteaba la blusa mojada como un pollito buscando granos. El viejo empezó a sacar la fruta y la verdura de la canasta apilándola sobre la mesada de la cocina. Hacía el trabajo lentamente, como para demostrar que no le correspondía terminarlo sin ayuda. Mamá sacó algunas naranjas, una por una, con la mano libre. El verdulero amarreteaba las bolsitas.

Una buena madre no encarga el pedido: una madre que realmente quiere a sus hijos va personalmente a la verdulería y elige una por una las frutas y verduras con que los alimentará. Cuando una mujer es lo bastante perezosa como para encargar los alimentos en lugar de ir a buscarlos personalmente, el verdulero trata de engañarla de dos maneras: en el peso de los productos y en su calidad. Mamá observó detenidamente cada pieza que salía de la canasta buscando algún motivo que justificara su protesta para poder demostrarle al viejo que ella, aunque se hiciera mandar el pedido, no era de las que se conforman con cualquier cosa.

—Las papas—dijo por fin—. ¿No son demasiado grandes?

—Cuanto más grandes mejor—dijo el hombre—lo malo son las papas chicas. Mire ésta—tomó una de las papas más grandes y la

She patted the dough into the pan, added the filling that she had prepared earlier, fastened the top with a clumsy push of her thumbs, and put it in the oven. Through the infernal barrage of noise coming from the TV, the cries of the baby now came filtering through. Automatically, her body responded as milk began to flow from her left breast, soaking the front of her blouse. The door bell rang.

"Just a minute," Mommy yelled toward the door.

She went to the children's room and returned with the baby in her arms. She opened the door. It was her order from the vegetable market. The delivery man was older, proud to be able to continue to do that type of work, and too fat for his age. Mommy had seen him once, during an outage, climbing the stairs with his basket on his shoulders, huffing and puffing, but proud.

"The kids are too close to the TV," said the man, making his way to the kitchen.

"You're right," said Mommy. Now there was even a witness; someone else had noticed and knew what kind of a mother she was.

The smell of the milk drove the baby crazy as he cried and pecked at the wet blouse like a baby chick looking for grain. The old man began to take the fruit and vegetables out of the basket, piling them on the kitchen counter. He did his work ever so slowly, as if to indicate that he wasn't responsible for finishing it without help. Mommy removed some oranges, one by one, with her free hand. The delivery man gathered up the empty little bags.

A good mother wouldn't order groceries to be delivered: a mother who really cares about her children would go personally to the market and select one by one the fruit and vegetables with which she would feed them. When a woman is so lazy that she has to order the food she wants instead of going to buy them herself, the delivery man will try to cheat her in two ways: by weight and by quality. Mommy scrutinized each piece that came out of the basket, looking for some reason to justify her dislike for something he had brought which, in turn, would demonstrate to the old man that, even though she had placed the order, she was not one of those who accepted just anything.

"The potatoes," she said finally. "Aren't they too big?"

"The bigger, the better," said the man, "small potatoes are no good. Look at this one," taking one of the bigger ones and holding

acercó a la cara de mamá—. Es ideal para hacer al horno. Usted la pela y le hace cortes así, ¿ve? como tajadas pero no hasta abajo del todo. En cada corte, un pedacito de manteca. Después en el horno la papa se abre y queda como un acordeón doradito, riquísima, hágame caso.

Mamá le dijo que sí, que le iba a hacer caso. Le pagó, y el hombre se fue, pero antes volvió a mirar con reprobación a los chicos, que seguían pegados al televisor.

Mamá se preparó un vaso grande lleno de leche y se sentó en la cocina para amamantar al bebé. Cuando se le prendía al pecho ella sentía una sed repentina y violenta que le secaba la boca. Sentía también que una parte de ella misma se iba a través de los pezones. Mientras el bebé chupaba de un lado, del otro pecho partía un chorro finito pero con mucha presión. Una buena madre no alimenta a sus hijos con mamadera. Mamá tomaba la leche a sorbos chicos, como si ella también mamara. Cuando el bebé estuvo satisfecho, se lo puso sobre el hombro para hacerlo eructar. Ahora había que cambiarlo. También ordenar la cocina. Organizarse. Primero cambiar al bebé.

Le sacó los pañales sucios. Miró con placer la caca de color amarillo brillante, semilíquida, de olor casi agradable, la típica diarrea posprandial, decían sus libros, de un bebé alimentado a pecho. El chiquitito se sonrió con su boca desdentada y agitó las piernas, feliz de sentirlas en libertad. Lo limpió con un algodón mojado. ¿Era suficiente? Otras madres lavaban a sus bebés en una palangana o debajo del chorro de la canilla. Tenía la cola paspada. A los bebés de otras madres no se les paspaba la cola. Una buena madre, una madre que realmente quiere a sus hijos, ¿usaría, como ella, pañales descartables? Usaría pañales de tela, los lavaría con sus propias manos, con amor, con jabón de tocador.

—¡Soledad! ¡Me alcanzás del baño la cremita para la cola del bebé!—pidió mamá.

Soledad apareció con inesperada, inhabitual rapidez. Traía el frasco de dermatol y las manos mojadas.

—¿Qué estabas haciendo en el baño?

—Nada mamá, lavándome las manos.

Tom gritó. Mamá dejó al bebé, limpio y seco pero todavía sin pañales, en la cuna corralito. Los gritos eran muy fuertes y venían del baño. Soledad se plantó delante de la puerta.

it toward her face, "these are great for baking. Peel it and cut it like this, into pieces without cutting all the way through, get it? Place a pat of butter in each slice. Later, in the oven, the potato opens up like an accordion, browned, and delicious, believe me."

Mommy said yes, she would follow his advice. She paid him and the man left, but not without looking disapprovingly at the children, who were glued to the TV.

Mommy fixed a big glass of milk and sat down in the kitchen to nurse the baby. When he would start to suck, Mommy would suddenly and urgently become thirsty and her mouth would dry up. She would also feel how a part of her was abandoning her body through her nipples. While the baby would suck on one side, the other breast would spurt a fine spray, with great pressure. A good mother doesn't bottle feed her children. Mommy would take small sips of milk as if she, herself, were nursing. When the baby was satisfied, she put him on her shoulder to burp him. Now it was time to change him. Also clean up the kitchen. Get organized. First, change the baby.

She removed his dirty diapers. She looked approvingly at the watery, shiny yellow, almost pleasant smelling excretion, the typical post-nursing diarrhea, her books had described, of the breast-fed baby. The little thing smiled, toothless, and kicked his legs, happy to be free of the diapers. She cleaned him with a moistened cotton ball. Had she done enough? Other mothers would wash their babies in a washbasin or would stick them directly under the faucet. His rump was chapped. Other mothers wouldn't let their babies' rumps get chapped. A good mother, a mother who really cares about her children, would they use, like her, disposable diapers? They would use cloth diapers, and they would wash them with their own hands, lovingly, with toilet soap.

"Soledad! Can you get me the cream for the baby's butt from the bathroom?" asked Mommy.

Soledad appeared in a flash, which was quite unusual and uncustomary. She brought the jar of lotion, along with wet hands.

"What were you doing in the bathroom?"

"Nothing, Mommy, washing my hands."

Tom screamed. Mommy left the baby in his playpen, clean and dry but without diapers. The screaming was very loud and it came from the bathroom. Soledad blocked the doorway.

—No entres ahí mamita, de verdad, por favor, no entres, perdonáme.

Los alaridos de Tom eran más fuertes que el mismísimo sonido del televisor, inútilmente encendido en el living. Deslizándose por debajo de la puerta del baño, un flujo lento y constante de agua jabonosa inundaba la alfombra del pasillo haciendo crecer una mancha de color oscuro. Mamá empujó a Soledad y abrió la puerta. Tom tenía la cara pintada de varios colores y en el pelo un pegote de pasta dentífrica. Sus cosméticos estaban tirados en el suelo, empapados, en medio del charco de agua que provocaba el desborde del bidet. Soledad había salido corriendo, seguramente para esconderse en el ropero.

Mamá sacó el tapón del bidet y forcejeó con las canillas.

—No pude cerrarlas—lloriqueó Tom.

Para mamá tampoco era fácil. Habían sido abiertas hasta su punto máximo y giraban en falso. Después de varios intentos lo consiguió. Sonó el teléfono. Mamá se obligó a quedarse en el baño hasta ver el bidet vacío y asegurarse de que no salía más agua. Después fue a atender.

Al levantar el tubo escuchó el caracteristico sonido que precedía las comunicaciories de larga distancia.

—Es llamado de afuera, chicos, ¡es papito!—gritó, feliz.

Soledad salió de la pieza arrastrando la cuna donde el bebé lloraba.

—¡Mamá!—gritó—. Tom lo quiere matar al bebé pero no sin querer. ¡Lo quiere matar a propósito!

—¡Mentira!—gritó Tom, que venía detrás—. Sos un culo cagado con olor a culo cagado Soledad, ¡caca caca caca con olor!

—¡Lo odio!—gritó Soledad—. Quiero que no exista más, mamá por qué tengo que soportarlo. ¡Hijo de culo! IHijo de mierda! ¡Ano con pelos!

—Cállense—pidió mamá—. ¡No oigo nada! ¡Hagan lo que quieran pero cállense! Soledad apagá la tele, es papito de afuera y no oigo nada.

—Mamá dijo hagan lo que quieran—le dijo Soledad a Tom. Tom sonrió y dejó de gritar. Empujando la cuna se fueron a la cocina.

"Don't go in, Mommy, really, please, don't go in, I'm sorry."

Tom's screams were even louder than the TV, now serving no function in the living room. From underneath the bathroom door came a slow but steady flow of soapy water that was inundating the hallway carpet and beginning to form a dark-colored stain on it. Mommy pushed Soledad aside and opened the door. Tom's face had been painted up with several colors and toothpaste had been plastered into his hair. Her cosmetics were strewn all over the floor, soaking wet in the pool of water coming from an overflowing bidet. Soledad ran out, probably to hide in the clothes closet.

Mommy removed the plug from the bidet and strained to turn off the faucets.

"I couldn't turn them off," whimpered Tom.

It wasn't easy for Mommy either. They had turned them on as far as they would go and now the knobs twirled around freely. After several attempts, she was successful. The telephone rang. Mommy made herself remain in the bathroom until the bidet was flushed empty and she could make sure no more water was escaping from it. Afterward she went to the phone.

Upon picking up the receiver she could hear that characteristic sound one gets from a long distance call.

"Kids, it's long distance, it's Daddy," she yelled happily.

Soledad came out of the bedroom, pulling along the playpen with the crying baby.

"Mommy!" she screamed. "Tom is trying to kill him on purpose!"

"Liar!" Tom yelled, who followed behind. "You're a shitty ass that smells like an ass that just shit, Soledad, shit, shit, shit that smells!"

"I hate him!" screamed Soledad. "Just make him disappear, Mommy. Why do I have to put up with him? He's an asshole! A shit! A hairy asshole!"

"Shut up," begged Mommy. "I can't hear a thing. Do whatever you want, just shut up! Turn off the TV, Soledad. It's Daddy long distance and I can't hear a word he's saying."

"Mommy said do whatever we want," Soledad said to Tom. Tom stopped screaming and smiled. Pushing the playpen along, they went to the kitchen.

Mamá volvió a prestar atención a la voz lejana, con ecos, que venía desde el tubo del teléfono. Entregaba una atención absoluta, concentrada. Al principio sonreía. Después dejó de sonreír. Después habló mucho más alto de lo necesario para ser oída. Después hizo gestos que eran inútiles, porque su interlocutor no los podía ver. Después cortó y sintió que tenía ganas de llorar y que quería estar sola. Después escuchó un ruido largo, complejo y violento. Tom gritó. Mamá corrió a la cocina.

Parado sobre la mesada, entre lechugas y berenjenas, Tom gritaba asustado. Soledad trataba de no llorar, milagrosamente entera en medio de una pila de escombros: restos de platos y vasos rotos. Tom se había trepado a la mesada para alcanzar los frascos de mermelada del estante y, apoyándose con todas sus fuerzas, lo había hecho caer. El bebé estaba bien. Habían volcado deliberadamente la azucarera sobre la cuna para mantenerlo entretenido. Lamía el azúcar con placer y agitaba los brazos y las piernas emitiendo sonidos de alegría. En la batita y en el pelo también tenía azúcar. Mamá miró los restos de un plato azul, de loza, con el dibujo de un perrito en relieve, un plato que había pertenecido a su propia madre. Nadie que no tuviera ese platito azul en un estante de la alacena podría llegar a ser una buena madre. Tuvo más ganas de llorar.

Tom y Soledad habían estado jugando al pic nic en el suelo de la cocina, sobre el mejor mantel blanco, el de las cenas con invitados. Habían sacado pan, queso, mostaza, ketchup y coca de la heladera y habían usado algunas de las frutas y verduras que estaban todavía sobre la mesada. En el mantel había dos tomates y una manzana mordisqueados, unas papas sucias y manchas de mostaza.

Mamá quería estar sola y quería llorar. Pensar en lo que le estaba pasando. También quería pegarles muy fuerte a Tom y a Soledad. Pero antes tenía que sacar al bebé de ahí para que el azúcar no le provocara gases, tenía que asegurarse de que los tres estaban bien y barrer los restos peligrosos de la cocina. Alzó a Tom, que estaba descalzo, y lo llevó a su pieza.

—Andate de acá, Soledad, salí que voy a barrer—dijo con voz controlada, contenida.

Mommy turned her attention to the distant voice that echoed in the background of the receiver. Concentrating, she forgot about everything else. At first she was smiling. Then she stopped smiling. Then she talked louder than necessary in order to be heard. Then she made useless gestures, because the listener couldn't see them. Then she hung up, felt like crying and wanted to be alone. Then she heard a long, undefined, violent noise. Tom screamed. Mommy ran to the kitchen.

Standing on the kitchen counter among heads of lettuce and eggplants, Tom was screaming with fright. Soledad was trying not to cry, still miraculously intact amid a pile of rubble of broken dishes and glasses. Tom had climbed up on the kitchen counter in order to reach some jelly on the shelf and, leaning on it with all his weight, pulled it down. The baby was OK. They had purposely poured the contents of the sugar bowl all over the playpen in order to keep the baby occupied. He was licking up the sugar with pleasure, moving his arms and legs all about and was all gooey. There was even sugar in his hair and it was all over his little night shirt. Mommy stared at the remains of a blue ceramic plate with an embossed image of a little dog on it that had belonged to her own mother. Any mother who doesn't have a little blue plate like that on the kitchen shelf could never become a good mother. Now she felt like crying even more.

Tom and Soledad had been playing picnic on the best white table cloth, the one for dinners with invited guests, that was now spread out all over the kitchen floor. They had gotten out bread, cheese, mustard, ketchup and Coke from the refrigerator and had taken some of the fruit and vegetables from the counter. There were two half-eaten tomatoes, an unfinished apple, some dirty raw potatoes and mustard stains on the table cloth.

Mommy wanted to be alone and she wanted to cry; and to think about what was happening. She also wanted to spank Tom and Soledad very hard. But first she had to get the baby out of there before the sugar made him pass gas; she had to make sure all three of them were OK, and sweep up the dangerous shards in the kitchen. She picked up Tom, who was barefoot, and carried him to his room.

"Go on, out of here, Soledad, leave, I need to sweep up in here," she said, controlled and restrained.

—Vos dijiste hagan lo que quieran.

—Soledad no te estoy retando ahora, solamente te dije que salgas.

—El estante lo tiró Tom—dijo Soledad.

—¡Porque vos me mandaste a buscar la mermelada!—gritó Tom, que había vuelto a acercarse, todavía descalzo, a la puerta de la cocina—. ¡Sos una acusadora y una basura con ano y porquería cagada!

—¡Basta!—gritó mamá. Y ella misma se asustó al notar la carga de furia en su grito—. Basta basta basta, no aguanto más gritos, hiciste un desastre y encima gritás gritás gritás.

Atrapó a Tom de un brazo y le dio un chirlo en la cola sabiendo que estaba siendo injusta, que Soledad había sido tan culpable como él o más. El bebé lloraba ahora y también Tom. Soledad le dio un empujón a mamá con bastante fuerza como para hacerla caer de rodillas, con las manos hacia adelante. Sintió un dolor afilado en la palma de la mano derecha.

—¡No le vas a pegar a mi hermanito!

—¡Mamá es un dedo en la nariz!—gritó Tom.

Mamá había caído sobre un vidrio roto. Se miró la mano lastimada. El tajo era profundo y sangraba.

—Mama, ¿por qué la sangre es colorada?—preguntó Tom.

—Mirá lo que le hiciste a mamá, Soledad—dijo mamá, mostrándole la herida.

Pero después vio la carita asustada, los ojos grandes de Soledad y pensó que había sido cruel. Una buena madre, una madre que realmente quiere a sus hijos, no los carga de innecesaria culpa.

—No es nada, linda, no te asustes, ya sé que fue sin querer, ahora me pongo agua oxigenada y una curita y ya está—agradecía casi el dolor físico que le permitía evitar las sonrisas, hasta llorar un poco. Levantó la mano por encima del corazón para parar la sangre.

—Mamá, ¿por qué la sangre es colorada?—preguntó Tom.

—Porque sí—dijo mamá distraída, apretándose la mano con un repasador. Tenía que barrer y sacar al bebé. ¿Qué primero? Organizarse.

—Soledad, haceme un favor, levantá un minutito al bebé mientras yo me voy a poner una venda.

—Pero yo también quiero ver cómo te curás.

"You said we could do whatever we wanted to."

"Soledad, I'm not scolding you now, I only told you to leave."

"Tom was the one who pulled the shelf down."

"Because you told me to look for the jelly!" screamed Tom, who had returned, still barefoot, to the door of the kitchen. "You're a tattletale, you're garbage with an asshole, you're a shit."

"Enough!" screamed Mommy. And she even frightened herself upon noting the fury with which she had screamed. "Enough is enough, I can't take any more screaming, you've created a catastrophe and all you do is scream, scream, scream."

She grabbed Tom by the arm and gave him a swat on his rear, knowing that she was being partial, for Soledad was as much to blame as he was, or more. The baby was crying now and so was Tom. Soledad pushed her mother hard enough to make her fall to her knees, hands outstretched, and feel a sharp pain on the palm of her right hand.

"You're not going to hit my little brother!"

"Mommy is a finger stuck up the nose!" Tom screamed.

Mommy had fallen onto a piece of broken glass. She looked at her cut hand. The gash was deep and bleeding.

"Mommy, why is blood red?" asked Tom.

"Soledad, look at what you did to your Mommy," said Mommy, showing her the gash.

But then she saw Soledad's frightened face and bulging eyes, and thought she had been cruel to her. A good mother, a mother who really cares about her children, wouldn't burden them with unnecessary guilt.

"It's nothing, precious, don't be frightened, I know it was an accident, I'll just put some hydrogen peroxide on it and put on a band-aid, that'll take care of it," almost thanking the physical pain that allowed her to avoid smiling and even cry a bit. She raised her hand above her heart to stop the bleeding.

"Mommy, why is blood red?" asked Tom.

"It just is," said Mommy not paying attention, applying a dishtowel to her palm. She had to sweep up and take the baby to the other room. What's first? Get organized.

"Soledad, do me a favor, hold the baby a minute while I put a bandage on."

"But I want to see how you do it."

—Sí, levantalo al bebé y vení con él al baño y ves todo.

—Mamá, por qué la sangre es colorada, porque sí no me digas—dijo Tom.

—No quiero levantar al bebé porque está sin pañales—dijo Soledad—. Me va a cagar y mear toda.

—¡Soledad cagada y meada!—gritó gloriosamente Tom.

Mamá terminó de atarse torpemente el repasador con ayuda de los dientes. Necesitaba estar un momento, nada más que un momento sola. Y en silencio. Pensar en la voz lejana, con ecos. Y llorar. Levantó al bebé y mientras lo sostenía con el brazo izquierdo usó la mano herida para inclinar la cunita y tratar.de sacudir el grueso del azúcar. Acostó al bebé y empezó a barrer los restos de vidrios y loza. La tarea hizo que se aflojara el repasador mal anudado y la mano herida volvió a sangrar. Dolía mucho. Juntó lo que pudo con la pala. Levantó al bebé y lo llevó a la pieza para ponerle un pañal limpio. En el camino, el bebé regurgitó una bocanada de leche semidigerida sobre su ropa.

—Mamá por qué la sangre es colorada, porque sí no me digas—preguntó Tom.

—Porque está compuesta por glóbulos rojos—dijo mamá mientras le ponía el pañal al bebé y le limpiaba la boca con un trapito. Tom se quedó desconcertado por unos segundos, pero Soledad estaba atenta.

—¿Por qué son rojos los glóbulos de la sangre?—preguntó.

—Porque el libro del porqué tiene muchas hojas—contestó Marná

Puso una sábana limpia sobre la cuna y unos cuantos chiches de goma. Todo lo que tocaba se ensuciaba con manchitas de sangre. El bebé se largó a llorar en cuanto lo puso boca abajo. Pero esta vez mamá estaba decidida a curarse la mano. También quería estar sola. Soledad la siguó al baño para ver cómo se vendaba.

—¿Ves lo que hace mamita? Así también tenés que hacer vos cuando te lastimás. Primero lavarse bien a fondo con agua y jabón.

El baño seguía encharcado de agua jabonosa. Levantó los cosméticos mojados. Tendría que secarlo enseguida, antes de que alguien se resbalara. En el botiquín encontró agua oxigenada,

"Of course you can, just pick up the baby and bring him with you to the bathroom and you'll learn how to do it."

"Mommy, why is blood red, and don't tell me it just is," said Tom.

"I don't want to pick up the baby because he doesn't have a diaper on," said Soledad. "He's going to pee and shit all over me."

"Soledad, all peed and shit on," Tom yelled gloriously.

Clumsily, Mommy finished tying the dishcloth with her teeth. She needed to be alone, if only for a moment, just for a moment. And where it was quiet. To think about that distant voice, echoing in the background. And cry. She picked up the baby and while she was holding him with her left arm, she used her wounded hand to tip the playpen and brush out most of the sugar. She laid the baby down and began to sweep up the rest of the broken glass and porcelain. As a result, the dishrag came loose and the gash began to bleed again. It hurt a lot. She gathered up what she could with the dustpan. She picked up the baby and carried him to the bedroom to put on a fresh diaper. On the way, the baby regurgitated a mouthful of partially digested milk on her clothes.

"Mommy, why is blood red, and don't tell me it just is," asked Tom.

"Because it's made up of red corpuscles," said Mommy as she put the diaper on the baby and wiped his mouth with a rag. Tom was baffled for a few seconds, but Soledad was listening carefully.

"Why are corpuscles red?" she asked.

"Because the book of why's has a lot of pages," Mommy answered.

She put a clean sheet in the playpen and tossed in some rubber toys. Everything she touched was spotted with blood. The baby began to cry as soon as she put him down on his stomach. But this time Mommy was determined to fix her bandage right. She also wanted to be alone. Soledad followed her to the bathroom to see how she would put the bandage on.

"Do you see how Mommy is doing it? This is the way you'll have to do it when you cut yourself. First, wash the wound well with soap and water."

The bathroom was still full of puddles of soapy water. She picked up the wet cosmetics. She would have to dry the floor immediately before someone slipped on it. She found hydrogen

vendas, tela adhesiva. Iba a necesitar ayuda. Vertió el agua oxigenada sobre la herida, que tenía los bordes separados. Probablemente necesitara unas puntadas pero se sentía incapaz de llegar con los tres chicos hasta el hospital. Apretó una compresa de gasa con mucha fuerza contra la herida, para parar la hemorragia. Después se puso otra gasa limpia y, con ayuda de Soledad, la tela adhesiva. Entonces percibió el silencio. El bebé había dejado de llorar.

—Soledad, andá a ver qué pasa con Tom y el bebé.

A Soledad le gustaba proteger al bebé casi tanto como pegarle a Tom. Apenas había salido cuando se escuchó su desesperado aullido de socorro.

—Lo está matando, mamá mamá mamá, lo va a destrozar, mamá, mamá, ¡vení ahora! Lo está revoleando, ¡Lo MATA MAMA!

Mamá quiso correr a la velocidad que exigían los gritos enloquecidos de Soledad, se resbaló y se cayó torciéndose un tobillo de mala manera. Se levantó y siguió como pudo hasta la pieza donde el bebé dormía tranquilamente en su cuna mientras Tom revoleaba por el aire un perrito de paño relleno de mijo. El perrito ya estaba en parte roto y el mijo salía por el agujero, impulsado por la fuerza centrífuga, chocando contra las paredes, cayendo al suelo, sobre las camas, en la cuna. Soledad gritaba histéricamente. Mamá la hizo callar de una bofetada, le sacó a Tom el perrito de paño y se sentó sobre una de las camitas porque el tobillo lastimado ya no la sostenía. Vio sangre en la cara de Soledad y sintió un golpe en el corazón. Después se dio cuenta de que le había pegado con la mano herida, que volvía a sangrar. Vio el dibujo de globos y payasos que ella misma había elegido para la colcha y otra vez tuvo ganas de llorar.

—Tráeme el costurero que voy a curar a tu perrito: lo voy a coser—le dijo a Soledad. El tobillo empezaba a hincharse.

—Tráeme esto, tráeme aquello, qué te creés que soy—dijo Soledad—. ¿Te creés que soy la Cenicienta de esta casa?

—Entonces no te coso nada el perrito y no me importa nada si se le sale todo el relleno—lloriqueó mamá. ¿Como una buena madre? ¿Lloriqueando?

peroxide, bandages, and adhesive tape in the medicine cabinet. She was going to need help to fix the bandage. She poured the peroxide over the gash that was now open. She was probably going to need some stitches, but it was going to be impossible to go to the hospital with three kids in tow. She pressed the gauze hard against the wound in order to stop the bleeding. Then she applied another piece of gauze and, with Soledad's assistance, secured it with adhesive tape. It was then she heard the silence. The baby had stopped crying.

"Soledad, go see what's happening with Tom and the baby."

Soledad liked protecting the baby almost as much as she liked beating on Tom. No sooner had she left the bathroom than a desperate cry for help was heard.

"He's killing him, Mommy, Mommy, Mommy, he's going to destroy him, Mommy, Mommy, come quick! He's thrown him into the air, he's KILLING HIM, MOMMY!"

Mommy wanted to take off running at a speed that matched Soledad's maddening screams, but she slipped and fell, twisting her ankle badly. She got up and continued as best she could to the room where the baby was sleeping calmly in his playpen while Tom flung a stuffed teddy bear through the air. The animal was ripped and the stuffing was coming out through a hole, activated by the centrifugal forces at work, flying against the walls, falling to the floor, all over the beds, into the playpen. Soledad was screaming hysterically. Mommy shut her up with a slap on the face, took the stuffed animal away from Tom, and sat down on one of the little beds because she was unable to continue standing on her twisted ankle. She saw blood on Soledad's face and felt her heart sink; but then she immediately realized she had slapped her with her wounded hand that had begun to bleed again. She looked at the balloon and clown design that Soledad herself had chosen for her bedspread and, once again, Mommy felt like crying.

"Bring me the sewing basket so I can bandage your little teddy bear; I'll sew him up," she told Soledad. Her ankle had begun to swell.

"Bring me this, bring me that, who do you think I am?" said Soledad. "Do you think I'm the Cinderella in this house?"

"Then I'm not going to sew up your teddy bear and I don't care a bit if all the stuffing comes out," sobbed Mommy. Like a good mother? Sobbing?

—Quiero panquenques rellenos—dijo Tom—. Mamá le pegó a Soledad. Mamá es un ano con pelotudeces.

Mamá rengueó hasta su dormitorio. En el cajón de la cómoda encontró un pañuelo del tamaño adecuado para hacerse un vendaje en el tobillo. Un esguince, nada grave, si mañana empeoraba iría al médico. El pie ya no le cabía en el zapato. Trató de hacer el vendaje bien apretado (la mano herida no le facilitaba el trabajo) y se puso encima un zoquete de los que su marido odiaba y que ella usaba solamente para dormir. Sintió en el aire un olor a quemado y se acordó de la torta pascualina.

Caminando despacio (el tobillo latía dolorosamente) fue a la cocina. Se agachó para abrir la puerta del horno y vaya a saber por qué alcanzó a darse vuelta justo a tiempo para ver a Tom y Soledad ya definitivamente aliados (pero qué bueno que los hermanos sean unidos, que se ayuden entre ellos), sus cuatro manitas empujándola desde su inestable posición, en cuclillas, contra el horno caliente. Pudo moverse hacia un costado antes de caer, quemándose solamente el antebrazo izquierdo, que rozó la puerta abierta. Puteó de dolor y también de miedo. Sin decir nada, mirándolos fijamente, jadeando, puso la zona quemada debajo del chorro de agua fria. Eso la alivió enseguida.

—Mamá dijo una mala palabra—dijo Tom.

—De veras no sabíamos que el horno estaba caliente de verdad, mamita, perdoname, queríamos jugar a Hansel y Gretel, de veras que no sabíamos.

—La bruja mala se quemó en el horno y se hizo de chocolate rico y se la comieron—dijo Tom—. Mamá dice malas palabras.

—De veras que no sabíamos—repitió Soledad, con cierta monotonía.

Mamita pensó que no le creía y también que estaba loca por no creerle. Sus hijos. Los quería. La querían. El amor más grande que se puede sentir en este mundo. El único amor para siempre, todo el tiempo. El Amor Verdadero. Necesitaba estar un momento sola, pensar en la llamada, en la voz lejana, con ecos. Llorar. Ponerse Cicatul en la quemadura, que ardía ferozmente. Fue al baño. Una mujer organizada ya lo hábría secado. El baño seguía mojado. Una buena madre. Tom la siguió.

"I want pancakes," said Tom. "Mommy hit Soledad. Mommy is a hairy asshole."

Mommy limped to her bedroom. In the chest of drawers she found a handkerchief big enough to bandage her ankle. A little sprain, nothing serious, but if it gets worse, she'd go to the doctor tomorrow. She couldn't get her foot into her shoe. She tried to tie the bandage as tightly as possible (her wounded hand didn't make it any easier) and she put on a sock, one of the ones that her husband detested so much and that she used when she slept. She smelled something burning in the air and remembered the quiche Lorraine.

Walking slowly (now her ankle was throbbing painfully), she made her way to the kitchen. She bent over to open the oven door and God only knows why she turned her head just in time to see Tom and Soledad, having definitely formed an alliance (but isn't it nice that they are together now, that they help each other), their four little hands pushing her from an unstable squatting position as they pushed her off balance against the hot oven? She managed to move to one side before falling down, but burned her left forearm that rubbed against the open door. She swore over the pain and also because of her fear. Remaining silent, she just stared at them, panting, and put her burned arm under the faucet and turned on the water. She felt better immediately.

"Mommy said a bad word," said Tom.

"Honest, we didn't know the oven was hot, really, Mommy dear, I'm sorry, we wanted to play Hansel and Gretel, honest, we didn't know."

"The bad witch was burned in the oven and turned to yummy chocolate and they ate her up," said Tom. "Mommy says bad words."

"Honest, we didn't know," Soledad repeated monotonously.

Mommy dear thought she didn't believe her and also that she was crazy not believing her. They were her children. She loved them. They loved her. That was the greatest love one could experience in this world. The only love, forever, always. True Love. She needed to be alone for a moment, think about the phone call, that distant voice, echoing in the background. Cry. Put some lotion on the burn that was stinging fiercely. She went to the bathroom. An organized woman would have already dried the floor. The bathroom was still wet. A good mother. Tom followed her.

—Tom, mi vida, mamita tiene que estar un momentito sola en el baño.

—¿Para qué?

—¡Para hacer CACA! A mamita le gusta estar sola cuando hace caca, ¿sabés?

—A mí no. A mí me gusta más que me hagan compañía cuando hago caca.

—Pero a mí me gusta estar sola.

—A mí también—intervino Soledad—. Porque yo ya soy grande. Tom es un bebé.

—Yo no soy ningún bebé—aulló Tom.

—Quiero ver cómo mamá se saca la bombacha. Quiero verte los pelitos de abajo—dijo Soledad.

—Yo también quiero ver la concha peluda de mamita—dijo Tom.

—Cuando yo sea grande voy a tener una concha peluda—dijo Soledad.

—¡Pero nunca de nunca vas a tener un pito.—dijo Tom.

—¡Y vos nunca de nunca vas a tener mis años! ¡Por más que cumplas y cumplas años nunca vas a tener mis años!—dijo Soledad.

—Quiero que se vayan—dijo mamá en voz muy baja, temblorosa, amenazadora.

—Y yo quiero verte las tetas—dijo Tom—. Al bebé lo dejás chupar y a mí no.

—Sí, sí, eso queremos, tetas tatas titas totas tetas tetas— canturreó Soledad.

Con todo su peso Soledad se abalanzo sobre mamita para desabrocharle la blusa, mientras Tom le metía las manitos por abajo. El ataque fue repentino, mamá no lo esperaba y su nuca golpeó fuerte contra los azulejos blancos y celestes, con motivos geométricos. El golpe la atontó y al mismo tiempo la hizo perder el control. Agarró a cada uno de un brazo, apretando con bastante fuerza como para dejarles marcadas las huellas de sus dedos. Casi no sentía dolor en la mano herida. Caminar, en cambio, era un puro esfuerzo de voluntad. Los arrastró fuera del baño, por el pasillo.

Cuando calculó que estaba lo bastante lejos los soltó de golpe, empujándolos para asegurarse de que se cayeran. Corrió hacia el baño apoyándose en las paredes, sintiendo que Tom y Soledad se

"Tom, honey, Mommy dear needs to be alone in the bathroom for a moment."

"What for?"

"In order to take a SHIT? Mommy dear likes to be alone when she takes a shit, you know."

"Not me. Nope. I like someone to be with me when I take a shit."

"But I like to be alone."

"So do I," intervened Soledad. "Because I'm bigger now. Tom is still a baby."

"I'm no baby," howled Tom.

"I want to see how Mommy takes off her underwear. I want to see that hair down below," said Soledad.

"Me too, I want to see Mommy dear's hairy cunt," said Tom.

"When I'm big I'm going to have a hairy cunt," said Soledad.

"But you'll never, ever, have a peepee," said Tom.

"And you'll never, ever, be as old as I am! No matter how many birthdays you have you'll never be as old as me!" said Soledad.

"I want you both to leave," said Mommy in a low, trembling, threatening voice.

"And I want to see your tits," said Tom. "You let the baby suck them but not me."

"Yes, yes, that's what we want, tits, tats, tots, tits, tits," sang Soledad.

With all of her might, Soledad pounced on Mommy dear, trying to unbutton her blouse while Tom was sticking his hands up her dress. Mommy wasn't expecting this sudden attack and she struck the back of her head against the white and light blue bathroom tiles with geometric designs. The blow not only stunned her but also made her lose control. She grabbed each one by the arm, squeezing them with enough force so as to leave fingerprints on them. And she almost didn't feel any pain in her wounded hand. Walking, on the other hand, took all she had. She dragged them out of the bathroom and down the hall.

When she calculated that she had gotten them far enough away, she suddenly let go, pushing them to make sure they would fall down. She ran back to the bathroom, bracing herself against the

levantaban, escuchando sus pasitos livianos y veloces otra vez hacia ella, alcanzó sin embargo a meterse en el baño y cerrar la puerta sobre un pie de Soledad, que no gritó. Empujó la puerta hasta que Soledad, jadeando de dolor pero todavía en silencio, tuvo que sacar el pie. Pudo cerrar la puerta y dar vuelta la llave.

Mamá se sentó en el inodoro, apoyó la cabeza en un toallón y se puso a llorar. Lloró y lloró, aliviándose, sintiendo que un sollozo provocaba al otro, lo buscaba. Lloró como quien vomita hasta escuchar, de pronto, a través de su propio llanto, otro llanto nítido, distinto, que se acompasaba extrañamente con el suyo. El bebé. Su bebé. Se acercó a la puerta, apoyó el oído. Se oían risitas ahogadas. Estaban allí. Ahora la tenían en sus manos, sin defensas. Un rehén. Rescatarlo.

Muy lentamente, tratando de no hacer ruido, dio vuelta la llave en la cerradura y abrió la puerta de golpe. Tom, que estaba del otro lado apoyándose con todo su peso, cayó sobre los mosaicos golpeándose la cabeza. Mamá rengueó hasta la pieza de los chicos. Soledad, sentada, sostenía al bebé sobre su falda. La golpeó en la cara, con la mano abierta, arrancándole al bebé de los brazos. Soledad tropezó contra una sillita baja y eso le dio tiempo a mamá a adelantarse. Pronto estuvo otra vez en el baño con el bebé. Tom seguía en el suelo, gritando y pateando. Lo empujó afuera con el pie y volvió a cerrar con llave.

Su bebé. Chiquito. Indefenso. Suyo. Mamá lo abrazó, lo olió. La leche empezó a fluir otra vez, mansamente, de sus pechos. Se tocó la nuca. Apenas un chichón. Puso su cara contra la del bebé, tan suave, cubierta por un vello rubio casi invisible. Despedía calor, amor. Mamá lo acunó mientras cantaba una dulcísima melodía sin palabras. El bebé era todavía suyo, todo suyo, una parte de ella. Movía incontroladamente los bracitos como si quisiera acariciarla, jugar con su nariz. Tenía las uñitas largas. Demasiado largas, podía lastimarse la carita: una buena madre, una madre que realmente quiere a sus hijos, les corta las uñas más seguido. Algunos movimientos parecían completamente azarosos, otros eran casi

walls as she went, perceiving that Tom and Soledad were getting up and, hearing their little, quick, light steps right behind her, she still managed to reach the bathroom and shut the door on one of Soledad's feet, although she didn't scream. Mommy pushed against the door until Soledad, panting from the pain but not saying a word, finally had to pull her foot out of the door. Then Mommy shut the door and locked it.

Mommy sat down on the toilet seat, buried her head in a bath towel and began to cry. She cried and she cried, lessening the pain, feeling that one sob provoked another, and she sought more sobs. She cried like someone who vomits until she hears, all of a sudden, through her own sobbing, another sobbing, clear and distinct, that oddly had the same rhythm as hers. The baby. Her baby. She drew close to the door, putting her ear next to it. She could hear muffled snickering. They were there. Now they had her in their hands: defenseless. They had a hostage. Rescue him.

Very slowly, trying to avoid making any noise, she turned the key and abruptly opened the door. Tom, who was on the other side of the door leaning against it, fell down and hit his head on the tiled bathroom floor. Mommy limped to the children's bedroom. Soledad was sitting down holding the baby on her lap. Mommy slapped her in the face open-handedly, yanking the baby from her arms. Soledad fell over a child's chair which gave Mommy time to get away. Now she was in the bathroom with the baby. Tom was spread out on the floor, screaming and kicking. She pushed him out the door with her foot and locked the door again.

Her baby. Tiny little thing. Defenseless. Hers. Mommy hugged him and smelled him. Her milk began to flow once again, slowly, from her breasts. She felt the back of her head, there was a slight swelling. She put her face up against her baby's face, so tender and covered with an invisible white down. Warmth and love radiated from him. Mommy rocked him while she hummed a pleasant melody. The baby was still hers, all hers, a part of her. He waved his arms uncontrollably, as if he wanted to caress her, and tried to play with her nose. His little fingernails were long, too long: he could scratch his face. A good mother, a mother who really loves her children, would cut his fingernails more frequently. Some of his movements seemed haphazard, others seemed almost deliberate, as

101

deliberados, como si se propusieran algún fin. El índice de la mano derecha del bebé entró en el ojo de mamá provocándole una profunda lesión en la córnea. El bebé sonrió con su sonrisa desdentada.

if they intended to communicate something. He stuck the index finger of his right hand into her eye, causing a serious lesion on the cornea. The baby, toothless, smiled.

OCULTEN LA LUNA

HIDE THE MOON

Asa Zatz, translator of Jorge Lanata

Asa Zatz lives in New York City. He has translated Gabriel García Márquez's *Clandestine in Chile*, Alejo Carpentier's *Concierto Barroco*, Tomás Eloy Martínez's *The Perón Novel*, Arturo Arias's *After the Bombs*, and works by the Spaniard Miguel del Valle Inclán.

"A creativity-gene defect" is Zatz's explanation for his continuing participation in the field of translation. "Some kind of strange biological mutation," he wrote in his reply to the questionnaire, "disabled me from writing my own stuff." (Though Zatz later expressed concern that this response might seem "flip," he reassures that instead it should be gamely considered "antisolemne.") He first discovered the uses of "my defect" translating Pierre Loti and Caesar's *Gallic Wars* in his Brooklyn High School. Later, he translated a play by Ferdinand Bruchner as a favor for the author, and finally entered the field professionally in 1973 with Oscar Lewis's *Children of Sánchez*. Zatz prefers to work independently on a text without collaboration with the author, unless "enigmaticalness, crypticalness, sui generisness and the like" impede him from making satisfactory decisions. He describes his changing perspective on his career in eloquent terms: "My approach was that of a bricklayer until I began translating Latin American literature circa 1981 and beautiful poetry later on; then it changed to that of a lover."

Zatz's motivation for selecting a story by Jorge Lanata emerges in part from the pleasure of reading him. Born in 1954, Lanata is one of Argentina's brilliant young journalists. At thirty he became editor of *Página 12*, the second most important daily in Buenos Aires, and is responsible for a handful of novels, as well as *Polaroids*, a collection of stories published in 1991 from which "Hide the Moon" is taken. Its English translation is in need of an American publisher.

Jorge Lanata
OCULTEN LA LUNA

"La naturaleza humana antes era muy diferente de lo que es hoy en día. Al principio hubo tres clases de hombres: los dos sexos que subsisten hoy en día y un tercero compuesto de estos dos y que ha sido destruido. Este tercero era una especie particular, llamada andrógina, porque reunía el sexo masculino y el femenino. La diferencia con los otros dos tipos estaba en sus principios: el sexo masculino está reproducido por el Sol, el femenino por la Tierra y el andrógino por la Luna. Júpiter encontró un medio de tener más reprimidos a los andróginos y disminuir su fuerza:—Los separaré en dos—dijo. Una vez hecha esta división, cada mitad trató de encontrar a la otra y, cuando se encontraban, se abrazaban y unían con tal ardor que morían de hambre en aquel abrazo, no queriendo hacer nada la una sin la otra. Estas dos mitades se buscan siempre. El único objetivo de estos seres, sean amantes o amados, es reunirse con sus semejantes."
(Aristófanes, en El banquete, de Platón).

Cuando a las cinco en punto de la tarde el destino golpeó a la puerta del Cadogan Hotel, Oscar Wilde pensaba en el amor. Las cortinas cerradas permitían que se dibujara un pequeño triángulo de sol en el piso. Sobre la cama había una valija a medio preparar. Oscar estaba sentado en un sillón al lado del armario. Tenía los brazos cruzados y las piernas vencidas. En la sala de estar se oyó un murmullo: el mismo cuchicheo que acompaña una convalecencia o un velorio.

Se oyó a lo lejos el golpe seco sobre la puerta y Oscar supo que ése era el momento en que comenzaba el juego. Imaginó sus manos, húmedas de transpiración sobre el paño verde de la mesa, atentas al reparto de las cartas. Había vivido cada momento de su vida en dirección a esos nudillos que insistían contra la puerta.

Podía describir cada detalle del futuro, dirigirlo amablemente, como quien inicia la mano de un niño en la escritura. Pero en ese

Jorge Lanata
HIDE THE MOON
Translated by Asa Zatz

"Human nature then was very different from what it is today. In
the beginning, there were three variants of humankind: the two
sexes now in existence and a third, since destroyed. Its members
constituted a special species and were called androgynes, because
they were a combination of the sexes. The difference from the
other two lay in their origins, the males being reproduced by the
Sun, the females by the Earth, and the androgynes by the Moon.
Jupiter found a means of lessening the androgynes' strength and
keeping them more submissive: "I will separate them into two,"
he said. The division having been made, one half sought the
other half and, on finding each other, they embraced and joined
with such ardor that they starved to death in that embrace,
preferring to do nothing, the one without the other, each half
seeking the other forever. The only objective of these beings,
whether lovers or beloveds, is to unite with their counterpart."
(Aristophanes, in Plato's *Banquet*)

When fate knocked on the door of the Cadogan Hotel punctually at
five o'clock in the afternoon, Oscar Wilde was thinking of love. The
drawn curtains allowed a tiny triangle of sunlight through to paint
itself on the floor. A suitcase, partially packed, lay open on the bed.
Oscar sat in an armchair beside the clothespress, arms crossed, legs
lax. A murmuring could be heard in the sitting room, the same
hushed sound that is associated with convalescence or a wake.

The crisp stroke upon the door sounded far away and Oscar
recognized it for the signal that the game was to begin. He imagined
his hands, moist with perspiration, resting on the green table top
waiting for the cards to be dealt. He had lived every moment of his
life attendant upon those insistent knuckles rapping on the door.

He was able to describe every detail of the future, to direct it
kindly, amiably, like one guiding a child's hand in penmanship. But

momento se asombró por su pasado, que a veces le dolía de tan ajeno y otras de tan pesadamente propio.

Supo que, si se miraba de pronto en el reflejo de la ventana, encontraría los rasgos de Bosie sobreimpresos en los suyos. No el rostro inerte de Bosie en una fotografía, sino alguna de sus miradas, su risa, un sonido de cristal, otro de caballos, su indefensión y su peligro.

Oscar pensó en el amor cuando golpearon la puerta. Pensó si quería a Bosie. Se dijo que sí, y también se repitió por enésima vez que jamás podría tenerlo.

—La felicidad, no. Sobre todo, nada de felicidad. ¡El placer! Hay que preferir siempre lo más trágico—mintió una vez.

—Feasting with panthers—dijo otra.

Festejó con panteras, y también Bosie lo hizo. Felinos ingenuos, inconscientes de los que daban, ávidos y sedientos. Tensos como panteras. El mismo Bosie fue pantera alguna vez, pero una pantera demasiado ocupada en sí misma como para pensar en su presa. Una pantera que entraba en un hotel de lujo a lamer su imagen en el espejo.

Se dijo una vez más que lo quería cuando recordó los ojos de aquella pantera, que eran a veces selva y otras desierto; un animal tan simple que resultaba una complicación. Porque Bosie no buscaba nada.

Ahora que se acercaba el final del juego, Oscar sentía una compulsión hacia el recuerdo, similar a la que antecede a la muerte. Había muerto otras veces. Recordó una tarde en Venecia cuando necesitaron aire y un café, y se sentaron a una mesita en la terraza del hotel. Bosie dijo algo sobre su padre: no era importante, y ahora no podía recordarlo. Oscar disparó alguno de sus epigramas, y ambos rieron. Hubo un largo silencio y fue entonces la primera vez que oyó en Venecia el discreto sonido del agua. Miró a Bosie. Leía el periódico con desinterés; en realidad sólo lo tenía frente a sí para lograr un poco de sombra sobre su rostro. Oscar escuchó el agua, destinada desde siempre a mover los cimientos de la ciudad. Era una misión lenta e inexorable.

No hacía frío, ni calor, y desde la costa llegaba una brisa agradable. Oscar jugó con la cuchara contra la taza de café hasta que la cuchara acarició la taza y cayó en el plato; entonces espió a Bosie con interés. Llevaban varias semanas juntos en Venecia y,

his past, which pained him at times for being so alien, at times for being so burdensomely his, at this moment dismayed him.

He knew that if suddenly he were to look at his reflection on the window pane he would see Bosie's face superimposed upon his own. Not Bosie's inert features in a photograph but one of his glances, his smile, a sound of crystal, another of horses, his defenselessness and his danger.

Oscar's thoughts were on love when the knock came. He wondered if he loved Bosie. He told himself that he did and also repeated for the nth time that he could never have him.

"Happiness, no. Above all, no happiness whatsoever. Pleasure! The most tragic always the most preferable," he had once lied.

"Feasting with panthers," he said on another occasion.

He feasted with panthers and so did Bosie. Ingenuous felines, avidly, hungrily unaware of those who gave. Tense as panthers. Bosie was once himself a panther, but too self-centered a panther to think of his prey. A panther that entered a posh hotel to lick at his image in the mirror.

He told himself once more that he loved him, as he recalled that panther's eyes, sometimes a jungle, sometimes a desert; an animal so simple that he became a complication. Because Bosie was not after anything.

Now that the end of the game was nigh, Oscar felt a compulsion to remember, akin to that which precedes death. He had died other times. He remembered one afternoon in Venice when, needing fresh air and coffee, they had sat down at a little table on the hotel terrace. Bosie made some remark about his father, nothing of any importance, that he could now no longer remember. Oscar came out with one of his epigrams and they both laughed. A long silence followed and it was the first time that he heard the discreet sound of the water in Venice. He looked at Bosie who was reading the newspaper disinterestedly. Actually, he was holding it up merely for the bit of shade it provided his face. Oscar listened to the water, destined from the beginning to shift the city's foundations. A mission slow and inexorable.

It was not cold, not warm, and a pleasant breeze was blowing in from the coast. Oscar toyed with his spoon against the coffee cup until the spoon, grazing the cup, fell into the saucer; he then peeped at Bosie with interest. They had been together in Venice for several

aunque Bosie había sufrido cierto ahogo días atras, todo se resolvió con facilidad. Miraban el atardecer en la terraza cuando Bosie comenzó a estornudar y retornaron a la habitación, quejándose por el polvo de la ciudad. Esa tarde en la que casi no cruzaron palabra y el silencio fluía con naturalidad—Oscar supo que no lo tendría jamás.

En aquella terraza miró un largo rato a ese ángel rebelde, joven y tenso, que aceptaba su compañía como una equivocación, o como un resultado del azar que no procuraba entender. Solo le quedaba amarlo.

Esa tarde lo llevó a una noche en Londres, en la que se miraron profundamente a los ojos. Fue sólo un segundo, que no pudieron soportar y terminó con un portazo. Bosie estaba borracho, un camarero cruzó a medio vestir la habitación y discutió con Oscar en el pasillo. Esa noche Oscar fue la pantera y Bosie la presa, aunque quizá siempre hubiera sido de esta forma.

A las cinco de la tarde de aquel 5 de abril pensó en Bosie y se repitió que lo quería: lo quería cuando el sonido discreto del agua en los canales, y quería su robe golpeando la puerta, y quería su manera de preguntar indagando, cómplice y divertido, y su modo trágico de convertirse en niño.

Ross y Wyndham discutían en la recámara, después del mediodía, cuando Bosie abrió la puerta y se llevó a Wyndham a buscar ayuda. Ross quedó solo en la sala y dio vueltas en círculo, lentamente, hasta que abrió la puerta de la habitación muy despacio. Oscar sonrió desde el sillón:

—Es necesario—dijo Ross.

—El tren ya se ha marchado—dijo Oscar, que de inmediato bajo los ojos hacia el apoyabrazos. Rascó el terciopelo con la uña, cuidándose de no rayarlo, y luego tosió.

Ross estaba abandonado contra la pared. Se cruzó de brazos y miró un largo rato por la ventana.

—Oscar, esto no es un juego—insistió.

—Lo sé—dijo Oscar, pero quiso decir: "Lo es". No valía la pena aclararlo.

Los dos miraron molestamente al suelo, parecían víctimas de un bochorno. Por un instante Oscar pensó en volver a las valijas. No lo hizo. Estaba cansado.

weeks and, although Bosie had been bothered by shortness of breath a few days before, it had been readily cleared up. As they watched the sunset from the terrace, Bosie began to sneeze and they returned to their room complaining of the city's dustiness. That same afternoon—during which they exchanged hardly a word and silence seemed the natural course—Oscar knew he would never have him.

There on the terrace, he gazed long at that rebel angel, young and tense, who accepted his company as a misunderstanding or a consequence of chance there could be no accounting for. There was nothing he could do but love him. That afternoon took him back to a night in London when they looked deep into each other's eyes. It lasted only a second, which they could not endure, and it ended with the door being slammed. Bosie was drunk; a bellboy, half-dressed, crossed the bedroom and argued with Oscar in the hall. That night Oscar was the panther and Bosie the prey, although it would probably have been like that always.

On that April 5th at five o'clock, he was thinking of Bosie and repeating that he loved him: loved him to the discreet sound of the canal water, loved his dressing gown brushing the door, loved his manner of asking a question, searchingly, in complicity and amusement, and the tragic way he had of changing into a child.

Ross and Wyndham were arguing in the bedroom in the afternoon when Bosie opened the door and took Wyndham with him to get help. Ross remained alone in the sitting room, walking about in a circle slowly until, very gingerly, he opened the bedroom door. Oscar, in the armchair, smiled.

"It's the only way," Ross said.

"The boat has sailed," replied Oscar, immediately dropping his gaze to the arm of the chair. He drew his nail over the velvet, careful not to leave a mark, then coughed.

Ross, against the wall, abandoned, crossed his arms and looked out the window for a long time.

"Oscar, this is no game," he insisted.

Wanting to say "It is," Oscar said "I know." There was no use explaining.

They both stared at the floor in annoyance, like the victims of an embarrassing incident. For a moment, Oscar considered going back to his packing. He didn't. He was weary.

Comenzó a imaginarse el momento en que se anunciara la sentencia: ¿que pasaría después: habría un silencio? ¿Un abucheo? Supo que el juez—a quien no conocería hasta semanas después— tendría voz estridente y aguda. Con esa voz leería el veredicto del Reino Unido contra Oscar Wilde.

Un murmullo, sí; después de la sentencia serpentearía un murmullo por todo el tribunal: rostros flojos, abatidos, frases dichas de soslayo, indignación ante un final tan previsible que solo podía ser cierto en un mal vaudeville. Construyó cada detalle de la escena con temor: podía ver a los demás, pero no podía verse a sí mismo, y lo acorralaba el miedo de perder el equilibrio.

A las cuatro y media de la tarde Ross salió a fumar a la sala. Oscar miraba el reloj cada dos o tres minutos. Se sentía obligado a recordar cada momento de ese 5 de abril. Había sufrido otras veces esa repentina neurosis de biógrafo, acompañada de la obligación de recordar como un testigo.

Oyó en la sala la repentina voz de Ross y otra más joven, de uno de los camareros:

—No—decía Ross.

—Le pido disculpas, pero eso me dijeron en el desk...—dijo el mozo.

Oscar imaginó al mozo que trataba de espiar por la abertura de la puerta.

—No pedimos nada, gracias.

—¿No quiere nada, entonces?

—No.

—Disculpe, entonces.

—Está bien. Puede retirarse.

—¿Tampoco agua?

—Tampoco, gracias.

En el sillón, Oscar tenía la sonrisa de un padre. Le provocaban ternura aquellos personajes anónimos que luchaban por entrar en la historia: seres mediocres y acorralados pugnando por acercarse a la vida. Siempre había alguien que llevaba un jarro con agua fresca al condenado a muerte, o un niño que lustraba las armas con placer y desesperación, a la madrugada, minutos antes del duelo. En el fondo buscaban acercarse a la muerte; para todos ellos la muerte estaba más viva que su propia vida.

He began imagining the moment when sentence would be passed and what might happen immediately after. Would it be followed by silence? Hooting? He knew that the judge—whom he wasn't to meet until weeks later—would have a high-pitched, strident voice. He would pronounce the verdict in the case of the United Kingdom vs. Oscar Wilde in that voice.

A murmuring, yes; after the sentence, a murmur would slither through the courtroom: sagging, disheartened faces, snatches of furtive remarks, indignation at such a predictable finale worthy only of a cheap vaudeville. He anxiously reconstructed the scene, detail by detail. He was able to visualize the other people, but not himself, and was beset by fear of losing his balance.

At 4:30, Ross went to the sitting room to have a smoke. Oscar was consulting his watch every two or three minutes. He felt compelled to recall every moment of that April 5th. He had been attacked by the same sudden biographer's neurosis on other occasions, coupled with the obligation, as a witness, to remember.

He suddenly heard Ross in the other room and then a more youthful voice, a bellboy's.

"No," Ross was saying.

"I beg your pardon, but they did tell me at the desk..." said the youth.

Oscar imagined the boy trying to see into the room through the crack in the door.

"We didn't ring for anything, thank you."

"There's nothing you'd be wanting, then?"

"No."

"I beg pardon, then."

"Very well. You may go."

"Not even water?"

"Not even, thank you."

Oscar, in the armchair, smiling paternally. He was moved to tenderness by the way anonymous characters try to force their way into history; mediocre, cornered beings fighting to draw close to life. There was always someone on hand to bring the condemned man a pitcher of water, or the boy, anxiously, eagerly polishing the weapons at daybreak, minutes before the duel. What they are actually seeking is to get close to death; death, for them, is more alive than their own lives.

El tiempo era sólo un capricho. Oscar miró las agujas del reloj y pensó que se equivocaban. El tiempo no podía correr de esa manera. Recordaba semanas, y solo habían pasado algunos minutos. Hubiera dado su vida por esta velocidad en aquellos momentos en que el tiempo transcurría lento por una palabra hasta que permitía, finalmente, que ella saltara sobre el papel.

Ahora su futuro colgaba de una palabra:

—Culpable—diría el juez de la voz aguda.

O aquellas ocho palabras que le rogó Lady Wilde para que se reconciliara con su hermano Willie. "Solo ocho palabras", le escribió: He olvidado la enemistad. Volvamos a ser amigos. Solo eso". Oscar nunca las escribió.

Cuando encontraba las adecuadas era distinto: cada palabra se acomodaba allí donde él la ponía, como si nunca hubieran conocido otro lugar mejor, y convertían a la realidad en un accidente trivial:

Oculten la Luna

podía escribir. Y miles de brazos se prestaban, obedientes, a ocultarla. Ahora sólo esperaba en su sillón que saliera la Luna. No quería impedirlo.

* * *

Bosie nunca pudo llorar. En su cuarto de estudiante, en Oxford, se paró varias veces frente al espejo mirándose a los ojos, tratando de forzar el llanto. Pero las lágrimas no salían.

No podía llorar. El dato le preocupó al punto de atribuirlo a alguna lesión en los lagrimales, quizá congénita, o a una completa falta de interés por el resto del mundo. Una vez, en El Cairo, cuando las cartas de Oscar se demoraban en llegar—nunca llegaron, en realidad—y sus propias cartas a Londres volvían con el sobre cerrado, se creyó capaz de llorar en los brazos de cualquier desconocido. Pero no lo hizo. A las tres de la tarde de aquel 5 de abril caminó por los pasillos del Parlamento consciente de que el destino de Oscar estaba sellado. Se compadeció de sí mismo; no podía encontrarle cauce al llanto. De poder hacerlo, ¿lloraría por Oscar? ¿Por sí mismo? ¿Por Queensberry? ¿Por esa imposibilidad física de llorar? Un vidrio sucio, tocado por demasiadas manos, lo

Time was only a fancy. Oscar looked at his watch and thought that it must be wrong. Time could not pass by like that. He was remembering weeks and no more than a few minutes had gone by. He would have given his life for such rapidity at those moments when time moves so slowly until a word is finally permitted to spring onto the page.

His future now hung on a word:

"Guilty," the judge with the shrill voice would say.

Or those eight words with which Lady Wilde begged him to reconcile with his brother Willie. "A mere eight words," she wrote him: "*I've forgotten the enmity. Let's be friends again.*' Only that." Oscar never wrote them.

It was different when he found the right words. Each settled in just where he placed it, as though they could never have known a better place, and turned reality into a commonplace accident:

Hide the Moon

he could write. And thousands of obedient hands were there to hide it. Now, he simply waited in his chair for the Moon to come out. He had no desire to prevent it.

* * *

Bosie could never cry. As a student at Oxford, he had stood before the mirror in his room a number of times trying to force tears. But they would not come.

He could not cry. This worried him to such an extent that he attributed it to a possible malformation of the tear ducts, probably congenital, or to utter disinterest in the rest of the world. Once, in Cairo, when Oscar's letters were late in arriving—never arrived, actually—and his own to London had come back unopened, he felt himself capable of weeping in the arms of any stranger. But he did not. At three o'clock in the afternoon on that April 5th, he walked through the halls of Parliament aware that Oscar's fate was sealed. He felt sorry for himself; he could not find the conduit for his tears. Were he able to, would he weep for Oscar? For himself? For Queensberry? For that physical incapacity to cry. A dirty window glass, fingered by too many hands, distanced him from everything.

alejaba de todo. Caminó hasta el Holborn Viaduct Hotel y se sentó en el bar. Pidió un licor, y miró en torno. Era excitante y perverso sentirse dueño de un futuro ajeno. Bebió un sorbo pensando que era la única persona en la ciudad que conocía el sitio de la bomba y la hora en que ésta iba a explotar.

No le sentaba la vida de los mártires: podría levantarse en ese instante y correr hacia el Tribunal y declarar a favor de Oscar: lo salvaría de la prisión. Pero no iba a hacerlo.

Además, era Oscar quien había armado este juego y era a él a quien le correspondía mover las piezas. Revisó cada detalle de su relación con Oscar hasta que concluyó, como siempre: el dinero era lo único que los mantenía unidos. Pedirle dinero a Oscar era una dulce humillación, y un exquisito placer, para ambos. Eso los hacía fieles. Tal vez sólo a eso fueran fieles los hombres.

Oscar lo había asediado durante meses hasta aquella noche de primavera en que perfumó su cuarto de la Universidad. Aquella noche Bosie era una estatua. Serena, fría y perfecta. Tenía las curvas y la tensión y los relieves de las estatuas clásicas y cumplía con naturalidad la misión de ser adorado.

Pero Oscar era el Dios; un dios fláccido y presuntuoso, expulsado del Olimpo y condenado a escribir su propia historia.

Cuando las manos de Oscar recorrían su cuerpo sentía que lo creaban de la nada, como si nunca hubiera existido. Esa noche sintió asco, y luego lo odió.

—Bosie. Querido Bosie—lo bautizó Oscar, tomándole la mano. Aquella noche había asistido a la creación de alguien mejor que él mismo. Oscar era un mundo: con millones de habitantes, de vidas truncas, de voces.

A la mañana siguiente Bosie se levantó sabiendo que jamás tendría su propio destino, y aquella certeza lo ensombreció.

Después de la tercera copa en el bar del hotel, Bosie dejó de llevar la cuenta; el mozo le servía con intervalos de quince minutos. Notó que, desde una de las mesas del fondo, lo miraban dos mujeres y comentaban algo. Una de ellas sonrió. Bosie desvió los ojos y se miró las manos, que sostenían la copa en el centro de la mesa y se multiplicaban en un espejo de pared, ubicado a todo lo largo del salón. Pensó en inclinarse hasta mirar su rostro. Se imaginó triste, y despeinado, aunque no lo estaba. Se pasó la mano por el pelo.

He walked to Holborn Viaduct Hotel and sat in the barroom. He ordered a liqueur and looked about. It was perverse and exciting to feel oneself master of another's future. He took a sip, thinking that he was the only person in the city who knew where the bomb was and at what time it was set to go off.

A martyr's life was not for him. He could have gotten to his feet that very moment, run to the Court, testified in Oscar's defense and saved him from prison. But he was not going to.

Besides, it was Oscar who had set this game up and it was for him to move the pieces. He went back over every detail of his relationship with Oscar until he concluded, as always: it was money alone that kept them together. Asking Oscar for money was a sweet humiliation and, for both, an exquisite pleasure. It kept them faithful. Perhaps that is the only thing people are faithful to.

Oscar had laid siege to him for months until the spring night that he perfumed his room at the University. That night, Bosie was a statue. Serene, cold and perfect. He had the curves, the tension, the reliefs of classical statues and he fulfilled his mission naturally of being adored.

But Oscar was the God, a flabby, presumptuous god, ejected from Olympus and condemned to write his own story.

When Oscar passed his hands over his body, he felt them creating him out of nothingness, as though he had never existed. His feeling that night was one of disgust and after that he hated him.

"Bosie. Dear Bosie," Oscar baptized him, taking his hand. He had been present that night at the creation of something better than himself. Oscar *was* a world—with millions of inhabitants, of stunted lives, of voices.

Bosie rose the next morning aware that he would never have a destiny of his own and that certainty cast a pall over him.

After his third drink at the hotel barroom, Bosie lost count. The waiter served him at fifteen-minute intervals. He noticed two women at a table in the rear looking at him and commenting. One of them smiled. Bosie looked away and stared at his hands holding the glass in the center of the table which was reflected in the wall mirror that ran the length of the room. He thought of leaning over far enough to see his face. He imagined himself sad-looking and unkempt, though he wasn't. He smoothed his hand over his hair.

—¡Oscar!—dijo una voz en la mesa de al lado.

Bosie se dio vuelta de inmediato y vio a un hombre mayor que sonreía ante la llegada de un amigo. El hombre observó extrañado a ese joven que, sin ningún motivo, lo observaba con tan poca educación. Bosie enrojeció y volvió a su copa.

—¡Oscar!—recordó—. ¡Vamos, Oscar! ¡Cuenta otra historia de la Iglesia Primitiva!—Acababa de terminar la cena en casa de Saint Giles, y era Grant el que quería recordar los viejos tiempos de Oxford, cuando todos se sentaban alrededor de Wilde, para escuchar sus historias.—Una historia—dijo Grant—, sólo una.

Oscar se hacía rogar, aunque cada negativa era parte del juego. Bosie sonreía entre el círculo de amigos.

—Ya que insisten—cedió Oscar. Hubo un par de aplausos y. un silbido. Bosie recordaba cada palabra con exactitud:

—Hace poco—comenzó Oscar, y se produjo el silencio—, hace poco recorría la biblioteca de una casa de campo y tomé al azar un mohoso volumen encuadernado en cuero. Lo abrí en cualquier parte y mis ojos dieron con la frase: "Ese año el Papa Juan XXII murió de una muerte vergonzosa". Eso me intrigó: ¿que clase de muerte vergonzosa? Hojeé el libro una y otra vez en busca de la respuesta, pero sin éxito. De modo que decidí buscar la verdad con certeza: haciéndola surgir de mi conciencia interior. En el silencio de la noche se me presentó la verdad desnuda. Era ésta.

Oscar miró cada una de las caras del pequeño auditorio. La cuerda de la intriga estaba tensa. Prosiguió:

—En aquellos días el Papa no llevaba una vida aislada detrás de las murallas del Vaticano, sino que intervenía libremente en la sociedad de Roma. No es de extrañar que, al poco tiempo de ser elegido, el Papa Juan, al frecuentar diariamente las más bellas mujeres de la capital, se enamorase. La dama objeto de su amor era la joven esposa de un noble anciano. Primero se amaron con el amor que muere: el amor del alma por el alma; y luego se amaron con el amor que nunca muere: el amor del cuerpo por el cuerpo. Pero incluso en la Roma de esa época sus oportunidades eran escasas: por ello resolvieron fijar sus encuentros en un lugar apartado, lejos de la ciudad. El marido de la dama tenía una pequeña villa con un huerto a pocos kilómetros de distancia. El día designado, el Papa Juan se atavió con las ropas comunes de un noble romano y montando su caballo, cabalgó con el corazón exultante

"Oscar!" said a voice at a neighboring table.

Bosie quickly looked around and saw an older man smiling as a friend approached. The man was taken aback at the sight of this young person who with no justification was staring at him so rudely. Bosie blushed and returned to his drink.

"Oscar!" he remembered. "Come on, Oscar! Tell us another about the Primitive Church." Supper at the Saint Giles house had finished and it was Grant who wanted to reminisce about the old days at Oxford when everybody would gather around Wilde to listen to his stories. "One story," said Grant, "just one."

Oscar let himself be coaxed, each refusal part of the game. Bosie, one of the circle, smiled.

"Since you insist," Oscar gave in. A few applauded and one whistled. Bosie could recall every word.

"Not long ago," Oscar began, and all fell silent, "not long ago, I was browsing through the library in a country house and happened to pick up a moldy, leather-bound volume. I opened it at random and my eyes lit on these words: 'That year, Pope John XXII died a shameful death.' I was intrigued. What sort of a shameful death? I leafed through the book several times looking for an answer, but could find none. And so, I decided to ascertain the truth—by calling it up from my inner consciousness. In the silence of the night, the naked truth came to me. It was this."

Oscar looked into the faces of his small audience. The thread of intrigue was taut. He continued.

"In those days, the Pope did not lead a cloistered life within Vatican walls, but moved about freely in Roman society. It should come as no surprise that soon after his election, Pope John, who was in daily contact with the city's most beautiful women should have fallen in love. The object of his infatuation was the young wife of an elderly nobleman. First, they loved with the love of soul for soul, the love that dies; then, they loved with the love that never dies, the love of body for body. But, opportunities were few, even in the Rome of those times, and they decided to hold their trysts in a remote place outside the city. The lady's husband owned a small villa with an orchard not many kilometers away. On the appointed day, Pope John, clad in the ordinary garb of a Roman nobleman, mounted his horse and rode off to the villa, his heart exultant. A few kilometers along the way, he came to a small, humble church

hacia la villa. Cuando había hecho unos kilómetros se topó con la pequeña y humilde iglesia donde había sido sacerdote tiempo antes. Entonces se adueñó de él un extraño capricho: ponerse las vestiduras y sentarse en el confesionario como tantas veces había hecho. A los pocos minutos se abrió la puerta y entró un hombre a toda prisa, en un evidente estado de perturbación. "Padre", dijo con voz quebrada. "¿Hay algún pecado tan grande que Cristo no pueda absolverme de él?" "No, hijo mío, no hay tal pecado", contestó el Papa. "¿Qué pecado tan terrible has cometido para que me preguntes eso?" "No he cometido ningún pecado aún", le dijo el otro, "pero estoy a punto de cometer un pecado tan horrible que ni siquiera el mismo Cristo podría absolverme: voy a matar al vicario de Cristo en la Tierra, voy a matar al Papa Juan XXII". "Hasta de ese pecado Cristo podría absolverte", dijo con seguridad y pavor el Papa Juan. El hombre salió precipitadamente de la iglesia y el Papa se levantó, se quitó las vestiduras de sacerdote, montó su caballo y cabalgó hasta donde esperaba su amante. Allí, sobre el verde césped, en un claro iluminado entre los árboles, vio a su dama. Ella lanzó un grito de alegría, corrió hacia él y se arrojó en sus brazos. Mientras se amaban, surgió una figura entre los árboles y clavó una daga hasta la empuñadura en la espalda del Papa Juan. Con un gemido la víctima cayó al suelo, agonizante. Luego, haciendo un supremo esfuerzo, elevó su mano y, mirando a su atacante, pronunció la absolución: "Quod ego possum et tu eges, absolve te". Así murió el Papa Juan XXII, de una muerte vergonzosa.

Bosie miró el reloj: faltaba poco para las cinco. Decidió caminar hasta el Cadogan Hotel. Bebió lo que quedaba de su copa, pagó al mozo y, antes de levantarse, se inclinó para ver su rostro en el espejo del salón. Advirtió que estaba llorando.

* * *

Cuando Marlowe golpeó a la puerta del Cadogan Hotel, a las cinco en punto de la tarde, sabía que hasta el lobo podía pasar por momentos de debilidad, ponerse del lado del cordero y pensar: "Ojalá que huya". Cuando sus nudillos golpearon a la puerta de la habitación creyó oír movimientos en el interior.

—No te preocupes—alcanzó a descifrar en una voz apagada.

where, as a priest, he had once officiated. Suddenly, he was seized by an inexplicable urge: to don his vestments and sit in the confessional as he had so often done. Shortly thereupon, the door opened and a man entered, evidently overwrought and in great haste. "Father," he said in a hoarse voice, "is there a sin so great that Christ could not absolve me of it?" "No, my son, there is no such sin," the Pope replied. "What sin did you commit so heinous that you should ask me this?" "I have as yet committed no sin," he told him, "but I am about to commit one so terrible that not even Christ himself could absolve it. I am going to kill Christ's vicar on earth; I am going to kill Pope John XXII." "Christ could absolve even that sin," said Pope John in certainty and in fear. The man rushed from the church, the Pope stepped out of the confessional, removed the priestly vestments, mounted his horse, and rode off to where his lover awaited. There, upon the green lawn, in a clearing between the trees lit by the sun, he saw his lady. She gave a cry of joy, ran to him, and threw herself into his arms. As they loved, a figure stepped out from among the trees and plunged a dagger up to the hilt in Pope John's back. With a gasp, the victim fell to the ground, dying. Making a supreme effort, he raised his hand and, looking at his assailant, gave absolution: "*Quod ego possum et tu eges, absolve te.*" And so did Pope John XXII die a shameful death.

Bosie looked at his watch and decided to walk to the Cadogan Hotel. It was close to five o'clock. He drained his glass, paid the waiter, and before getting to his feet, bent over to look at his reflection in the mirror and saw that he had been crying.

* * *

When Marlowe knocked on the door at the Cadogan Hotel at five o'clock sharp, he was aware that even the wolf may have a moment of weakness and take the lamb's part, thinking: "I hope it gets away." When his knuckles struck the door of the room, he seemed to hear movement inside.

He could make out a muffled voice saying, "Don't worry." Then,

Después oyó pasos acercándose. Reconoció el rostro apenas se abrió la puerta y dijo:

—Mister Ross, soy Marlowe, periodista del Star—y alargó la mano.

Ross iba a cerrar cuando Marlowe se precipitó a explicar:

—Es imperioso que hablemos. Traigo una noticia importante.

Ross dudó, Marlowe ya estaba en el centro de la sala.

—Mister Marlowe—repitió Ross.

—Del Star.

—El señor Wilde no va a dar ninguna entrevista a la prensa—recitó Ross.

—Lo sé, lo sé. No vengo por eso.

Marlowe caminó hasta la ventana. Sentía cierto placer en demorar las frases. Observó la expresión de Ross, en ascuas ante sus palabras. Una semana antes hubiera dado un año de su vida por una entrevista con Oscar Wilde. Su periódico, el Star, como la mayoría de la prensa británica, no había ahorrado calificativos frente a ese "artista corruptor de menores", esa "verdadera vergüenza de una sociedad civilizada". Marlowe no tenía ningún sentimiento especial por Wilde, ni siquiera había visto sus obras, ni leído sus poemas. No sentía repugnancia ante los homosexuales, solo tristeza o desinterés. Definitivamente no era el lobo; sí quizás una pequeña pulga en el lomo del lobo. Si se enteraban en el periódico de esta visita, iban a despedirlo. Había sido el azar aquello que lo acercó a la puerta. Hasta Oscar Wilde merecía una oportunidad:

—Van a detenerlo. Esta tarde. A las seis—dijo Marlowe por fin.

—¿Cómo lo sabe?

—Me lo dijo un periodista del diario hace una hora en Bow Street. Charles Russell en persona fue a solicitar el arresto, y Sir John Bridge aceptó.

Ross se llevó la mano a la frente y se alisó el pelo. Marlowe miró el reloj.

—Falta poco menos de una hora—dijo.

Ross asintió en silencio.

—¿Él está aquí?—preguntó Marlowe.

—Sí—dijo Ross, y señaló el cuarto con la cabeza.

—Tiene que irse, todavía hay tiempo.

Ross tomó a Marlowe del brazo y lo acompañó hasta la puerta.

—Gracias—le dijo, mirándolo a los ojos—. Muchas gracias.

there were steps approaching. The moment the door opened, he recognized the face, and stretching out his hand, said, "Mister Ross, I'm Marlowe, reporter of the *Star*."

As Ross made to close the door, Marlowe hastened to explain, "It's urgent that we talk. I have important news."

Ross hesitated but Marlowe was already in the middle of the room.

"Mr. Marlowe," repeated Ross.

"Of the *Star*."

"Mr. Wilde is not giving interviews to the press."

"I know, I know, that's not what I'm here for."

Marlowe walked towards the window. He felt a certain pleasure in holding back his words. He noted Ross's expression on edge with expectancy. A week before he would have given an eyetooth for an interview with Oscar Wilde. Like most of the British press, the *Star* had minced no words about the "artist corrupter of youth," that "unmitigated disgrace to civilized society." Marlowe had no special feelings about Wilde, had never seen a play of his nor read his poems. He felt no repugnance for homosexuals, merely sadness or indifference. He was certainly not the wolf though possibly a little flea on the wolf's back. If his paper learned of this visit, he'd be sacked. Being there had been fortuitous. Even Oscar Wilde deserved a chance.

"He's going to be arrested. This evening. At six o'clock," said Marlowe, finally.

"How did you find out?"

"A reporter at Bow Street told me an hour ago. Charles Russell personally presented the petition and Sir John Bridge granted it."

Ross brought his hand to his forehead. Marlowe looked at his watch.

"There's a bit less than an hour to go," he said.

Ross assented with silence.

"He's here, is he?" asked Marlowe.

"Yes," replied Ross, tilting his head in the direction of the bedroom.

"He must leave. There's still time."

Ross took Marlowe by the arm and accompanied him to the door.

"Thank you," he said looking into his eyes. "Very much."

* * *

—¿Lo escuchaste?—preguntó Ross, entrando a la habitación.

—¿Qué?—dijo Oscar.

—Van a detenerte a las seis. Son las cinco y diez.

—Voy a quedarme—dijo Oscar, y una sombra pasó frente a sus ojos.—Voy a cumplir la sentencia, cualquiera que sea—agregó.

Ross tuvo la convicción de que Oscar necesitaba la cárcel por algún motivo pero sólo entendió ese motivo años después, cuando Wilde publicó La balada de la cárcel de Reading. Todos sus pasos lo habían conducido a ese libro. Oscar recordó miles de veces la escena siguiente: el camarero que entró a las seis y diez del 5 de abril, seguido por dos detectives. El más alto de los detectives, que dijo:

—Tenemos aquí una orden, señor Wilde, para su detención bajo la acusación de realizar actos indecentes.

—¿Me concederán la libertad bajo fianza?—preguntó Oscar.

Los detectives dudaron. Oscar se levantó y caminó a tientas por la habitación. Buscó su abrigo y un libro de tapas amarillas. Pidió a Ross que le preparara una muda de ropa y se la alcanzara más tarde.

—¿Adónde me llevan?—preguntó Oscar.

—A Bow Street—dijo uno de los detectives.

Media hora después Bosie llegó al hotel.

* * *

"Did you hear?" asked Ross, entering the bedroom.

"What?" asked Oscar.

"They're coming to arrest you at six o'clock. It's now ten minutes past five."

"I'm staying," said Oscar, and a shadow passed before his eyes. "I shall serve out the sentence, whatever it is."

Ross was convinced that Oscar needed prison for some reason, but it was not until years later, when Wilde published *The Ballad of Reading Gaol*, that he understood why. His every step had led to that poem. Oscar recalled the following scene a thousand times: the bellboy entering at 6:10 on April 5th, followed by two detectives, the taller of whom said, "We have here an order for your arrest, Mr. Wilde, under the accusation of having committed acts of indecency."

"Will I be released on bail?" Oscar asked.

The detectives were dubious. Oscar stood up and walked through the room, groping his way. He picked up his overcoat and a book with a yellow cover. He asked Ross to pack a change of clothing and bring it to him later.

"Where are you taking me?"

"To Bow Street," one of the detectives told him.

Bosie arrived at the hotel half an hour later.

LA MÚSICA DE LA LLUVIA

THE MUSIC OF THE RAIN

Suzanne Jill Levine, translator of Silvina Ocampo

Suzanne Jill Levine teaches literature at the University of California at Santa Barbara. She has translated Guillermo Cabrera Infante's *Three Trapped Tigers*, Manuel Puig's *Tropical Night Falling*, and Adolfo Bioy Casares's *Adventures of a Photographer in La Plata*, among other Latin American works. Authors and their translators often converse on an intimate plane, and Jill Levine has especially benefited from a prolific number of such relationships. She views friendships with the writers she has translated essential to her success. Some of her experiences of collaboration "with authors who become dear and close friends" appear in her book *The Subversive Scribe: Translating Latin American Fiction*, which includes correspondence with Puig discussing her work on *Heartbreak Tango* and *Tropical Night Falling*.

As early as high school Levine recognized translation as a means of integrating her love of French, modernist literature and "playing with words." She was not inspired to pursue Spanish translation seriously until she encountered post-Boom authors who, she said, "made the spoken literary," who loved movies even more than she did, who—with extraordinary wit and originality—took language to its limits," and whose writings share a "challenge to programmatic thinking, and an affirmation of life." Along with her mentor, Gregory Rabassa, Levine believes that a translator must have a fine-tuned ear. "It isn't surprising that many translators and writers are also musicians or music fans," she writes.

Two of the things she finds fascinating about Silvina Ocampo is the notion of music as intrinsic to the story, and that she makes Levine laugh. Ocampo, who died in December 1993, is a crucial name in contemporary Argentine letters. Sister of Victoria Ocampo, the *grand dame* of national letters and editor of *Sur*, Silvina, born in 1906, wrote numerous collections of short stories, including *Antología de Ireneao, Las invitada,* and *Y así sucesivamente,* the latter being the source of Levine's choice for this anthology. It is sad that, in spite of her relevence and prodigious output, only a fraction of her work is available in English (this includes Daniel Balderston's translation of *Leopoldina's Dream*). Ocampo is best known in the United States as the wife of Adolfo Bioy Casares and as co-editor, with Jorge Luis Borges and her husband, of the influential *Antología de literatura fantástica,* published in 1988 north of the Rio Grande as *The Book of Fantasy.*

Silvina Ocampo
LA MÚSICA DE LA LLUVIA

Las piedritas del camino cantaban bajo las ruedas del coche de plaza. En el atento jardín no podía confundirse el ruido pausado y rítmico del coche de caballos con el ruido seco y rápido del automóvil. Aquel día todo parecía musical: la roldana del aljibe que subía el balde, las voces, las toses, las risas.

—¿Quién llegó?—preguntaron gritos aflautados.

—Octavio Griber—contestó una voz grave.

—¿Quién?—insistió la pregunta impaciente.

—El pianista—contestó la voz grave.

—¿En coche de plaza? En un día de lluvia. ¿Acaso no pudieron venir en automóvil?

—El pianista está loco por los coches de caballos y la lluvia; dice que son musicales. Por lo menos relinchan a veces los caballos.

En la sala se sentó la gente, en los sillones demasiado cómodos, tan cómodos que después de un rato era difícil para algunas personas incorporarse, de modo que la actitud que tomaron sugería la permanencia. En el jardín, de vez en cuando, un relámpago seguido de un trueno iluminaba la sala.

El dueño de casa, que sabía tocar el piano, se apostó junto a la ventana. Estaba tan habituado en su ilusión a que lo retrataran que adoptó esa postura romántica.

Iluminado por un relámpago, el pianista entró por fin. Ninguna timidez suavizaba su rostro. Saludó con un movimiento de cabeza, que lo despeinó a todos los invitados. Cuando vio el enorme espejo que había junto al piano, ordenó que lo taparan. (Esta exigencia causó revuelo. No había con qué taparlo. Por fin encontraron un edredón floreado y lo colocaron, como pudieron, sobre el espejo.) Luego el pianista se dirigió ceremoniosamente a un rincón donde había un biombo decorado con espigas, racimos de uvas y palomas, sacó de un portafolio una chaqueta de terciopelo, con alamares dorados, y se la puso después de quitarse el abrigo, los zapatos y las medias.

Silvina Ocampo

THE MUSIC OF THE RAIN

Translated by Suzanne Jill Levine

The pebbles on the road clattered beneath the wheels of the hired coach. From the silent garden the steady rhythm of a horse-drawn carriage could be heard clearly, distinct from the dry swift sound of an automobile. Everything seemed musical that day, the pulley-wheel raising the bucket from the well, the laughter, the voices, the coughs.

"Who's there?" voices piped in unison.

"Octavio Griber," a deep voice answered.

"Who?" the impatient voices refrained.

"The pianist," the deep voice responded.

"In a hired coach? On a rainy day? Couldn't they come by car?"

"The pianist is crazy about rain and horse-drawn carriages. He says they're musical, at least when the horses whinny."

The guests seated themselves in the drawing room in armchairs that were so comfortable that after a while they swallowed the people up and turned them into permanent fixtures. From the garden the room was lit by an occasional flash of lightning followed by thunder.

The owner of the house, who knew how to play the piano, posted himself near the window. He adopted a romantic pose, as if fantasizing that he was having his portrait painted.

Amid flashing bolts of lightning, the pianist finally entered. No sign of humility softened his features. He greeted the guests with an extravagant wave of his head that mussed his hair. When he saw the enormous mirror beside the piano, he ordered it to be covered. (This caused a commotion; there was nothing to cover it with. Finally they found a flowered quilt and draped it, as best they could, over the mirror.) Then the pianist ceremoniously sauntered over to a corner where there was a screen decorated with doves, ears of grain and bunches of grapes. Next he proceeded to pull out of his briefcase a velvet jacket adorned with golden loops and put it on after taking off his coat, his shoes and his socks.

Obedeciendo a su pedido, varias manos anilladas levantaron la tapa del piano. El pianista sacó de su bolsillo diminutos papeles de seda blanca y los puso cuidadosamente, uno por uno, debajo de cada martillo de felpa, en el interior del piano, que previamente había examinado, como un médico a un enfermo. El dueño de casa disimuló su inquietud al ver debajo de los martillos todos esos papelitos, pero no pudo contener su impaciencia y exclamó con una voz incongruente:

—Es un excéntrico.—Y preguntó amablemente a la madre del pianista—: ¿Por qué hace eso?

—Es un nuevo sistema que «ensueña» los tonos del piano. Suena como un clavicordio.

—¿Sueña o suena? Un sistema no es más nuevo que otro, pues ningún sistema es nuevo. El clavicordio es un instrumento antiguo. ¿Qué ventaja hay en utilizar efectos modernos para conseguir antigüedades? Pero ante todo no me gusta que me toquen el interior del piano. Ya bastantes polillas le han entrado.

Octavio Griber miró con severidad al dueño de casa, encendió un cigarrillo y murmuró:

—Yo no toco sin papel de seda.—Siguió acomodando sus papelitos y murmuró dirigiéndose al dueño de casa—: Me han dicho que usted es un gran pianista. ¿No nos hará oír su repertorio?

—Sí, pero no toco con los pies—contestó el dueño de casa secamente.

Era muy celoso. Cuando lo estaba, se le notaba en la barba: se le ponía tan áspera que ni un beso podían darle, por suave que fuera la brillantina que usaba.

—Después de estas reuniones me siento más viejo—me susurró al oído.

Advertí por primera vez que era bizco, de tanto mirar su barba, y que esto era el secreto de la inteligencia de su mirada.

La lluvia arreciaba en el jardín. Se la oía golpear los vidrios como si fuera piedra en vez de lluvia. En ese momento se distribuyeron los programas manuscritos con letra de colegial. De Liszt figuraban varias obras: Al borde de una fuente, San Francisco de Paula sobre las aguas, Juegos de agua en la Villa d'Este. Los nombres de Debussy, Ravel, Chopin, Repighi estaban escritos en tinta verde. Los papeles volaban de mano en mano.

Upon his request, various ring-laden fingers raised the piano lid. The pianist pulled tiny white silk papers out of his pocket and tucked them carefully inside the piano, one by one, under each felt hammer he had previously examined as a doctor would a patient. The owner of the house tried to conceal his discomfort upon seeing all those pieces of paper under the hammers, but finally gave into his impatience and awkwardly exclaimed:

"He's an eccentric," and politely asked the pianist's mother, "Why is he doing this?"

"It's a new system that 'dreams up' the piano tones. It sounds like a clavichord."

"Dreams up or drums up? One system can't be any newer than the next because no system is new. The clavichord is an old instrument. What advantage is there in using modern devices to attain antiquity? But most of all, I don't like them playing around with the inside of the piano. Enough moths have already snuck in."

Octavio Griber looked sternly at the owner of the house, lit a cigarette and murmured:

"I never play without silk paper." He continued arranging the papers while he mumbled to the owner of the house: "I've been told you are a great pianist. Won't you let us hear your repertoire?"

"Yes, but I don't play with my feet," the owner of the house answered dryly.

He was a very jealous type. It was his beard that gave him away: it became so prickly you couldn't even give him a kiss, no matter how slick a hair tonic he used.

"These gatherings always take ten years off my life," he whispered in my ear.

For the first time I noticed he was cross-eyed. Before, I had always stared at his beard, but now this explained the wisdom behind his gaze.

In the garden the rain kept coming down harder. The drumming of the rain could be heard against the windows as they distributed the hand-scrawled programs; it sounded as if stones, rather than raindrops, were falling. Several works from Liszt appeared: *Au bord d'une source, St. Francois de Paule marchant sur les flots, Les jeux d'eau a la Ville d'Este*. The names of Debussy, Ravel, Chopin, and Respighi were written in green ink. The leaflets flew from hand to hand.

Cuando cesaron de volar los papeles de los programas, que sirvieron de abanico, el pianista se sentó en el taburete, colocó el cigarrillo encendido sobre el borde del piano y giró varias vueltas buscando la altura que convenía a su estatura. Miró sus pies, los pedales, sus pies, los pedales y luego comenzó a tocar escalas con el dedo gordo del pie. Las notas se sucedían con un staccato originalísimo. Los invitados no sabían si tenían que admirar o reír.

—Qué gracia—dijo alguien—. Yo también puedo hacer lo mismo.

—Pero ¿por qué no toca como la gente con todos los dedos?—preguntó una voz femenina como un alfiler.

—Porque sería muy difícil. Tendría que ser equilibrista para tocar con los cinco dedos del pie.

—Pero yo digo con las manos, como Dios manda. ¿Por qué hay que tocar con los pies?

—Hay personas que pintan con los pies o con la boca. ¿Qué tiene de malo?

—Pero son inválidos.

—Es su manera de tocar; toca a veces con el dedo gordo del pie. Fiel a la primera composición que interpretó, vuelve a repetirla siempre. El comienzo de su carrera fue brillante. Nunca siguió los consejos de ningún maestro—dijo la señora de Griber, lentamente extasiada—. Cuando mi hijo empezó a estudiar, me decía, mirándose el pie: «¿Por qué tantos dedos?». Inútil fue que la profesora le diera caramelos de naranja, de limón o de frambuesa, hasta de chocolate, que le provocaban urticaria. Rehusaba tocar el piano con todos los dedos. Tocaba exclusivamente con el dedo gordo. Después de aquella primera experiencia recurrió a los papelitos de seda y luego a la desafinación del piano para conseguir, según lo proclamaba, sonidos mas naturales. Un afinador le reveló todos los secretos del instrumento. Solía exclamar: «Voy a desafinarlo en mi bemol y en re menor». Nadie sabía lo que esto quería decir. Tal vez él mismo no lo sabía, pero los sonidos que obtenía del mismo eran tan extraordinarios que del piso de abajo de mi casa vinieron un día a averiguar qué disco de Wanda Landowska habíamos puesto en el fonógrafo, porque nunca habían oído algo tan maravilloso. Aquí no se atreve, pero en otras casas desafina los pianos. No hay que contrariar a los genios—decía la señora de Griber.

When the programs, now being used as fans, ceased to fly, the pianist sat down on the stool, positioned his lit cigarette precariously on the edge of the piano, and spun around several times, seeking the appropriate chair height. He looked at his feet, the pedals, his feet, the pedals, and then began to play scales with his big toe. The notes that followed were an extravagant *staccato* and the guests didn't know whether to admire or to laugh at his performance.

"What a feat!" someone said, adding, "which anybody can perform."

"But why doesn't he play with all his toes like everyone else?" asked a woman with a piercing voice.

"Because it would be too difficult. He would have to be as dexterous as a tightrope walker to play with all five toes."

"I say he should use his hands, as God intended. I mean, why does he have to use his feet?"

"There are people who paint with their feet, or with their mouths. What's wrong with that?"

"But those people are invalids."

"It's his way of playing. Sometimes he plays with his big toe only. The beginning of his career was brilliant; forever faithful to the first composition he performed, he always repeated this method. He never followed the advice of any teacher," Mrs. Griber said, mildly enthused.

"When my son began to study he would tell me, looking at his foot: Why so many toes?' It was useless for the teacher to give him lemon, orange, or raspberry suckers, or even chocolate, which made him break out in hives. He refused to play the piano with all his toes. He played only with his big toe.

"After the first experience he reverted to the silk papers and later to tuning the piano off-key in order to obtain, as he proclaimed, more natural sounds. A tuning key revealed all the secrets to him. He would always exclaim, 'I'm going to untune my E-flat and D minor. Nobody knew what this meant. Maybe even he didn't know, but the sounds he produced were so extraordinary that one day the neighbors came up from the apartment downstairs to find out what record of Wanda Landowska we had put on the phonograph because they had never heard anything so marvelous. Here he doesn't dare, but in other homes he untunes the pianos. You never question a genius," Mrs. Griber said.

Octavio Griber, que ya estaba tocando el piano con todos los dedos de la mano, de improviso giró en el taburete y miró a la concurrencia, como diciendo: ¿Quién se atreve a hablar, cuando sólo están aquí para escuchar? No dijo nada, pero moviendo la cabeza impuso el silencio, para que pudieran oír su interpretación de la Balada en si menor, de Brahms.

—Esta música no tiene nada que ver con el agua—dijo alguien que comprendía el sentido acuático del concierto hasta en los más mínimos detalles.

—Con los relámpagos—contestó imperiosamente Octavio.

Jardín bajo la lluvia, La catedral sumergida, Pez de oro, de Debussy, y Juegos de agua, de Ravel, adquirían una sonoridad perfecta a pesar de la sordina impuesta por el papel de seda. Cuando tocó la canción A orillas del agua, de Fauré, otra de sus innumerables originalidades, tarareó la melodía con tanta suavidad que desencadenó un aplauso estruendoso: el Preludio de la gota de agua, de Chopin, alcanzó un éxito mayor. Indudablemente, el contacto de los pies desnudos del virtuoso en los pedales influía sobre la interpretación de cada obra. Había que atenerse a la crítica que salió el día anterior en el diario; había que admitirlo como el público lo admiró en el último concierto del teatro Colón.

—Pero todas las piezas que toca son de músicos franceses.— protestó una señora.

—Chopin no es francés, Liszt tampoco, Respigni tampoco.

—Van Gogh fue el primer pintor en pintar la lluvia. ¿No es extraño?

—¿Qué tiene que ver la pintura con la música?

—Van Gogh asociaba la música con la pintura. Y el primer músico en cantar la lluvia fue Debussy.

—No es exacto.

—¿Qué es lo que no es exacto?

—Que Van Gogh asociara la música con la pintura. Si lo hizo fue en uno de sus desvaríos, cuando mandó de regalo una de sus orejas envuelta. Además no era francés. Handel, Grieg, Schubert, hasta Wagner en El oro del Rin, se inspiraron en el agua.

—Pero se trata de música de orquesta y no de piano. ¡El oro del Rin, a quién se le ocurre!

Octavio Griber, who was already playing the piano with all of his fingers, suddenly spun around on the stool and glared at the assembly, as if to say, "Who dares to speak when you are all here to listen?" He didn't say a word, but by turning his head he imposed total silence so that they would listen to his performance of the *Ballad in B Minor* by Brahms.

"This music doesn't have anything to do with water," said someone who obviously understood the aquatic meaning of the concert down to the last detail.

"It goes with the lightning bolts," Octavio pompously answered. *Jardin sous la pluie, La cathedrale engloutie* and *Poissons d'or* by Debussy, and *Jeux d'eau* by Ravel acquired a perfect resonance despite the silk paper's muting effect. When he played the song *Au bord de l'eau* by Fauré, another of his innumerable innovations, he hummed the melody so smoothly that it released a thunderous applause, and *The Raindrop Prelude* by Chopin was met with resounding success. Undoubtedly, the master's naked foot on the pedals had an impact on the performance of each piece.

He had to live up to the rave reviews that had appeared in the previous day's newspaper, and confessed that the audience had admired his last concert at the Colon Theater.

"But all the pieces he plays are by French musicians," a woman protested.

"Chopin isn't French, and neither are Liszt or Respighi."

"Van Gogh was the first painter to paint the rain. Isn't that strange?"

"What does painting have to do with music?"

"Van Gogh associated music with painting. And the first musician to sing to the rain was Debussy."

"Not exactly."

"What do you mean, not exactly?"

"That Van Gogh associated music with painting. If he did, it was in one of his fits of delirium as when he wrapped up one of his ears and mailed it off as a present. Besides, he wasn't French. Handel, Grieg, Schubert, even Wagner in *Das Reingold*, were others who were inspired by water."

"But it's performed by an orchestra, not a piano. *Das Reingold*, who would think!"

—¿Cuál pieza era la de Chopin?—interrogó un joven.

—¿No leíste el programa?

—Uno de los Estudios, el de La gota de agua.

—¿Quién tiene gota?—preguntó una señora que estaba en la otra punta de la sala.

—Es una pieza de música—le contestaron.

—Es el colmo de la aberración: inspirarse en una enfermedad.

Resonaba el piano con un misterio nuevo. Nadie lo escuchaba, salvo una invitada, que exclamó:

—¡Hay músicas que matan!—sollozaba con la cara entre las manos—. Nunca pude oír Jardín bajo la lluvia sin llorar.

A través de los vidrios de las ventanas parecía que los árboles del jardín crecían. De pronto el concertista se detuvo. Pidió que le abrieran las ventanas y dijo:

—Que me escuchen por lo menos los árboles o la lluvia.

Vio mil hermosos ojos con lágrimas, lágrimas más bien con ojos. Sonrió. Si hubiese podido guardar esas lágrimas en un frasquito, las hubiera guardado como una esencia de azahar, para su amargura. «Las lágrimas de la novia, mi próxima obra, llevará ese título», pensó. Pero le ofrecían una naranjada helada y una fuente con tarteletas de frutilla. Bebió la naranjada y comió las tarteletas con apremio. Entre cada bocado se chupó algún dedo como si fuera una golosina. Le ofrecieron en bandeja una servilleta de hilo bordada para que se limpiara. Miró la bandeja, tomó la servilletita y la metió en el bolsillo rápidamente. Giró de nuevo en el taburete y volvió a posar las manos sobre el teclado del piano, mirando el cielo raso, como lo había visto hacer a Paderewski, en un teatro de Rino Bandini. Una señora se le acercó, le tomó del mentón y le dijo:

—Qué amor de niño precoz: pensativo como sus tatarabuelos.

Cuando volvió a resonar el piano, algo le molestó. Inclinó la cabeza hasta tocar las teclas con la oreja. Se agachó para examinar los pedales. Una nota resaltaba más que las otras. Se incorporó, hurgó en el interior del piano, descubrió que uno de los martillos no tenía su papelito. Octavio Griber pidió que trajeran un papel de seda. Buscaron el papel por todos los rincones de la casa, con linternas, porque ya se hacía de noche y los altillos sin luz eran

"Which was the piece by Chopin?" a young boy inquired.

"Didn't you read the program?"

"One of the *Etudes*, the one about the raindrop."

"Who's got dropsy?" asked a woman from the other side of the room.

"It's a musical piece," they answered.

"That's the peak of insanity—to be inspired by a disease!"

The piano echoed with a new sense of mystery. Nobody listened except one guest who exclaimed:

"There are some pieces that just kill me!" she sobbed with her head between her hands, "I've never been able to hear *Jardin sous la pluie* without crying."

Through the windowpanes it seemed as if the trees in the garden were growing. Suddenly the pianist paused, asked them to open the windows and said:

"At least let the rain and the trees listen to me."

He saw a thousand beautiful eyes filled with tears, or rather, tears with eyes. He smiled. If he had been able to save those tears in a tiny bottle, he would have saved them with lemon essence because they were so bitter. "My next work will be titled *The Bride's Tears*," he thought to himself. But they offered him a cold orangeade and a platter filled with strawberry tarts. He drank the orangeade and ate the tarts with constraint. Between bites he licked each finger as if it were a delicacy. On a silver platter they offered him an embroidered silk napkin so he could wipe his hands and mouth. He looked at the platter, took the delicate napkin and hastily stuffed it into his pocket. He spun around again on his stool and once more posed his hands above the keyboard, watching the satin sky, as he had seen Paderewski do in a play by Rino Bandini. A woman approached him, took him by the chin and said:

"What a dear precocious boy, pensive like his great grand-parents."

When the piano sounded once again, something bothered him. He lowered his head to the point of touching his ear to the keys, and squatted to examine the pedals. One note stood out over the others. He sat up, poked around inside the piano, and discovered that one of the hammers did not have its tiny paper. Octavio Griber asked them to bring a silk paper. They searched for the paper in all the nooks and crannies of the house, with lanterns, because night

inaccesibles. Finalmente encontraron unas manzanas envueltas en papel verde, que trajeron a la sala en una bandeja. ¿Serviría este papel, aunque no fuera del más fino?

Octavio Griber colocó las tiras de papel en el sitio donde faltaban, cuidadosamente hizo repicar las notas y apreció la superioridad del papel de envolver manzanas.

Juegos de agua resonó nuevamente en el piano, como nunca había resonado, con el nuevo aditamento de papel verde. A veces un trueno precedido de un relámpago conmovía los caireles de la araña, pero no a las personas que oían, cuando no hablaban, resonar aquel piano. Los aplausos, tímidos al principio, llenaron después la sala de entusiasmo. Octavo, temblando de ambición, pidió a dos jóvenes que estaban a su lado que abriesen de nuevo el piano. Indicó los pormenores de la operación. De su bolsillo sacó lo que nos pareció una pequeña pinza, que era un diapasón, y se acercó a los jóvenes que abrían enérgicamente las entrañas del piano.

—Es cosa de un momento—dijo Octavio al piano, como si se tratara de una operación quirúrgica.

Alguien protestó, pero la vergüenza se apoderó del que protestaba. ¿Cómo prohibir a un genio las manifestaciones de su originalidad? Para distraerlo, alguien llevó al dueño de casa al antecomedor a buscar unos cubiertos que faltaban. Octavio ajustó o aflojó algunas cuerdas del piano. Consiguió la total desafinación del instrumento, con la máxima rapidez.

No se reconocía ni Carnaval, de Schumann, ni Jardin bajo la lluvia, de Debussy, ni Juegos de agua, de Ravel. Todo se había transformado en algo diferente, que él solo interpretaba.

La tormenta no amainaba. La lluvia golpeteaba sobre los vidrios.

Después de servir el chocolate a la española y las masitas de distintas formas y colores, después de rogar al dueño de casa que tocara su repertorio, Octavio Griber, suspirando, se quitó la chaqueta de terciopelo en el mismo rincón en donde se la había puesto, la guardó en el portafolio, se vistió, se alisó el pelo, se puso las medias y los zapatos. Cuando me miró para despedirse le presenté mi álbum para que firmara un autógrafo.

¿Cómo te llamas?—preguntó.

was falling and without light the attic was inaccessible. They finally found some apples wrapped in green paper which they brought to the room on a platter. Would this paper do even though it wasn't the finest?

Octavio Griber placed the strips of paper in the spot where they were missing, carefully made the notes chime, and acknowledged the superiority of the apple wrapping paper.

With the new addition of the green paper, *Jeux d'eau* echoed in the piano as it had never before. Once in a while a roll of thunder preceded by lightning shook the crystals of the chandelier, but not the people who listened—when they weren't talking—to the piano play. The applause, timid at first, gradually filled the room with enthusiasm. Trembling with excitement, Octavio asked two boys near him to open the piano again. He orchestrated the minor details of the operation. From his pocket he removed what seemed to us to be a pair of tweezers but what was really a tuning fork, and he approached the youths who were energetically exposing the bowels of the piano.

"It will take just a minute," Octavio told the piano, as if this were a surgical operation.

Someone protested, but this person's embarrassment got the best of him. Who could prevent a genius from demonstrating his originality? In order to distract the owner of the house, someone took him into the dining room to search for some serving trays. Octavio tightened or loosened some of the piano chords and with great speed obtained complete discord with the instrument. Schumann's *Carnival*, Debussy's *Jardin sous la pluie*, and Ravel's *Jeux d'eau* were unrecognizable. Every piece had been transformed into something different that only he could perform.

The storm didn't let up and the rain drummed against the window panes.

After the thick hot chocolate and assorted cookies had been served, and after they had begged the owner of the house to play his repertoire, Octavio Griber sighed as he took off his velvet jacket in the same corner where he had put it on, stored it in his briefcase, got dressed, smoothed his hair, and put on his shoes and socks. When he looked at me to say good-bye, I offered him my album so that he would autograph it.

"What's your name?" he asked.

—Anabela—respondí.

Firmó «Para Anabela, su admirador, Octavio».

Ya estaba esperando el coche en la puerta.

El dueño de casa corrió a buscar algo y volvió con un sobre y un pianito de juguete, con un pianista.

—Para Octavito—dijo amargamente, como si estuviese repitiendo una lección aprendida.

—No—susurró la señora de Griber, deteniéndolo—. Puede ofenderlo. No le gustan los diminutivos.

—Los japoneses regalan juguetes a los grandes. Además no tiene edad de ofenderse—dijo el dueño de casa, acariciándose la barba, áspera como un felpudo.

—Algunos nacemos ofendidos—exclamó la señora de Griber.

—Pero ¿qué edad tiene su hijo, señora?

—Es un secreto. Se quita la edad. La poquita edad que tiene. Nunca quiso mirarse en un espejo, en la ilusión quizá de conservarse siempre niño. Me dijo una vez a los cinco años, cuando insistí para que se mirara: «La música no se ve en el espejo» Le parece avejentado?

—De ninguna manera. Toca el piano como un niño de cinco años.

El dueño de casa entregó el sobre a la señora de Griber, que subía al coche, y el pianito a Octavio, que se demoraba en la puerta, bajo la lluvia. Octavio examinó el juguete, le dio cuerda, lo dejó en el suelo. El pianista de lata se puso en movimiento y la cajita de música entonó el principio de un vals. Octavio recogió el juguete, quería y no quería oír esa música, quería y no quería mirar al pianista de lata. Luego, con ímpetu, arrojó el juguete y subió al coche. Cuando el coche doblaba en la curva del camino, Octavio se asomó detrás de la cortinita negra de hule para mirar; la lluvia, los árboles escuchaban el vals de Brahms interpretado por el pianista de juguete.

"Anabela," I answered.

He signed it "For Anabela, from your admirer, Octavio."

The coach was already waiting at the door.

The owner of the house ran to look for something and returned with an envelope and a toy piano with a pianist.

"For little Octavio," he said wryly, as if he were repeating a memorized lecture.

"No," whispered Griber's mother, holding him back. "It may offend him. He doesn't like diminutives."

"The Japanese give toys to adults. Besides, he's not old enough to be offended," the owner of the house said, caressing his beard that was as rough as a doormat.

"Some of us are born offended," exclaimed Griber's mother.

"But how old is your son, Mrs. Griber?"

"It's a secret. He rejects his age, the little age he has. He never wanted to look at himself in the mirror, hoping always to remain a child. Once, when he was five years old, and I insisted that he look at himself in the mirror, he told me, 'Music can't be seen in a mirror.' Don't you think he was wise beyond his years?"

"Absolutely not. He plays the piano like a five-year-old."

The owner of the house handed the envelope to Griber's mother who was entering the coach, and the little piano to Octavio, who hesitated at the door in the rain. Octavio examined the toy, pulled the cord, and set it on the ground. The tin pianist started moving and the little music box played the tune of the beginning of a waltz. Octavio gathered up the toy. He wanted but didn't want to watch the tin pianist. Then, violently, he hurled the toy away and climbed into the coach. As the coach wound its way around a curve, Octavio poked his head out from behind the black curtain to see out: the rain and the trees were listening to the Brahms Waltz played by the toy pianist.

COTO DE CAZA

GAME OF SHADOWS

Donald A. Yates, translator of Rubén Loza Aguerreberre

Donald A. Yates taught at the University of Michigan and now lives in California. He has translated for Jorge Luis Borges, Manuel Peyrou, Julio Cortázar, and Marco Denevi, among many other Latin American authors, and is the editor of *Latin Blood*. He is a frequent contributor to *Ellery Queen's Mystery Magazine* and a member of the Mystery Writers of America.

One reading, according to Yates, is enough to pronounce a story fit or unfit for the English language, and by that standard the works of Jorge Luis Borges have consistently proved worth Yates's while. Long an aficionado and writer of detective stories, Yates discovered translation when he stumbled upon a wealth of "original and marketable crime stories" in Spanish—among these the intriguing tales of Borges. Yates enjoyed startling successes at translating and finding places for the stories in English-language mystery digests, and, he recalls, "After that, there was no stopping me." He became a prolific translator of Borges when the author gave Yates a translator's "carte blanche" in 1955, to produce a collection that eventually turned into the manuscript of the extraordinarily successful *Labyrinths*, published in 1962. Without hesitation Yates cites his work on Borges as the most thrilling experience of his career: "To have discovered the experience of reading Borges in 1954, to have been the first to see that he needed to be done into English," he calls his source of greatest satisfaction as a translator.

Yates's first translation of Uruguayan author Rubén Loza Aguerreberre's work was the story "The Man Who Stole from Borges," published in 1987 in *Ellery Queen's Mystery Magazine*. Born in 1945, Aguerreberre spent more than thirty years as a journalist writing for Montevideo's newspapers, and during this period brought out his highly praised volumes of short stories: *La espera, La casa al atardecer, El hombre que robó a Borges,* and *Pasado en limpio.*

Rubén Loza Aguerreberre
COTO DE CAZA

Para Carlos Meneses

"Lo que cuenta es lo que no se ve"
— Germán Yanke

I

Yo maté a un hombre.

Si hablo de una serie de episodios de los que fui protagonista, en forma involuntaria, durante cuatro días, es porque siento algo parecido al remordimiento. En la desventura nos queda el consuelo de las palabras, como han observado escritores más sutiles que yo.

Los hechos ocurrieron hace tres meses. Una fotografía y pocos ahorros de la memoria me ayudarán, espero, a no ser infiel a esta historia que, ahora, se cierra en círculos a mi alrededor.

II

En el pasado mes de noviembre me tocó hablar en un congreso de escritores, en París. Fui el último expositor de esa tarde; advertí que la platea estaba bastante raleada, razón por la cual apresuré mis palabras.

Al terminar me saludaron algunos fieles amigos. Entre ellos, se abrió paso una mujer muy joven, linda, de pelo corto y rubio. No recuerdo el fulgor de la mirada, sino que era ojerosa. La noté un poco tímida; hablaba con palabras atropelladas.

Ella quería conocerme porque había leído (con entusiasmo, dijo) una novela mía, traducida hace poco. Me obsequió uno de sus

Rubén Loza Aguerreberre
GAME OF SHADOWS

Translated by Donald A. Yates

For Carlos Meneses

"What counts is what you don't see."
— Germán Yanke

I

I killed a man.

If I speak now of that period of four days—in which I was a prominent, if involuntary participant—it is because I am feeling something akin to remorse. As writers more subtle than I have observed, in the midst of unhappiness we have the consolation of words.

It all happened three months ago. A photograph and a collection of memories will, I hope, help me remain faithful to the sense of this experience that seems now to have become oppressive for me.

II

Last November I was scheduled to speak to a writers' conference in Paris. I was the last speaker on that afternoon's program, and I noted that the audience had noticeably thinned out, which encouraged me to hasten my presentation.

After I finished, a group of loyal friends came up to congratulate me. Among them I observed an attractive young woman with short, blond hair who had also come forward. It was not the intensity of her gaze that attracted my attention, but rather the fact that there were circles under her eyes. I sensed that she was shy; she spoke haltingly and with effort.

She wanted to meet me because she had read (with pleasure, she said) a novel of mine that had recently been translated. She

libros de poemas, que tengo por ahí; demuestran talento, sensibilidad y una escritura acaso demasiado premeditada.

Al revés que los avaros, dejo entrar a mi casa a quien quiera, así que esa tardecita dimos un largo paseo por las calles de París, que estaban humedecidas y reflejaban las luces de colores de los edificios, quebrándose en los adoquines.

Llegamos hasta el Centro Pompidou. Largo rato miramos una exposición sobre "Apollinaire journaliste"; abundaban manuscritos, revistas y fotografías. Como ella, más tranquila, hablaba con entusiasmo y erudición, me dio vergüenza decirle que me estaba aburriendo. Finalmente, cuando salimos de allí, las sombras y la llovizna nos envolvieron.

En medio del bullicio, unos músicos muy bien ataviados, bajo un refugio de paraguas que sostenían manos de chicas jóvenes, tocaban la Pequeña Serenata Nocturna. Mi compañera de paseo se abrió camino hacia ellos y se quedó escuchándolos. Unas lágrimas, que vanamente procuraba disimular, le humedecían las mejillas. Se envolvió el rostro en su larga bufanda y les dejó una generosa propina; se echó a andar en silencio, ensimismada, como buscando recomponer el ánimo.

Una vendedora de castañas, que orinaba, agachada, en plena calle, nos guiñó un ojo; la curiosa situación le devolvió la sonrisa al rostro.

Esa primera noche cenamos en un restaurante griego de Montparnasse. Me acuerdo que estaba adornado con unas redes colgadas a las paredes como enormes telarañas; entre ellas había remos, boyas, restos de naufragios.

Bebimos un vino Bocussa, áspero y negro, en la sobremesa, y conversamos largamente.

Me preguntó que hacía en "las Sudamérica" (así dijo). Le expliqué que administraba un campo de mi familia, y aproveché a decirle que la Argentina, como el Uruguay y una parte de Chile, no se parecía al resto del continente. Aquí me interrumpió para decirme que lo sabía, pues había leído a Hudson, cosa que me llamó la atención.

Con sorpresa, casi con ingenuidad, me preguntó si andaba a caballo. Le respondí que sí, que era un diestro jinete. "Antes, cuando era muchacho, hasta domé algunos potros", agregué.

gave me a copy of a book of her poetry, which I have. Her verses showed talent, sensitivity and perhaps a bit too deliberate execution.

Having an open mind, I allow most persons easy access to me, and so it was effortlessly arranged for us to take a stroll through the city. That afternoon, glistening with the rain, the streets reflected the facades of the bordering rows of buildings, broken up into fragments by the wet paving stones.

We stopped at the Centre Pompidou, where we spent a long time viewing an exhibition entitled "Apollinaire, Journalist". There were dozens of manuscripts, magazine issues, and photographs. Because, now more relaxed, she so candidly expressed her enthusiasm for the display, I couldn't bring myself to tell her that I found it all boring. When finally we left, darkness and mist enveloped us.

Along the boulevard we came across several extravagantly attired street musicians who, sheltered under umbrellas held by young girls, were playing *Eine Kleine Nachtmusik*. My walking companion moved through the crowd and stood listening to them. Tears that she vainly tried to conceal ran down her cheeks. She wrapped her long scarf around her face and gave them a generous offering. Walking on in silence, withdrawn into herself, she seemed to be trying to regain her composure.

A woman chestnut vendor, who was squatting in the street relieving herself, winked an eye at us. The amusing situation brought a smile back to my friend's face.

That first evening we dined at a Greek restaurant in Montparnasse. I recall that it was decorated with huge fishing nets that hung from the walls like enormous spiderwebs. Scattered about were also oars, buoys and assorted flotsam. After dinner we drank a dark and coarse Bocussa wine and talked at great length.

She asked me what I did in "the South Americas," as she called them. I explained that I oversaw a family ranch, and took the opportunity to point out that Argentina, Uruguay and a good part of Chile were different from the rest of the continent. She interrupted me to say that this she already knew, since she had read W. H. Hudson (which somewhat surprised me.)

Ingenuously, she asked if as a ranch foreman I rode horseback. I said that I did, that in fact I was an accomplished rider. "Once," I added, "when I was much younger, I even tamed horses."

—Cuándo leés?

—Después de la cena. Como en el campo me acuesto temprano, las noches se me hacen muy largas. Tengo una buena biblioteca, porque si un libro me aburre antes de las cien páginas no lo leo más.

Se escandalizó. No entendía muy bien como llevaba una vida con oficios tan dispares, pero, sobre todo, cómo dejaba un libro sin haber llegado hasta el final. Con algunos ejemplos, que no importan ahora, procuré explicarle qué lecturas me aburrían y cuáles no, y concluí señalando que la literatura, aunque hable de la muerte, es el habitáculo de la vida.

Apoyó ambos codos sobre la mesa y me miró decididamente a los ojos para contradecirme. Apeló a demasiados especialistas; algunos los conocía y a otros los había oído nombrar vagamente, como disecadores de libros ajenos. Naturalmente, no me convenció y, al final, presentí que ella misma dudaba un poco.

III

He omitido su nombre. Se llamaba (se llama) Annie y su apellido es Maalhouf. Bien: a la mañana siguiente, Annie pasó por el hotel donde yo me hospedaba. Por las dudas le dije que no pensaba ir al coloquio y que mi intención era pasear un rato y comprar unos regalos para mi familia.

De inmediato se ofreció a llevarme en su pequeño automóvil. Cuando me abrió la portezuela, vi en el asiento trasero un par de raquetas y una gran cantidad de pelotas de tenis, desparramadas por el piso. Le comenté que una de mis frustraciones era no haber ganado el "Roland Garrós", lo que la hizo sonreír.

—Antes jugaba bien—insistí—, pero después el destino me llevó para otro lado. Todo se pierde, mañana o pasado, así que no me preocupo, ni me quejo.

Con su ayuda elegí algunas cosas para mi esposa y mis hijos. Almorzamos liviano y, como la lluvia arreciaba, entramos en un cine. Eligió una película venezolana, porque le gustaba el color local, de la que no recuerdo nada, salvo un indiecito medio desnudo que, creo, andaba buscando a su madre.

"When did you read?"

"After dinner. In the country bedtime is early, so the nights can be long. I have a good library because if I find a book uninteresting after a hundred pages, I get rid of it."

She seemed perturbed. She didn't understand very well how I had managed a life with such disparate interests. She was especially puzzled over how I could abandon a book before getting to the ending. Giving a few examples, which I need not repeat here, I tried to show her what types of reading I did and didn't like, and ended up suggesting that even though it might tackle death, literature was the vital dwelling place of life.

With her elbows on the table and her chin in her hands, she looked me in the eye and shook her head in disagreement. She alluded to the opinions of a number of literary specialists, some of them known to me and others names I had only a vague knowledge of as arid dissectors of other people's books. Naturally, she failed to change my opinions and in the end, I sensed that she was beginning to have some doubts about her own beliefs.

III

I have failed to mention her name. It was (it is) Annie, Annie Maalhouf. The next morning she stopped by my hotel. So as to leave things open, I told her that I didn't plan to attend that day's sessions because I wanted to see more of the city and buy some gifts for my family. She immediately offered to chauffeur me around in her small car. When she opened the car door for me I saw a couple of tennis racquets on the back seat and tennis balls scattered on the floor. I told her that one of my unfulfilled dreams was to win the French Open. This brought forth an amused grin.

"No, really," I said. "I used to play very well, but fate moved me in another direction. We lose everything anyway, sooner or later, so it doesn't bother me and I don't complain."

With her help I picked out a few things for my wife and children. We had a light lunch and, since it was raining harder, we decided to see a movie. She picked a Venezuelan film because she said she liked the jungle setting. I don't recall a thing about the movie except that there was a half-naked Indian in it who, I seem to recall, was searching for his mother.

En la oscuridad de la sala me tomó de la mano; la sorpresa me impidió hacer ademán alguno. Poco después giró el rostro y me besó. Recapacité: "Esto se está poniendo serio. Mejor buscarle una 'solución platónica', como dice mi amigo Landaburu".

Yo soy un hombre hecho y derecho, y vagamente presentía que Annie me tenía una cierta admiración, un cierto respeto. Así que hice como si nada hubiera pasado y, al salir, cuando me tomó del brazo volví a decirme que tenía que ser precavido.

IV

Esta fotografía donde Annie y yo estamos ante la fachada multicolor de la librería "Shakespeare and Company", en la vereda, mirando entre las mesas de libros, corresponde al tercer día. Ella trajo consigo una máquina fotográfica, de revelado instantáneo, y le pidió a alguien que pasaba por allí que nos tomara unas fotos. Me regaló ésta y se guardó otras más o menos parecidas.

Me acuerdo que compré una biografía de Kipling y, para ella, "Aspectos del Amor", el librito de David Garnett, pues lo desconocía. "Es una novela divertida—le dije—, con mujeres que sólo existen en la imaginación de los hombres". Ella se entusiasmó tanto que me pidió una dedicatoria; en la primera página le escribí unas palabras galantes.

Luego la invité a pasar por la casa donde había vivido Hemingway, en París en el 74 de la rue Cardinal Lemoine, por caminar un rato bajo el sol. No soy un gran admirador de el; sólo me gusta su estilo para contar.

Ella no la conocía. Llegamos. Una señora baja y gorda, vestida de negro, estaba barriendo la vereda. Annie le pidió que nos sacara una fotografía en la puerta del edificio. Cuando la mujer estaba por presionar el disparador, Annie se me colgó del cuello y me besó. Rápidamente se hizo de la máquina, quitó la foto y la guardó en el bolsillo.

En un pequeño local de la place Contrescarpe bebimos unas copas de vino blanco. Ella me preguntaba sobre mis libros, de lo que no me gusta mucho hablar. Sé que le dije que la realidad es fantástica en cualquier momento, y que muchas historias de mis novelas me las han contado algunas amigas mías.

In the darkness of the theater she took my hand. I was so surprised that I didn't even react. Then, after a bit, she turned her head and kissed me. My first thought was: "This is getting serious. Best to keep things platonic," as my friend Landaburu puts it.

I am a straightforward and reasonable person, and I had begun to sense that Annie had developed a certain respect and admiration for me. I thought it best to try to act as if nothing had happened between us. When she took my arm as we left the theater, I renewed my resolve to be cautious.

IV

The photograph before me, in which Annie and I are seen going through the tables of sale books in front of the colorful facade of the Shakespeare and Company Bookstore, goes back to our third day. She had brought along a Polaroid camera and asked someone passing by to take a few photos of us. She gave me this one and kept the others herself.

I remember that I bought a biography of Kipling and for her a copy of David Garrett's *Aspects of Love,* which she hadn't heard about. 'It's an entertaining novel," I told her, "with women who exist only in the minds of men." She was so pleased with the gift that she asked me to dedicate the book to her. On the flyleaf I wrote a fanciful dedication.

Then, so we could enjoy a walk in the sunshine, I invited her to visit the house where Hemingway lived in Paris, at 74 rue Cardinal Lemoine. He is not a novelist I particularly admire, but I have always been impressed by his original style. Annie was pleased since she said she had not known about that residence. When we arrived there, a short, fat woman dressed in black was sweeping the sidewalk. Annie asked her to take our photo in the doorway. As the woman was about to snap the picture, Annie threw her arms around my neck and gave me a kiss. She then quickly took back the camera, removed the photo and put it in her purse.

At a small cafe in the Place Contrescarpe we had a few glasses of white wine. She questioned me about my books, which I really don't enjoy talking about. I recall saying to her that reality is unreal at any given moment and mentioning that many of the plots for my novels had been given to me by some of my women friends.

Cuando cambié de tema y hablé de mi regreso ella se puso un poco triste. Salió del paso, tras beber un sorbo, diciéndome que los visitantes del lugar donde estábamos, cosa que comprobé con una rápida ojeada, escribían sus nombres en las paredes,. Me pidió que lo hiciera. Me pasó un lápiz y desganado, sin levantarme de la silla, escribí: "Annie y Adolfo". Pensé: "Sólo me falta dibujar un corazoncito".

Cuando dijo que vendría seguido a mirarlos me dije: "Todo esto es muy literario; qué le vamos a hacer".

V

En la noche del cuarto día yo partía hacia Madrid, donde pensaba visitar algunos amigos, antes de regresar a Buenos Aires. Temprano hice las valijas, desayuné y salí a la calle. Me gusta deambular sin rumbo, recorrer algunos lugares ya visitados, mirar a la gente, leer los diarios en esos cafés con terrazas tranquilas.

Annie no había dado señales de vida y sentí una especie de alivio.

A las siete de la tarde me llamó a la habitación y calmosamente exclamó: "Te estoy esperando para llevarte al aeropuerto".

Tomamos un café mientras me preparaban la cuenta y bajaban las valijas. Me dejé estar. Ella pasaba revista a los buenos momentos y me miraba como si buscara algún indicio revelador. Sólo dije que lo había pasado muy bien y sintió esas palabras como una caricia.

De pronto, nerviosa, buscó en su cartera; me entregó un paquete y se quedó expectante. Lo abrí: era un cenicero de color gris, un poco estrafalario. Al agradecerlo noté una indisimulada ansiedad por decirme algo. Me dije: "Lo mejor es que me diga todo; tal vez quiera que le tenga lástima". La estimulé, con dos o tres preguntas; bastó para que largara el rollo. Me contó que el cenicero lo había hecho un escultor de nombre Alban, que era un muchacho muy erudito y un poco bohemio, por el que ella sentía cariño; agregó

When I changed the subject and spoke about my trip home, she turned sad. She took a sip of wine and avoided the topic by pointing out that the people who visited the cafe we were in were allowed to write their names on the walls. I looked around and saw that this did appear to be the case. She handed me a pencil and suggested that we go along with the custom. Reluctantly, without moving from my chair, I wrote "Annie and Adolfo." I thought to myself that all that was missing was a heart drawn around the names. When she said that she would come often to look at the inscription, I considered that the whole business was straight out of a cheap romance novel, but I didn't see what could be done about it.

V

On the night of the fourth day I was to leave for Madrid, where I planned to visit a few friends before returning to Buenos Aires. I got up early and packed my bags, had breakfast and went out. I like to stroll about aimlessly, visiting familiar places, observing the people who pass by, and then go to read the newspaper in a quiet sidewalk cafe. Annie had not been in touch with me, and for that I felt a sense of relief.

At seven o'clock in the evening she called me in my room and calmly declared: "I'm downstairs in the lobby, waiting to take you to the airport."

We ordered coffee while they got the bill ready and brought down my bags. I was quiet. She went on at length, reviewing the good times we had had together and watching me closely, as if to pick up some encouraging signal. I simply said that I had enjoyed myself, but these words seemed to please her enormously.

At this point, nervously, she drew something out of her purse. It was a small package, which she handed to me expectantly. I opened it and found a gray ashtray of somewhat unusual design. When I thanked her for it, I noted in her an apparent urgency to say something. It seemed to me that the best thing would probably be for her to get it off her chest. Most likely she wanted me to feel sorry for her. So I encouraged her with a few questions and that was enough to start her talking.

She told me that the ashtray had been made by a sculptor named Alban, that he was a very sensitive fellow with a Bohemian streak,

que de chico había perdido una pierna en un accidente de auto. Supe, también, que la madre de Annie, una señora de fortuna, se negaba a tratarlo y a que ella lo frecuentara.

Después hicimos el viaje a marcha nerviosa, silenciosos, con el auto inundado de Mozart.

Llegué sobre la hora y cuando anunciaron el vuelo por los altoparlantes empecé unas palabras de despedida que ella cortó poniéndome un dedo en los labios.

Me preguntó si podía escribirme. Anotó la dirección en mi libro que traía consigo y se lo firmé. Hubo un instante de expectativa que me pareció muy largo cuando se lo devolví y le dije adiós.
Annie me abrazó con fuerza. Sin quererlo, una de mis manos rozó su pecho y, estremecida, dijo "¡No, por favor!". Hice un gesto, disculpándome, pero de inmediato tomó mi mano derecha y bruscamente la llevó hacia sus senos. Me acordé de la frase: "La mujer guía y el hombre sigue"; y me alegré de que todo llegaba, ya que había llegado algo, bastante tarde.

Ella ahogó unos sollozos y me marché con esa imagen de Annie, que me hizo pensar en la pura desesperanza.

VI

Con el paso de los días, ya de regreso, me fui olvidando de los sucesos narrados, hasta que una carta, recibida la semana pasada, me llevó a unirlos en este inventario.

Yo estaba en el campo (no sé si dije que mi familia, salvo en las temporadas de verano, vive en Buenos Aires) cuando, por los ladridos de los perros, me di cuenta de que llegaba mi hermano en su auto. Me trajo unos libros que le había pedido a mi esposa por teléfono y nutrida correspondencia.

Encontré una carta de París y me senté a leerla junto a la chimenea; no sé por que un vago temor me empujó a buscar la soledad.

Annie escribía abundamente; no menores eran sus revelaciones. Alban, el escultor, estaba casado con ella cuando yo la conocí; llevaban ocho meses de matrimonio. Que su madre se había opuesto

and that she was fond of him. She added that as a child he had lost a leg in a car accident. I learned, too, that Annie's mother, a wealthy woman, disliked him and wanted her to have nothing to do with him. After she had said all this, we drove to the airport, speechless and uneasy, the car reverberating with the music of Mozart.

We arrived with no time to spare and they were already announcing the boarding of my flight. I began to mumble a few words of farewell, but Annie silenced me, placing her finger on my lips. She asked if she could write to me, then took down the address in my book, which she had brought along and which I now signed for her. There was a long moment of expectant silence when I handed the book back to her and said goodbye.

Annie put her arms around me and held me tightly. Unintentionally, one of my hands brushed her breast and, with a tremor she said: "No, please don't." Apologizing, I tried to disengage myself, but she now took hold of my right hand and moved it quickly to her breasts. I remember her saying: "Women guide and men follow." I felt relieved that this moment, which was probably inevitable, had arrived late in the game. She tried to hold back her sobs and I turned and left her that way—the image of inconsolable despair.

VI

As the days wore on after I returned home, I gradually let the events recounted here fade from my mind. Until, that is, a letter I received last week led me to gather them in this account.

I was at our country estate (I don't recall if I mentioned that the rest of my family, except for summer vacation months, lives in Buenos Aires) when the barking of the dogs announced the arrival of my brother's car. He had brought me a couple of books that I had asked my wife for by phone and a large pile of accumulated correspondence. I found a letter from Paris, and I sat down by the fireplace to read it, making sure—I don't know why—that I wouldn't be interrupted. It was a long letter from Annie, full of revelations. Alban, the sculptor, was her husband. They had been married for eight months when I met her. Her mother had indeed opposed the marriage. She was a woman who wanted for her

era verdad: ella quería para su hija uno de esos muchachos que todas las madres quieren y que casi nunca son escultores, pintores o poetas.

Me detuve varias veces en la tercera y última hoja. Allí decía que todas las noches, durante mi permanencia en París, ella le contaba a Alban, quien la aguardaba en la cama, los detalles de nuestra común relación. Y le hablaba, según sus propias palabras, del "encuentro de dos almas gemelas". En este punto me acordé de las fotos, del libro dedicado, de la mala película venezolana.

Un poco desorientado me representé al joven escultor, sostenido en sus muletas, mirando detrás de una ventana a Annie, cuando ella se marchaba en mi busca. Lo que no pude (ni puedo) es ponerle un rostro a ese muchacho. Esto me pareció patético.

Seguí leyendo.

El día de mi partida, Alban terminó una estatua que lo mostraba de cuerpo entero, desnudo, y que según dice Annie no era muy grande. La ubicó (supongo yo que trabajosamente) en un lugar visible de su estudio. Cuando ella retornó a su casa desde el aeropuerto, donde aguardó hasta que mi avión se perdió en el cielo nocturno, se enteró de que Alban se había lanzado al vacío por la ventana. Lo buscó en varios hospitales; él murió al segundo día de agonía.

La carta tenía un estilo candoroso y la lectura de este episodio me provocó una suerte de vahído.

Apenas tuve fuerzas para decirme: "Qué bien cumplí mi parte".

daughter the kind of young man who is almost never a sculptor, a painter, or a poet.

I suspended my reading several times on the third page. There she related that every night, while I was in Paris, she would recount to Alban, who waited up in bed for her, the details of our relationship. And she told him of—in her words—"the meeting of our attuned souls." At this point I remembered the photographs, the book with the dedication, the artless Venezuelan film.

Disturbed, I imagined the young sculptor, leaning on his crutches, watching from a window as Annie went off to see me. What I could not do—and still cannot—is give a face to that figure. That upset me.

I continued reading. On the day I left, Alban had finished a small nude sculpture of himself. He had situated it (with some difficulty, I imagined) in a prominent spot in his studio. When Annie returned home from the airport, where she had waited until the plane had disappeared into the evening sky, she had learned that Alban had jumped to the street from his studio window. She searched the hospitals for him. He died the next day.

Her letter was written in a tone of complete candor and her recounting of this tragedy left me weak and trembling. I scarcely had the strength to utter the words: "How well I played my role."

INCIDENTE EN LA CORDILLERA

INCIDENT IN THE CORDILLERA

James E. Maraniss, translator of Antonio Benítez-Rojo

James E. Maraniss translated Antonio Benítez-Rojo's *Sea of Lentils* and is the author of *On Calderón*. He studied at Harvard and Princeton, is married to photographer Gigi Kaeser, and has translated and adapted works by Sor Juana Inés de La Cruz and Angel Cuadra.

Maraniss claims not to stop reading and re-reading the text he is translating until the final draft has gone to press. "The real writing is the writing of the last draft," is one among many insights gleaned by him over the course of what he terms "a very small career," highlighted by work with authors who are friends. As a professor of Romance Languages at Amherst College, Maraniss wrote a libretto based on Pedro Calderón de la Barca'a *La vida es sueño* for the operatic composition of a colleague in the music department. This then encouraged a group of students to approach him for a translation of Calderón's *El gran teatro del mundo* for performance at the college's theater.

Maraniss claims to have made a commitment to become a translator after rendering several works by his colleague at Amherst, Antonio Benítez-Rojo, a Cuban novelist, editor and critic born in 1931. In the early seventies, before going to Amherst, Benítez-Rojo had been director of Cuba's publishing house Casa de las Américas, and during his tenure he edited books by Joaquim María Machado de Assis and Juan Rulfo. His most celebrated critical work, *The Repeating Island: The Caribbean and the Postmodern Perspective*, which Maraniss has also translated, has received wide critical attention. Maraniss claims that working with a colleague process permitted him to "know him more completely." He added during an interview: "I selected this story because I like it, had it at hand, was short enough for didactic use, and is the first piece that Benítez-Rojo has written after thirteen years of non-fictional theorizing."

Antonio Benítez-Rojo
INCIDENTE EN LA CORDILLERA

Para Julio, donde quiera que esté

El desfiladero es estrecho. Aquí y allá la vegetación crece pobre, rastrera, enmarañada. El camino que lo atraviesa es un camino colonial, uno de esos malos caminos, apenas apisonados, que serpenteaban por entre las cordilleras evitando torrentes y volcanes. Este en particular, está blanqueado por el ir y venir de mulas y borricos sobre el cascajo de piedra pómez, y corre de oeste a este a través de la vieja Guatemala. Ahora parece humear bajo el sol del mediodía, pues un súbito ventarrón se ha encajonado entre los paredones de granito que se alzan a sus lados, y levanta el polvo, lo arremolina y lo lanza hacia el lejano bosque, apenas una ceja verde en el reducido confín que se observa desde el paraje. La recua de mulas, con sus arrieros esclavos y su guardia de soldados españoles, penetra lentamente en la árida garganta. Los cencerros de las bestias se dejan oír en medio del viento, pero el sonido, al igual que el polvo, es arrojado hacia adelante, de modo que para la hilera de tamemes y los hombres de la retaguardia que justo ahora entran en el paso, el batir de las chapas de cobre debe ser inaudible. Un gran lagarto, de pellejo costroso y fláccido, atraviesa el camino y se hunde en un matorral de espinos, y uno de los soldados, un mozo que marcha junto al mensajero indio a la cabeza de la recua, cambia de mano la ballesta, se lleva los dedos a la visera del morrión y hace una apresurada señal de la cruz. Entonces, de improviso, una densa columna de pájaros de diferentes tamaños y colores sobrevuela el desfiladero; trinan, graznan, baten las alas con desesperación; se alejan en dirección al bosque. Abajo, en el camino, las mulas se detienen en seco y echan a temblar, estremeciendo las alforjas repletas de mercaderías y las cajas que llevan la plata del rey. Los negros tiran de los cabestros con denuedo, dan broncas voces que el viento desgarra, asestan furiosos palos, pero no consiguen que los

Antonio Benítez-Rojo
INCIDENT IN THE CORDILLERA

Translated by James E. Maraniss

For Julio, wherever he might be

It is a narrow pass. Plants are growing here and there, meager, creeping, snarled. The road that winds through it is a colonial highway, one of the poor, unleveled ones that snake their way across the cordilleras circuiting the volcanoes and torrents. This one in particular, blanched by the back and forth of mules and donkeys on the pumice, runs east-west through old Guatemala. It seems to exhale vapor in the midday sun, as a sudden gust has squeezed between the granite steeps on either side to lift the dust and whirl it toward a distant forest, a mere green eyebrow on the narrow prospect visible from here. The pack train, with its slave muleteers and guard of Spanish soldiers, creeps through the arid slot. The animals' bells can be heard above the wind, but the sound, like the dust, is hurled ahead, so that to the row of Indian *tameme* porters and the rearguard now entering the pass this coppery tolling must be inaudible. A big lizard, crusty, floppy-skinned, walks over the road and darts into a thornbush; one of the soldiers, a youth marching with the Indian messenger at the head of the train, shifts his crossbow to one hand, lifts his other hand to helmet height, and crosses himself hurriedly. Then, all of a sudden, a dense column of variously sized and colored birds flies over the gorge; they screech and caw in a desperate beating of wings. Beneath them on the pathway, the mules stop cold and begin quaking, rattling the goods inside their packsaddles, boxes filled with silver for the king. The slaves pull bravely on the lead ropes, launch harsh noises rent by the wind, strike furious blows, but never get the animals to lift a

animales desclaven del camino siquiera una herradura. Los tamemes rompen la fila, hacen grupos y cambian miradas y gestos de inquietud; llevan a la espalda, sostenidos por tiras de cuero que se hincan en sus frentes, abultados fardos, cofres, canastos que les sacan cuatro palmos por sobre las orejas y que se bambolean en la ventolera; arracimados, doblados por el peso de la carga, con los brazos plegados sobre el ayate descolorido, recuerdan parvadas de pollos al filo de la tormenta. Ahora el viento se detiene. Cesa el enloquecido aleteo de las aves en fuga. Los remolinos de polvo se asientan, se deshacen y, cual rociada de harina, caen a plomo sobre la recua, blanqueando el fardaje, las grupas y crines, las capas y morriones. Ahora el tiempo es silencio y eternidad, blancor deslumbrante. Los tamemes callan; los esclavos dejan caer los palos y, haciendo visera con sus manos, miran el cielo ardiente. Un vaho denso, azufrado, salido de no se sabe dónde, se estanca poco a poco en el desfiladero; el aire se empaña y verdea como una charca de aguas podridas, y los rostros de los españoles se desencajan y parecen pender de los cascos, y la piel de los esclavos se ablanda y transpira un sudor que huele a cieno, y los tamemes, jadeantes en la calma, se doblan sobre sus piernas arqueadas y arcillosas, sobre sus tobillos hinchados, sobre sus míseros pies de uñas desportilladas. Uno de los más jóvenes deja resbalar su fardo sobre el espinazo, y los rollos de mantas, incrustadas con vistosas plumas de quetzal, se despliegan con parsimonia por el camino; enseguida otro desparrama, como un puñado de relampagüeantes doblones, una docena de vasos de plata, y así, en breve, todos se desembarazan de sus cargas, y junto con la plata labrada ruedan los panes de azúcar moscavado, las marquetas de índigo, las tortas de achiote, las untuosas barras de chocolate; de las cajas y bolsas saltan conservas de ananás y de guayaba, manojos de flores de mesasuchil, raíces de zarzaparrilla; polvos encarnados, pardos, marrones, sazonan las calcinadas piedras con la especiería de Indias. Los tamemes, sin hacer caso de las amenazas que profieren los soldados, retroceden despacio andando de espaldas, inclinados, como si quisieran escapar a hurtadillas de un jaguar acechante. A la delantera de la comitiva, arrimados a las mulas, están los esclavos; aún no se han percatado de la callada rebelión de los tamemes y, sin saber que hacer, comienzan a cantar con la esperanza de tranquilizar a las bestias y lograr que éstas prosigan la marcha; pronto los rudos cantos van decayendo, se

hoof they've planted on the roadway as if nailed. The *tamemes* break the line and bunch together, gesturing and squinting; on their backs they're carrying, held with leather straps that cut into their foreheads, big bundles, coffers, baskets jutting two feet over the ears and wobbling in the wind; clustered, bent over with the weight, arms folded over their faded *ayates*, they call to mind a flock of chickens before a storm. Now the wind stops, as does the fleeing birds' mad flapping. The dusty whorls break up and fall straight down like flour sprinkling on the mule train, whitening the bundles, manes and haunches, helmets, capes. Now the air is dazzling whiteness, silence, endless time. The *tamemes* stop their talking; the slaves drop their staffs and, eyes visored with their hands, look up at the burning sky. A thick steam, sulphurous, seeped out from who knows where, starts pooling in the notch, the air grows dim and greenish like a wash of putrid water, the Spaniards' faces seem to crumple, dangle from their helmets, and the slaves' skin goes soft and begins oozing out a mucky-smelling sweat, and the *tamemes*, panting in the calm, bend forward over arched, buttery legs, over swollen ankles, over miserable feet with riven toenails. One of the youngest slips the bundle from his back, and the rolled blankets, with their embroidered quetzal plumes, unfurl deliberately along the road, and then another spills a clutch of glittering doubloons, a dozen silver goblets; then quickly all the loads are shed, and with the tooled silver there tumble out brown sugarloaves, bricks of indigo, *achiote* cakes, oily chocolate ingots; now the chests and pouches spill out pineapple and guava preserves, clumps of *mesasuchil* flowers, sarsaparilla roots, and spices of the Indies season the chalky rocks. The *tamemes*, paying no attention to the soldiers' shouted threats, step slowly backward, bent, as though trying to sneak from a stalking jaguar. At the head of the procession, leaning on the mules, stand the slaves; they have yet to notice the *tamemes'* mute rebellion, and, not knowing what to do, they start singing, to lull the animals and to get them going once again; quickly the rough chorus begins to trail off, withered in the narrow notch's stinking

marchitan en el vaho hediondo del desfiladero, y las cabezas permanecen alzadas con estupor hacia el último eco que flota entre los paredones de granito. El joven soldado que va al frente, el mismo que se sobrecogiera al ver el lagarto cruzar su paso, deja la ballesta sobre una piedra, saca el puñal, se acerca a la primera de las mulas y la desjarreta; el animal cae pesadamente, y con odiosa torpeza el hombre lo acuchilla en medio de lacerantes relinchos y revolcones; luego, ensangrentado y rígido va hacia el indio mensajero, un hombre tuerto y esmirriado que, tendido en el camino, pega su oreja al polvo en actitud de escucha. El español, con la siniestra calma de un hechizado, se agacha y apoya la punta de la hoja en el cuello del indio; éste fija su ojo redondo, como de pájaro, en el rostro del mozo, y desvía la cabeza hacia las altas masas de piedra. Entonces, sin decir palabra, se incorpora y echa a correr camino abajo. Pasado un instante, un prolongado tronido retumba en el desfiladero, y de inmediato el camino empieza a temblar, a remecerse, a ondularse y abrirse en grietas, en zanjas resollantes. Sobre uno de los paredones se dibuja un fisura, de abajo a arriba, que toma la forma sesgada del rayo, y la montaña se desmorona sobre los hombres y las bestias.

* * *

"¿Venís?", pregunta el tameme más corpulento, al tiempo que anuda sobre la oreja las puntas del sucio pañuelo que cubre su herida, todavía sangrante. Pero el esclavo dice que no con la cabeza y se pone a contemplar, con cierta altiva indiferencia, el lejano bosque hacia el cual desciende el camino. Los cuatro indios sobrevivientes, todos heridos, se ayudan unos a otros a cargar lo poco que se ha salvado del derrumbe. Después, dan la espalda al esclavo, tiran de la mula y comienzan a subir el escarpado túmulo que ciega ahora el paso de la montaña. El maltrecho grupo, seguido por la mirada del esclavo, prosigue su trabajosa marcha de regreso. Al llegar a la cima del túmulo, los tamemes se detienen para tomar aliento. Con objeto de hacer más fácil la ascensión, han acomodado los canastos al través de las espaldas, y sus siluetas, recortadas por la contraluz de la tarde, permanecen estáticas y tristes como cruces de camposanto. El esclavo, después de palparse la magulladura del hombro, intenta meter su pelambre, blanca de polvo, en el morrión de un soldado

vapors, and every head stands upraised, stupefied, to hear the latest echo float between the granite walls. The young soldier at the point, the one who started when he saw the lizard cross his path, lays his crossbow on a rock, pulls out a dagger, then walks up and hocks the first mule in the line; the animal falls heavily, and with cool deliberation the man begins to stab it amid lacerating neighs. Now stiff and bloodied, he walks up to the Indian messenger, a skinny, one-eyed man who, stretched out on the road, has pressed ground. The Spaniard, with the sinister calm of one bewitched, kneels down to place the blade of his knife on the Indian's throat; the latter trains his rounded, birdlike eye upon the soldier's, then turns his head to face the overhanging stone. Then, with nothing said, he gets up and sets off running down the road. After an instant, a steady rumble is resounding in the pass, and now the road starts trembling, swinging, swaying, cracking open into spluttering ditches. A fissure draws a line from top to bottom on the wall, a lightning shape, the mountain sunders, crumbles over man and beast.

* * *

"Are you coming?" the most corpulent *tameme* asks, as he knots a dirty handkerchief behind his ear to cover a still-bleeding cut. The slave shakes his head to say no and starts to survey, with a kind of haughty indifference, the distant forest at the bottom of the road. The four Indian survivors, each one mangled, work together gathering the few things that they've rescued from the cave-in. Then they turn their backs to the slave, tug at the mule, and begin to climb the sheer mound that has entombed the mountain pass. This battered group, which the slave is now following with his glance, proceeds laboriously rearward. As they reach the top of the mound, the *tamemes* halt to catch their breath. To make their climb easier they have slung the baskets over their backs, and their silhouettes, cut into the evening light, are as still and cheerless as crosses in a cemetery. The slave, having fingered the bruise on his shoulder, tries to stuff his bushy head, white with dust, into the dead soldier's helmet; with a disgusted look, he tosses it away, and the noise of

muerto; con un ademán de disgusto lo arroja lejos de sí, y el ruido del metal que rueda sobre las piedras tiene un timbre de arenosa desolación. Ahora el hombre se inclina sobre el cuerpo del soldado, y con ambas manos comienza a halar un objeto oculto a medias en el polvo; después de un tirón que abulta sus músculos, aparece una ballesta; entonces, con el pie, voltea boca abajo al muerto y lo despoja rápidamente de la aljaba de saetas, de la espada, del zurrón de cuero y la botella de agua. Un grito distante lo hace volverse. Es uno de los tamemes que desciende a saltos por los escombros de la montaña, dejando tras de sí una polvareda. "¡Negro, negro! ¡Espera, que voy con vos!"

El esclavo lo aguarda cabizbajo; escarba en el polvo con los dedos de los pies; su semblante se ha tornado hosco, cerrado.

"¿Onde vas?", pregunta el tameme jadeando, sujetándose el cabestrillo en que lleva su brazo derecho. A juzgar por el aspecto de su mano, ligada por sobre la muñeca con una tira de cuero, es difícil que recupere la destreza; una piedra pesada debió caer sobre ella. "¿Onde vas?", repite. "¿No ves que no podés ir solo por estas tierras? ¿No ves que si el español te ve te echa los perros? Los perros son malos. Siempre son muchos, tres, cuatro, cinco perros". El esclavo se encoge de hombros y vuelve la mirada hacia el lejano bosque. "Vente conmigo, negro. Vente conmigo que mejor se es dos que uno", dice el indio sacudiéndose con su mano sana el polvo del ayate. "Bien se ve que sos novicio en los caminos. ¿Como vas andar por ai con ballesta y espada? ¡Ni que jueras capitán, carajo! Tíralas, negro. Tíralas, que por tu bien te lo digo. ¿Que decís? Hablá como los cristianos, que no te hacés entender".

El esclavo alza la cabeza y señala a su garganta. Bajo los pelos enroscados de su barba hay una horrible cicatriz.

"¡Ah, negro, suerte que has tenido! Mordida de perro es, que si juera de jaguar ya no andabas por el mundo. De seguro te huiste". El esclavo frunce el ceño y responde con un gruñido. "Suerte también tenés de ir conmigo, que tres veces he hecho el camino a la costa, y tres veces la vuelta a Quetzaltenango. No más unos días de camino y te muestro onde viven los esclavos fugitivos", agrega señalando al naciente. "De seguro te toman en su banda de salteadores, que eres mozo y aprestado. A cinco jornadas están, en las Montañas del Mico". El esclavo, ahora mostrando sus dientes limados en una amplia sonrisa, se lleva la mano al pecho y asiente

metal on the stones has a timbre of sandy desolation. Now the man bends over the soldier's body; he starts to pull with both hands on a thing half-hidden in the dust; after a hard tug that knots his muscles, a crossbow is produced; then he turns the dead man face-down with his foot and strips him quickly of his quiver, its arrows, his sword, his leather pouch, his water bottle. A distant shout spins him around. It is one of the *tamemes*, who comes leaping down the rubble, raising a cloud of dust behind. "*Negro! Negro!* Wait! I'm going with you!"

The slave waits for him with head down; he rubs his toes in the dust, his face grown sullen, shut.

"Where you going?" the *tameme* asks, wheezing, clutching the splint on his right arm. To judge from the way his hand looks, held to the wrist by a bloody tatter, it will not now nor perhaps ever be of any use to him; a big rock must have fallen on it. "Where you going?" he inquires. "You think you can get through here by yourself? The Spanish find you, don't you know, they'll feed you to the dogs. They're bad. And always lots. Three, four, five, dogs." The slave shrugs and looks back toward the forest in the distance. "Come on, *Negro*, come with me. Two's better," the Indian says, shaking dust from his *ayate* with his good hand. "You don't know these roads. How you going walk through here with a sword and a crossbow? Hell, who you think you are? You're no *capitán*. Drop them, *Negro*. For your own sake, man. What? Talk like a Christian. What you say?"

The slave lifts his chin and puts his finger to his throat. There is an awful scar beneath the curly bristles of his beard.

"Christ, *Negro*, you've been lucky! A dog bit you. A jaguar and you wouldn't be here walking around. You ran off, right?" The slave frowns and answers with a grunt. "Lucky for you you're with me, too; I've been down by this road three times to the coast, and back then to Quetzaltenango. In four, five days I'll show you where the *cimarrones* live," he adds, pointing toward the east.

"They'll make a bandit out of you; you're young and fit for anything. Five days' walk from here. The Mico mountains." The slave, showing his filed, shiny teeth in a broad smile, brings hand to

repetidamente. "Mejor te quedás las armas. No más llegados al bosque, dejamos el camino, que por ai debe andar el tuerto Felipe, el que hacía de mensajero. De seguro fue dar cuenta del suceso al alcalde de Acazabastlán, que ofrece buenas monedas a cambio de malas noticias".

Los hombres echan a andar uno al lado del otro, rodeando las grietas que el terremoto ha dejado en el camino. El indio mira el lejano túmulo por sobre el hombro y, sin dejar de caminar, hace la señal de la cruz. "Que Dios se apiade de sus almas", murmura.

El desfiladero ha quedado atrás. En ese punto el camino se aparta de la cordillera y desciende bruscamente hacia un bosque de pinos, muchos de ellos inclinados de norte a sur. El polvo se torna terracota, y la vegetación, aunque todavía rala, refresca un tanto el aire y lo llena de olores a resina y a flores silvestres. "Mira", dice el tameme, señalando una ruinosa construcción de piedra en la cima de un peñasco. "Hasta ai llegaron los quichés en sus guerras con los tzutuhiles". Y lleno de orgullo, añade: "Sabes, el padre de mi abuelo era señor de Huehuetenango. Murió en la hoguera con los señores de Sololá y de Atitlán, que no quisieron renunciar a la adoración de los viejos dioses, Tepeu, Gugumatz y... ¡A la mierda!", grita asustado, y de repente se escucha un tronido apagado y la tierra empieza a temblar de nuevo. Instintivamente, los hombres corren lo mejor que pueden hacia un macizo de hierba, hasta que el tameme, luego de un fuerte remezón, rueda por el camino.

"¡Carajo!", dice el indio incorporándose, en su rostro una expresión de intenso dolor. "Ya vuelve a sangrar esta mierda de mano", se queja metiendo el brazo en el trapo manchado que lleva alrededor del cuello. El esclavo se acerca y examina la mano del tameme, que cuelga desarticulada y sangrante; bajo los gemidos del hombre, aprieta la ligadura de la muñeca hasta que la mano cesa de gotear; luego ata el zurrón del indio al suyo y se lo echa a la espalda junto con las armas. "Parece una rata aplastada", dice el tameme mirando su mano con una expresión de triste incredulidad. "¡Ay, negro, carajo!", se lamenta. "¿Cómo crees que puedo pagar el tributo a don Esteban, mi señor, con esta mierda de mano? ¿Quién me va a alquilar como tameme? Mi mano ya no sirve, negro. Soy un hombre de mierda, un hombre lisiado. Mi mujer se meterá a puta y mis hijos a ladrones. Si lo sabré yo, que ansina jue con mi hermano Anselmo. Mejor morir, hombre. Te lo digo que sí".

chest and nods agreement. "You better ditch those weapons," the Indian says. And he tries to take the crossbow away from the slave. But the latter, lifting it over his head, holds it out of the *tameme's* reach. "All right, *Negro*, whatever you want. Soon as we get to the forest we leave the road. One-eyed Felipe must be on the loose around there, the messenger. You can bet he went to Acazabastlán to see the mayor, who pays good money for bad news."

The two men begin walking, side by side, skirting cracks left by the earthquake in the road. The Indian glances backward at the now-distant tumulus; he starts to cross himself, with no pause in his stride. "May God have mercy on their souls," he murmurs.

They leave the pass behind. At this point the road leaves the cordillera, goes down brusquely to a sea of pines, many of them knocked over north to south. The dust is terra-cotta and the vegetation, though still sparse, freshens the air a little, sends out a whiff of wildflower and resin. "Look," says the *tameme*, signaling a wrecked stone structure on a crag. "The Quichés got as far as this against the Tzutuhiles." And he adds proudly: "You know, my great-grandfather was the lord of Huehuetenango. They burned him at the stake, next to the lords of Atitlán and Sololá; they wouldn't stop adoring the old gods, Tepeu, Gugumatz, and...Shit!" he shouts, frightened, and suddenly they hear a stifled thunder as the earth begins to tremble for a second time. Instinctively, the two men start to run as quickly as they can up toward a patch of grass, until the Indian, after a savage temblor, bites the dust.

"Son of a bitch!" the Indian growls as he gets up, pain showing on his face. "This God damned hand is bleeding again," he says, inserting his arm once more into the soiled rag that hangs from his neck. The slave comes up to take a look at the *tameme's* hand, which dangles bloody, loose and disarticulate; he tightens the sling around the Indian's wrist until the bleeding stops. Then he ties the Indian's pouch to his own and throws them both across his back beside the weapons. "It's like a squashed rat," the *tameme* says, looking sadly at his hand, incredulous. "Oh, Christ, *Negro*," he complains. "How the hell will I put up Don Esteban's tribute with this shitty hand? The hand's no good now, *Negro*. I'm not worth shit. I'm a cripple. My wife's going to be a whore, and the kids will have to rob. I know it. That's what happened to my brother Anselmo. You're better off dead."

El esclavo descorcha la botella de agua y le ofrece de beber al tameme. Luego de un largo trago, éste se serena y trota hacia su compañero, que ha reiniciado la marcha. "¿Sabés qué voy a hacer?" dice al cabo del rato. "Me voy a las tierras bajas, a las tierras de los lacandones, más allá de la Vera Paz. Son indios paganos y brutos. Diz que andan en cueros como monos y son muy poco de fiar. Pero, quién sabe, a lo mejor me acogen por las muchas cosas que sé, que además de tameme sé ayudar en muchos oficios". Y después de una breve pausa, agrega malhumorado: "Y si me matan, carajo, qué voy a hacer si muerto estoy para los míos, que eso quedamos con mi primo Tomás y los dos tamemes tzutuhiles. Sí señor. Todos dirán que me aplastaron las piedras, que es mejor que me sepan muerto que viviendo de caridad por las iglesias".

El esclavo asiente y pasa su brazo sobre los hombros del tameme. Y asi, arrimados uno al otro, marchan un corto trecho hasta que el indio se detiene y saca por debajo de su ayate un cuchillo de trinchar con rico mango de plata. "¿Me hacés una merced?", dice mirando al esclavo a los ojos. "¿Me cortás la mano?" Y agrega sombrio: "Algo sé de curar heridas". El esclavo toma el cuchillo y pasa el dedo por el filo. "Mirá, si no lo haces se me pudre en dos días, que ansina mesmo pasó con el pobrecito Anselmo. Primero la mano, en seguido el brazo y dispués se murió jediendo y rabiando, sin querer ver al cura ni a nadie, que Dios perdone su alma".

* * *

Desde el parapeto de la atalaya quiché se domina el camino de Acazabastlán y la ancha y boscosa barranca que éste bordea. Del lado interior del parapeto, roídos por la intemperie y los años, los muros emergen de entre la maleza como grandes dientes de piedra renegrida. En un rincón despejado de arbustos, el único propiamente dicho, el tameme dormita mientras el esclavo asa a la barbacoa una bestezuela, tal vez un cachorro de puma. Un precario colgadizo, hecho con sus desgarradas mantas, los cobija del sol. El indio, sentado en un colchón de hierba recién cortada, la espalda recostada al muro, ha inclinado la cabeza sobre el pecho; aún lleva el brazo en cabestrillo, pero ya no en un pedazo de su ayate sino en una envoltura de corteza de árbol; emplastos de hojas intensamente verdes empaquetan su muñón. El esclavo, en cuclillas, con el torso

The slave unstops the water bottle, offers it to the *tameme*. After a long swallow, the Indian jogs up next to his companion, who had walked ahead. "Know what I'll do?" he says. "I'll go down there with the Lacandones in the jungle, beyond Vera Paz. They're wild Indians, pagans. People say they run around bare as monkeys and you can't trust them at all. But, who knows? Maybe they'll take me in because of all the things I know about. I'm not just a carrier; I can help out on some other jobs." And following a brief pause he adds, sourly: "Even if they kill me, shit, what am I going to do anyway, if I'm as good as dead to my own, that's what it came to with Tomás, my cousin, and the two Tzutuhil *tamemes*. *Sí señor*. They'll all say that I got flattened by the rocks, and I'd sooner be dead to them all than a beggar at the church door."

The slave nods in understanding. He takes the *tameme* by the shoulder, and stuck together in this way they walk ahead for a short while, until the Indian stops to pull a curved, silverhandled knife from his *ayate*. "Do me a favor, *Negro*," he says, looking into the black man's eyes. "Cut this hand off." And he adds, dismally: "I know how to heal a cut." The slave takes the knife and runs his finger down the blade. "Look, if you won't do it this hand rots in two days, that's how it went with poor Anselmo. First the hand and then the arm, then he died screaming and shaking and not wanting to see anybody, God's mercy on him."

* * *

From the parapet of the Quiché lookout tower you can see the road to Acazabastlán and the broad, forested ravine that it skirts. Eaten away by time and weather, the walls jut from the underbrush like huge teeth of blackened stone. Just one cranny has been cleared of bushes; in it the *tameme* drowses while the black man barbecues a little beast, perhaps a puma cub. A dubious awning, put together from their ragged blankets, shields them from the sun. The Indian, sitting cushioned in some cut grass, his back against the wall, hangs his head down over his chest; his arm is still in a sling, but not one made from his *ayate*, rather one wound together out of tree bark; his stump is packed in dark green leaves. The slave, crouching, his torso bare, stares thoughtfully into the pale wood fire. His thoughts

desnudo, mira absorto el fuego casi incoloro de la leña. Sus pensamientos se entrelazan, se alargan y repliegan junto con las llamas; conceptos, imágenes, sonidos de palabras, deseos, crepitan con desasosiego, se sobreponen unos a otros y lamen la lumbre de sus ojos quietos. Una escena, sin embargo, permanece estable el tiempo suficiente para ser descrita: junto a un río lento, de aguas amarillas y bajas riberas, hay una empalizada circular de troncos robustos, aguzados; un sendero polvoriento lleva al portón que se abre de súbito en la empalizada, a través de cuyo vano se descubre una aldea con chozas de techado cónico; en el interior de una de ellas aparece una mujer alta y ancha de caderas; canta plácidamente mientras maja en un pequeño mortero pedazos de ñame hervido; su cráneo rapado reluce de aceite y en su brazo resalta una ajorca de cobre; ahora se escucha un llanto de niño y la mujer, dejando de cantar, se vuelve hacia el lugar más oscuro de la choza y alarga los brazos de manera acogedora, maternal. Esta escena, o más bien cuadro imaginativo que forma el recuerdo, empieza a temblar, a doblarse por los bordes como una hoja caída al fuego, y los contornos y colores enseguida se agostan, se hacen humo, mientras dos lágrimas asoman a los ojos del hombre.

En el sueño del tameme, o tal vez en una memoria que presiente no del todo suya, hay, en primer término, oscuridad. No se trata de la oscuridad de la noche sin luna, incluso de la noche encapotada que ciega las estrellas; es la oscuridad de un tiempo sin estaciones, sin semanas y calendarios. En esta oscuridad primigenia hay agua; no es posible verla, por supuesto, pero sí sentirla como un abrazo helado, inmóvil, que yace bajo el cielo negro y vacío. También parece haber tierra, tierra sumergida, légamo que sirve de sostén a las plantas desnudas del tameme. Entonces, en esta suerte de sueño mítico, el hombre echa a andar, o más bien a vagar con frío y agobio por el silencio, por el tiempo ausente. En algún lugar—no se puede apreciar si queda próximo o distante—surge una débil claridad, apenas un resplandor de rescoldo, de la cual parten murmullos, voces bajas, profundas, que llenan el espacio inconmensurable del piélago y lo hacen vibrar. El tameme, esperanzado, se acerca al luminoso cuchicheo con pasos cautos, espesos de légamo: de algún modo sabe que allí están, ocultos bajos sus mantos de plumas verdes y azules, Tepeu y Gugumatz, el Creador y el Formador; tal vez se animen a darle de nuevo su mano derecha, piensa en el sueño.

entwine, uncoil, fold over with the flame; images, conceits, word sounds, desires crackle briskly, falling one upon another, giving luster to his quiet eyes. A single scene, however, plays out long enough to be described; beside a sleeping river, with low-lying banks, there is a circular stockade of strong sharpened posts; a dusty path leads up to the gate, which opens suddenly, and through the portal one can see a village of cone-roofed huts, and inside one of them there is a tall, broad-hipped woman; she sings staidly as she mashes something in a mortar; her shaven head is oiled and gleaming; she flaunts a copper bracelet on her arm. Now you can hear a bawling child, and the woman stops her singing, turns her body toward the darkest corner of the hut and stretches out her arms in a gathering, motherly way. This scene, or rather imagined picture formed in memory, begins to tremble, to fold over at the edges like a leaf that's fallen in the fire, and the shapes and colors quickly wither, turn to smoke, as two tears surface in the black man's eyes.

In the *tameme*'s dream, or perhaps in a memory that he reads as not entirely his own, there is, in the first place, darkness. Not the darkness of a moonless night, nor even a night of star-obliterating cloudiness; it is the darkness of an era without seasons, weeks or calendars. There is water in this primeval dark, not visible of course, but one can feel it, like a frozen still embrace beneath a sky that's black and empty. There is land here, too, submerged, a loam supporting the *tameme*'s naked feet. Then, in this mythic dream, the man starts walking, wandering cold and wasted through the silence and lost time. At a certain place—whether near or distant one can't tell—there is a burst of pallid light, almost like a glow of smoldering ashes, out of which come murmurings, deep muffled voices to fill the measureless pelagic void and set it vibrating. The *tameme*, heartened, walks toward this luminous pulsation with careful, muddy footsteps; he knows somehow that right there hidden underneath the blue and green plumed blankets lie Tepeu and Gugumatz, the Creator and the Shaper; in his dream he hopes they'll give back his right hand.

Al romper la aurora, el bosque de pinos que crece en la barranca hace un paisaje lamentable; por entre los bancos de neblina, las copas de los árboles se ven tumbadas de norte a sur, formando calles, o más bien canelones de terreno breñoso, a veces rasgados al centro por largas y dentadas grietas; también hay árboles volteados, por lo general al borde de las quebraduras, y sus raíces se descubren como enormes nudos de lombrices. Quizá allí tuvo su centro el terremoto, pues suman millares los pinos abatidos, tronchados, desgajados, y un tupido tapiz de agujas verdes cubre el declive del terreno, salvo en los surcos en que voló la tierra. El olor salvaje y penetrante de la resina ha atraído a las hormigas de las tierras altas. Formadas en columnas, pintan de un negro rojizo la vertiente oeste de la barranca, y van cubriendo los árboles heridos, los pellejos ondulantes de las serpientes, los nidos reventados; hay algo tenebroso en esta exterminadora marcha de minúsculas patas y tiento de pinzas, algo profundamente viejo y terrible que irrumpe de un mundo de galerías carbonosas, de secretos oficios y profanaciones, y se ordena como una feroz y ciega plaga a la luz del amanecer.

El negro y el indio, que duermen arrebujados en sus mantas, despiertan por el dolor de las picadas. Sobresaltados por el voraz rumor que se les viene encima, apenas atinan a desembarazarse de sus mantas y a sacudirse las ropas uno al otro. Abandonando a las hormigas los zurrones, huyen despavoridos barranca abajo, pisando alimañas en fuga, botando de piedra en piedra, los ojos grandes y las bocas abiertas.

Al saltar por sobre un tronco atravesado en su carrera, el indio tropieza y rueda por el declive con un largo aullido; finalmente, su cuerpo se detiene al golpear contra un árbol. Una vez más ha caído sobre el brazo lastimado, y su rostro, apenas alzado de las agujas de pino, es ahora un ovillo de terror salpicado de hormigas. Trata de incorporarse apoyándose en su brazo izquierdo, pero cae resoplando. Sólo le quedan fuerzas para alzar de nuevo la cabeza. "¡Negro, negro!", grita angustiado.

El esclavo, saltando limpiamente el tronco atravesado, da varias zancadas y cae en cuclillas junto a su compañero; enseguida lo vuelve boca arriba y lo arrastra hasta una piedra. "Mátame pronto,

At daybreak the pine trees growing in the gap make a sorry landscape; seen among the fogbanks, the trees' crowns lie knocked down north to south, forming streets, or rather gutters, of uneven ground, some with long toothed cracks; there are uprooted trees, usually at the edges of the cracks, their roots huge wormlike knots. The epicenter may have been here, for there are thousands of torn, battered pines and a slope covered in a thick carpet of green needles everywhere except in furrows where the earth went flying. The savage, penetrating smell of resin has brought in the upland ants. Massed in columns, they paint the hollow's western face a rusty black and cover the wounded trees, the snakes' undulating skins and broken nests. There is something tenebrous in this annihilating march of tiny feet, this grabble of pincers, something profoundly old and terrible erupting from a world of carbonous galleries, from secret rites and profanations, to come out at daybreak like a fierce, blind plague.

The black man and the Indian, wrapped up sleeping in their blankets, are wakened by the sting of biting ants. Startled in the devouring buzz that has landed on them, they can barely think to throw off their blankets and shake ants off one another's clothes. Abandoning their pouches to the ants, they run helter-skelter down the gully, terrified, stepping on small animals in flight, bouncing rock to rock, gaping, openmouthed.

As he jumps over a trunk fallen in his path, the Indian trips and rolls howling down the slope; his body stops against a tree. He has landed on his wounded arm again, and his face, barely raised from the green needles, is now a gnarl of terror flecked with ants. He tries getting up, pushes on his left arm, but then collapses, wheezing. He has strength left only to lift up his hand. "*Negro! Negro!*" he shouts in anguish.

The slave jumps cleanly over the fallen trunk, takes a few long strides and falls kneeling by his companion; then he turns him face-up and drags him toward a rock. "Come on, kill me, *Negro*. I can't

negro. Mátame, que ya no puedo más", gime el tameme mientras se da manotazos en la cara. "No dejés que me coman vivo", solloza. El esclavo se vuelve y mira barranca arriba: el que fuera su campamento ha desaparecido bajo la bullente masa de insectos. Entonces, con un rápido gesto, desenvaina la hoja de acero que lleva a la espalda y mide con su punta la yugular del tameme. "Vamos, hombre, acabá de una vez", suplica. "Recordá, negro bruto", dice ahora intentando sonreír, "cuatro largas jornadas hacia el naciente y verás un río. Del otro lado están las Montañas del Mico. ¡Mátame, carajo!"

El esclavo mira fijamente al tameme. A pesar de la caída y las volteretas, el muñón permanece cubierto. Una lívida hinchazón trepa por el brazo mutilado, alcanzando el lado derecho de la cara; el carrillo semeja una vejiga fofa y el ojo es un pliegue costroso y enrojecido. Con un ronco grito de furia, el hombre arroja lejos la espada, toma al tameme por el brazo izquierdo y se lo echa al hombro de golpe; sin mirar atrás comienza a correr.

Allá en lo alto, para el indio tuerto que observa desde la atalaya, los hombres del bosque apenas se distinguen por entre las copas de los árboles. Por un momento piensa que podrán escapar de las columnas de hormigas que convergen hacia el naciente, pero enseguida, al medir de nuevo la distancia con su redondo ojo de pájaro, hace la señal de la cruz y se retira del parapeto.

bear it!" the *tameme* wails, beating his face with his hands. "Don't let them eat me alive," he sobs. The slave turns to look up the ravine; what had been their camp has disappeared under the boil of insects. Then with a quick gesture he draws the steel blade from on his back, touching its point to the *tameme*'s jugular. "End it now," the Indian implores. "Listen, you dumb slave," he says, trying to smile, "four long days toward sunrise and you see a river. Mico mountains on the other side. Kill me, damn it!"

The slave looks straight at the *tameme*. Despite the fall, and all the rolling, his stump is still covered. An angry swelling climbs along his mutilated arm, reaching the right side of his face; his jowl is a loose bladder, his eye a scabby, reddened wrinkle. With a hoarse, furious yell, the black man throws away his sword, grabs the *tameme* by the left arm, hoists him on his back in a single swoop; not looking backward, he starts running.

To the one-eyed Indian observing from the lookout tower in the upland, the two men below in the forest are barely visible among the trees. He thinks for a moment that they might escape the columns of ants that are converging in the east, but soon, as he calculates the distances with his rounded, birdlike eye, he crosses himself and leaves the parapet.

Movimiento perpetuo

Perpetual Motion

Edith Grossman, translator of Augusto Monterroso

Edith Grossman, born in Philadelphia in 1936, spent part of her adolescence and young childhood in California and Spain, and has lived in Manhattan since 1963. She received her Bachelors and Masters degrees from the University of Pennsylvania and a Doctorate from New York University. Grossman translated Gabriel García Márquez's *Love in the Time of Cholera* and *The General in his Labyrinth*, as well as Alvaro Mutis's *Maqroll*, among other works. A scholar and critic, she teaches at Dominican College in Orangeburg, New York, and is the author of *The Anti-Poetry of Nicanor Parra*.

Her beginnings as a translator date back to the early seventies, when Ronald Christ, then the editor of *Review: Latin American Literature and Art*, asked her to translate a story by Macedonio Fernández. Her working method is as follows: "I usually read the text once and then begin to translate. In fact, though, I read the original text at least ten times, since the translation undergoes countless revisions. I don't have a fixed working schedule: I work when I can, and for as long as I can. Sometimes I put in 8-10 hours a day and at other times, I can't write at all." Grossman believes that it is very helpful to consult with the author. "Inevitably there are words or phrases that I don't know, that are in none of my dictionaries, or that my Spanish-speaking friends can't help me with. Ralph Manheim once said that translators are like actors: we speak lines by someone else. Knowing the author sometimes makes it easier for the translator to imagine how the author would say these words if he or she spoke English. As for the text: the better the writing, the more inspired I feel."

In her eyes, Augusto Monterroso, born in Guatemala City in 1921 and a resident of Mexico City since 1944, is a master of what Irving Howe called "short shorts," and certainly deserves a wider readership north of the Rio Grande. Monterroso has published more than 14 volumes of satirical fiction and fables. In English, his work is collected in *The Black Sheep and Other Fables* and *Complete Works and Other Stories*.

Augusto Monterroso
MOVIMIENTO PERPETUO

Pape: Satan, pape: Satan Aleppe.
DANTE, *Inferno,* VII

—¿Te acordaste?

Luis se enredó en un complicado pero en todo caso débil esfuerzo mental para recordar qué era lo que necesitaba haber recordado.

—No.

El gesto de disgusto de Juan le indicó que esta vez debía de ser algo realmente importante y que su olvido le acarrearía las consecuencias negativas de costumbre. Así siempre. La noche entera pensando no debo olvidarlo para a última hora olvidarlo. Como hecho adrede. Si supieran el trabajo que le costaba tratar de recordar, para no hablar ya de recordar. Igual que durante toda la primaria: ¿Nueve por siete?

—¿Qué te pasó?

—¿Que qué me pasó?

—Sí; cómo no te acordaste.

No supo qué contestar. Un intento de contraataque:

—Nada. Se me olvidó.

—¡Se me olvidó! ¿Y ahora?

¿Y ahora?

Resignado y conciliador, Juan le ordenó o, según después Luis, quizá simplemente le dijo que no discutieran más y que si quería un trago.

Sí. Fue a servirse él mismo. El whisky con agua, en el que colocó tres cúbitos de hielo que con el calor empezaron a disminuir rápidamente aunque no tanto que lo hiciera decidirse a poner otro, tenía un sedante color ámbar. ¿Por qué sedante? No desde luego por el color, sino porque era whisky, whisky con agua, que le haría olvidar que tenía que recordar algo.

—Salud.

—Salud.

Augusto Monterroso
PERPETUAL MOTION
Translated by Edith Grossman

Pape: Satan, pape: Satan Aleppe.
Dante, *Inferno*, VII

"Did you remember?"

Luis became involved in a complicated but basically weak mental effort to remember what it was he was supposed to have remembered.

"No."

Juan's gesture of disgust indicated that this time it must have been something really important and his having forgotten would bring the usual negative consequences. It was always the same. The whole night thinking I mustn't forget only to forget at the last minute. As if he did it on purpose. If they only knew the effort it cost him trying to remember let alone remembering itself. Just like elementary school: 9x7?

"What happened?"

"What do you mean what happened?"

"Just what I said. How could you forget?"

He didn't know what to say. An attempt at counterattack:

"Nothing happened. I just forgot."

"I just forgot! And now?"

"And now?"

Resigned and conciliatory, Juan ordered, or according to Luis afterward, perhaps he simply said that they wouldn't discuss it anymore and did he want a drink.

Yes. He helped himself. Whiskey and water. He put in three ice cubes that began to melt rapidly in the heat, although not enough to make him decide to put in another one. It had a soothing amber color. Why soothing? Not of course because of the color but because it was whiskey, whiskey with water that would make him forget that he had to remember something.

"Cheers."

"Cheers."

—Qué vida—dijo irónico Luis moviéndose en la silla de madera y mirando con placidez a la playa, al mar, a los barcos, al horizonte; al horizonte que era todavía mejor que los barcos y que el mar y que la playa, porque más allá uno ya no tenía que pensar ni imaginar ni recordar nada.

Sobre la olvidadiza arena varios bañistas corrían enfrentando a la última luz del crepúsculo sus dulces pelos y sus cuerpos ya más que tostados por varios días de audaz exposición a los rigores del astro rey. Juan los miraba hacer, meditativo. Meditaba pálidamente que Acapulco ya no era el mismo, que acaso tampoco él fuera ya el mismo, que sólo su mujer continuaba siendo la misma y que lo más seguro era que en ese instante estuviera acariciándose con otro hombre detrás de cualquier peñasco, o en cualquier bar o a bordo de cualquier lancha. Pero aunque en realidad no le importaba, eso no quería decir que no pensara en ello a todas horas. Una cosa era una cosa y otra otra. Julia seguiría siendo Julia hasta la consumación de los siglos, tal como la viera por primera vez seis años antes, cuando, sin provocación y más bien con sorpresa de su parte, en una fiesta en la que no conocía casi a nadie, se le quedó viendo y se le aproximó y lo invitó a bailar y él aceptó y ella lo rodeó con sus brazos y comenzó a incitarlo arrimándosele y buscándolo con las piernas y acercándosele suave pero calculadoramente como para que él pudiera sentir el roce de sus pechos y dejara de estar nervioso y se animara.

—¿Te sirvo otro?—dijo Luis.

—Gracias.

Y en cuanto pudo lo besó y lo cercó y lo llevó a donde quiso y le presentó a sus amigos y lo emborrachó y esa misma noche, cuando aún no sabían ni sus apellidos y cuando como a las tres y media de la mañana ni siquiera podía decirse que hubieran acabado de entrar en su departamento—el de ella—, sin darle tiempo a defenderse aunque fuera para despistar, lo arrastró hasta su cama y lo poseyó en tal forma que cuando él se dio cuenta de que ella era virgen apenas se extrañó, no obstante que ella lo dirigió todo, como ese y el segundo, el tercero y el cuarto año de casados, sin que por otra parte pudiera afirmarse que ella tuviera nada, ni belleza, ni talento, ni dinero; nada, únicamente aquello.

—El hielo no dura nada—dijo Luis.

—Nada.

"What a life," said Luis ironically, shifting in the wooden chair and looking calmly at the beach, the ocean, the boats, the horizon— the horizon that was even better than the boats and the ocean and the beach because out there you didn't have to think or imagine or remember anything anymore.

On the oblivious sand several bathers were running in the last light of dusk with their soft hair and their bodies darker than tan after several days of daring exposure to the severity of the sky king. Juan watched them thoughtfully. He was thinking, palely, that Acapulco was no longer the same, that perhaps he was no longer the same either, only his wife was the same and the one certainty was that right now she was embracing another man behind some rocks or in some bar or on some boat. He didn't really care, but that didn't mean he didn't think about it all the time. The two things had nothing to do with one another. Julia would go on being Julia forever, just as he had first seen her six years ago when, without provocation and with some surprise on his part, she stared at him at a party where he hardly knew anyone and came up to him and asked him to dance and he said yes and she put her arms around him and began to excite him rubbing up against him and searching for him with her legs and moving against him gently but with calculation so he would feel the brush of her breasts and stop being nervous and not be afraid.

"Would you like another one?" said Luis.

"Thanks."

And as soon as she could she kissed him and encircled him and led him away and introduced him to her friends and got him drunk and that same night, when they didn't even know each other's last names, when they were in her apartment at three-thirty in the morning and he didn't even have time to defend himself she pulled him into bed and possessed him in such a way that when he realized she was a virgin he wasn't even surprised though she controlled everything that year and the second, third, and fourth year of their marriage. He couldn't say she had anything else—not beauty or talent or money—she had nothing but that.

"The ice doesn't last at all," said Luis.

"Not at all."

Unicamente nada.

Julia entró de pantalones, con el cabello todavía mojado por la ducha.

—¿No invitan?

—Sí; sírvete.

—Qué amable.

—Yo te sirvo—dijo Luis.

—Gracias. ¿Te acordaste?

—Se le volvió a olvidar; qué te parece.

—Bueno, ya. Se me olvidó y qué.

—¿No van a la playa?—dijo ella.

Bebió su whisky con placer: no hay que dejar entrar la cruda.

Los tres quedaron en silencio. No hablar ni pensar en nada. ¿Cuántos días más? Cinco. Contando desde mañana, cuatro. Nada. Si uno pudiera quedarse para siempre, sin ver a nadie. Bueno, quizá no. Bueno, quién sabía. La cosa estaba en acostumbrarse. Bien tostados. Negros, negros.

Cuando la negra noche tendió su manto pidieron otra botella y más agua y más hielo y después más agua y más hielo. Empezaron a sentirse bien. De lo más bien. Los astros tiritaban azules a lo lejos en el momento en que Julia propuso ir al Guadalcanal a cenar y bailar.

—Hay dos orquestas.

—¿Y por qué no cuatro?

—¿Verdad?

—Vamos a vestirnos.

Una vez allí confirmaron que tal como Juan lo había presentido para el Guadalcanal era horriblemente temprano. Escasos gringos por aquí y por allá, bebiendo tristes y bailando graves, animados, aburridos. Y unos cuantos de nosotros alegrísimos, cuándo no, mucho antes de tiempo. Pero como a la una principió a llegar la gente y al rato hasta podía decirse, perdonando la metáfora, que no cabía un alfiler. En cumplimiento de la tradición, Julia había invitado a Juan y a Luis a bailar; pero después de dos piezas Juan ya no quiso y Luis no era muy bueno (se le olvidaban afirmaba los pasos y si era mambo o rock). Entonces, como desde hacía uno, dos, tres, cuatro años, Julia se las ingenió para encontrar con quién divertirse. Era fácil. Lo único que había que hacer consistía en mirar

Nothing, nothing at all.

Julia came in wearing slacks, her hair still wet from the shower.

"Aren't you going to offer me a drink?"

"Sure. Help yourself."

"How nice."

"I'll get it for you," said Luis.

"Thanks. Did you remember?"

"He forgot again. Can you believe it?"

"That's enough. I forgot and so what?"

"Aren't you two going to the beach?" she asked.

She drank her whiskey with pleasure. No need to be cruel.

The three of them were silent. Don't speak or think about anything. How many more days? Five. Four counting from tomorrow. Nothing. If only you didn't have to see anybody. Well, maybe not that. Well, who knows. The thing was to get used to it. They're all suntanned. Dark, dark.

When dark night spread its blanket they asked for another bottle and more water and ice and then more water and more ice. They began to feel good. Really good. The stars were twinkling a distant blue when Julia suggested going to the Guadalcanal to eat and dance.

"They have two bands."

"Why not four?"

"Okay?"

"Let's get dressed."

When they got there they saw it was too early for the Guadalcanal, just as Juan had said. A few scattered gringos drinking sadly and dancing seriously, animatedly, in boredom. And a few of us, much too drunk too early. But at about one o'clock people started to come in and soon, if you'll pardon the metaphor, there wasn't room for a pin. In obedience to tradition, Julia invited Juan and Luis to dance, but after two numbers Juan didn't want to anymore and Luis was not very good (he said he forgot the steps, forgot if it was a mambo or rock). Then, as she had for one, two, three, four years, Julia found someone to have a good time with. It was easy. All she had to do

de cierto modo a los que se quedaban solos en las otras mesas. No fallaba nunca. Pronto vendría algún joven (nacional, de los nuestros) y al verla rubia le preguntaría en inglés que si le permitía, a lo que ella respondería dirigiéndose no a él sino a su marido en demanda de un consentimiento que de antemano sabía que él no le iba a negar y levantándose y tendiendo los brazos a su invitante, quien más o menos riéndose iniciaría rápidas disculpas por haberla confundido con una norteamericana y se reiría ahora desconcertado de veras cuando ella le dijera que sí, que en efecto era norteamericana, y pasaría aún otro rato cohibido, toda vez que a estas alturas resultaba obvio que ella vivía desde muchos años antes en el país, lo cual convertía en francamente ridículo cualquier intento de reiniciar la plática sobre la manoseada base de si llevaba mucho tiempo en México y de si le gustaba México. Pero entonces ella volvería a darle ánimo mediante la infalible táctica de presionarlo con las piernas para que él comprendiera que de lo que se trataba era de bailar y no de hacer preguntas ni de atormentarse esforzándose en buscar temas de conversación, pues, si bien era bonito sentir placer físico, lo que a ella más le agradaba era dejarse llevar por el pensamiento de que su marido se hallaría sufriendo como de costumbre por saberla en brazos de otro, o imaginando que aplicaría con éste ni más ni menos que las mismas tácticas que había usado con él, y que en ese instante estaría lleno de resentimiento y de rabia sirviéndose otra copa, y que después de otras dos se voltearía de espaldas a la pista de baile para no ver la archisabida maniobra de ellos consistente en acercarse a intervalos prudenciales a la mesa separados más de la cuenta como dos inocentes palomas y hablando casi a gritos y riéndose con él para en seguida alejarse con maña y perderse detrás de las parejas más distantes y abrazarse a su sabor y besarse sin cambiar palabra pero con la certeza de que dentro de unos minutos, una vez que su marido se encontrara completamente borracho, estarían más seguros y el joven nacional podría llevarlos a todos en su coche con ella en el asiento delantero como muy apartaditos pero en realidad más unidos que nunca por la mano derecha de él buscando algo entre sus muslos, mientras hablaría en voz alta de cosas indiferentes como el calor o el frío, según el caso, en tanto que su marido simularía estar más ebrio de lo que estaba con el exclusivo objeto de que ellos pudieran actuar a su antojo y ver hasta dónde llegaban,

was look a certain way at the men sitting alone at other tables. It never failed. Soon some young man would come over (a national, one of us) and seeing she was blonde would ask her if she would care to dance, and she would answer looking not a him but at her husband, asking permission that she knew ahead of time he would not deny, and she would stand up and stretch her arms toward the man who more or less laughing would begin his rapid excuses for mistaking her for an American and then, really disconcerted, would laugh when she told him yes, in fact she was an American, and for a while he would be self-conscious since it was obvious she had lived in the country for many years making it utterly ridiculous to try to begin the conversation again with the well-worn had she been in Mexico long and did she like Mexico. But then she would raise his spirits with the never failing tactic of pressing her legs against him so he would understand this was a matter of dancing not of asking questions or tormenting himself in an effort to find things to talk about, since if it was true that feeling physical pleasure was good, what she liked best was to be carried away by the thought that her husband would be suffering as usual knowing she was in another man's arms or imagining that with this one she would use exactly the same tactics she had used with him and at this moment he would be full of resentment and anger and have another drink and after two more he would turn his back so he wouldn't see the maneuver he knew by heart and they would come to the table at prudent intervals with more distance between them than there had to be like two innocent doves and talk almost in shouts and laugh with him and then immediately skillfully move away to lose themselves beyond the most distant couples and embrace to their heart's content and kiss without saying a word but certain that in a few minutes when her husband was completely drunk they would be safe and the young national could take them all in his car with her in the front seat not close to him at all but in fact more united than ever because his right hand was searching for something between her thighs while she talked in a loud voice about trivial things like the heat or the cold, depending, while her husband pretended to be drunker than he really was with the sole object of letting them do as they pleased and seeing how far they would go

y emitiría de vez en cuando uno que otro gruñido para que Luis lo
creyera en el quinto sueño y no pensara que se daba cuenta de
nada. Después llegarían a su hotel y su marido y ella bajarían del
coche y el joven nacional se despediría y ofrecería llevar a Luis al
suyo y éste aceptaría y ellos les dirían alegremente adiós desde la
puerta hasta que el coche no arrancara, y ya solos entrarían y se
sirvirían otro whisky y él la recriminaría y le diría que era una puta
y que si creía que no la había visto restregándose contra el
mequetrefe ese, y ella negaría indignada y le contestaría que estaba
loco y que era un pobre celoso acomplejado, y entonces él la
golpearía en la cara con la mano abierta y ella trataría de arañarlo y
lo insultaría enfurecida y empezaría a desnudarse arrojando la ropa
por aquí y por allá y él lo mismo hasta que ya en la cama, empleando
toda su fuerza, la acostaría boca abajo y la azotaría con un cinturón
destinado especialmente a eso, hasta que ella se cansara del juego y
según lo acostumbrado se diera vuelta y lo recibiera sollozando no
de dolor ni de rabia sino de placer, del placer de estar una vez mas
con el único hombre que la había poseído y a quien jamás había
engañado ni pensaba engañar jamás.

—¿Me permite?—dijo en inglés el joven nacional.

and from time to time he would grunt so Luis would think he was sound asleep and wouldn't think he knew about anything. Then they would reach their hotel and she and her husband would get out of the car and the young national would say good night and offer to take Luis to his hotel and he would accept and they would happily say goodbye at the door until the car pulled away and when they were alone again they would go in and have another whiskey and he would reproach her and tell her she was a whore and did she think he hadn't seen her rubbing up against that idiot and she would deny it with indignation and say that he was crazy and that he was a poor jealous neurotic and then he would slap her face and she would try to scratch him and would insult him in a fury and begin to undress throwing her clothes around the room and he would do the same until they were in bed and using all his strength he would throw her face down and whip her with a belt made especially for the purpose until she wearied of the game and as always would turn over and let him enter sobbing not with pain or rage but with pleasure, the pleasure of being once again with the only man who had ever possessed her, the only man she had never deceived and had never even thought of deceiving.

"May I have this dance?" the young national said in English.

LA NOCHE CLARA
DE LOS CORONELES

THE COLONELS'
LAST BLAST

Jo Anne Engelbert, translator of Jorge Medina García

Jo Anne Engelbert, born in Cincinnati, Ohio, in 1943, was raised in Kentucky. She has published *Macedonio Fernández and the Spanish American Novel* and has translated works by Julio Cortázar, Isabel Allende, and Roberto Sosa. She teaches at Montclair State University in Montclair, New Jersey.

"I think I became a translator," writes Engelbert in a letter, "the night a teacher at Adelphi University gave our Spanish American literature class the assignment of translating a poem into English. I choose 'Meciendo' by Gabriela Mistral because it was short and I knew almost all the words. Within minutes of beginning, I was hopelessly hooked in the most absorbing of all pursuits. Forty years and hundreds of poems later, I am still trying to approximate Mistral's perfect little lullaby and am still awed by the complexity of tying to translate the simplest phrase from one language into another." Engelbert generally reads the text over and over "to get it into my head and to try to figure out how it works. I eventually make a very careful first draft, often quite close to the original. As soon as I think it is safe to do so, I put the original away for a time and concentrate on trying to move my successive versions progressively toward the norms of English. Whenever the translation begins to sound really terrific to me, I put it in a special drawer I have that turns great writing into gibberish. When I take it out a few days later, I sigh and begin the slow labor of making repairs. Finally, I compare the translation to the original, a terrible moment, and make more adjustments. Eventually I simply run out of time or carrot sticks, or discover I have switched from carrot sticks to Haagen Daaz, and have to stop. For me, no translation is ever really finished...Let me add that I physically sit at the computer late at night, but I am thinking about translation most of the time. Like most translators I know, I occasionally solve translation problems in my sleep." Engelbert says that she needs to feel affinity for the text, to feel that the author is totally serious about his or her use of language. "I love to translate a writer who shows me that every syllable is intended and essential."

Engelbert selected this story by Jorge Medina García because, she tells us, "it seemed like a good opportunity to introduce to readers of English a writer few people know even in Central America." Born in 1947 in San Lorenzo, Honduras, Medina García now works as a high school teacher in his home town. In 1989 he published his story collection *Pudimos haber llegado más lejos*. Since that year, when Engelbert received a copy from a friend, she had been hoping to do something with the stories. "I love their outrageous political humor and their goofy, surreal situations."

Jorge Medina García
LA NOCHE CLARA
DE LOS CORONELES

Mientras le ceñían sobre el pecho la llamativa banda presidencial, el licenciado Marco Tulio Alcántara se persuadió de que estaba respirando el aire y absorbiendo la luz del mejor día de su existencia. Alzó los brazos, dibujó la V de la victoria con dos dedos de la mano derecha y sintió en toda su piel el hormigueo rojiblanco de las banderas que atestaban el Estadio Nacional.

Cuando en sus años de adolescencia, siendo aún un pillo de barriada, reunió a sus diez más íntimos camaradas en la francachela de graduación de la secundaria y les dijo entonces, llanamente, que se proponía llegar a ser, algún día, Presidente de la República con el objeto primordial de instaurar el gobierno más democrático, independiente y civilista que se hubiese visto por estos andurriales, el carácter acrítico y la capacidad de perplejidad de su auditorio le permitió reconocer la fórmula que le abriría tantas compuertas en su azarosa vida de político de país tercermundista: hacerse tomar en serio.

El esqueleto de su proyecto era de una sencillez elemental. No habría acto en sus vidas que no estuviera encaminado al logro de dos fines: él a lograr el control total de algún partido político importante, ellos a copar la cúpula militar del país.

No los seleccionó sin criterio definido. Conocía sus debilidades y sus fuerzas, sus placeres primitivos, sus limitaciones intelectuales y sus curiosas habilidades como la capacidad de imitar voces de Saldívar, la de caminar con las manos de Calixto, la de tocar la guitarra con los pies de Medina, conocía a fondo las raíces de sus respectivas intimidades y, día con día, mes con mes, año con año, estimuló sus esfuerzos, arbitró sus pleitos, favoreció sus amoríos, toleró sus defectos y en cada uno armonizó sus complejos de inferioridad y sus contradicciones esenciales, logrando de ellos el juicio unánime de que él, indiscutiblemente, era el mejor amigo

Jorge Medina García
THE COLONELS' LAST BLAST

Translated by Jo Anne Engelbert

As the colorful presidential band was fastened across his chest, Marco Tulio Alcántara felt that he was breathing the air and absorbing the light of the best day of his life. He raised his arms, made a V for victory with two fingers of his right hand and felt his skin tingle with the red and white excitement of the flags filling the National Stadium.

The night of his high school graduation party—he was still just the neighborhood wise guy—when he gathered his buddies around him and told them outright that he was planning to become President of the Republic for the sole purpose of founding the most democratic, independent and non-military government ever known in that part of the world, he had learned something: the uncritical response of his audience, its capacity to be snowed, showed him the formula that was to open so many doors for him in his perilous career as a politician in a Third World country: the trick was to get people to take you seriously.

The plan they developed was exquisitely simple. No one would take a step that did not contribute to achieving one or the other of two goals: his, to gain total control of an important political party; theirs, to gain access to the inner sanctum of the country's military establishment.

He had not selected them at random. He knew their strengths and weaknesses, their visceral pleasures, their intellectual limitations and their peculiar talents: Saldívar's ability to imitate voices, Calixto's knack of walking on his hands, Medina's gift for playing the guitar with his feet; he knew about their friendships, their liaisons and day by day, month by month and year by year he cheered them on, facilitated their love affairs, tolerated their shortcomings. He worked hard to harmonize their hang-ups, their inferiority complexes, their contradictions and earned their

que jamás tuvieron, escapándosele no obstante un hilo de inestimable valor tanto o más que los enumerados: su extraña preferencia de andar y divertirse con gente pobre siendo hijo de uno de los hombres más ricos de la nación.

Formaron una hermandad secreta que se reunía cada semana, y en la segunda y conflictiva sesión acordaron que López, Saldívar, Pérez y Asterio se matricularían en la Escuela Militar Francisco Morazán; Medina, Cálix y George en la Escuela Militar del Norte y Antúnez, Fernández y Chévez en la Escuela de Aviación.

Esa prueba fue para Marco Tulio Alcántara la clarinada de la resurrección, pues todos ellos coincidieron en traicionar naturales vocaciones que estaban a distancias siderales de las aceptadas, tras extenuar, desde luego, los argumentos de una encarnizada defensa.

Los días subsiguientes se disolvieron en preparar los exámenes de admisión. Marco Tulio Alcántara se dio mañas para conseguir pruebas escritas de años anteriores, adquirió textos de Castellano Actual, Matemáticas Modernas, Física Simplificada, Química a su Alcance, Inglés Inmediato y Economía Política; libros de ficción como La Gesta de San Rafael de Las Mataras, Informe Militar de Los Horcones y la Constitución Política de la República, obras todas que diseccionaron en sórdidas hermenéuticas nocturnas.

Subieron cien veces a paso redoblado la cuesta de El Picacho, se adormecieron haciendo lagartijas y culucas, practicaron hasta el agotamiento boxeo, futbolito y baloncesto, se abonaron a la rueda de Chicago para tonificarse el estómago con sus vueltas alucinantes, organizaron prácticas de escupidas a la calle desde la azotea del hotel "Honduras Maya" para domesticar el vértigo, consiguieron recomendaciones y salvoconductos mágicos y al final, todos aprobaron con facilidad los exámenes a excepción de Asterio Molina, quien tras múltiples súplicas y el soborno de doscientos lempiras mensuales sacados de la bolsa de Alcántara tuvo que aceptar su ingreso al Primer Batallón de Artillería con el rango de Cabo y mientras ellos iniciaban el apostolado de la Lealtad, Honor y Sacrificio, Marco Tulio Alcántara desplegaba sus alas en la Facultad de Derecho de la Universidad Nacional Autónoma de Honduras.

unanimous conviction that he was the best friend they ever had. It somehow escaped them that he had a trait that was even more endearing: his inexplicable liking for hanging out and enjoying himself with poor folks—he, son of one of the richest men in the nation.

They created a secret society that met weekly. At the stormy second session, it was decided that López, Saldívar, Pérez and Asterio would enter the Francisco Morazán Military Academy; Medina, Cálix and George would attend the Northern Military Academy and Antúnez, Fernández and Chévez, the Air Force Academy.

For Marco Tulio Alcántara, these decisions were a critical test of his ability, and his success was a clarion call to glory, for in the end they all agreed—after a knock-down, drag-out battle—to betray their personal vocations, which were light-years away from those they accepted.

The days that followed that session were a blur of preparations for the entrance exams. Marco Tulio Alcántara managed to get hold of the written tests from previous years, bought copies of Standard Spanish, Modern Mathematics, Physics Made Simple, Chemistry at Your Fingertips, English at a Glance and Political Economy as well as fictional works like the Epic of the Soccer War, the Military Report on Los Horcones and the Constitution of the Republic, all of which they dissected in horrendous all-night cram sessions.

They ran double time up Picacho Hill a hundred times, fell asleep doing push-ups and sit-ups, practiced boxing, soccer and basketball till they dropped, rode the Ferris wheel to tone their stomach muscles on its delirious plunges, organized drills of spitting into the street from the roof of the Honduras Maya Hotel to overcome dizziness, obtained recommendations and magical letters of safe conduct and in the end, everyone passed the exams like a breeze except Asterio Molina, who after much pleading and a bribe of two hundred *lempiras* per month, which came out of Alcántara's pocket, finally agreed to enter the Artillery Battalion with the rank of corporal. And as they began the apostolate of Loyalty, Honor and Sacrifice, Marco Tulio Alcántara was trying his wings in the Law School of the Autonomous University of Honduras.

* * *

Alzó los brazos de nuevo para acallar la aullante multitud y los plagios de corridos mejicanos del partido.

—Entrañables conciudadanos hombres y mujeres. Honorables Diputados al Congreso Nacional. Honorables Miembros de la Corte Suprema de Justicia. Conspicuos Mandatarios y Representantes de los países hermanos que nos honran con su presencia. Excelentísimos Miembros del Cuerpo Diplomático. Pueblo de Honduras y pueblos del mundo entero que testifican este histórico momento por medio de los nunca bien ponderados alcances de la ciencia y la tecnología..."

* * *

No conoció el amor. Su enlace matrimonial con la que estaba llamada a ser la Primera Dama de la Nación lo hizo apresuradamente y por conveniencia. Nunca logró entender su sensiblería de poetisa de acrósticos ni mucho menos comprender a cabalidad la mediatización de la conducta de esposa con su vocación de estéril cortesana. Por el contrario, su ascenso personal en la jerarquía del Partido Liberal fue vertiginoso. Vio en esa entidad el caldo de cultivo de rencores y ambiciones particulares que más se ajustaba a sus propósitos, no por ser la institución que cobija a las milicias eternamente jóvenes o mayoritarias, como decían los periódicos locales y él mismo lo predicaba en sus campañas politiqueras.

Sus armas más afiladas las esgrimía desde su capacidad de manipulación. Poseía una oratoria sulfúrica y sus equívocas habilidades acabaron abriéndole puertas sin tocarlas, arrimándole sillas sin buscarlas y poniéndole en la mira posiciones sin solicitarlas, como aconteció con la Presidencia del Comité Central Ejecutivo al rechazar su candidatura de primer diputado por el departamento de Comayagua y se encontró sin sentirlo con la reputación intacta y los hilos completos en la mano.

* * *

He raised his arms again to silence the howling multitude and the blare of the plagiarized Mexican ballads that were his party's songs.

"Beloved fellow citizens. Honorable Deputies of the National Congress. Honorable Members of the Supreme Court. Illustrious Heads of State and Representatives of sister countries who honor us with your presence. Most Excellent Members of the diplomatic corps. People of Honduras and of the entire world who witness this historic moment through the medium of the never sufficiently understood achievements of science and technology."

* * *

He never knew love. His matrimonial liaison with the woman called to be the First Lady of the Nation was arranged hastily and for the sake of convenience. He understood neither the sensibility of this poetess of acrostic verses nor her evolution in the direction of her true vocation, that of fashionable slut. On the other hand, his ascent in the hierarchy of the Liberal Party was dizzying. He saw that entity as the perfect broth for the cultivation of the rivalries and ambitions so necessary to his ends—not as the institution that nurtured the eternal youth (the eternal majority) of the armed forces, as the local papers said and he himself proclaimed in his campaign speeches.

The sharpest weapon in his arsenal was his capacity for manipulation. He had a gift for sulfurous oratory and his equivocal skills opened doors for him that he hadn't knocked on, proffered him chairs he hadn't asked for and put in his sights positions he hadn't even sought, as happened with the Chairmanship of the Central Executive Committee when, after declining to run for first deputy of the Department of Comayagua, he suddenly found himself with his reputation intact and all the reins of power in his hands.

"...De este Estadio Nacional—templo del músculo, la bravura y la inteligencia—sólo saldremos para entrar en la página virginal de nuestra Historia. Las masas populares de Honduras inauguran hoy la primera República y el Gobierno más civilista, libre, popular y democrático desde México a la Tierra de Fuego y de más de dos cuartas partes del mundo que conocemos..."

Un muro de alaridos lo cercó.

* * *

Mucho más complicado resultó controlar a los otros copartícipes. Medina había muerto deshecho por una granada de fragmentación mientras participaba en el 905° Ejercicio Militar Conjunto "Around the eagle" con tropas norteamericanas en una montaña de Yoro. López, con todos sus esfuerzos, no logró traspasar la barrera de Teniente de Infantería, adscrito luego como Delegado de la Fuerza de Seguridad Pública en un pueblecito del departamento de Copán, y el Sargento 1° Asterio Molina despertó a última hora alarmantes sospechas de infidencia. Hacia éste dirigió entonces los golpes rítmicos de su persuasión en las reuniones ahora individuales que sostenía con los viejos y los nuevos prosélitos en la clandestinidad cada quince días, pero fue una labor de readoctrinamiento innecesaria. La sanguijuela de la traición se había incubado en el sobaco de uno de sus discípulos más amados y mejor ubicados en el gallinero militar, el Teniente Coronel de Aviación Calixto Antúnez Suazo.

A desgano había concedido una nueva audiencia a uno de los choferes privados del Ejército, quien deseaba agradecerle personalmente la beca conseguida a su hijo a través del partido.

—Ayer era que te esperaba—le dijo a modo de saludo en cuanto lo vio.

El soldado le explicó que había sido llamado a emergencia para llevar al Coronel Téllez a una reunión con el Coronel Antúnez Suazo.

—¿Se reúnen con frecuencia?—indagó el licenciado con la traza de quien finge interés por cortesía.

* * *

"...From this National Stadium—temple of muscle, courage and intelligence—we shall step out onto a virgin page of our history. On this day the people of Honduras inaugurate the First Republic and the most civilian, democratic, popular, free government anywhere from Mexico to Tierra del Fuego, anywhere in the two-fourths of the world we know..."

A wall of cheers rose around him.

* * *

Controlling the co-participants was a much more complicated affair. Medina had died, blown apart by a fragmentation grenade on a mountain in Yoro while participating in the 905th Combined Military Exercise "Around the Eagle" with US troops. López, try as he might, was unable to clear the hurdle of Lieutenant in the Infantry and ended up being stationed as a Delegate of the Public Security Force in a little town in the Department of Copán. First Sergeant Asterio Molina suddenly began to arouse suspicions of disloyalty. Tulio then began to center on him the rhythmic blows of his persuasiveness in the now separate meetings of new and old proselytes held secretly every two weeks, but the work of reindoctrination was in vain. The leech of betrayal had already fastened itself in the armpit of one of his most beloved disciples, Lieutenant Colonel of the Air Force Calixto Antúnez Suazo, who now occupied a high roost in the military henhouse.

With some annoyance he had rescheduled an appointment with one of the Army's private chauffeurs who wanted to thank him personally for the scholarship he had obtained for his son through the good offices of the party.

"You were supposed to be here yesterday," he said to him by way of greeting as soon as he came in.

The soldier explained to him that he had been called in for an emergency trip, to take Colonel Téllez to a meeting with Colonel Antúnez Suazo.

"Do they meet often?" inquired Alcántara with the air of one who makes a show of interest in order to be polite.

—Yo he ido sólo dos veces, señor—le contestó el subalterno. Alcántara sonrió.

—Son puterías—dijo—los dos se cogen a dos hermanas que viven en...

—En Zambrano—se animó el chofer—eso ha de ser porque sólo entran ellos dos a esa casa.

—No te digo pues, regresate y me seguís informando cómo le va al muchacho—le repuso despidiéndolo con una palmadita en la espalda.

No había concluido su tercera llamada telefónica en clave cuando su secretaria le anunció la invitación perentoria del Coronel Téllez, Jefe de Inteligencia Militar, para que asistiera a su despacho.

Un vehículo sin identificación ocupado por dos hombres taciturnos esperaba estacionado frente a la puerta principal de las oficinas del partido.

* * *

"...Desde que se instituyeron en el país las Fuerzas Armadas, con raras treguas de conveniencia, ningún Presidente libremente electo por el pueblo ha gobernado realmente otra cosa que no sea su dormitorio familiar, porque han sido los militares en cínica violación a los preceptos constitucionales, no un poder paralelo como se cree erróneamente, sino el único y terrible poder del Estado, maniobrado siempre por intereses extranjeros que no se han tocado jamás el alma para depositar a la patria en las aras más cimeras de la hecatombe, la indignidad y el desprestigio internacional..."

Una corriente de estupor se deslizó entre los asientos de honor, pero una gritería unánime conmovió los cimientos de las graderías donde se encaramaba el bajo pueblo embanderado.

El licenciado sonrió lleno de júbilo.

* * *

—Buena la pendejada liki—le dijo el Coronel Téllez, fumándose un puro—lo creí un hombre de honor y me resulta usted un sinvergüenza y un papo.

—¿Lo sabe alguien más Coronel?—repuso Alcántara sentándose sin invitación.

"I have only gone there twice, sir," his subaltern answered. Alcántara smiled.

"Probably whoring. They've been balling a couple of sisters who live in..."

"Zambrano," offered the driver. "That must be it, because they both go to the same house."

"Didn't I tell you? Well, you run along and be sure to let me know how that son of yours is doing," he said, dismissing him with a pat on the shoulder.

He had not completed his third encoded phone call when his secretary announced a peremptory invitation from Colonel Téllez, Chief of Military Intelligence, to go to his office.

An unmarked vehicle occupied by two taciturn men was parked in front of the main entrance of party headquarters.

* * *

"In the entire history of the Armed Forces in this country, with only rare moments of truce, not a single President freely elected by the people has really governed anything more than the family bedroom, because the military, in cynical violation of constitutional principles, have not been a parallel power as is mistakenly believed, but the one and only terrible power of the state, manipulated by foreign interests who have never hesitated to lead the country directly to the slaughterhouse, disgraced in the eyes of the world..."

A current of disbelief rippled along the seats of honor, but a unanimous cheer shook the foundations of the bleachers where the poor sat clutching their flags.

* * *

"Nice try, sport. You are a piece of work," Colonel Téllez told him, puffing on a cigar. "I thought you could be trusted, but you turn out to be a son-of-a bitch and dumb as dog dirt."

"Does anybody else know, Colonel?" Alcántara asked, sitting down without waiting to be invited.

—Negativo liki pero en veinte minutos destapo la olla, me cago en ustedes y me arreglo el pecho para la condecoración.

—Bueno Coronel, a usted le he dispensado admiración y aprecio y le daré una oportunidad—expresó Alcántara como hablándose a sí mismo.

—Déjese de mierdas. Solo quiero que me dé una confesión completa por las buenas para no tener que sacársela por las malas— barbotó el militar, comenzando a perder la serenidad—. No me va a negar que usted es un traidor a la patria que planeaba dominar las Fuerzas Armadas infiltrándonos unos pelagatos que sólo han ascendido por nuestra buena voluntad y solidaridad de soldados. No me ha de negar que quiere ser Presidente de la República para cambiar las estructuras democráticas que disfrutamos. ¿O niega que quiere implantar un gobierno comunista cumpliendo consignas exóticas de malos hondureños?...¡Ah pendejo! Usted no es más que un tonto útil. ¿Cree que me estoy chupando el dedo?

El licenciado Marco Tulio ratificó su opinión de que no estaba hablando precisamente con un caballero. Se inclinó sobre su interlocutor con la elegancia que desplegaba en las cenas diplomáticas, pero esta vez con un fulgor demoníaco en la mirada y sin tomar aliento y sosteniendo la dureza de sus ojos en las adiposidades visuales del militar, le dijo:

—Escúcheme bien barrigón estúpido. En este momento su confidente, el coronelito Antúnez, está siendo sacado con acetileno del amasijo de hierro de su carro, que tuvo la desgracia de chocar contra un camión de asalto del ejército, y mire lo que son las cosas, en una revisión a fondo le hallarán una buena cantidad de cocaína y algunos papeles comprometedores donde estará su nombre, Coronel. Se descubrirán algunas inexplicables citas en una solitaria casa de Zambrano y mire qué cosa, también hallarán polvo—se le arrimó más aún—. ¿Sabrá el inteligente Coronel Téllez que todo está prácticamente consumado? No, usted no sabe que contamos con las comandancias de cinco Batallones de Infantería y dos de Artillería, con la Fuerza Naval, la Fuerza Aérea, el Comando en Jefe del Estado Mayor, y no lo sabe porque no confían en su lengua como yo no confié en Antúnez, pero debe entender, guerrero de escritorio, que estamos construyendo una revolución pacífica sin parangón en América Latina, que estamos destruyendo el mito de

"Negative, sport, but in twenty minutes I'm going to blow the lid off of everything, shit all over you creeps and get my chest ready for a decoration."

"Well, Colonel, I've always admired and appreciated you and now I'm going to give you an opportunity," said Alcántara as if talking to himself.

"Cut the shit. I only want you to confess nice and easy so I don't have to bother getting rough," the officer muttered, beginning to lose patience. "You can't deny that you're a traitor to the country and that you were going to take over the Armed Forces by bringing in a bunch of assholes who have only been promoted out of the kindness of our hearts. You can't deny that you want to be President of the Republic in order to change the democratic structure we enjoy. Or do you deny that you want to set up a communist government that will carry out the alien orders of bad Hondurans?...You stupid prick. You're nothing but a useful moron. Do you think I sucked this out of my thumb?"

Marco Tulio confirmed his impression that he was not talking to what one might refer to as a perfect gentleman. He leaned toward his interlocutor with the demeanor he displayed at diplomatic dinners, but this time with a demonic gleam in his eye; without pausing to breathe and fixing the steel of his gaze on the adipose pouches that were the eyes of the officer, he said:

"Listen to me, you potbellied piece of shit. At this moment your confidant, dear Colonel Antúnez, is being extracted with acetylene from the wad of metal that used to be his car, which had the misfortune of colliding with an army personnel carrier and—funny how things work out—the inspection of the wreckage is going to turn up a large quantity of cocaine and a bunch of compromising papers with your name on them, Colonel. They will lead to the discovery of some unexplainable meetings in an isolated house in Zambrano and, you know what else? A stash of explosives." He moved even closer to him. "I wonder if brilliant Colonel Téllez knows that the whole operation is practically complete. No, you don't know, how could you? that we can count on the top command of five infantry battalions and two artillery battalions, the Navy, the Air Force, the Chief of Staff and the reason you don't know it is that they don't trust your tongue—just like I couldn't trust Antúnez, but you should understand, you paper-pushing wonder, that we are

que los verdaderos patriotas sólo podrán tomar el poder con la fuerza de las armas, que sacaremos a la patria del lupanar donde la han metido y la presentaremos de nuevo al mundo digna y respetada sin derramar una gota de sangre. ¡Despierte Coronel!—alentó— Sienta de qué lado sopla el viento y elévese con nosotros. Si cree que yo le miento, llame al General Cruz. Tome ese teléfono y hágalo ahora mismo porque ya no hay tiempo para usted, óigame bien, sólo yo estoy creyendo contra el criterio de sus colegas que puede sernos útil y que será leal. Llame, porque su tiempo se termina y después será imposible salvarlo...¡Llame, desgraciado, que nada le cuesta!!—bramó el licenciado fuera ya de sí.

El Coronel Téllez vio el teléfono de soslayo como si fuera un platillo volador, trató de rehacerse y de recuperar su vanidad herida de profesional asignado a la inteligencia militar. Lo intentaba aún cuando marcó el número telefónico.

—¿Mi General?—se envaró—, el Coronel Téllez, señor. Tengo aquí al licenciado Alcántara porque detecté una maniobra de peligro extremo. Pero me ha cantado...—palideció notablemente— ¡Positivo, señor!...Perdone, señor...Así lo haré, mi General...¡A la orden, mi General!!—y se derrumbó en el asiento casi loco.

Alcántara quedó convencido una vez más de que el Teniente Coronel DEM Efraín Saldívar, Secretario Privado del Señor Jefe de Estado Mayor del Ejército de la República, seguía conservando la eficacia de sus habilidades para imitar en forma convincente hasta la voz de su jefe y tuvo la clarividencia de presentir que el Coronel Téllez llegaría a ser uno de los mejores cuadros políticos de su causa.

* * *

"...Ese baldón, como la clásica y mitológica ave de negro plumaje, se esfumó, esta vez de verdad—aclaró—porque las Fuerzas Armadas están ahora comandadas por legítimos patriotas, por guerreros heroicos de estirpe espartana..."

* * *

Más tarde se produjo la elección condicionada del nuevo Jefe de las Fuerzas Armadas por el Congreso Nacional con mayoría a su favor.

building a peaceful revolution without parallel in any country of Latin America. We are destroying the myth that real patriots can only take power by armed force. We are going to take the country out of the cathouse you put it in and give it back to the world clean and worthy of respect—without shedding one drop of blood. Wake up, Colonel! See which way the wind is blowing. Stand up and be counted alongside us. If you think I'm lying, call General Cruz. Pick up the telephone and do it, because your time is running out. You'd better listen, because unlike your colleagues, I think you could be useful to us and that you have the capacity to be loyal. Make the call, because time is short and later I won't be able to save you... Call, you stupid bastard, what have you got to lose?" bellowed Alcántara, beside himself.

Colonel Téllez looked at the telephone obliquely, as if it were a flying saucer, tried to compose himself and to recover his shattered pride as an intelligence professional. He was still working on this when his finger began to dial the number.

"General?" He squared his shoulders. "Colonel Téllez, sir. I have brought in Marco Tulio Alcántara because I detected an extremely dangerous maneuver. But he told me..." He paled noticeably. "Affirmative, sir. I'm sorry, sir... I'll do that, my General... At your orders, General." He fell back in his chair with a crazed look.

Alcántara was reassured that Lieutenant Colonel Efraín Saldívar, Private Secretary of the Chief-of-Staff of the Army of the Republic, was as good as ever at imitating voices, even that of his boss. He also had the clear premonition that Colonel Téllez would become one of the most stalwart pillars of his cause.

* * *

"...That stain on our honor, like the mythological bird of black plumage, has vanished, this time for good," he explained, "because the Armed Forces are now commanded by genuine patriots, by heroic warriors of Spartan stripe..."

* * *

A little later, the election of the new Chief of the Armed Forces was carried out by the National Congress with a majority in his favor.

El cultivo de los más variados matices de la clientela política. Los nombramientos, ascensos y cambios de oficiales, clases y soldados que se materializaron por intermedio de sugerencias manejadas subterráneamente por el licenciado Alcántara y finalmente la candidatura, su elección y la consolidación definitiva de sus ocho camaradas del alma en la cúpula militar.

* * *

"...No sólo porque los hombres de uniforme, brazo armado del pueblo y apoyo logístico de la justicia, han sido tocados por el hálito de los grandes soldados americanistas desde Morazán hasta Bolívar, sino porque el pueblo, motor y combustible de las más altas transformaciones sociales de la Historia, han electo como Presidente de la República a un hombre que tiene bien amarrados los pantalones".

Era cierto. Cuando la bomba estalló bajo la tribuna presidencial y la onda expansiva lanzó por los aires el cuerpo desarticulado del licenciado Marco Tulio Alcántara y cayeron en el centro del engramado del Estadio Nacional la pelvis y las extremidades inferiores, la muchedumbre pudo ver los pantalones de gala deshechos y ensangrentados, pero eso sí, bien amarrados.

Cultivation of political supporters of the most varied hue. Appointments, promotions and transfers of officers and soldiers, managed behind the scenes by Alcántara, and finally, his candidacy, his election and the consolidation of his eight bosom friends in the cupola of military power.

* * *

"...Not only because men in uniform, heroic defenders of the people and logistical support for the judiciary, have been inspired by the great Americanist soldiers, from Francisco Morazán to Simón Bolívar, but because the people, engine and fuel of the greatest social transformation in History, have elected as President of the Republic a man who has his trousers on tight."

It was true. When the bomb exploded under the presidential tribune, sending skyward the dismembered body of Marco Tulio Alcántara, his pelvis and lower extremities landed on the well-manicured turf of the National Stadium, and the crowd could see that his elegant striped trousers, though bloody and ripped to shreds, were indeed on tight.

Tres pesadillas

Three Nightmares

Harry Morales, translator of Ilan Stavans

Harry Morales lives in New York City. He has translated works by Reinaldo Arenas and Mario Benedetti. Morales says that tuning his skills as a translator, a career he began in 1989, "out of pure curiosity," is like developing film in "complete darkness." In his own words, there is "something emotionally attractive and comforting about hearing how a section of text, whether in prose or poetry, written in Spanish, sounds in English." This sounding-out process, for Morales, begins with drafting a first version, usually without reading the whole text he has made a commitment to translate. The act of translation, thus, constitutes something of a leap of faith. His translation of poetry and short stories by Uruguayan Mario Benedetti, along with an in-progress translation of Benedetti's novel, *La tregua*, are the products of this sort of enriching relationships.

Morales first became acquainted with Ilan Stavans, a Mexican novelist born in 1961, as a neighbor in Manhattan's Upper West Side. Stavans's books in English include *Imagining Columbus*, *Growing Up Latino*, *Tropical Synagogues* and *The Hispanic Condition*, and he is a recipient of the Latino Literature Prize and has been nominated to the National Book Critics Circle Award. One day Morales asked to translate a story or two ("I truly enjoy this kind of fiction in Spanish," he adds, "which very rarely one comes across in English"), and these were published in *TriQuarterly*, the *Literary Review*, and other journals, and are now part of Stavans's *The One-Handed Pianist and Other Stories*. The two have since collaborated on various projects. Morales writes: "There is no question that the translator has to respect, enjoy, and believe in the author's work—that, in fact, is a sine qua non turning a mere professional activity into an artistic endeavor."

Ilan Stavans
TRES PESADILLAS

Recordar a Betzi es invocar tres pesadillas, con sus interludios. Ninguna da suficientes detalles sobre nuestra relación. Lo sé. Quizás esconden su significado. La verdad es que tampoco yo entiendo detalles. Vivir con Betzi fue para mí una manera de funcionar. Mientras la tuve, sus besos y caricias despertaban sensaciones deliciosas. Daba mi reino por prolongarlas. Pero vino después el chubasco de discordias. Nos gritamos, nos dijimos, nos desdijimos y todo se volvió caos. Dejé de entender. Hoy me he curado de las caricias, pero no de los sueños.

* * *

Todo comenzó cuando irresponsablemente perdí nuestro anillo de compromiso. Era un anillo sencillo de oro. Lo habíamos adquirido en una joyería pequeña, abarrotada, del centro. No pude recordar dónde lo extravié. ¿En la oficina? ¿Durante algún almuerzo? Lo busqué hasta el cansancio y regrese a casa avergonzado, con la intención de explicarle lo sucedido a Betzi. Se enfureció. Pegó un grito del tamaño del mundo. Me disculpé. ¿Qué podía hacer? Prometí buscarlo mejor. Jamás pensé que el incidente pudiera alcanzar tales connotaciones. En f una noche después, tras una agitada sesión de póker. Nos habíamos reunido en casa varios cuates. Compramos whisky, tequila, aperitivos que la sirvienta mejoró con queso, cebolla y salsas. Bebimos bastante. Era después de las 12:00. Betzi había llegado tarde y de mal humor de la oficina. Parecía tener resortes en la cara, muecas gruñonas, pétreas. A mí se me estaba subiendo el alcohol. Estaba mareado, con la difusa sensación de ahogarme en una pecera. Barajas iban. Venían. Ruido. El agudo golpeteo de dos botellas que se estrellaban. Humo de cigarros. Quise vomitar y, disculpándome, corrí al baño a encerrarme durante

Ilan Stavans
THREE NIGHTMARES
Translated by Harry Morales

To remember Betzi is to invoke three nightmares, with their interludes. None of them give enough details about our relationship, I know. Perhaps they even hide its significance. The truth is that I don't understand details either. Living with Betzi was a way of functioning for me. While we were together, her kisses and caresses would awaken delightful feelings. I would turn over my realm if I could prolong them. But then came the shower of disagreements. We shouted at each other, cursed at each other, contradicted each other and everything turned into chaos. I stopped understanding. Today I'm cured of the caresses, but not of the dreams.

* * *

It all started when I irresponsibly lost my wedding ring. It was a plain gold ring. We had bought it at a small, cramped downtown jewelry store. I couldn't remember when and where I misplaced it. In the office? During lunch? I looked for it until I was exhausted and returned home feeling ashamed, with the intention of explaining to Betzi what had happened. She was furious and let out a scream as big as the world. I apologized. What could I do? While I did promise to look for it better, I never thought the incident could have such connotations. Well, the first nightmare occurred the following night, after an exciting game of poker. Several friends of mine and I had gathered together at home. We bought whiskey, tequila, and appetizers that the maid improved with cheese, onions, and dip. We drank quite a bit. It was after midnight. Betzi had arrived home late from the office and in a bad mood. She seemed to have springs in her face and a grumpy, stony grimace. The alcohol was starting to go to my head. I was dizzy and had the vague sensation that I was drowning in a fish tank. Packs of cards would go. Come back. Noise. The piercing rattling of two bottles that would shatter. Cigarette smoke. I wanted to vomit and, excusing myself, ran to the bathroom and locked myself in for fifteen

quince minutos. Exacto quince minutos devolví el estómago. El foco sobre el espejo me hería la vista. Sentía escalofríos. Betzi me gritaba, «¿estás bien, Messeguer?». Sentía vergüenza, «Sí...», le contesté. Ahora que reflexiono, sé que Betzi me controlaba como una bruja. Más tarde tocó a la puerta. Le abrí. Me observó y corrió al comedor donde estaban los amigos. «Vaya alguien a la farmacia», dijo. «Necesito una botella de leche de magnesia para Messeguer...» ¡Qué vergüenza! Emborracharse es uno de los más duros desafíos...y yo fracasé. ¿Desde cuándo no bebía? Tiempo suficiente para perder la resistencia...para volver a ser niño. Hubiera querido vomitarle a Betzi mi incomodidad. Una ducha no me hubiera caído mal pero ni siquiera lograba abrir el grifo. Esperé a que Betzi viniera a curarme. Después salí y estuve derrumbado en el sofá. Desaparecieron mis amigos. ¿Había terminado el juego? En mis tímpanos algodonados, las voces sonaban como chillidos de rata, como cerraduras oxidadas. Fue entonces cuando tuve la pesadilla, que de un salto me hizo despertar. Habrán pasado horas. Betzi estaba en la recámara. Subí las escaleras. El cuarto estaba a oscuras. Me escabullí cabizbajo entre las sábanas. «Muy calladito, ¿eh?», balbució. Temblaba mi corazón. «Taquicardia», le respondí. «Me duelen los pulmones. Mi corazón sistea demasiado. Fueron esos aperitivos que sirvió la sirvienta. Me provocaron una horrenda pesadilla.» Ella prendió la lámpara. «Plaltícame». Me resistí. «Cálmate... ya, ya...», me arruyaba. «Estás nervioso. Perdiste el ritmo. ¿Que sucedió?» Entonces le platiqué la secuencia del sueño: estaba en un cuarto sombrío, pardo, con paredes altísimas, heladas. No era un cuarto sino un almacén. O un refrigerador. Uno de esos viejos refrigeradores que apestan a humedad porque el dueño ha olvidado limpiarlo. Sentía sofocación. Buscaba alguna ventana o puerta, un espacio para respirar. Nada. ¿Por qué estaba enlatado en esa caja? Había un banco de madera al centro. ¿Sentarme? Caminaba en círculos, sin dirección, como un loco. Caminaba rodeando al banco. De pronto, un guardia uniformado con guantes, casco con visera y botas aparecía en la esquina. Sus pupilas seguían el compás de mis talones, la coyuntura de mis rodillas. Uno, dos... Uno, dos... Uno, dos... Absurda circunstancia. Uno, dos... Uno, dos... Me acercaba a él pero me rehuía. Seguro estaba prohibido mezclarse con los reos.

minutes. For exactly fifteen minutes I threw up my stomach. The light bulb over the mirror hurt my eyes. I felt chills. Betzi was shouting at me, saying, "Are you all right, Messeguer?" "Yes," I replied, feeling embarrassed. (Now that I think about it, I know that Betzi controlled me like a witch.) Later on she knocked on the door. I opened it, she looked at me and ran into the dining room where my friends were. "Someone go to the drug store," she said. "I need a bottle of milk of magnesia for Messeguer..." How embarrassing! Getting drunk is one of the hardest challenges a man can undergo...and I had failed. How long had it been since I last drank? Long enough to lose my resistance...to become a child again. To be honest, I would have wanted to vomit my discomfort at Betzi. A shower wouldn't have done me any harm, but I didn't even manage to open the faucet. I waited for Betzi to come and cure me. I later came out of the bathroom and collapsed on the sofa. My friends disappeared. Had the game ended? In my cotton-filled eardrums the voices sounded like squeaking rats, like rusty locks. That was when I had the nightmare that woke me in a single bound. Hours had gone by. Betzi was in the bedroom. I walked up the stairs. The room was dark. Depressed, I slipped into bed between the sheets. "Very quiet, aren't you?" she stammered. My heart trembled. "Tachycardia," I replied. "My lungs hurt. My heart beats too fast. It was those appetizers that the maid served. They provoked a horrible nightmare." She turned the lamp on. "Talk to me," she said. I resisted. "Relax... now, now...," she said, soothing me. "You're nervous. You lost your rhythm. What happened? Then I told her the sequence of the dream: I was in a grayish room, with very high walls, frozen. Actually, it wasn't a room but a warehouse. Or a refrigerator. One of those old refrigerators that smell damp because the owner forgot to clean it. I felt I was suffocating. I looked for some window or door, an area in which I could breathe. Nothing. Why was I encased in that box? In the center of the box there was a wooden bench. Should I sit down? I walked around in circles, without direction, like a madman. I walked around the bench. Suddenly, a uniformed guard, wearing gloves, a helmet with a visor, and boots, appeared at the corner. His pupils followed the outline of my heels, the joints of my knees. One, two... One, two... One, two... Absurd situation. One, two... One, two... I would approach him, but he would back away. Surely he was prohibited to mingle

Enguantadas, sus manos detenían su cinturón...o el cinturón las manos. Tenía un bigote hirsuto, convexo. «Oiga», le decía. Pero me ignoraba. Cerca de mí descubrí un portafolios. Era uno barato, oficial, de fabricación italiana, con una franja verdeamarillenta en sus costados. Antes no había estado ahí, seguro. Me intrigaba su contenido. Sin tener todavía la oportunidad de acercarme, un monstruo abominable brotaba de su interior. Era transparente. Tenía una docena de tentáculos en cada lado, y joyas. Perlas y anillos con diamantes, con gemas hindues, con rubíes, le colgaban de la nariz, las orejas y la cabellera. No era pelo lo que florecía en su cabeza: eran cables, miles de cables multicolores de distinto calibre. Un adefesio mohoso, putrefacto. Sus pestañas largas, negruzcas, estaban envueltas entre bulbos eléctricos. Era una medusa mecánica que vomitaba (igual que yo en el baño), no residuos estomacales, sino semen. Escupía semen al hablar mientras sus tentáculos oscilaban campantes, de acá para allá, encogiéndose como gusanos. «Benito Messeguer, hemos decidido su sentencia.» Pronunciaba mi nombre, lo que implicaba que sabía quién era. «Deberá usted presentar en el plazo de una semana tres cartas de recomendación.» ¿Tres cartas? ¿Por qué? ¿Dirigidas a quién? «Messeguer, tenga en consideración lo que digo. Esto no es una broma. Su vida corre peligro. Usted perdió ese anillo y merece los peores castigos. Queremos ayudarlo. Queremos que traiga esas cartas. A través de ellas podremos comprobar que usted merece perpetuarse...seguir siendo Benito Messeguer... ¿Entiende?» No, no entendía. No había sospechado siquiera la relación del refrigerador con el anillo. «Esto es una pesadilla. ¿Sabe lo que es una pesadilla? Recibimos reportes de mala conducta. Usted es igual a toda la gente, Messeguer, pero un poco más. No le permitiremos mayores libertinajes. ¿Desea seguir siendo usted? Muy bien...entonces, ¡comprométase!» Estaba confundido. ¿De que me culpaban? «Conviene no pasarse de listo. La gente de su calaña merece las cloacas, arrastrarse como un reptil. Nosotros vamos a darle una tentadita en el culo.» Yo miraba soslayadamente al guardia, quien hasta entonces había estado distraído y que ahora, complaciente, aplaudía las palabras de su jefe. «Le advierto, Messeguer, que repelar no le servirá. Tenemos espías colocados en sitios estratégicos. Siguen cada uno de sus actos. Conocen lo que conoce su mente.» Sentí vértigo y respondí: «No

with the prisoners. With gloves on, his hands held up his belt...or perhaps his belt held up his hands. He had a hairy, curved mustache. "Listen," I told him. But he would ignore me. Nearby, I discovered a briefcase. It was inexpensive, conventional, and Italian-made, with a greenish-yellow band on the side. Surely it hadn't been there before. I was intrigued by its contents. But before I even had the chance to approach it, an abominable monster, a strange medusa, sprung out of its interior. Transparent, it had a dozen tentacles on each side of its body, and wore jewelry. Pearls and rings with diamonds, Hindu gems and rubies were hanging from its nose, ears, and long hair. But it wasn't hair that flourished on its head: it was cables, miles of multicolored cables of different calibre. A moldy, rotten and ridiculous looking sight. Its long, blackish eyelashes were surrounded by electric bulbs. It was a mechanical medusa that vomited (like me in the bathroom), not stomach residue, but semen. It spit semen when it spoke while its tentacles oscillated happily, to and fro, contracting like worms. "Benito Messeguer, we've decided on your sentence." He was saying my name, which implied that he knew who I was. "You have one week to present three letters of recommendation." Three letters? Why? Addressed to whom? "Messeguer, think about what I'm saying. This isn't a joke. Your life is in danger. You lost that ring and deserve the worst punishments. We want to help you. We want you to bring those letters. Through those letters we can prove that you deserve to go on living interminably...to continue being Benito Messeguer...understand?" No, I didn't understand. I hadn't even realized the connection between the refrigerator and the ring. "This is a nightmare. Do you know what a nightmare is? We receive reports of bad behavior. You're just like everyone else, Messeguer, and then some. We won't allow serious depravity. Would you like to continue being Benito Messeguer? Very well then..., commit yourself!" I was confused. What were they blaming me of? "It's advisable that you not be too clever. People like you deserve to be in the sewers, crawling like reptiles. We're going to give you a little pat on the rear." I was looking at the guard out of the corner of my eye, who until then had been daydreaming and that now, obligingly, applauded his bosses' words. "I warn you, Messeguer, refusing won't do you any good. We have spies placed in strategic areas. They're following your every move. They know what your mind knows." I felt dizzy and replied: "I don't

pienso cooperar». La medusa se enfurecía. «Messeguer, ¡por favor! Sepa que al no cooperar, estará cooperando con nosotros mucho mejor. Recuerde: tres cartas de recomendación en una semana. Y sea estólido, amigo. Vamos, despiértese. La semana acaba de comenzar.»

Betzi soltó una carcajada. Se burlaba y su sonrisa me inspiraba todavía más terror. «Te matarán», anunció. «No sabes siquiera con que pretexto pedir esas cartas. ¡Estás jodido, Messeguer!, y se le escurrían lágrimas de risa. «Pero...si acaso te matan», pronunció luego con majestuosidad, «ten por seguro que lo harán de la forma más delicada posible». «¿De qué hablas?», le pregunté. «¿Te has vuelto loca? Tú pareces espiar para ellos.» Siguió Betzi: «¡Ese es tu castigo por haber perdido el anillo!». Detestable me resultaba la discusión, detestable Betzi. Todavía se dio el lujo de terminar: «¡Lástima, Benito! Servirías mejor estando en la basura». Sentí una furia inaudita. «¡Cállate!», dije. «¡Cállate! Me vas a destrozar. Eres una bruja. ¡Déjame tranquilo, por favor!» Salí del cuarto aventando la puerta. Hubiera querido matarla.

* * *

En los días siguientes me descubrí ahuyentando fantasmas que se posaban en mis rodillas y sombras que me atacaban. (Lo sé: no existen los fantasmas, por eso los ahuyentaba.) Sentía embrutecer. Perder los estribos. Existen hombres resistentes que saben amar...y otros débiles, pigmeos, que son atrapados por la pasión. Mi amor por Betzi era el espejo fidedigno de mis incapacidades y temores. Conforme caminaban los días ella actuaba más y más extrañamente. Se levantaba del desayuno sin darme mi beso acostumbrado de despedida. Se metía en el grueso abrigo de piel de zorro, se perfumaba mientras fruncía el ceño, asquerosa. Sí, ninguneándome. Dolido, tristón, me encerraba en el baño. Me encerraba más de quince minutos. No salía aunque sonara el teléfono. O me rasuraba por horas. Dejé de ir a trabajar. Si llamaban del despacho, no contestaba. ¿Y si la sirvienta fuera un espía?, me preguntaba. Todo era confusión. Betzi también telefoneaba. Preguntaba si el tanque

plan to cooperate." The medusa was becoming furious. "Messeguer, please! Know that by not cooperating, you'll be helping us even more. Remember: three letters of recommendation in one week. Come now, my friend, wake up. The week has just begun."

Betzi burst out laughing. She was making fun of me and her smile was terrifying. "They'll kill you," she announced. "You don't even know under what pretext you should ask for those letters of recommendation. You're screwed, Messeguer!" And as she said this, tears of laughter trickled down her face. "But...in case they do kill you," she then said with dignity, "make sure they do it in the most delicate way possible." "What are you talking about?" I asked. "Have you gone crazy? You seem to be spying for them." And Betzi continued: "That's your punishment for having lost the ring." The discussion and Betzi were both proving to be detestable. Still, she gave herself the luxury of finishing, by saying: "What a pity, Benito! You would be better off dead." I felt an unprecedented rage. "Shut up," I said. "Shut up. You're going to destroy me. You're a witch. Please, leave me alone." I left the room, slamming the door behind me. I wanted to kill her.

* * *

In the days that followed I found myself driving away ghosts that perch themselves on my knees and shadows that attack me. (I know ghosts don't exist, that's why I would drive them away.) I felt like brutalizing someone, like losing control. There exist resistant men who know how to love...and others who are weaker, and dwarfish, who are trapped by passion. My love for Betzi was the trustworthy mirror of my inabilities and fears. Similar were the days that went by during which she acted more and more strangely. She would get up from eating breakfast without giving me my customary good-bye kiss. And she would get into her heavy fox fur coat, and would put perfume on while she frowned, loathsome—yes, ignoring me. Hurt and very sad, I would lock myself in the bathroom for more than fifteen minutes and wouldn't come out even if the telephone rang. Or I would shave for hours. I even stopped going to work. If they would call from the office, I wouldn't come to the phone. And what if the maid was a spy?, I would ask myself. Everything was in a state of confusion. At noon, Betzi would also call. She would ask if

de gas estaba lleno o si las cobijas estaban oreándose...y sólo al final, al colgar, preguntaba por mí. Una vez le contesté el teléfono: «¿Por qué no te despediste?» le dije. Ella respondió cualquier insensatez y luego yo de nuevo: «¿Qué crees que hagan conmigo, Betzi, si no entrego esas cartas de recomendación?». «Messeguer, eres un imbécil», y cortó la comunicación. Me llamó imbécil.

Mi mente comenzó a tramar solicitudes, a imaginar parientes o allegados a quien pudiera pedirles cartas. Tenía que buscar a alguien que me conociera bien. Que me tuviera confianza. Pensé en los amigos del póker, en mi jefe en la oficina. En mi hermano. ¿Y qué iba a decirles? Pensarían que había perdido la razón. (¿La había perdido?) ¿Qué necesitas probar, Messeguer?, me dirían.

Una mañana subí al camión de la ruta No. 5, el que todas las mañanas me llevaba al despacho. Fue horrible. Los pasajeros me observaban. Parecían espías al servicio de la medusa. Una niña vigilaba mis manos y su madre tenía la atención centrada en mi zipper. (Pensé por un momento que lo traía abierto, pero no.) Otro sujeto con corbata de moño doblaba la boca hacia abajo. Me tenía lástima. Incluso el chófer, al pagarle, me aventó el cambio. Quería evitar tocarme. «¡Aléjense!», les grité sin contenerme más. Una anciana quiso ayudarme. La empujé. Bajé del camión. Me tumbé en un camellón público. Tenía dolor de cabeza. Estaba agotado. Regresé a la casa. La sirvienta me abrió la puerta porque no podía encontrar la llave. Me vio con ojos temerosos. Es chistoso: tenía tomado del manguillo en la mano derecha una maleta. Hubiera jurado que era el portafolios de la medusa. «Habló la señora Betzi», dijo. «Ha tenido que partir rumbo a Rotschester. Es un congreso innacional.» Deduje que innacional quería decir internacional. Sonaba simpática la palabra: innacional. Betzi era modista. Diseñaba vestidos para invierno, cinturones, zapatos. Sus compromisos profesionales la hacían viajar con frecuencia, alejarse. Entendí el mensaje. Entendí que los congresos internacionales pueden improvisarse. ¿Que hacía la sirvienta con aquella maleta? «¿En dónde la has obtenido?», le pregunté. «Estará dos días en Rotschester. Dijo la señora que tenía

the gas tank was full or if the bed clothes were being aired out...and only at the end, when she was about to hang up, would she ask about me. One time I answered her phone call, saying: "Why didn't you say good-bye?" She replied with whatever stupidity and then again I said: "What do you think they'll do to me, Betzi, if I don't turn in those letters of recommendation?" "Messeguer, you're an imbecile," she replied, and then she cut me off. She had called me an imbecile.

My mind started to plan requests, think of relatives or close friends of whom I could ask for letters of recommendation. I had to look for someone who knew me well, who had confidence in me. I thought about my poker friends, my boss at the office, my brother. And what was I going to tell them? They would think that I had lost my mind. (Had I?) What do you need to prove, Messeguer?, they would ask.

One morning I got on the route number 5 bus, the same bus that would take me to the office every morning. It was horrible. The passengers were watching me. They looked like spies who were working for the medusa. A little girl kept looking at my hands, while her mother had her attention focused on my zipper. (For a moment I thought it was open, but no.) Another individual wearing a silly tie was bending his mouth downward. He felt sorry for me. Even the bus driver, when I went to pay him, waved away the change. He avoided touching me. "Go away!" I shouted, without holding myself back any longer. An old woman tried to help me, but I pushed her. I got off the bus and stumbled into a concrete median. I had a headache and I was exhausted. I returned home and the maid had to open the door for me because I couldn't find the key. She looked at me with fearful eyes. It's funny: hanging from a handle in her right hand was a suitcase. I could have sworn that it was the medusa's briefcase. "Ms. Betzi called," she said. "She's had to leave for Rochester. It's a *ternational* conference." I deduced that *ternational* meant international. Ternational: the word sounded nice. Betzi was a fashion designer. She designed winter dresses, belts, and shoes. Her professional commitments would call for her to travel frequently, go away. I understood the message. I understood that international conferences could be improvised. What was the maid doing with that suitcase? "Where did you get it," I asked her. "She'll be in Rochester for two days," said the lady who owned an inn... She

un inn...» Repetía mecánicamente la misma frase. «Te he preguntado algo distinto», dije. «¿De dónde sacaste esa petaca?» ¿Qué petaca? ¿Cuál maleta? La sirvienta tenía las manos vacías. Yo había soñado. Mi garganta estaba seca. «¿Qué le pasa, señor Messeguer?», me preguntó. Había sido un tipo normal hasta anteayer y ahora estaba bajando la guardia. Tomé dos aspirinas. «¿Dos?» Tomé también una cápsula de antibiótico que sobraba en el botiquín y me eché a dormir.

* * *

Aquella tarde llamó mi hermano. «Benito, ¿por qué no estás en el despacho?» «Necesito de favor una carta de recomendación tuya», le dije. «Estoy dejando de ser quien soy», y revelé mis trances, las alucinaciones. «Has perdido la sesera, querido. Es Betzi, que te está embrujando.» Me puse a la defensiva: «No, ella es inocente. Es la crisis de la edad adulta. Tengo miedo». «Despreocúpate. Sepárate de esa mujer, yo sé lo que te digo. Jamás fuiste tan frágil. Tenías fama de responsable. ¡Despreocúpate! Gente muere de tifoidea, de cáncer...nunca de haber soñado una pesadilla...y menos debiendo tres cartas de recomendación.» Se rió. La conversación era alentadora. Una palabra hacía eco en mi mente: frágil...frágil. Colgué el auricular y de inmediato sentí una mejoría. Es una convalecencia del alma, pensé. Debo recuperarme. Tu hermano tiene razón: tienes miedo de Betzi. Ella te ha embrujado. Esa insatisfacción íntima está generando esta secuencia de espantos... Debes apaciguar tu ansiedad.

Otros tres días pasaron sin Betzi, sin controlar la paciencia. Sin lógica. Tres días absurdos. Seguí buscando el anillo. Escombré la oficina, el sótano de la casa—donde había arreglado una podadora. Mandé colocar unos anuncios clasificados en el periódico Excélsior. Nada. Decidí entonces comprar otro anillo. Es necesario, me dije. Su materia escondía secretos tonificantes. Reemplazarlo me devolvería la felicidad perdida. Fui a la misma joyería del centro. Describí al vendedor exacto lo que quería: un anillo sencillo, nada lujoso aunque de oro, sustituto del anterior. Habían discontinuado el modelo pero podían imitarlo bajo pedido. Costaría más, el doble.

mechanically repeated the same phrase. "That's not what I asked you," I said. "Where did you get that suitcase?" "Which suitcase?" she replied. The maid's hands were empty. I had been dreaming. My throat was dry. "What's the matter, Mr. Messeguer?" she asked. I had been a normal guy until the day before yesterday and now I was lowering my guard. A bit later I took two aspirin. I also took an antibiotic capsule remaining in the medicine chest and lay down to sleep.

* * *

My brother called that afternoon. "Benito, why aren't you at the office?" he said. "As a favor, I need a letter of recommendation from you," I told him. "I'm ceasing to be who I am," and I disclosed my critical moments, the hallucinations. "You've lost your mind, dear. It's Betzi, she's bewitching you." I got on the defensive: "No, she's innocent. It's the mid-life crisis. I'm afraid..." "Stop worrying. Separate yourself from that woman, I know what I'm telling you. You've never been so frail. You had a reputation for being responsible. Stop worrying! People die of typhoid, cancer...but never from having had a nightmare...and even less, from owing three letters of recommendation." He laughed. The conversation was encouraging. One word echoed in my mind: frail...frail. I hung up the receiver and immediately felt better. It's the convalescence of my soul, I thought. I should recover. Your brother is right: you're afraid of Betzi. She's bewitched you. That innermost dissatisfaction is creating this sequence of apparitions... You should alleviate your anxiety.

Another three days went by without Betzi, without controlling my patience, without logic. Three absurd days. I kept looking for the ring. I cleaned the office, and the basement of the house—where I had repaired a pruning hook, looking for the damned ring. And I had a few classified ads placed in the newspaper *Excelsior*. Nothing. That's when I decided to buy another ring. It's necessary, I told myself. Its importance hid powerful secrets. Replacing it would return some lost happiness to me. I went to the same downtown jewelry store and explained to the salesman exactly what I wanted: a plain ring, not luxurious, although made of gold, to replace the previous one. Although they had discontinued the style, they could

Y no me aseguraban que fuera idéntico. «Sin embargo...nada es idéntico a nada», dijo el vendedor. «Las cosas se parecen a sí mismas.» Se asemejaría, sí, pero también tendría cualidades propias. En fin, acepté. Estaría listo hasta dentro de dos semanas: el oro sería fundido, tenían que conseguir el antiguo molde. Eso tardaría varios días. Tenían que hacer el trabajo con cuidado... No, mi urgencia era demasiada. Debía tenerlo listo cuando la semana terminara, la fecha de la segunda pesadilla. El vendedor dijo que haría el intento, aunque no me lo prometía. Esto fue motivo suficiente para alegrarme. Regresé a la casa. Ninguna noticia de Betzi había llegado, ni un telegrama. Pensé en el chance de haber sido engañado durante años en mi propio matrimonio. Mientras ella provocaba esta crisis emocional, seguramente tenía otro metido entre las piernas. Todas las mujeres son putas, pensé. Todas son brujas. Quise vengarme. Vengarme de algún modo. Caminé por la recámara. Subí las escaleras. Las bajé. Daba vueltas como loco.

* * *

Llegó el día séptimo. En la joyería no tuvieron listo el anillo. Yo estaba agotado. Aun así, hice lo imposible por no dormir. No, no quería. No. Me resistía pero al final...caí. Frente a mí estaba el mismo refrigerador. El mismo guardia con el cinturón deteniéndole las manos. La misma visera. Yo estaba sentado en aquel banco. En la esquina más lejana estaba el portafolios, que irradiaba calor. Pasaban horas...y nada. Seguro que se han olvidado de mí, pensaba. Estarán ocupados leyendo otras cartas de recomendación...o soñándolas. De pronto el guardia se acercaba a mí: «Felicitaciones. Sabemos que no ha conseguido ni una sola carta». ¿Por que me felicitaba? De inmediato apareció del portafolios la medusa transparente. Sus cables estaban peor enrollados, sucios de grasa. Tenía la apariencia de una esponja marina calenterosa. «Despreocúpese», me decía. «Por fortuna nosotros hemos encontrado su anillo. Lo dejó usted acá.» ¿Qué? Imposible. «Lo extravié dos o tres días antes de venir. Ustedes no pueden haberlo hallado.» «No se pase de listo, Messeguer. Si le digo que encontramos el anillo...es porque

match it by request. The replacement would be more expensive and they couldn't assure me it was going to be identical. "However... nothing is identical," said the salesman. "Things look like themselves." Yes, there would be a similarity, but it would also have its own qualities. After much talk, I accepted. It would be ready in two weeks: the gold would be melted down, and the original mold would have to be found. That would take several days. They would have to work very carefully... No, my urgency was too great. He should have it ready by the end of the week, the date of the second nightmare. The salesman said that he would try, though he couldn't promise. This was enough reason to make me happy. I returned home. There was no news from Betzi, not even a telegram. I thought about the possibility of having been deceived for years during my marriage. While she provoked this emotional crisis, she surely had another man inserted between her legs. All women are bitches, I thought. They're all witches. I wanted to get revenge, to avenge myself somehow. I walked around in the bedroom, went up the stairs, down, and walked around in circles like a madman.

* * *

The seventh day arrived and the jewelry store didn't have the ring ready. I was exhausted. Even so, I did everything possible not to fall asleep. No, I didn't want to. I resisted, but in the end...I dropped off. In front of me was the same refrigerator. The same guard with the belt holding up his hands. The same visor. I was sitting on that bench. In the farthest corner was the briefcase radiating heat. Hours would go by...and nothing. Surely they've forgotten about me, I thought. They must be busy reading other letters of recommendation...or dreaming them. Suddenly the guard approached me: "Congratulations. We know that you haven't obtained a single letter." Why was he congratulating me? Immediately the transparent medusa appeared out of the briefcase. Its cables were coiled and dirty with grease. It looked like a bubbling sea sponge. "Stop worrying," it was telling me. "Luckily, we've found your ring. You left it here." What? That's impossible. "I misplaced it two or three days before coming here. You couldn't have found it." "Don't be clever, Messeguer. If I tell you we found the ring...it's because we found the ring. Look at it." He extended one of its

encontramos el anillo. ¡Mírelo!», y extendía uno de sus tentáculos, mostrándomelo entre tanta joyería. «Tómelo, Messeguer. Y manténgase atento. Nos disgustaría mucho tenerlo que juzgar nuevamente», decía mientras me lo entregaba. Yo lo deslizaba en el metacarpo de mi dedo meñique izquierdo. «¡Alégrese!», finalizaba. «Esta pesadilla también ha terminado.»

¿Cómo? Me desperté empapado de sudor. Había sido utilizado. Como una marioneta. Jamás había perdido el anillo. Tampoco nunca lo había tenido. Todo era confusión. Revisé mi mano: ahí estaba. ¡Qué sorpresa! Palpitaba mi corazón a ritmo diabólico. Volví a adormecerme de súbito, dejando así emerger la pesadilla final. Su secuencia era la siguiente: estoy en una calle penumbrosa, recargado bajo la luz de un farol, fumando, con un gabán gris, dispuesto a ir al cine. Sé que exhiben el film Shanghai Express con Marlene Dietrich a una o dos cuadras de ahí. Llego a la taquilla. Encuentro una mujer hermosa, robusta. Ella ha perdido su billetera. Quiero ayudarla pero mi timidez me lo impide. Luego ella me pregunta: «¿podría usted prestarme dinero? Quiero entrar al cine». Accedo. (Se parecía a Betzi, pero no.) Le doy el dinero, ella paga y me da la espalda. «¡Qué falta de educación!», pienso. En fin, me despreocupo. Entro también sin mirarla siquiera. La descubro después, sin quererlo, comprando un cartón de palomitas. Aguardo. Veo que, silenciosa, entra en la sala. Busca una butaca. Indiscreto, la sigo y me siento junto a ella. Bien, perfecta movida Messeguer. Miro con el rabillo del ojo sus formidables pechos, su esbeltez. Pronto comienza la película y se apagan las luces. Intento concentrarme. No puedo. Mantengo la atención en ella. Siento incomodidad. Vergüenza. Más obligado al instinto que a la conciencia, pongo sobre su rodilla mi mano. Ella usa medias de nylon que hacen suavecita su piel delgada. Aguardo. Sé que de un momento a otro me cacheteará. Mi mano está tiesa. Sudorosa. Dios, la cachetada no llega. ¡Qué alegría! Pero la mano comienza a sudar. Me veo forzado a retirarla. Saco el pañuelo de mi bolsillo y la limpio. Coqueta, ella mientras tanto se arregla el vestido. Jalonea eróticamente el tirante de su sostén. Me estimula. Supongo que también ella sentirá apetito. Pronto recuerdo que estoy casado con Betzi. ¡Mierda! Pongo de nuevo la mano en su rodilla y dejo que se deslice. Fascinada, nerviosa, ella mueve hacia arriba la nalga. Se acomoda. Me está pidiendo más...lo sé. Más le daré. Con suavidad

tentacles, showing me the ring amongst so much other jewelry. "Take it, Messeguer, and be attentive. It would displease us very much if we had to judge you again," it was saying while it gave it to me. I slipped it onto the knuckle of my left pinkie finger. "Be happy!" said the medusa, in conclusion. "This nightmare has also ended."

What? I woke up drenched in sweat. I had been used like a puppet. I had never lost the ring, nor did I ever have it. Everything was in a state of confusion. I examined my hand, and there it was. What a surprise! My heart was beating at a wicked pace. Suddenly, I fell asleep again, thus allowing the final nightmare to begin. The following was its sequence: I'm on a shadowy street, standing feverishly under the light of a lamppost, and smoking. I'm wearing a gray suit and preparing to go to the movies. I know that they're showing the film *Shanghai Express* with Marlene Dietrich one or two blocks away. I arrive at the ticket booth and find a beautiful, robust woman there. She's lost her ticket. I want to help her but my shyness impedes me. Immediately she asks me: "Could you lend me some money? I want to go in." I agree to. (She looked like Betzi, but no, it wasn't her.) I give her the money, she pays, and then turns her back on me. "How rude!" I think. Eventually, I stop concerning myself about it. Then I too go in without even looking at her. Later, I unintentionally discover her buying a box of popcorn. I wait. I see that she quietly enters the auditorium and looks for an orchestra seat. Indiscreetly, I follow her and sit down next to her. Good, perfect move, Messeguer. Out of the corner of my eye I look at her tremendous breasts, her slender body. As soon as the film begins the lights go out. I try to concentrate. But I can't. I keep my attention on her. I feel uncomfortable, embarrassed. More out of an obligation to instinct than to conscience, I put my hand on her knee. She wears nylon stockings that make her thin legs smooth. I wait. I know that from one moment to the next she would slap me. My hand is stiff. Sweaty. God, the slap doesn't arrive. What joy! But the hand starts to sweat. I see myself forced to remove it and pull a handkerchief out of my pocket to dry it. Flirting, in the meantime, she tidies up her dress and erotically pulls on the strap of her bra. I'm aroused. I suppose that she too felt desire. Quickly I remember that I'm married to Betzi. Shit! Once again I place my hand on her knee and I let it slide. Fascinated, nervous, she lifts her buttock upwards and gets comfortable. She's asking me for more... I know it. And I'll give

llevo mi mano hasta sus muslos y ¡oh sorpresa!, noto que bajo las
enaguas, entre esos ligamentos tan confusos, protectores...no trae
calzoncillos. Mi respiración se acelera. El calvo que está sentado en
la butaca de adelante sospecha. Sabe que no estamos atendiendo la
película. Voltea para asegurarse que todo esté en orden. No. Voltea
porque me tiene envidia. Quiere arrebatarme a mi mujer. Saco la
mano traviesa pues no me gusta que me vean. Es probable que sea
su esposa, pienso. No, si fuera su esposa estarían sentados juntos.
Vuelvo a poner la mano en la rodilla, y rápido encuentro su parte
pudenda. Encuentro esa jungla salvaje que tanto me apasiona. Me
enloquece. Intento atraparla. Ella como si nada ocurriera, no se
inmuta. ¡Es lindo el jugueteo, eh! Sigo manoseando. Debo sugerirle
ir a un hotel o invitarla a cenar. Saco la mano y rápido descubro...
¡oh, no!... descubro que otra vez he perdido mi anillo. Imposible, es
una trampa. Soy un pendejo. «Señora, perdí mi anillo», le digo. Ella
no reacciona. Vuelvo entonces al sitio del delito. Introduzco mi
mano. Me agacho. Busco. Y nada. Ni rastro del maldito anillo. Meto
la mano entera. Nada. Entonces meto la otra. Es un agujero
profundo, amplísimo, sin fondo. Es una cueva invernal. Levanto la
vista: ella sigue mirando a Marlene Dietrich. ¡Mierda!, en qué
embrollo me he metido. Decidido, me agacho. Las dos manos van
hacia dentro, y luego la cabeza. Tengo miedo. El calvo podría
denunciarme. Silencio, hazlo con cuidado Messeguer. Meto los pies,
el cuerpo enterito. Me meto completo en ese abismo...y la oscuridad
es total. Prendo un cerillo. Imposible que se haya desvanecido el
anillo. Alumbro con el cerillo hacia acá o hacia allá. Nada. ¡Dios
mío!, tengo la sensación que la medusa aparecerá pronto. Empiezo
a caminar. Camino. Escucho a lo lejos voces guturales. Quizás sean
los ruidos del filme. Un líquido gelatinoso, escurrido en el suelo,
dificulta mis pasos. Mi respiración es torpe. ¿Y si quisiera regresar?
Sí, quiero regresar. Quiero regresar pero estoy extraviado. He
perdido la ubicación. Grito. Me digo: Grita, Messeguer. Fuerte...más
fuerte. Devuélvanme el anillo. Ojalá que el calvo pueda venir a
salvarme. Nada. Están sudándome las manos. Veo de pronto a una
pareja. Me acerco y descubro que es Betzi—acompañada de algún
extraño. Claro, era obvio su engaño. Me estaba engañando. Mi

her more. I gently bring my hand up to her thighs and oh, what a surprise!, I realize that underneath her slip, amongst those very confused, protective ligaments...she wasn't wearing any underwear. I started breathing faster. The bald headed man sitting in the orchestra seat in front of us suspected something. He knows that we're not watching the film. He turns around to make sure that everything is all right. No. He turns around because he's jealous of me. He wants to snatch *my* woman away from me. I place my hand across my face because I don't want him to see me. She's probably his wife, I think. No, if she was his wife they would be sitting next to each other. I place my hand on her knee again and quickly find her private part. I find that savage jungle that fills me with passion. I become insane. I try to trap her. Meanwhile, she acts as if nothing was happening, not even batting an eyelid. Hey, this frolicking is nice! I keep fondling her. I should suggest that we go to a hotel or ask her out to dinner. I remove my hand and I quickly discover... oh, no!... I discover that once again I've lost my ring. Impossible, it's a trick. I'm an idiot. "Lady, I lost my ring," I tell her. She doesn't react. I return to the scene of passion. I introduce my hand again, and then bend down to look. Nothing, not a trace of the damned ring. I insert one of my hands completely, then the other hand. It's a very large, deep, and bottomless hole—a wintry cave. I look up and she's still watching Marlene Dietrich. Shit! What a mess I've gotten myself into. Determined, I bend down once more. Both of my hands and then my head go inside. I'm afraid the bald headed man could report me. Quiet, Messeguer, do it carefully. I insert my feet and then my entire body. I completely enter that abyss...and it is totally dark. I light a match. It's impossible that the ring could have vanished. I illuminate from one side to the other with the lit match. Nothing. My God! I have the feeling that the medusa is going to appear soon. I start walking. I walk. I hear deep voices in the distance. Perhaps they're sounds coming from the film. A jelly-like liquid, having dripped onto the floor, makes it difficult for me to walk. My breathing is awkward. And what if I wanted to return? Yes, I want to return. I want to return but I'm lost. I've lost myself. I scream. I tell myself: Scream, Messeguer, louder...louder. "Give me back my ring." I hope that the bald-headed man can come to save me. Nothing. My hands are sweating. Suddenly I see a couple. I get closer and discover that it's...Betzi—accompanied by some stranger.

hermano tenía razón. Oigo que menciona algo sobre Rotschester aunque apenas descifro las sílabas. Enfocando, descubro que el extraño trae en el dedo meñique izquierdo mi anillo. Betzi menciona algo más sobre la salida. Sí, ellos deben conocer a la perfección el camino de regreso. ¿Sería indiscreto pedirles que me devuelvan mi anillo? «Eh, amigo», le digo disimulado, «trae usted puesto mi anillo». Lo veo a la cara. Imposible...quien acompaña a Betzi soy yo.

Esa fue la última vez que nos vimos.

Sure, her deception was obvious. My brother was right. I hear her say something about Rochester even though I can barely decipher the syllables. I soon discover that the stranger standing beside her is wearing my ring on the pinky finger of his left hand. Betzi then says something more about the trip. Yes, they should know the way back perfectly. Would it be indiscreet to ask them to return my ring? "Hey, friend," I tell him slyly, "you're wearing my ring." I look at his face. It's impossible...the person who is accompanying Betzi is me.

That was the last time we saw each other.

Tres tiros na tarde

Three Shots in
the Afternoon

Gregory Rabassa, translator of Dalton Trevisan

Gregory Rabassa has translated over 30 books of Latin American literature during the past three decades, among them Gabriel García Márquez's *One Hundred Years of Solitude* and Julio Cortázar's *Hopscotch*. He has received a National Book Award, the PEN Translation Prize, and the Wheatland Foundation Award. He is Distinguished Professor at Queens College of The City University of New York. Rabassa claims in his reply to the questionnaire: "I got into translation through serendipity. When I was an Associate Editor of *Odyssey* my mission was to scout out good literary stuff from Latin America. As we also needed the items translated, I tried my hand at it and did quite a few of the entries. Then Sara Blackburn from Pantheon Books asked me if I would consider translating *Hopscotch* by Julio Cortázar. I did some samples: I liked them, she liked them, and Julio liked them too. Happily, I went on to win a National Book Award in 1967. I have been translating ever since. I find that translation is little more than the closest possible reading of a text. With *Hopscotch* I translated the book as I read it for the first time, a rather daring way to do things but one which over time I've found to be more rewarding and creative than a pseudoscientific and pompous "deconstruction" of the text. In the case of *One Hundred Years of Solitude*, I read the book before I undertook the translation, but as a novel, not with an eye to doing it." As for the relationship with each author, "it usually depends on him or her and also on geographical circumstance. I developed a grand rapport with Julio Cortázar and we got to be great friends over the years. We both liked Jazz (I'd known Charlie Parker) and had a kind of impish outlook in common. My proudest award is being named Cronopio by Julio."

Rabassa chose Dalton Trevisan's story for two reasons: "To get recognition for Brazil in the Latin American context, and to bring some attention to Dalton, who has gone almost unrecognized despite a collection I did of his stories in 1972 *(The Vampire of Curitiba and Other Stories)*." Trevisan was born in Curitiba, Brazil, in 1925, and since his publishing debut at age 34 has published some four hundred short stories. Rabassa adds: "Trevisan may be a forerunner of what has come to be called post-modernism (whatever that is, Brazil went through that phase long ago). He is what we think of as a minimalist, to borrow a term from musical composition. He writes short-short stories and has said that his ultimate aim is to reduce the story to its essential haiku. The wickedness of his themes is based on marital fights and squabbles, often leading to murder and mayhem. This genre of his—the microstory—is almost his alone, which makes him a master of it. The characters are inevitably João and María—everyman and everywoman. He finally unmasks the bourgeois image of the happy couple and thereby the sham of our accepted relationships."

Dalton Trevisan

TRES TIROS NA TARDE

Primeiro ela deitou uma droga no licor de ovo—a garganta em fogo,
João correu para a cozinha e tomou bastante leite. Depois ela
misturou soda cáustica na loção de cabelo, que lhe queimou as
mãos. O vidro moído no caldo de feijão rangia—lhe nos dentes—e
rolava no chão do banheiro, as entranhas fervendo.

Chaveados no guarda-roupa o creme de barba, o talco, o
perfume. João decidiu só comer na companhia dos filhos—e se,
para matá—lo, envenenasse María também os filhos?

Ele dormia, cansado da viagem de negócio. María abriu o gás
do aquecedor apagado. Salvo por um dos meninos, que bateu na
porta e já tossindo:

—Pai, acorde. Que cheiro é esse, pai?

—Esqueci o cigarro aceso.

Já dormiam em quartos separados. Ela recebia flores de antigos
namorados. Fim de semana viajou sozinha para o aborto de um
filho que não era dele.

—Os dias que passei longe de João e dos meninos—anunciou
para uma amiga—foram os melhores de minha vida.

O pai de João foi procurá-lo no escritório:

—Meu filho, que está esperando? Você quer morrer—é isso?

Sem coragem de abandonar os meninos com aquela doida. Ou
quem sabe amava a doida?

Na poltrona da sala, o copo de uísque na mão, lia em voz alta o
programa dos cinemas:

—Que filme gostaria de ver, María?

Um dos guris brincando a seus pés no tapete.

—Para você, querido.

Dalton Trevisan

THREE SHOTS IN THE AFTERNOON

Translated by Gregory Rabassa

First she put a drug in his egg brandy—his throat on fire, João ran
to the kitchen and downed a lot of milk. Then she mixed caustic
soda in with his hair tonic, which burned his hands. The ground
glass in his bean soup was gritty on his teeth—and he rolled on the
bathroom floor, his insides all aboil.

He put his shaving cream, talcum powder, and lotion under
lock and key in his bureau drawer. João decided to eat only in the
company of his children—but what if, in order to kill him, María
killed the children too?

He was sleeping, worn out from a business trip. María opened
the jet on the unlighted gas heater. He was saved by one of the kids
knocking on the door, already coughing:

"Wake up, father. What's that smell, father?"

"I forgot and left a cigarette burning."

They were already sleeping in separate bedrooms. She would
get flowers from old boyfriends. One weekend she took a trip to get
an abortion for a child that wasn't his.

"The days I spent away from João and the kids," she told a girl
friend, "were the best I ever had."

João's father went to see him at his office:

"What are you waiting for, son? Do you want to die—is that
it?"

Without the courage to abandon the children to that madwoman. Or maybe he loved the madwoman.

In the armchair in the living room, a glass of whiskey in his
hand, he was reading aloud the list of movies being shown:

"What picture would you like to see, María?"

One of the kids was playing on the rug by his feet.

"This is for you, dear."

Voltou-se e recebeu os três tiros no rosto—o filhinho abraçou-se no pai.

—Mãe, por que a senhora fez isso?—e esfregava no pulôver branco a mãozinha peganhenta.

—Agora não adianta mais.

Olho arregalado, a sogra surgiu na porta:

—O meu filho essa desgraçada matou.

Deitado o seu menino no sofá de palhinha, vertia sangue das feridas e pingava numa bacia no chão.

—Tao bonito, nem tinha pêlo no braço. No carnaval saiu de mulher e ninguém desconfiou.

De joelhos, com o lenço enxugava a sangueira no bigode:

—Por que não dá o tiro de misericórdia?

María virou-lhe as costas:

—Tirem essa louca de perto de mim.

Sozinha no quarto, vestiu-se de vermelho, pintou os olhos, enfeitou-se de brincos e, toda em sossego, sorria para o espelho.

He turned and caught the three shots in the face—the little boy embraced his father.

"Mother, why did you do that?" and he wiped his sticky little hand on the white sweater.

"It doesn't matter now."

Wide-eyed, the mother-in-law appeared in the doorway:

"That bitch has killed my son."

Her boy, lying on the wicker couch had blood pouring from his wounds and dripping into a basin on the floor.

"So nice-looking, he didn't even have any hair on his arms. During carnival he went out dressed as a woman and no one was any wiser."

On her knees, she was sopping up the blood on his mustache with her handkerchief.

"Why didn't you give him the coup de grace?"

María turned her back on her:

"Get that crazy woman away from me."

Alone in her room, she dressed all in red, made up her eyes, put on earrings, and, completely relaxed, smiled at herself in the mirror.

Mangos de Enero

Mangoes in January

Leland H. Chambers, translator of Jorge Turner

Leland H. Chambers earned a Ph.D. from the University of Denver, after submitting as his dissertation a translation of Baltasar Gracián's *The Mind's Wit and Art*. He has translated Julieta Campos and Ezequiel Martínez Estrada, among others, and was editor of *Denver Quarterly* in the late seventies and early eighties. He co-edited *Contemporary Short Stories from Central America* (University of Texas Press). In keeping with a life's trend of "one thing leading to another," Chambers gradually entered his field via translations prepared on an impromptu basis for his comparative literature classes at the University of Denver. Since his unpublished dissertation, Chambers has translated four major novels and stories that have appeared in more than twenty literary magazines and five anthologies. Also, he has had the good fortune to work with the esteemed author Enrique Jaramillo Levi, with whom he co-edited *Contemporary Short Stories from Central America*.

His translation of a poem by Nicaraguan Joaquín Pasos was discovered by composer Norman Lockwood, who set Chambers's words to music. Chambers, who admits to being "a little of the activist," selected "Mangoes in January" by Jorge Turner, a lawyer from Panama born in 1922, who has been a journalist, university professor, and Panama's ambassador to Mexico. Turner is the author of a collection of short stories, *Viento de agua,* as well as the nonfiction, *Raíz, historia y perspectiva del movimiento obrero panameño,* a work that "raises a perspective on Panamanian affairs traditionally unobserved from the North American vantage point." Chambers writes: "I prefer to translate fiction, but I do a fair amount of poetry. My approach is rather different in the two cases. With poetry I read the original carefully before starting to translate. With prose I do this much less (I've actually started some projects blind)...If I need to consult with a native speaker or look up technical words, I usually put these tasks off until it seems to me the rest of the translation is in pretty good shape. As for close working relationships with the authors, I don't feel it's necessary. Which says something about me as a person, I guess. It is true that the more I know about this or that author, the better I feel about translations."

Jorge Turner
MANGOS DE ENERO

A Dení Claudia y a Clarita Xóchitl

Lo que son las cosas de la vida. El caso es como el asunto que sirvió
de base a un relato de Neco Endara. Se sostiene que un gringo se
convirtió en pez por bañarse en el río en Viernes Santo. Pero la
versión actual tiene ángulos originales. En primera, el gringo no se
bañó porque quiso sino porque lo echaron al agua; en segunda el
nombre del río aparece cambiado. Es decir que al parecer quien
empujo al gringo fue un muchacho, es decir que si lo hizo se debió
a que tenía sus motivos; es decir que el verdadero río de los hechos
se llama Juan Díaz... Basta.

Con energía Edi reitera su relato al fiscal. Sobre el 9 de enero de
1964, cuando mataron a su hermano Vicente, puede hablar; sobre
el gringo del viernes santo, muy poco. No va a resultar sospechoso
debido a su participación en el nueve porque entonces gran parte
del pueblo panameño también resultaría sospechoso. El fiscal tiene
que descartar la idea de la venganza. El gringo era un viejo jubilado
y capaperro, vecino suyo. ¡Qué interés tenía causarle daño! Pero el
fiscal sí lleva razón en desear enterarse de los detalles del nueve,
pues siempre debe refrescarse lo que pasó en aquella fecha, aunque
de allí sería absurdo apresurarse a sacar conclusiones.

Al caer la noche de ese día el cielo es un periódico gris con
anuncios de arrebol. Ambulancias y automóviles, bocina abierta,
convergen al edificio de la Sala de Urgencia. Estacionan sobre el
pasto verde, al pie de un letrero que dice: zona de silencio. El calor
insoportable parece producto de las emanaciones de un gran lago
de azufre hirviente. Pero un lago así no existe. En realidad el calor
se debe a los efluvios llegados de los puntos fronteros que

Jorge Turner
MANGOES IN JANUARY
Translated by Leland H. Chambers

To Dení Claudia and Clarita Xóchitl

That's the way life goes. This whole thing is like the case that was the basis for a story by Neco Endara. Some claim this gringo got turned into a fish because he went swimming in the river on Good Friday. But the actual version has some original angles. First, the gringo didn't go swimming there because he wanted to but because he was thrown into the water. Second, the name of the river was changed. That is, it seems that whoever pushed the gringo was a boy; and if he did it he must have had his reasons; and the real river of these events is the Juan Díaz... Well, that's enough.

Eddie, full of spirit, is repeating his story for the district attorney. Concerning the 9th of January of 1964, now, when they killed his brother Vicente, he can talk about that; concerning this gringo on Good Friday, there isn't much to say. He isn't going to come out a suspect just because of his participation in the doings of the 9th, because then a whole lot of the Panamanian public would also turn out to be suspects. The district attorney has to put aside any idea of revenge. The gringo was an old man, retired, about as useless as tits on a boar hog, a neighbor of his. What reason would he have for doing him any harm? But the district attorney surely has the right idea to want to be informed about the details of the 9th, since you should always keep reminding yourself what happened that day, though it always be absurd to jump to conclusions too quickly from there.

At nightfall that day the sky is a gray newspaper with ruddy headlines. Ambulances and cars, horns blowing wide open, converge on the building where the emergency room is located. They park on the green grass, at the foot of a sign saying: SILENT ZONE. The unbearable heat seems to be the product of emanations from a big lake of boiling sulphur. But that kind of lake doesn't exist. In reality the heat is due to the effluvia coming from the border points that

resguardan la zona del canal. Los efluvios que el viento arrastra desde la linde (convertida en frente bélico), de aquella antilla de la misma hierba, los mismos mangos y las mismas palmeras del mismo paisaje nacional pero de otro paisaje humano que disloca la continuidad mestiza, en la que la realidad de los anuncios también exhibe otro idioma, tallado a salivazos; "KEEP OFF THE GRASS!" "RESERVED AREA, WARNING!" "MILITARY AREA, NO ENTRANCE!" "NO TRESPASSING!" "NO DOGS ALLOWED!" "PROHIBITED!"

El vehículo en el que Edi acompaña a Vicente, herido de bala, se vacía de su carga humana y parte de una vez. En la sala de Urgencia, tras rápido examen clasificatorio de muerto o vivo, o sobre el tipo de lesión, acuestan a los pacientes en camillas de ruedas. A Vicente lo instalan como a centenares de personas. Las camillas rodantes empiezan a circular por la calle, dirijidas por enfermeras improvisadas, hacia su destino. Las camillas con muertos encima, a la morgue, donde se van apiñando. Las camillas con heridos, al pabellón correspondiente. Edi camina pegado a la camilla donde yace inmóvil su hermano Vicente. Les indicaron el pabellón ginecológico, habilitado para atender algunos heridos. Se hace desesperadamente lenta la marcha de los camilleros y la de los carretilleros que trasladan de un lado a otro tanques de oxígeno. No avanzan gran cosa porque la angustia colectiva presente en el centro hospitalario constituye el obstáculo. A lo largo y ancho del área se encuentran: guardias nacionales, bomberos, "boy scouts," mulatos, cholos, negros, blancos, ricos, pobres, viejos y jóvenes. A muchos de ellos les cuelgan del hombro radios portátiles, sintonizados a todo volumen. De los radios claramente se escucha: "En la Avenida Cuatro de Julio, sobre la línea divisoria, continúa la matanza del ejército norteamericano contra los panameños. El Presidente de la República, ante el clamor popular, acaba de romper relaciones diplomáticas con Estados Unidos.."

El fiscal debe conocer la vida de ellos, como la de tantos jóvenes, para comprender las inquietudes que los mueven, en vez de estar averiguando si el gringo pendejo de verdad se convirtió en pez o no. Ese gringo era hipócrita. Con la casa llena de gatos. Siempre andaba sudando la borrachera y diciendo: Christmas: gringo viejo

protect the Canal Zone. Effluvia that the wind carries from the boundary (become a war zone) of that island of the same grass, the same mangoes and palm trees as the landscape of the nation itself—but also of another landscape, this time a human one that dismembers the mestizo continuity, in which the reality of the spittle-smeared signs—in English—also displays another language: "KEEP OFF THE GRASS!" "RESERVED AREA, WARNING!" "MILITARY AREA, NO ENTRANCE!" "NO TRESPASSING!" "NO DOGS ALLOWED!" "PROHIBITED!"

The vehicle in which Eddie accompanies Vicente, wounded by a bullet, empties its human cargo and departs at once. In the emergency room after a rapid examination classifying him on whether he is dead or alive, and the type of wound he has, they put the patient on wheeled stretchers. Vicente is settled down just like hundreds of others. The rolling stretchers begin to circulate through the halls pushed toward their destinations by impromptu nurses. Those with corpses on them to the morgue, which is getting more and more jammed. Those with the wounded to the corresponding wing. Eddie walks as if tied to the stretcher where his brother Vicente lies motionless. They have been sent to the gynecological wing which is equipped to take care of some of the wounded. The march of the stretcher bearers and those with the pushcarts moving oxygen tanks from one place to another becomes desperately slow. They don't move ahead very fast because of the obstacle at the heart of the hospital which is presented by the collective agony. Throughout the length and breadth of the area they encounter national guardsmen, firemen, boy scouts, mulattos, cholos, blacks, whites, the rich and the poor, the old and the young. Many of them have portable radios hanging from their shoulders, tuned full blast. On the radios it is clearly heard: "On the Avenida Cuarto de Julio, over the dividing line, the slaughter of Panamanians by the US army continues. In the face of popular outcry the President of the Republic has just broken diplomatic relations with the United States."

The district attorney should become familiar with their lives, like those of so many young people, in order to understand the restlessness that moves them, instead of trying to verify whether that dumb gringo really was turned into a fish or not. That gringo was a hypocrite. With a house full of cats. He was always going around, dripping with his drunken sweat, saying, "Christmas! me

quiere Panama, ¿sabi? Ellos, desde chicos, le tomaron sabor a los gringos. Edi y Vicente frecuentemente iban a buscar mangos. Una vez, a la salida de la escuela, se internaron con los amigos de la Zona. Los amigos treparon a los árboles, ellos quedaron abajo con las bolsas. Edi miraba un árbol, ancho y umbroso, como mamá Juana, gorda y buena con su abundante pelo cus cus... Más allá, una palma doblegada por el viento: como el viejo, de regreso del trabajo. Vicente tampoco ponía atención a la placa brillante en el uniforme. Suena el pito. A la distancia, el policía norteamericano pita y pita, enrojecido por la ira. Los muchachos se descuelgan rápidamente. Antes de cruzar corriendo la línea divisoria sonó un balazo. Es lo prohibido: "NO TRESPASSING". El pito el disparo, corrieron como conejos. Se leía "CANAL ZONE," pero no soltaron las bolsas.

Vicente en el pabellón ginecológico. Queda en una banca, al lado de una mujer embarazada que explica el vuelco sufrido allí. Cuando llega, todo tranquilo. De repente, el manicomio. La mujer dice que no se puede atender a las parturientas y al mismo tiempo intervenir a los baleados. La sala principal se llena de gente. El público se confunde con los heridos y las mujeres preñadas. Las puertas de resorte se abren y se cierran sin descanso dejando escapar su agudo chirrido. Con cada portazo salen gritos y entran gritos. Y con los nuevos gritos: más personas, nuevas noticias. La gente informa. Muchos médicos han sido convocados y vienen en camino; dos muchachos actuaron como kamikazes, carajo; se robaron una avioneta para estrellarla en la zona del canal pero no tenía gasolina suficiente y cayó al mar; se quiso meter fuego al Hotel Tivoli y no le entra la candela, la madera está curada. Gringos hijueputas. La mujer, que friega la paciencia como pocas, grita: Me estoy pariendo. Nadie le hace caso. La mujer insiste en que el feto está acomodando, se le está jodiendo, mientras su marido se cree muy macho, no está ahí, anda de juma, la deja sola, anda de poco importa, se cree vivo, anda con los amigos, se cree berraco, celebrando por anticipado... Lo viera como los muchachos, lo viera con una bala adentro, lo

old gringo love Panama, savvy?" Since they were kids they had been hassling the gringos. Eddie and Vicente used to go scouting for mangoes all the time. Once after school they went into the Zone with some friends. Their friends climbed the trees, they stayed down below with the bags. Eddie was looking up into a tree, broad and shady, like Mama Juana, fat and good with her plentiful, curly hair. Over there, a palm tree bent down by the wind: like the old man coming home from his job. Vicente wasn't paying attention to the shining badge on the uniform, either. Whistle sounds. In the distance the US policeman is blowing and blowing, getting all red in the face from anger. The boys jump down quickly. Before they cross the dividing line a shot sounded. This is the prohibited area: NO TRESPASSING. The whistle, the shot, they ran like rabbits. The sign said CANAL ZONE but they didn't let go of their bags.

Vicente in the gynecological ward. He is on a bench beside a pregnant woman who is telling about the fuss out there. When she arrived, everything was calm. Suddenly it was a madhouse. The woman says they can't take care of the childbirths and operate on those who have been shot at the same time. The main waiting room is full of people. The public is mixed in with the wounded and the pregnant women. The swinging doors open and shut ceaselessly, giving off their high-pitched creaking. Each time the door slams, screaming goes in, and screaming comes out. And with the new screams, more people, new news. The people are reporting. A lot of doctors have been rounded up and are on their way. Two kids did like the kamikazes, shit, they stole a little plane in order to crash it into the Zone but it didn't have enough gasoline and went down over the ocean. Someone tried to set fire to the Hotel Tivoli and they couldn't get it to light, the wood had been treated. Fucking gringos! The woman, who would put anyone's patience to the test like nobody else, screams out, "I'm having the baby!" No one pays any attention to her. The woman insists that the fetus is settling, they're all just fooling around with her while her husband thinks he's so great, he's not here, he's out getting drunk, leaves her here alone, as if there isn't much to it, thinks he's hot enough to make a good dog laugh, going around with his friends like that, just a little boy celebrating in advance... She'd like to see him like these kids, see him with a bullet inside him, see him going up against the

viera contra los gringos, lo viera en este escándalo, lo viera pariendo como yo. Entonces se cagaría en los pantalones.

Qué clase de marido; Se llena la boca diciendo del marido, bah marido: resistir, resisto, resistol, resistencia, dedos tronados, labios mordidos. Serenidad, para qué serenidad, serenidad, ¡A la mierda la serenidad...! Olor de éter ajetreo sudor nerviosismo. Una enfermera le dice a la mujer: Buen día para parir, espera un poco. "Me estoy pariendo" grita de nuevo la mujer. Un hombre gordo tercia: Y cuando estabas con el gustito no gritabas así, ¿verdad? Al gordo lo empuja otro y le advierte: Busca tu torniscón, desgraciado; recuerda que tienes madre.

Si el fiscal es realmente representativo del interés de la sociedad debe enterarse como cayó cada uno de los mártires de ese día. Tras los primeros choques el pueblo se volcó para allá. Por eso la gente sencilla conoce bien muchos detalles. Los que necesitan informarse son los que quedaron cómodamente en sus Casas. Los estudiantes habían traspuesto la raya limítrofe. Vicente camina en primera fila. Lo sigue Edi. De las incursiones por mangos, los hermanos regresaron a la Zona en las "operaciones bandera", y de las "operaciones bandera" han llegado al nueve. Van a reforzar el grupo inicial con el que se suscitó el primer choque. Ascienden por la calle empinada. Los cerros laterales no anuncian peligro. Pero llegan a la parte más alta de la calle, continúan por la curva, y entonces advierten a los soldados gringos, en formación, rodilla en tierra. Se detienen. Los soldados están apuntando. El abanderado decide pasarle a Vicente su bandera. Empieza con disimulo el repliegue. Vicente, con Edi al lado, no se mueve de su sitio, enarbolando la bandera. "No la suelto, aunque me dé culillo, Edi", dice. La primera descarga. Caen algunos heridos. La mayoría retrocede o se echa al suelo. "No suelto la bandera, me dieron la responsabilidad". Intenta avanzar. El disparo se escucha con nitidez. El vidrio de la ventana, tric trac... Rafael metió el gol... El estómago se abre...tinaja rota...cae el agua...sangre. Un gran peso sobre los ojos de Vicente, sobre los párpados superiores un gran peso. Debilidad extrema. Sus dedos morenos y fuertes, argollas en el asta. La hierba está húmeda y le re

gringos, see him in this mess, see him having a baby like her. Then she shit in her underwear.

What kind of husband... Her mouth is full of her husband, bah! husband!: resist, resisting, resister, resistance, fingers worn out, lips bitten down. Calm, why calm? calm—to hell with being calm! Smell of ether bustling activity nervous sweating. A nurse tells a woman, "It's a good day to have a baby, just wait a while." The woman screams out again: "I'm having the baby NOW!" A fat man chimes in, "And when you were having your little fun you weren't screaming like that, were you?" Someone else gives him a little push and warns him, "You're asking for a poke, stupid; remember that you've got a mother."

If the district attorney is really representative of society's interest he should inform himself how every one of the martyrs went down that day. After the first clashes the people poured in toward the area. That's why the common folk pretty well know a lot of the details. Those who need to be informed are the ones who stayed comfortably in their homes. The students had crossed over the boundary line. Vicente is walking in the first rank. Eddie is following him. From the mango raids the brothers had gone back to the Zone with their "flag drills," and from the "flag drill" they have come to January 9th. They are going to reinforce the initial group that had sustained the first clash. They go up the steep street. The hills on their flanks do not warn of any danger. But they reach the highest part of it, follow the curve around, and then they notice the gringo soldiers, in formation, knees to the ground. They stop. The soldiers are aiming. The flag bearer decides to hand his flag to Vicente. The retreat begins furtively. Vicente, with Eddie by his side, does not move from his place; he brandishes the flag. "I'm not going to let go, even if they kick my ass, Eddie," he says. The first salvo. Some fall wounded. Most of them retreat or throw themselves to the ground. "I won't let go of the flag. They made me responsible." He tries to move ahead. The shot is heard clearly. Window glass, tric trac... Rafael scored a goal... His stomach is open...broken pot...water's falling...blood. A great weight over Vicente's eyes, a heavy weight upon his upper eyelids. Weakness in the extreme. His fingers dark and strong, like iron rings around the flag standard. The grass is damp and it cools his head. Thousands of cicadas

fresca la cabeza. Miles de cigarras corean en el tiempo indefinible de la tarde. En el cielo huyen los anuncios de arrebol.

La mujer embarazada advierte: ¡no aguanto más, me voy a parir ya! Con las manos cruzadas bajo el vientre corre rumbo a los ascensores. Allí nace el hijo. Nació vivo. El hombre gordo comenta que, por su origen, el recién nacido debe llamarse: Elevador Ramírez. El hombre flaco, que lo tiene amenazado con un torniscón, responde: No, así no se llamará; le pondrán: Enero Ramírez. Vicente le dice a Edi, en un murmullo, que los poros no le duelen. El dolor se fija abajo, en lo profundo del estómago, en el fondo de un pozo. La banca de madera lo estropea. Edi siente que le tiembla el brazo sobre el que su hermano tiene reclinada la cabeza: La enfermera pasa de regreso, observa a Vicente y manifiesta que es muy joven, que se está muriendo, que hay que atenderlo cuanto antes. Alguien empuja y reclama atención inmediata porque va a donar sangre. Le enrostran: coño, no emporres, qué pendejos son los viejos, gran vaina de sangre, los muchachos no la pasan a las probetas sino que la riegan en el suelo para fecundarlo. El gordo mira, en torno, escrutando a los heridos, se detiene en Vicente y dice: esas son las cosas, qué sabe de política ese chiquillo como de veinte años; ni idea tiene de la suma de cosas a que puede aspirar Panamá dentro del orden internacional a que pertenece, o sea dentro del orden internacional dirigido por Estados Unidos. El flaco vuelve a callarlo: Cierra el pico, gringófilo, te prometí un torniscón y te lo meto. La enfermera se acerca a Vicente empujando una silla de ruedas. Con cuidado lo acomoda y se lo lleva. El herido aparece con el rictus labial sufriente y la vista lánguida.

Cuando Edi refiere el instante en que ocurrió la muerte de Vicente la voz se le quiebra. Se impuso y logró entrar al cuarto de operaciones. En la ventana cruzada de barrotes verdes aparece un pedazo de la noche sin estrellas. El cirujano ordena la anestesia. Mira con calma su reloj. Vicente solloza, luego se queja débilmente primero para después delirar en voz alta y ronca: habla de mangos, de su novia Elsa. El doctor enjuga meticulosamente la sangre del estómago del herido, valiéndose de una gasa. Vicente insiste en los

chorusing in the indefinable atmosphere of the afternoon. The ruddy headlines are fleeing from the skies.

The pregnant woman warns, "I can't stand any more, I'm going to have my baby now!" With her hands crossed beneath her belly she runs in the direction of the elevators. That is where the child is born. It is born alive. The fat man remarks that because of his place of birth the newborn boy should be named Elevator Ramírez. The thin man who had threatened him with a poke in the nose answers, "No, he shouldn't be called that; they should name him January Ramírez." Vicente tells Eddie, murmuring, that his pores don't hurt him. The pain is settled down at the bottom of his stomach at the bottom of a well. The wooden bench really hurts him. Eddie feels the arm trembling on which his brother's head is reclining. The nurse returns, notices Vicente and sees how young he is, that he is dying, that they have to take care of him right away. Someone pushes through and wants attention now because he wants to donate blood.

They reproach him: "Don't be a nuisance, you bastard, what idiots these old men are, all this crap about blood; these boys aren't putting it into test tubes, instead they're watering the ground with it to fertilize it." The fat man turns around, scrutinizing the wounded, comes to a pause over Vicente and says, "That's the way things are, what does this twenty-year-old kid know about politics? He hasn't the faintest idea of the total picture of what Panama can expect to be within the international world it belongs to, or rather the world as led by the United States." The thin man quiets him down once more: "Shut your mouth, you gringo-brown-noser, I promised you a poke in the snoot and you're going to get it." The nurse approaches Vicente pushing a wheel chair. Carefully she gets him into it and carries him away, a pained rictus on his lips, his gaze listless.

When Eddie tells about the moment when Vicente's death occurred, his voice breaks. He prevailed and managed to get into the operating rooms. In the window criss-crossed with thick green bars appears a piece of the starless night. The surgeon orders anesthesia. He looks at his watch calmly. Vicente is sobbing, then he complains weakly at first and later grows delirious in a high, raucous voice: he is talking about mangoes, about his sweetheart Elsa. The doctor meticulously wipes the blood from the wounded man's stomach, using gauze. Vicente persists with the mangoes, he talks

mangos, habla de la bandera y de que desea casarse con Elsa. El médico con parsimonia pone en orden, en la mesilla auxiliar, tijeras y bisturíes, mientras la enfermera: Por vida de Dios, apure, doctor. Vicente dice una palabra rara: desalmarse, prefiere la muerte a desalmarse, nunca desalmarse. Enguantado en forma, el médico coloca sobre los bordes de la herida dos pinzas de apertura y a continuación empuña un instrumento, sus manos se mueven con rapidez. Vicente menciona a los viejos, quiere a su hermano. Edi llora en silencio. Las manos del doctor exploran con los dedos, dice: Es difícil por el lugar, hay mucha sangre, no aparece la bala. La enfermera advierte: El pulso se va, doctor, ya...es...tarde. El médico se deprime. Permanece con la cabeza gacha. Decide tomarse un descanso antes de ver a otro herido. Palmea en el hombro a Edi. Abandona la sala con éste, enciende un cigarrillo. Le explica que con todo y su experiencia no puede permanecer tranquilo ante la muerte. Le duele lo de Vicente y lo de todos los muchachos. Afirma que los jóvenes, con más vida que dar, la entregan generosamente, mientras los mayores se pudren en su vida vieja, en el cuidado conservador de su pedacito de existencia.

El fiscal no debe decir en ningún momento, mal interpretando el relato, que entonces los jóvenes como Vicente y Edi fueron a la Zona a pelear por razones originadas en cosas como unos simples mangos. Nada de simples. Aunque Edi se exponga a cualquier sanción está dispuesto a la protesta. Plantearlo así es reducir a su mínima expresión la jornada del nueve. Tal criterio es semejante al del gordo que tanto jodió el día de la tragedia en el Hospital Santo Tomás. Otro asunto es afirmar que la toma de conciencia anticolonialista se inicia, entre los panameños, por hechos que desde la niñez se graban para siempre. A partir de ahí se profundiza en una actitud superior a la del mero antiyanquismo. Edi, al igual que todo panameño consciente, rechaza cualquier forma, directa o indirecta, de dominación extranjera. No se constriñe a la zonofobia. El fiscal se equivoca si piensa que él vengó en el gringo jubilado el asesinato de su hermano. No cree que el gringo fuera la gran mierda. Pero tampoco tenía por qué martarlo o, si se quiere, convertirlo en

about the flag and how he wants to marry Elsa. The doctor imperturbably arranges scissors and scalpels on the auxiliary table, while the nurse says, "For God's sake, hurry, doctor." Vicente says a strange word: yearning, he prefers death to yearning, never to yearn. Gloved in due form, the doctor places two forceps around the lips of the wound for spreading it open and seizes another instrument; now his hands are moving swiftly. Vicente mentions his parents, he loves his brother. Eddie weeps silently. The doctor's hands are exploring with their fingers, and he says, "It's difficult because of the place, there's a lot of blood, the bullet isn't showing up." The nurse warns, "His pulse is going, doctor—there...too late." The doctor slumps, keeping his head bowed. He decides to take a rest before seeing another wounded patient. He puts his arm around Eddie's shoulder. Going out of the room with him, he lights up a cigarette. He explains that no matter what, and with all his experience, he can never remain calm in the face of death. This business with Vicente and with all the young men pains him. He declares that the young men, with more of life to give, hand it over generously, while their elders are putrefying in their old lives, in their circumspect care for their little pieces of existence.

The district attorney should never claim, not for a moment, as that would be misinterpreting the story, that the youths like Vicente and Eddie went into the Zone then to fight for reasons based on things like a few mangoes. They weren't simpleminded. Though Eddie opens himself up to some kind of punishment by doing so, he is ready to protest. For to set up the problem that way is to reduce the action on January 9th to its smallest dimensions. Just like the fat man did who got on everyone's nerves in Santo Tomás hospital the day of the tragedy. It is a wholly different matter to point out that, among the Panamanians, the development of an anticolonialist stance begins with events that from childhood on are engraved on their minds forever. From there they go on farther, into an attitude superior to that of mere anti-yankeeism. Eddie, like any conscientious Panamanian, rejects any form of foreign domination, direct or indirect. It is not restricted to zonophobia. The district attorney is mistaken if he thinks Eddie took vengeance on the retired gringo because of his brother's murder. He doesn't think the gringo was worth a pile of shit. But neither did he have any reason to kill him, or to turn him into a fish, if you like.

pez. Durante los hechos sangrientos del nueve, se pintaron letreros en las paredes: "Yanqui visto, yanqui muerto". Eso fue en aquel tiempo. Cuando se reanudaron las relaciones diplomáticas regresaron a la ciudad los gringos evacuados que vivían con mujeres panameñas. Nadie les hizo nada. ¡Qué caso tendría joder ahora al gringo gatófilo! El sabía que el gringo iba con frecuencia a pescar al río Juan Díaz. Como vecino, lo vio salir el viernes santo con su caña y arreos de pesca y obviamente dedujo que se encaminaba al río. Está enterado de que un testigo dijo haber visto cuando un muchacho empujó al gringo al agua. Hasta ahí. Si es cierto que el gringo se ahogó, no pudo decir porqué no ha aparecido flotando el cadáver. A ciencia cierta no está seguro de quién inventó la versión (porque era viernes santo y porque nunca más apareció el gringo) de que se había convertido en pez. Son cosas del pueblo. La negra Pastora, que tiene un negocio de venta de pescado frito al pie del río y que dice saber de macuá, sostiene que los seres humanos que se convierten en peces se conocen porque nadan rápido, soltando una tinta verde de la bilis que les da la tragedia que viven. Y lo que a Edi le parece la gran ahuevazón es que la semana pasada la fiscalía designara a un empleado con el fin de que espiara en el río para ver si de casualidad aparecía por alguna parte la estela verde que a su paso deja el gringo viejo que involucionó.

During the bloody event, of the 9th, inscriptions used to be painted on the walls: "Yankee seen, Yankee dead." That was back then, during those days. When diplomatic relations were renewed the evacuated gringos who lived with Panamanian women came back to the city. No one did anything to them. What point was there in messing around now with the gringo cat-lover? He knew the gringo frequently went fishing in the Juan Díaz. As any neighbor, he saw him go out with his rod and fishing gear on Good Friday, and obviously he deduced that he was on the way to the river. He is aware that a witness says he had seen a boy push the gringo into the water. So far, so good. Whether it is true that the gringo drowned he himself couldn't say, because the body has never appeared floating on the surface. He is not sure for an absolute fact who it was that invented the story of his being turned into a fish (just because it was Good Friday and because the gringo never was seen again). Things like that—well, that's the way the people are. Pastora, a black woman who has a little place where she sells fried fish at the edge of the river and says she knows all about evil spells, claims that human beings who turn into fish can be recognized because they swim rapidly and leave a green tint behind them because of the bile that the tragedy they are going through has brought out. And what seems to Eddie the biggest stupidity is that last week the District Attorney's office designated an employee to keep watch on the river to see if by chance there should appear the greenish wake of the old gringo who reversed his evolutionary development.

CON JIMMY EN PARACAS

IN PARACAS WITH JIMMY

Hardie St. Martin, translator of Alfredo Bryce Echenique

Hardie St. Martin was born in 1924 in Money River, British Honduras, now Belize, and raised in the United States. He currently lives in Barcelona. He has translated José Donoso's *The Garden Next Door* and Isaac Goldemberg's *Play by Play*. Other authors he has translated include Pablo Neruda, Gustavo Sainz, Roque Dalton and Juan Gelman. His anthology *Roots & Wings: Poetry from Spain 1900-1975* is considered a classic.

While a graduate at Columbia University, St. Martin started translating poetry and Miguel Angel Asturias's *Leyendas de Guatemala* for his own pleasure, without trying to publish. Then, in the fifties, he began to submit material to literary reviews. As for his liaison with the author, he argues: "I need no relationship with the prose writer to come up with a decent translation, though it can sometimes make it easier for me if I follow his work closely." He translated Bryce Echenique's story because he admires him very much and feels that he is eclipsed by other literary figures.

Alfredo Bryce Echenique was born in 1939 in Peru, taught at the Paul Valéry University in France for many years, and now lives in Madrid, where St. Martin met him. His novel *A World for Julius* won the prize for Best Novel in Peru in 1972 and the award for Best Foreign Novel in France in 1974. Gregory Rabassa once described him as "Peru's best novelist," and Fernando Alegría declared, "Bryce awakens curious echoes. His recreation of Lima's aristocracy awakens a sweet-and-sour nostalgia, even a drunken feeling like the one generated by Scott Fitzgerald when he manages to dislocate his novelistic characters."

St. Martin had already been a secret admirer when he began translating Bryce Echenique. "I've never tried to meet him," he says, "in spite of the fact that he lives in Madrid." In St. Martins eyes, translating follows a simple method: "I read the text once and then tackle it with a first draft quickly. After that I do one or two revisions. By the way, I try to stick to the original text but I don't believe in stepping on the original author's heels."

Alfredo Bryce Echenique
CON JIMMY EN PARACAS

Lo estoy viendo realmente; es como si lo estuviera viendo; allí está sentado, en el amplio comedor veraniego, de espaldas a ese mar donde había rayas, tal vez tiburones. Yo estaba sentado al frente suyo, en la misma mesa, y, sin embargo, me parece que lo estuviera observando desde la puerta de ese comedor, de donde ya todos se habían marchado, ya sólo quedábamos él y yo, habíamos llegado los últimos, habíamos alcanzado con las justas el almuerzo.

Esta vez me había traído; lo habían mandado sólo por el fin de semana, Paracas no estaba tan lejos: estaría de regreso a tiempo para el colegio, el lunes. Mi madre no había podido venir; por eso me había traído. Me llevaba siempre a sus viajes cuando ella no podía acompañarlo, y cuando podía volver a tiempo para el colegio. Yo escuchaba cuando le decía a mamá que era una pena que no pudiera venir, la compañía le pagaba la estadía, le pagaba hotel de lujo para dos personas. «Lo llevaré», decía, refiriéndose a mí. Creo que yo le gustaba para esos viajes.

Y a mí, ¡cómo me gustaban esos viaje! Esta vez era a Paracas. Yo no conocía Paracas, y cuando mi padre empezó a arreglar la maleta, el viernes por la noche, ya sabía que no dormiría muy bien esa noche, y que me despertaría antes de sonar el despertador.

Partimos ese sábado muy temprano, pero tuvimos que perder mucho tiempo en la oficina, antes de entrar en la carretera al sur. Parece que mi padre tenía todavía cosas que ver allí, tal vez recibir las últimas instrucciones de su jefe. No sé; yo me quedé esperándolo afuera, en el auto, y empecé a temer que llegaríamos mucho más tarde de lo que habíamos calculado.

Una vez en la carretera, eran otras mis preocupaciones. Mi padre manejaba, como siempre, despacísimo; más despacio de lo que mamá le había pedido que manejara. Uno tras otro, los automóviles nos iban dejando atrás, y yo no miraba a mi padre para que no se fuera a dar cuenta de que eso me fastidiaba un poco, en realidad me

Alfredo Bryce Echenique
IN PARACAS WITH JIMMY

Translated by Hardie St. Martin

I can actually see him now, sitting there in the dining room at the summer resort, his back to the sea with its stingrays, maybe even sharks. I am sitting across from him, at the same table, yet seem to be watching him from the doorway of that room everyone had already left, only he and I are still there, we had been the last to arrive and had just made it for lunch.

This time he had brought me along. They had sent him down just for the weekend, Paracas wasn't very far. I'd be back in time for school on Monday. Mother hadn't been able to come, so he had brought me instead. He always took me when she couldn't go with him and I'd be able to make it back in time for school. I'd listen when he told mother it was a pity she couldn't come, the Company was putting him up in a luxury hotel room for two. "I'll take him along," he said, meaning me. I think he liked to have me with him on those trips.

And how I loved them! This time it was to Paracas where I'd never been, and when my father started packing his suitcase on Friday evening I knew I wouldn't get much sleep that night and would wake up before the alarm went off.

We left quite early Saturday morning but had to lose a lot of time at the office before we got on to the southern highway. Apparently my father still had things to look into, maybe receive last minute instructions from his boss. I'm not sure, I stayed out in the car waiting and started to worry that we'd arrive much later than we'd planned.

Once we hit the highway, there were other things for me to worry about. My father drove as slowly as ever, more slowly than mother had begged him to. One after the other, cars kept passing and leaving us behind, but I never looked at him, so as not to let him see how much it upset me, how ashamed it really made me

avergonzaba bastante. Pero nada había que hacer, y el viejo Pontiac, ya muy viejo el pobre, avanzaba lentísimo, anchísimo, negro e inmenso, balanceándose como una lancha sobre la carretera recién asfaltada.

A eso de la mitad del camino, mi padre decidió encender la radio. Yo no sé qué le pasó; bueno, siempre sucedía lo mismo, pero sólo probó una estación, estaban tocando una guaracha, y apagó inmediatamente sin hacer ningún comentario. Me hubiera gustado escuchar un poco de música, pero no le dije nada. Creo que por eso le gustaba llevarme en sus viajes; yo no era un muchachillo preguntón; me gustaba ser dócil; estaba consciente de mi docilidad. Pero eso sí, era muy observador.

Y por eso lo miraba de reojo, y ahora lo estoy viendo manejar. Lo veo jalarse un poquito el pantalón desde las rodillas, dejando aparecer las medias blancas, impecables, mejores que las mías, porque yo todavía soy un niño; blancas e impecables porque estamos yendo a Paracas, hotel de lujo, lugar de veraneo, mucha plata y todas esas cosas. Su saco es el mismo de todos los viajes fuera de Lima, gris, muy claro, sport; es norteamericano y le va a durar toda la vida. El pantalón es gris, un poco más oscuro que el saco, y la camisa es la camisa vieja más nueva del mundo; a mí nunca me va a durar una camisa como le duran a mi padre.

Y la boina; la boina es vasca; él dice que es vasca de puta cepa. Es para los viajes; para el aire, para la calvicie. Porque mi padre es calvo, calvísimo, y ahora que lo estoy viendo ya no es un hombre alto. Ya aprendí que mi padre no es un hombre alto, sino más bien bajo. Es bajo y muy flaco. Bajo, calvo y flaco, pero yo entonces tal vez no lo veía aún así, ahora ya sé que sólo es el hombre más bueno de la tierra, dócil como yo, en realidad se muere de miedo de sus jefes; esos jefes que lo quieren tanto porque hace siete millones de años que no llega tarde ni se enferma ni falta a la oficina; esos jefes que yo he visto cómo le dan palmazos en la espalda y se pasan la vida felicitándolo en la puerta de la iglesia los domingos; pero a mí hasta ahora no me saludan, y mi padre se pasa la vida diciéndole a mi madre, en la puerta de la iglesia los domingos, que las mujeres de sus jefes son distraídas o no la han visto, porque a mi madre tampoco la saludan, aunque a él, a mi padre, no se olvidaron de mandarle sus saludos y felicitaciones cuando cumplió un millón de años más sin enfermarse ni llegar tarde a la oficina, la vez aquella en

feel. Still there was nothing I could do, the poor old Pontiac was ancient, very bulky, black, enormous, and lumbered on, rocking like a barge on the newly paved highway.

When we'd gone about halfway, my father decided to switch on the radio. I don't know what came over him; anyway, he always did the same thing, but he tried only one station—they were playing a *guaracha*—and turned it off right away, without saying a word. I'd have enjoyed a little music but didn't protest. I believe that's why he liked to have me on his trips, I wasn't a kid who asked a lot of questions, I was easygoing and was conscious of it. One thing, though I was a very sharp observer.

That's why I watched him out the corner of my eye, and now I still see him driving, pulling up his trouser legs at the knees, letting his spotless white socks show, and they're better than mine because I'm still just a kid; white and spotless because we're on our way to Paracas, luxury hotel, summer resort, big bank rolls and all that kind of stuff. His jacket is the same for all trips outside of Lima, very light gray, sporty; it's U.S.-made and will last him all his life. The trousers are gray too, a slight shade darker than the jacket, and his shirt is the newest old shirt in the world. No shirt is ever going to last me like my father's shirts last him.

And the beret, it's Basque; the real thing, he explains. Just right for his travels, for the wind, for his bald head. Because my father is bald, bald as an egg, and when I look at him now, he's not a tall man anymore. I've discovered that my father is not a tall man, he's on the short side. Short and skinny. Short, bald, skinny; but I hadn't come to see him like that yet, and all I know now is he's the finest man on earth, easygoing like me and really scared of his bosses, who are so fond of him because he has never been late for work in the last seven million years or out sick or failed to show up at the office, bosses who I've seen slapping him on the back and who are forever congratulating him at the church door on Sundays; but they've never said hello to me, and my father is forever reassuring my mother at the church door on Sundays that his bosses' wives are absentminded or haven't seen her, because they don't say hello to her either, and yet they didn't forget to send him greetings and good wishes when he rounded out another million years without getting sick or being late at the office, that time when he brought home the

que trajo esas fotos en que estoy seguro, un jefe acababa de palmearle la espalda, y otro estaba a punto de palmeársela; y esa otra foto en que ya los jefes se habían marchado del cocktail, pero habían asistido, te decía mi padre, y volvía a mostrarte la primera fotografía.

Pero todo esto es ahora en que lo estoy viendo, no entonces en que lo estaba mirando mientras llegábamos a Paracas en el Pontiac. Yo me había olvidado un poco del Pontiac, pero las paredes blancas del hotel me hicieron verlo negro, ya muy viejo el pobre, y tan ancho, «Adónde va a acabar esta mole», me preguntaba, y estoy seguro de que mi padre se moría de miedo al ver esos carrazos, no lo digo por grandes, sino por la pinta. Si les daba un topetón, entonces habría que ver de quién era ese carrazo, porque mi padre era muy señor, y entonces aparecería el dueño, veraneando en Paracas con sus amigos, y tal vez conocía a los jefes de mi padre, había oído hablar de él, «no ha pasado nada, Juanito» (así se llamaba, se llama mi padre), y lo iban a llenar de palmazos en la espalda, luego vendrían los aperitivos, y a mí no me iban a saludar, pero yo actuaría de acuerdo a las circunstancias y de tal manera que mi padre no se diera cuenta de que no me habían saludado. Era mejor que mi madre no hubiera venido.

Pero no pasó nada. Encontramos un sitio anchísimo para el Pontiac negro, y al bajar, así sí que lo vi viejísimo. Ya estábamos en el hotel de Paracas, hotel de lujo y todo lo demás. Un muchacho vino hasta el carro por la maleta. Fue la primera persona que saludamos. Nos llevó a la recepción y allí mi padre firmó los papeles de reglamento, y luego preguntó si todavía podíamos «almorzar algo» (recuerdo que así dijo). El hombre de la recepción, muy distinguido, mucho más alto que mi padre, le respondió afirmativamente: «Claro que sí, señor. El muchacho lo va a acompañar hasta su 'bungalow', para que usted pueda lavarse las manos, si lo desea. Tiene usted tiempo, señor; el comedor cierra dentro de unos minutos, y su 'bungalow' no está muy alejado.» No sé si mi papá, pero yo todo eso de «bungalow» lo entendí muy bien, porque estudio en colegio inglés y eso no lo debo olvidar en mi vida y cada vez que mi papá estalla, cada mil años, luego nos invita al cine, grita que hace siete millones de años que trabaja enfermo y sin llegar tarde para darle a sus hijos lo mejor, lo mismo que a los hijos de sus jefes.

photos where I'm sure one boss had just slapped him on the back and another had already left the cocktail party, but they had been there, my father said to you, showing you the first photo again.

All this is not then but now that I'm seeing him, watching him as we reached Paracas in the Pontiac. The Pontiac had kind of slipped to the back of my mind but the hotel's walls called my attention to it there: black, very ancient, poor bastard, and so bulky. "Where will all those people end up?" he asked me, and I'm sure my father was scared to death, seeing those great big hearses, I don't mean because they were big but because they looked so fancy. If he had run into one of them, he would have had to deal with whoever owned it—because my father was a real gentleman—, when its owner, summer vacationing in Paracas with his friends, turned up and would maybe know my father's bosses and would have heard of him, "It's nothing to worry about, Juanito," (that was and is my father's name), and they'd slap him all over his back, then there would be pre-dinner drinks, and they wouldn't say hello to me but I'd act naturally just so he wouldn't notice they hadn't said hello to me. It was a good thing my mother hadn't been along.

But nothing happened. We found a space with plenty of room for the black Pontiac and there, when I got out, it sure looked old to me. We were at our Paracas hotel, four-star and all. The boy who walked over to the car for the suitcase was the first person we greeted. He led us to the reception desk and my father signed in and asked if we could still have "some lunch" (I remember those were his words.) The man at the desk, very distinguished-looking, much taller than my father, said okay: "Yes of course, sir. The boy will take you to your 'bungalow' so that you can wash up, if you'd like to. You have enough time, sir, the dining room will close in a few minutes but your 'bungalow' *isn't* very far away." I didn't know about my father, but I understood the 'bungalow' bit very well because I was attending an English school, which is something I mustn't forget the rest of my life; every time my dad blows up once in a thousand years, and later treats us to a movie, he shouts out that he works even when he's sick and has never been late in seven million years so as to give his kids only the very best, same as his bosses' kids.

El muchacho que nos llevó hasta el «bungalow» no se sonrió mucho cuando mi padre le dio la propina, pero ya yo sabía que cuando se viaja con dinero de la compañía no se puede andar derrochando, si no, pobres jefes, nunca ganarían un céntimo y la compañía quebraría en la mente respetuosa de mi padre, que se estaba lavando las manos mientras yo abría la maleta y sacaba alborotado mi ropa de baño. Fue entonces que me enteré, él me lo dijo, que nada de acercarme al mar, que estaba plagado de rayas, hasta había tiburones. Corrí a lavarme las manos, por eso de que dentro de unos minutos cierran el comedor, y dejé mi ropa de baño tirada sobre la cama. Cerramos la puerta del «bungalow» y fuimos avanzando hacia el comedor. Mi padre también, aunque menos, creo que era observador; me señaló la piscina, tal vez por eso de la ropa de baño. Era hermoso Paracas, tenía de desierto, de oasis, de balneario; arena, palmeras, flores, veredas y caminos por donde chicas que yo no me atrevía a mirar, pocas ya, las últimas, las más atrasadas, se iban perezosas a dormir esa siesta de quien ya se acostumbró al hotel de lujo. Tímidos y curiosos, mi padre y yo entramos al comedor.

Y es allí, sentado de espaldas al mar, a las rayas y a los tiburones, es allí donde lo estoy viendo, como si yo estuviera en la puerta del comedor, y es que en realidad yo también me estoy viendo sentado allí, en la misma mesa, cara a cara a mi padre y esperando al mozo ese, que a duras penas contestó a nuestro saludo, que había ido a traer el menú (mi padre pidió la carta y él dijo que iba por el menú) y que según papá debería habernos cambiado de mantel, pero era mejor no decir nada porque, a pesar de que ése era un hotel de lujo, habíamos llegado con las justas para almorzar. Yo casi vuelvo a saludar al mozo cuando regresó y le entregó el menú a mi padre que entró en dificultades y pidió, finalmente, corvina a la no sé cuántos, porque el mozo ya llevaba horas esperando. Se largó con el pedido y mi padre, sonriéndome, puso la carta sobre la mesa, de tal manera que yo podía leer los nombres de algunos platos, un montón de nombres franceses en realidad, y entonces pensé, aliviándome, que algo terrible hubiera podido pasar, como aquella vez en ese restaurante de tipo moderno, con un menú que parecía para norteamericanos, cuando mi padre me pasó la carta para que yo pidiera, y empezó a contarle al mozo que él no sabía inglés, pero que a su hijo lo estaba educando en colegio inglés, a sus otros hijos

The boy who took us to the bungalow didn't smile much when my father tipped him, but I knew that when you traveled on the Company's pay roll you couldn't splurge, because if you did the poor bosses would never make a dime and would fold up, in the mind of my obliging father who was washing his hands while I opened the suitcase and, all excited, pulled out my swimming trunks. That's when I found out—he told me—I shouldn't go near the sea because it was infested with stingrays, and maybe even sharks. I rushed over to wash my hands, because they were going to close the dining room in a few minutes, and I left my trunks lying on the bed. We shut the bungalow door and went to the dining room. My father was also observant, but less than me; he pointed out the swimming pool, maybe because of my trunks. Paracas was beautiful, a kind of oasis, a spa; sand, palm trees, flowers, side paths and roads where girls I didn't have the nerve to look at, only a few of them now, the last ones, still hanging on, dawdled on their way to sleep the siesta of those who've already grown used to the luxury hotel. Timid but curious, my father and I went into the dining room.

And it's there, sitting with his back to the sea, the stingrays and the sharks, it's there I'm seeing him, as if I were in the dining room's doorway, and I'm really seeing myself too, at the same table, across from him, waiting for the waiter who had barely answered our greeting and had gone off for the menu (my father had asked for the bill of fare and the man had said he was going for the *menu)* and who according to Dad should have changed the tablecloth but we had better not say anything because it was a luxury hotel and we had arrived for lunch at the last minute. I almost greeted the waiter again when he came back and handed the menu to my father who, in way over his head, finally ordered corvina *a la* something or other because the waiter had been standing there waiting for ages. He left with the order and, smiling over at me, my father set up the menu on the table so I could read the names of some of the dishes, actually a bunch of French names, and I thought, relieved, that something terrible could have happened, like the time in an ultramodern restaurant with a menu that looked like it was for Americans, when my father passed me the menu to do the ordering and started telling the waiter he *didn't* know any English but he was putting his boy through an English school, and his other children too, money was

también, costara lo que costara, y el mozo no le prestaba ninguna atención, y movía la pierna porque ya se quería largar.

Fue entonces que mi padre estuvo realmente triunfal. Mientras el mozo venía con las corvinas a la no sé cuántos, mi padre empezó a hablar de darnos un lujo, de que el ambiente lo pedía, y de que la compañía no iba a quebrar si él pedía una botellita de vino blanco para acompañar esas corvinas. Decía que esa noche a las siete era la reunión con esos agricultores, y que le comprarían los tractores que le habían encargado vender; él nunca le había fallado a la compañía. En esas estaba cuando el mozo apareció complicándose la vida en cargar los platos de la manera más difícil, eso parecía un circo, y mi padre lo miraba como si fuera a aplaudir, pero gracias a Dios reaccionó y tomó una actitud bastante forzada, aunque digna, cuando el mozo jugaba a casi tirarnos los platos por la cara, en realidad era que los estaba poniendo elegantemente sobre la mesa y que nosotros no estábamos acostumbrados a tanta cosa. «Un blanco no sé cuántos», dijo mi padre. Yo casi lo abrazo por esa palabra en francés que acababa de pronunciar, esa marca de vino, ni siquiera había pedido la carta para consultar, no, nada de eso; lo había pedido así no más, triunfal, conocedor, y el mozo no tuvo más remedio que tomar nota y largarse a buscar.

Todo marchaba perfecto. Nos habían traído el vino y ahora recuerdo ese momento de feliz equilibrio: mi padre sentado de espaldas al mar, no era que el comedor estuviera al borde del mar, pero el muro que sostenía esos ventanales me impedía ver la piscina y la playa, y ahora lo que estoy viendo es la cabeza, la cara de mi padre, sus hombros, el mar allá atrás, azul en ese día de sol, las palmeras por aquí y por allá, la mano delgada y fina de mi padre sobre la botella fresca de vino, sirviéndome media copa, llenando su copa, «bebe despacio, hijo», ya algo quemado por el sol, listo a acceder, extrañando a mi madre, buenísima, y yo ahí, casi chorreándome con el jugo ese que bañaba la corvina, hasta que vi a Jimmy. Me chorreé cuando lo vi. Nunca sabré por qué me dio miedo verlo. Pronto lo supe.

Me sonreía desde la puerta del comedor, y yo lo saludé, mirando luego a mi padre para explicarle quién era, que estaba en mi clase, etc.; pero mi padre, al escuchar su apellido, volteó a mirarlo sonriente, me dijo que lo llamara, y mientras cruzaba el comedor,

no object, and the waiter, who couldn't have cared less, kept shifting from leg to leg because he just wanted to get away.

Then my father chalked up a real victory. While the waiter was on his way back with the corvina a la something or other, my father started talking about us splurging because the place called for it and it wouldn't break the Company if he ordered a small bottle of white wine to go with the corvinas. He said he'd be meeting with the big-time farmers that evening at seven and they would buy the tractors he had been asked to sell; he had never failed the Company. He was going on about this when the waiter appeared, doing his best to carry the dishes in the most impossible way, it looked like a circus act, and my father watching him as if he were ready to start applauding, but thank God he used his head and put on a pretty stiff but dignified pose while the waiter performed his trick of nearly spilling the dishes into our faces, he was really setting them down on the table elegantly and we weren't used to the fancy treatment. "A white such and such," my father said. I almost hugged him for the word he had just pronounced in French, the name of the wine, when he hadn't even checked it on the wine list, no, none of that; he had ordered it just like that, triumphant, a connoisseur, and the waiter could only write it down and go fetch it.

Everything was going smoothly. They had brought us the wine and now I remember that moment of perfect harmony: my father sitting with his back to the sea, not that the dining room was over the beach, but the wall holding up those picture windows kept me from seeing the swimming pool and what I'm looking at now is my father's head, his face, his shoulders, the sea beyond him, blue on that sunny day, the palm trees scattered here and there, my father's fine slender hand around the cool bottle of wine pouring me half a glass, filling his own, "drink slowly, son," already a bit sunburned, obsequious, lonely for my mother, the best in the world, and me there, almost letting the juice the corvina was swimming in run all over me, and then I saw Jimmy. I let it run all over me then. It never dawned on me why I was so scared to see him. I would soon find out.

He was smiling at me from the dining room entrance and I said hi, glancing at my father to explain who he was, he was in my class and so on, but when my father heard his last name he turned to him with a broad grin on his face, he said for me to call him over

que conocía a su padre, amigo de sus jefes, uno de los directores de la compañía, muchas tierras en esa región...

—Jimmy, papá.—Y se dieron la mano.

—Siéntate, muchacho—dijo mi padre, y ahora recién me saludó a mí.

Era muy bello; Jimmy era de una belleza extraordinaria: rubio, el pelo en anillos de oro, los ojos azules achinados, y esa piel bronceada, bronceada todo el año, invierno y verano, tal vez porque venía siempre a Paracas. No bien se había sentado, noté algo que me pareció extraño: el mismo mozo que nos odiaba a mi padre y a mí, se acercaba ahora sonriente, servicial, humilde, y saludaba a Jimmy con todo respeto; pero éste, a duras penas le contestó con una mueca. Y el mozo no se iba, seguía ahí, parado, esperando órdenes, buscándolas, yo casi le pido a Jimmy que lo mandara matarse. De los cuatro que estábamos ahí, Jimmy era el único sereno.

Y ahí empezó la cosa. Estoy viendo a mi padre ofrecerle a Jimmy un poquito de vino en una copa. Ahí empezó mi terror.

—No, gracias—dijo Jimmy—. Tomé vino con el almuerzo.—Y sin mirar al mozo, le pidió un whisky.

Miré a mi padre: los ojos fijos en el plato, sonreía y se atragantaba un bocado de corvina que podía tener millones de espinas. Mi padre no impidió que Jimmy pidiera ese whisky, y ahí venía el mozo casi bailando con el vaso en una bandeja de plata, había que verle sonreírse al hijo de puta. Y luego Jimmy sacó un paquete de Chesterfield, lo puso sobre la mesa, encendió uno, y sopló todo el humo sobre la calva de mi padre, claro que no lo hizo por mal, lo hizo simplemente, y luego continuó bellísimo, sonriente, mirando hacia el mar, pero mi padre ni yo queríamos ya postres.

—¿Desde cuándo fumas?—le preguntó mi padre, con voz temblorosa.

—No sé; no me acuerdo—dijo Jimmy, ofreciéndome un cigarrillo.

—No, no, Jimmy; no...

—Fuma no más, hijito; no desprecies a tu amigo.

and as he crossed the room, he told me he knew his father, a friend of his bosses, one of the company directors, with lots of land in that part of the country...

"Jimmy, Dad." And they shook hands.

"Sit down, boy," my father said, and it was only then he said hello to me.

He was absolutely beautiful; Jimmy's was an extraordinary beauty: a blond with curly gold hair, blue almond-shaped eyes and bronze skin, bronze all year round, winter and summer, maybe because he was always coming to Paracas. As soon as he sat down I noticed something strange: the same waiter who had looked down his nose at my father and me came over, all smiles now, fawning, scraping and bowing, and he greeted Jimmy in a servile way but Jimmy merely smirked. And the waiter wouldn't go away, just stayed put, stood there waiting for orders, dying for them, and I almost asked Jimmy to tell him to drop dead. Of the four of us there, Jimmy was the only cool one.

And that's where the whole thing got started. I'm watching Dad offer Jimmy some wine. That's when I began to feel scared.

"No, thanks," Jimmy said. "I had wine for lunch." And without wasting a glance on him, he asked the waiter for a whiskey.

I checked my father: eyes nailed to his plate, smiling, he stuffed down a mouthful of corvina that might have been loaded with millions of bones. He didn't stop Jimmy from ordering the whiskey, and here was the waiter on his way now, almost pirouetting with the glass on a silver tray, it was something to watch the wide grin on the son of a bitch's face. And then Jimmy pulled out a pack of Chesterfields, laid it on the table, lit one up, and blew all the smoke on to the top of my father's bald head, of course he didn't do it deliberately, he just did it, and then he went on being so beautiful, smiling, looking at the sea, but neither my father nor I wanted any dessert.

"How long have you been smoking?" my father asked in a quivery voice.

"I don't know, can't remember," Jimmy said, offering me a cigarette.

"No, no, Jimmy, no..."

"Go ahead and smoke, sonny; don't turn down your friend."

Estoy viendo a mi padre decir esas palabras, y luego recoger una servilleta que no se le había caído, casi recoge el pie del mozo que seguía ahí parado. Jimmy y yo fumábamos, mientras mi padre nos contaba que a él nunca le había atraído eso de fumar, y luego de una afección a los bronquios que tuvo no sé cuándo, pero Jimmy empezó a hablar de automóviles, mientras yo observaba la ropa que llevaba puesta, parecía toda de seda, y la camisa de mi padre empezó a envejecer lastimosamente, ni su saco norteamericano le iba a durar toda la vida.

—¿Tú manejas, Jimmy?—preguntó mi padre.

—Hace tiempo. Ahora estoy en el carro de mi hermana; el otro día estrellé mi carro, pero ya le va a llegar otro a mi papá. En la hacienda tenemos varios carros.

Y yo muerto de miedo, pensando en el Pontiac; tal vez Jimmy se iba a enterar que ése era el de mi padre; se iba a burlar tal vez, lo iba a ver más viejo, más ancho, más feo que yo. «¿Para qué vinimos aquí?» Estaba recordando la compra del Pontiac, a mi padre convenciendo a mamá, «un pequeño sacrificio», y luego también los sábados por la tarde, cuando lo lavábamos, asunto de familia, todos los hermanos con latas de agua, mi padre con la manguera, mi madre en el balcón, nosotros locos por subir, por coger el timón, y mi padre autoritario: «Cuando sean grandes, cuando tengan brevete», y luego, sentimental: «Me ha costado años de esfuerzo.»

—¿Tienes brevete, Jimmy?

—No; no importa; aquí todos me conocen.

Y entonces fue que mi padre le preguntó que cuántos años tenía y fingió creerle cuando dijo que dieciséis, y yo también, casi le digo que era un mentiroso, pero para qué, todo el mundo sabía que Jimmy estaba en mi clase y que yo no había cumplido aún los catorce años.

—Manolo se va conmigo—dijo Jimmy—; vamos a pasear en el carro de mi hermana.

Y mi padre cedió una vez más, nuevamente sonrió, y le encargó a Jimmy saludar a su padre.

—Son casi las cuatro—dijo—, voy a descansar un poco, porque a las siete tengo una reunión de negocios.—Se despidió de Jimmy, y se marchó sin decirme a qué hora debía regresar, yo casi le digo que no se preocupara, que no nos íbamos a estrellar.

I can see my father saying those words and then picking up a napkin he hadn't dropped, almost picking up the foot of the waiter who was still standing there. Jimmy and I smoked, while my father told us he had never been tempted to smoke, and then went on about a bronchial condition he had had at some time or other, but Jimmy started talking about cars, while I checked the clothes he was wearing, they looked like silk, and my father's shirt began to age pathetically, not even his American jacket would last him all his life.

"Do you drive, Jimmy?" he asked.

"I've been doing it ever so long. Now I have my sister's car; I smashed mine up the other day but Dad is expecting another one. We have several cars at the ranch."

And I was scared stiff, thinking about the Pontiac; maybe Jimmy would find out it was father's, maybe he'd laugh at it, it would look even older, bulkier, uglier to him than it did to me. "Why had we come there?" I was remembering when my father had bought the car, convincing mom, "a small sacrifice," and also the Saturday afternoon when we washed it, quite a family ritual, all of us kids with cans of water, Dad with the hose, mom on the porch, all of us dying to get in and take the wheel, and my father acting the boss: "When you boys grow up, when you have a driver's license," and then in a sentimental tone: "This has cost me years of hard work."

"Do you have a license, Jimmy?"

"No, it makes no difference; everybody around here knows me.

And that's when my father asked him how old he was and acted as if he believed him when he said he was sixteen, and so did I; I had been about to call him a liar, but what for, everybody knew Jimmy was in my class and I wasn't fourteen yet.

"Manolo's coming with me," Jimmy said, "we'll go for a drive in my sister's car."

And my father gave in, smiled once more and asked Jimmy to say hello to his father.

"It's almost four o'clock," he said, "I'm going to get some rest; I have a business meeting at seven." He said goodbye to Jimmy and left without telling me what time I should be back and I almost told him not to worry, we weren't going to crack up.

Jimmy no me preguntó cuál era mi carro. No tuve por qué decirle que el Pontiac ese negro, el único que había ahí, era el carro de mi padre. Ahora sí se lo diría y luego, cuando se riera sarcásticamente le escupiría en la cara, aunque todos esos mozos que lo habían saludado mientras salíamos, todos esos que a mí no me habían caso, se me vinieran encima a matarme por haber ensuciado esa maravillosa cara de monedita de oro, esas manos de primer enamorado que estaban abriendo la puerta de un carro del jefe de mi padre.

A un millón de kilómetros por hora, estuvimos en Pisco, y allí Jimmy casi atropella a una mujer en la Plaza de Armas; a no sé cuantos millones de kilómetros por hora, con una cuarta velocidad especial, estuvimos en una de sus haciendas, y allí Jimmy tomó una Coca Cola, le pellizcó la nalga a una prima y no me presentó a sus hermanas; a no sé cuantos miles de millones de kilómetros por hora, estuvimos camino de Ica, y por allí Jimmy, me mostró el lugar en que había estrellado su carro, carro de mierda ese, dijo, no servía para nada.

Eran las nueve de la noche cuando regresamos a Paracas. No sé cómo, pero Jimmy me llevó hasta una salita en que estaba mi padre bebiendo con un montón de hombres. Ahí estaba sentado, la cara satisfecha, ya yo sabía que haría muy bien su trabajo. Todos esos hombres conocían a Jimmy; eran agricultores de por ahí, y acababan de comprar los tractores de la compañía. Algunos le tocaban el pelo a Jimmy y otros se dedicaban al whisky que mi padre estaba invitando en nombre de la compañía. En ese momento mi padre empezó a contar un chiste, pero Jimmy lo interrumpió para decirle que me invitaba a comer. «Bien, bien; dijo mi padre. Vayan nomás.»

Y esa noche bebí los primeros whiskies de mi vida, la primera copa llena de vino de mi vida, en una mesa impecable, con un mozo que bailaba sonriente y constante alrededor de nosotros. Todo el mundo andaba elegantísimo en ese comedor lleno de luces y de carcajadas de mujeres muy bonitas, hombres grandes y colorados que deslizaban sus manos sobre los anillos de oro de Jimmy, cuando pasaban hacia sus mesas. Fue entonces que me pareció escuchar el final del chiste que había estado contando mi padre, le puse cara de malo, y como que lo encerré en su salita con esos burdos agricultores que venían a comprar su primer tractor. Luego, esto sí que es extraño, me deslicé hasta muy adentro en el mar, y desde allí empecé

Jimmy didn't ask which car was mine and I didn't have to tell him it was the black Pontiac, the only one there, my father's car. Now I would like to tell him and when he laughed sarcastically I'd spit in his face, even if all those waiters who had greeted him on our way out, all those who didn't give a damn about me, even if they would all jump me and try to kill me for having messed up that face gorgeous like a gold coin, those hands, like the hands of someone in love for the first time, opening the door of a car owned by my father's boss.

Traveling at one million miles per hour, we were in Pisco in no time at all and there Jimmy almost ran over a woman in the Plaza de Armas; going at God knows how many million miles per hour, with a special fourth drive, we were soon at one of their ranches where Jimmy had a Coke, pinched one of his cousins in the cheek of her ass and didn't introduce me to his sisters; at I don't know how many thousands of millions of miles per hour, we were on our way to Ica and near there Jimmy showed me the spot where he had wrecked his car, shitty car, he said, it was no damn good.

It was 9:00 p.m. when we got back to Paracas. I don't remember how but Jimmy took me to a lounge where my father was having a drink with a whole bunch of men. He sat there, with a pleased look on his face, I had known he would do a great job. All those men knew Jimmy. They were landowners from around there and they had just bought the Company's tractors. Some patted Jimmy's hair and others were busy with the whiskey my father was treating them to in the Company's name. Just then my father started telling a joke but Jimmy interrupted him to say he was inviting me to dinner. "Fine, fine," my father said. "Go right ahead."

That night I drank the first whiskeys in my life, the first full glass of wine in my life, at a spotless table, with a smiling waiter dancing attendance on us. Everyone was elegantly dressed in this dining room filled with lights and the laughter of lovely women, with big red-faced men who slid their hands over Jimmy's gold ringlets as they walked past on their way to their tables. That's when I seemed to hear the end of the joke my father had been telling, I scowled in his direction, and I kind of locked him into his little lounge with those redneck farmers who had come to buy their first tractor. Then, and this is something really strange, I slipped far out

a verme navegando en un comedor en fiesta, mientras un mozo me servía arrodillado una copa de champagne, bajo la mirada achinada y azul de Jimmy.

Yo no le entendía muy bien al principio; en realidad no sabía de qué estaba hablando, ni qué quería decir con todo eso de la ropa interior. Todavía lo estaba viendo firmar la cuenta; garabatear su nombre sobre una cifra monstruosa y luego invitarme a pasear por la playa. «Vamos», me había dicho, y yo lo estaba siguiendo a lo largo del malecón oscuro, sin entender muy bien todo eso de la ropa interior. Pero Jimmy insistía, volvía a preguntarme qué calzoncillos usaba yo, y añadía que los suyos eran así y asá, hasta que nos sentamos en esas escaleras que daban a la arena y al mar. Las olas reventaban muy cerca y Jimmy estaba ahora hablando de órganos genitales, órganos genitales masculinos solamente, y yo, sentado a su lado, escuchándolo sin saber qué responder, tratando de ver las rayas y los tiburones de que hablaba mi padre, y de pronto corriendo hacia ellos porque Jimmy acababa de ponerme una mano sobre la pierna, «¿cómo la tienes, Manolo?», dijo, y salí disparado.

Estoy viendo a Jimmy alejarse; tranquilamente; regresar hacia la luz del comedor y desaparecer al cabo de unos instantes. Desde el borde del mar, con los píes húmedos, miraba hacia el hotel lleno de luces y hacia la hilera de «bungalows», entre los cuales estaba el mío. Pensé en regresar corriendo, pero luego me convencí de que era una tontería, de que ya nada pasaría esa noche. Lo terrible sería que Jimmy continuara por allí, al día siguiente; pero por el momento, nada; sólo volver y acostarme.

Me acercaba al «bungalow» y escuché una carcajada extraña. Mi padre estaba con alguien. Un hombre inmenso y rubio zamaqueaba el brazo de mi padre, lo felicitaba, le decía algo de eficiencia, y ¡zas! le dio el palmazo en el hombro. «Buenas noches, Juanito», le dijo. «Buenas noches, don Jaime», y en ese instante me vio.

—Mírelo; ahí está. ¿Dónde está Jimmy, Manolo?

—Se fue hace un rato, papá.

—Saluda al padre de Jimmy.

—¿Cómo estás muchacho? O sea que Jimmy se fue hace rato; bueno, ya aparecerá. Estaba felicitando a tu padre; ojalá tú salgas a él. Le he acompañado hasta su «bungalow».

to sea and there I started to watch myself in a festive dining room while a waiter, on his knees, served me a glass of champagne under Jimmy's almond-eyed blue stare.

At first, I didn't quite get him, I really didn't know what he was driving at or what he meant with all his talk about underwear. I was still watching him sign the bill, scribbling his name over a monstrously high figure and then inviting me to go for a walk along the beach. "Come on," he'd said and I was keeping up with him on the dim boardwalk without quite getting all his talk about underwear. But Jimmy wouldn't let up, asking me what kind of undershorts I wore and adding that his were like this, like that, till we sat down or some steps facing the sand and the sea. Waves were crashing real close to us and now Jimmy was talking about genital organs, only about male organs, and me sitting next to him, listening, not knowing what to say back, trying to make out the stingrays and the sharks my father was always mentioning, and suddenly racing toward them because Jimmy had just put his hand on my leg, "What's yours like, Manolo?" he said and I took off like a streak.

I'm watching Jimmy move away, very cool, heading back toward the bright glow of the dining room and soon slipping out of sight. From the sea's edge, standing there with wet feet, I stared at the hotel studded with lights and at the row of bungalows, one of them mine. I thought of running back there but then decided it would be silly, nothing more would happen that night. The awful thing would be if Jimmy stuck around all of the next day but right now, forget it, I'd just turn back and go to bed.

I had almost reached the bungalow when I heard a strange laugh. My father was with someone. An enormous blond man was roughing up my father's arm, congratulating him, saying something about doing a great job and wham! slapped him on the back. "Good night, Juanito," he said. "Good night, don Jaime," and just then he noticed me.

"Look, there he is. Where's Jimmy, Manolo?"

"He left a while ago, Dad."

"Say hello to Jimmy's father."

"How are you, kid? So Jimmy took off a while ago, well, he'll show up. I was just congratulating your father: I hope you'll take after him. I walked him over to his bungalow."

—Don Jaime es muy amable.

—Bueno, Juanito, buenas noches.—Y se marchó, inmenso.

Cerramos la puerta del «bungalow» detrás nuestro. Los dos habíamos bebido, él más que yo, y estábamos listos para la cama. Ahí estaba todavía mi ropa de baño, y mi padre me dijo que mañana por la mañana podría bañarme. Luego me preguntó que si había pasado un buen día, que si Jimmy era mi amigo en el colegio, y que si mañana lo iba a ver; y yo a todo: «Sí, papá, sí, papá» hasta que apagó la luz y se metió en la cama, mientras yo, ya acostado, buscaba un dolor de estómago para quedarme en cama mañana, y pensé que ya se había dormido. Pero no. Mi padre me dijo, en la oscuridad, que el nombre de la compañía había quedado muy bien, que él había hecho un buen trabajo, estaba contento mi padre. Más tarde volvió a hablarme; me dijo que don Jaime había estado muy amable en acompañarlo hasta la puerta del «bungalow»—y que era todo un señor. Y como dos horas más tarde, me preguntó: «Manolo, ¿qué quiere decir bungalow en castellano?»

"It was very nice of don Jaime."

"Well, good night, Juanito." And he went off, enormous.

We shut the bungalow's door behind us. We were both a little tight, he more than me, and ready for bed. My trunks were still there and my father said that tomorrow I could go for a swim. Then he asked if I'd had a nice day and whether Jimmy was a school pal and was I going to see him tomorrow. And to all this I said yes: "Yes, Dad, yes Dad," till he switched the light off and got into bed. Lying in bed, I wracked my brain for a stomach ache or some other excuse to let me stay in bed the next day, and thought he had already fallen asleep. But no. In the dark, my father told me the company's name had come through with flying colors, he had done a good job, my father was happy. Later, he spoke again. He said it had been very nice of don Jaime to walk him to the "bungalow" door, he was a real gentleman. And a couple of hours later, he asked me: "Manolo, what does 'bungalow' mean in Spanish?"

EL COCODRILO

THE CROCODILE

Alfred J. MacAdam, translator of Felisberto Hernández

Alfred J. MacAdam teaches at Barnard College. He is the author of *Textual Confrontations* and has translated Carlos Fuentes, Juan Carlos Onetti, Oswaldo Soriano, José Donoso, Fernando Pessoa, and Mario Vargas Llosa, among others. MacAdam postponed the start of a serious translation career when, as an undergraduate at Rutgers College, his senior project (Vicente Huidobro's long poem *Altazor)* had what he calls "catastrophic results." Much later, after a more heartening encounter with Carlos Franqui's account of the Cuban Revolution, *Family Portrait with Fidel*, and other fiction projects, MacAdam began to consider translation seriously. He offers his gratitude to word processing technology, which enables him to practice a direct approach to the texts at hand: "I simply sit down and translate without really reading it through," he said during an interview, and then he revises at the computer. He cites his translation of the encyclopedic novel *Christopher Unborn*, done in close collaboration with author Carlos Fuentes, as one of his greatest challenges, along with Fernando's Pessoa's *Book of Disquiet*. According to MacAdam, the most essential aspect of the dynamic of author, editor and translator is that all three "must remember they are working toward the same goal."

MacAdam discovered Felisberto Hernández, the celebrated Kafkesque author of *Piano Stories*, when writing his doctoral dissertation on Julio Cortázar. Hernández, born in 1902 in Montevideo, was a pianist by profession who for years worked in silent screen theaters and afterwards became a government employee. He died in 1963. Some of Cortázar's stories are clearly inspired by Hernández's imagery, especially "House Taken Over," which resembles Hernández's "House Inundated." "The Crocodile," which is not included in *Piano Stories*, is a work MacAdam deems "nothing short of extraordinary."

Felisberto Hernández
EL COCODRILO

En una noche de otoño hacía calor húmedo y yo fui a una ciudad que me era casi desconocida; la poca luz de las calles estaba atenuada por la humedad y por algunas hojas de los árboles. Entré a un café que estaba cerca de una iglesia, me senté a una mesa del fondo y pensé en mi vida. Yo sabía aislar las horas de felicidad y encerrarme en ellas; primero robaba con los ojos cualquier cosa descuidada de la calle o del interior de las casas y después la llevaba a mi soledad. Gozaba tanto al repasarla que si la gente lo hubiera sabido me hubiera odiado. Tal vez no me quedara mucho tiempo de felicidad. Antes yo había cruzado por aquellas ciudades dando conciertos de piano; las horas de dicha habían sido escasas, pues vivía en la angustia de reunir gentes que quisieran aprobar la realización de un concierto; tenía que coordinarlos, influirlos mutuamente y tratar de encontrar algún hombre que fuera activo. Casi siempre eso era como luchar con borrachos lentos y distraídos: cuando lograba traer uno el otro se me iba. Además yo tenía que estudiar y escribirme artículos en los diarios.

Desde hacía algún tiempo ya no tenía esa preocupación: alcancé a entrar en una gran casa de medias para mujer. Había pensado que las medias eran más necesarias que los conciertos y que sería más fácil colocarlas. Un amigo mío le dijo al gerente que yo tenía muchas relaciones femeninas, porque era concertista de piano y había recorrido muchas ciudades: entonces, podría aprovechar la influencia de los conciertos para colocar medias.

El gerente había torcido el gesto; pero aceptó, no sólo por la influencia de mi amigo, sino porque yo había sacado el segundo premio en las leyendas de propaganda para esas medias. Su marca era "Ilusión". Y mi frase había sido: "¿Quién no acaricia, hoy, una media Ilusión?" Pero vender medias también me resultaba muy difícil y esperaba que de un momento a otro me llamaran de la casa central y me suprimieran el viático. Al principio yo había hecho un

Felisberto Hernández
THE CROCODILE
Translated by Alfred MacAdam

One hot, humid autumn night, I traveled to a city I knew only very slightly. The humidity and the leaves on the trees made the dim street lights even dimmer. I went into a cafe near a church, sat down at a rear table, and thought about my life. I had the ability to separate my hours of happiness and enclose myself inside them. First, using my eyes, I would steal some forgotten object on the street or inside a house and then carry it off to my solitude. I enjoyed myself so much when I contemplated it that if people knew how much they would have hated me. Perhaps I didn't have much time left for happiness.

I had toured cities like that one giving piano concerts. My hours of happiness were few and far between because I lived with the anxiety that I was bringing together people who only wanted the concert to end. I had to coordinate them, influence them, and try to locate some dynamic man among them. It was almost always like wrestling slow, distracted drunks: just when I managed to get one, another would wander off. Besides, I also had to practice and write newspaper articles.

For a long time, I was free of that last problem: I managed to get a job with a company that manufactured women's stockings. I reasoned that stockings were more necessary than concerts so it would be easy to sell them. A friend of mine told the company supervisor I had lots of female acquaintances because I was a concert pianist and visited many cities. Therefore, I could use the influence of the concerts to sell stockings.

The supervisor grimaced, but he took me on, not only because of my friend's influence but because I had won second prize in a contest for advertising slogans about the stockings. The brand was *Illusion*, and my slogan was, "What woman doesn't cherish her *Illusion*?" But selling stockings also turned out to be hard for me, and I expected to be called from the main office at any moment and told that my travel expenses were canceled. At the beginning, I

gran esfuerzo. (La venta de medias no tenía nada que ver con mis conciertos: y yo tenía que entendérmelas nada más que con los comerciantes.) Cuando encontraba antiguos conocidos les decía que la representación de una gran casa comercial me permitía viajar con independencia y no obligar a mis amigos a patrocinar conciertos cuando no eran oportunos. Jamás habían sido oportunos mis conciertos. En esta misma ciudad me habían puesto pretextos poco comunes: el presidente del Club estaba de mal humor porque yo lo había hecho levantar de la mesa de juego y me dijo que habiendo muerto una persona que tenía muchos parientes, media ciudad estaba enlutada. Ahora yo les decía: estaré unos días para ver si surge naturalmente el deseo de un concierto; pero le producía mala impresión el hecho de que un concertista vendiera medias. Y en cuanto a colocar medias, todas las mañanas yo me animaba y todas las noches me desanimaba: era como vestirse y desnudarse. Me costaba renovar a cada instante cierta fuerza grosera necesaria para insistir ante comerciantes siempre apurados. Pero ahora me había resignado a esperar que me echaran y trataba de disfrutar mientras me duraba el viático.

De pronto me di cuenta que había entrado al café un ciego con un arpa; yo le había visto por la tarde. Decidí irme antes de perder la voluntad de disfrutar de la vida; pero al pasar cerca de él volví a verlo con un sombrero de alas mal dobladas y dando vuelta los ojos hacia el cielo mientras hacía el esfuerzo de tocar; algunas cuerdas del arpa estaban añadidas y la madera clara del instrumento y todo el hombre estaban cubiertos de una mugre que yo nunca había visto. Pensé en mí y sentí depresión.

Cuando encendí la luz en la pieza de mi hotel, vi mi cama de aquellos días. Estaba abierta y sus varillas niqueladas me hacían pensar en una loca joven que se entregaba a cualquiera. Después de acostado apagué la luz pero no podía dormir. Volví a encenderla y la bombita se asomó debajo de la pantalla como el globo de un ojo bajo un párpado oscuro. La apagué en seguida y quise pensar en el negocio de las medias pero seguí viendo por un momento, en la oscuridad, la pantalla de luz Se había convertido a un color claro; después, su forma, como si fuera el alma en pena de la pantalla, empezó a irse hacia un lado y a fundirse en lo oscuro. Todo eso ocurrió en el tiempo que tardaría un secante en absorber la tinta derramada.

made a huge effort. (The sale of stockings was completely unrelated to my concerts; I only had to deal with store owners.)

Whenever I ran into people I knew, I would tell them that being a salesman for a large company allowed me to travel independently and relieved my friends of having to support concerts when it was inconvenient for them to do so. My concerts had never been convenient. In this same city, they'd stalled me with the strangest pretexts: the president of the Club was in a bad mood because I had caused the card table to be removed; he also told me that because a person with many relatives had died half the city was in mourning. So I told them: I'll stay for a few days to see if desire for a concert arises naturally. But the fact that a concert pianist was selling stockings made a bad impression on them.

As to selling stockings: every morning I worked up my courage and every night I was discouraged. It was like getting dressed and then having to strip naked. The hard thing was having to renew the brute force I needed to convince shop owners who were always busy. But now I was just waiting to be fired, so I tried to take advantage of my travel money as long as it lasted.

Suddenly I realized a blind man with a harp had entered the cafe. I'd seen him that afternoon. I decided to leave before I lost the will to enjoy life, but when I came close to him, I could see he was wearing a hat with a badly folded brim rolling his eyes toward heaven while he tried to play. A few strings of the harp had been replaced and the light wood of the instrument, as well as the whole man, were covered with a grime I'd never seen before. I thought about myself and felt depressed.

When I turned on the light in my hotel room, I saw the bed I slept in for those days. It was turned down, and the nickel-plated spokes on the headboard reminded me of an insane young woman offering herself to anyone who came along. I went to bed, turned off the light, but couldn't sleep. I turned it on again, and the bulb peeked out from under the shade like an eyeball under a dark eyelid. I quickly turned it off and tried to think abut the stocking business, but for a moment I went on seeing the lamp shade in the darkness. It had taken on a dark color. Then, its form, as if it were the damned soul of the shade, began to tilt to one side and blend into the darkness. All that happened in the time it would take for a blotter to absorb spilled ink.

Al otro día de mañana, después de vestirme y animarme fui a ver si el ferrocarril de la noche me había traído malas noticias. No tuve carta ni telegrama. Decidí recorrer los negocios de una de las calles principales. En la punta de esa calle había una tienda. Al entrar me encontré en una habitación llena de trapos y chucherías hasta el techo. Sólo había un maniquí desnudo, de tela roja, que en vez de cabeza tenía una perilla negra. Golpeé las manos y en seguida todos los trapos se tragaron el ruido. Detrás del maniquí apareció una niña, como de diez años que me dijo con mal modo:

—¿Qué quiere?

—¿Está el dueño?

—No hay dueño. La que manda es mi mamá.

—¿Ella no está?

—Fue a lo de doña Vicenta y viene en seguida.

Apareció un niño como de tres años. Se agarró de la pollera de la hermana y se quedaron un rato en fila, el maniquí, la niña y el niño. Yo dije:

—Voy a esperar.

La niña no contestó nada. Me senté en un cajón y empecé a jugar con el hermanito. Recordé que tenía un chocolatín de los que había comprado en el cine y lo saqué del bolsillo. Rápidamente se acercó el chiquilín y me lo quitó. Entonces yo me puse las manos en la cara y fingí llorar con sollozos. Tenía tapados los ojos y en la oscuridad que había en el hueco de mis manos abrí pequeñas rendijas y empecé a mirar al niño. Él me observaba inmóvil y yo cada vez lloraba más fuerte. Por fin él se decidió a ponerme el chocolatín en la rodilla. Entonces yo me reí y se lo di. Pero al mismo tiempo me di cuenta que yo tenía la cara mojada.

Salí de allí antes que viniera la dueña. Al pasar por una joyería me miré en un espejo y tenía los ojos secos. Después de almorzar estuve en el café; pero vi al ciego del arpa revolear los ojos hacia arriba y salí en seguida. Entonces fui a una plaza solitaria de un lugar despoblado y me senté en un banco que tenía enfrente un muro de enredaderas. Allí pensé en las lágrimas de la mañana. Estaba intrigado por el hecho de que me hubieran salido; y quise estar solo como si me escondiera para hacer andar un juguete que sin querer había hecho funcionar, hacía pocas horas. Tenía un poco de vergüenza, ante mí mismo, le ponerme a llorar sin tener pretexto, aunque fuera en broma, como lo había tenido en la mañana.

The next morning, after getting dressed and working up my courage, I went to see if the night train had brought me bad news. No letter and no telegram. I decided to visit the shops on one of the main streets. Where the street began, there was a store. When I entered, I found myself in a room filled with odds and ends and rags. There was a naked dummy made of red cloth with a black knob instead of a head. I clapped my hands, and the rags instantly swallowed the noise. From behind the dummy appeared a little girl about ten years old who asked me in an ill-mannered way:

"What do you want?"

"Is the owner in?"

"There is no owner. The person in charge is my mom."

"Isn't she in?"

A boy about three years old appeared. He grabbed onto his sister's skirt, and they stood there a while in a row: the dummy, the girl, and the boy. I said: "I'll wait."

The girl said nothing. I sat down on a box and began to play with the little brother. I remembered that in my pocket I had one of the chocolates I'd bought in the movies. I took it out. The boy instantly came over and grabbed it. I put my hands over my face and pretended to sob. I had my eyes covered, and I opened small cracks in the darkness behind the hollow of my hands and began to look at the boy. Standing stock still, he observed me, and I cried harder and harder. Finally he decided to put the chocolate on my knee. Then I laughed and gave it to him. But at the same time, I realized my face was wet.

I left before the owner came. Passing by a jewelry store, I looked at my face in a mirror: my eyes were dry. After lunch, I sat in the cafe, but I saw the blind man with the harp rolling his eyes up, so I left instantly. I went to a solitary plaza in a sparsely populated area and sat down on a bench opposite an ivy-covered wall. I thought about the morning's tears. I was intrigued by the fact that they'd poured out; and I wanted to be alone, as if I were hiding so I could play with a toy I'd accidentally made work a few hours earlier. I was a little ashamed of myself to start crying for no reason, even if it was a joke, as it had been that morning. A bit timidly, I wrinkled my

Arrugué la nariz y los ojos, con un poco de timidez para ver si me salían las lágrimas; pero después pensé que no debería buscar el llanto como quien escurre un trapo; tendría que entregarme al hecho con más sinceridad; entonces me puse las manos en la cara. Aquella actitud tuvo algo de serio; me conmoví inesperadamente; sentí como cierta lástima de mí mismo y las lágrimas empezaron a salir.

Hacía rato que yo estaba llorando cuando vi que de arriba del muro venían bajando dos piernas de mujer con medias "Ilusión" semibrillantes. Y en seguida noté una pollera verde que se confundía con la enredadera. Yo no había oído colocar la escalera. La mujer estaba en el último escalón y yo me sequé rápidamente las lágrimas; pero volví a poner la cabeza baja y como si estuviese pensativo. La mujer se acercó lentamente y se sentó a mi lado. Ella había bajado dándome la espalda y yo no sabía como era su cara. Por fin me dijo:

—¿Qué le pasa? Yo soy una persona en la que usted puede confiar...

Transcurrieron unos instantes. Yo fruncí el entrecejo como para esconderme y seguir esperando. Nunca había hecho ese gesto y me temblaban las cejas. Después hice un movimiento con la mano como para empezar a hablar y todavía no se me había ocurrido que podría decirle. Ella tomó de nuevo la palabra:

—Hable, hable nomás. Yo he tenido hijos y sé lo que son penas.

Yo ya me había imaginado una cara para aquella mujer y aquella pollera verde. Pero cuando dijo lo de los hijos y las penas me imaginé otra. Al mismo tiempo dije:

—Es necesario que piense un poco.

Ella contestó:

—En estos asuntos, cuanto más se piensa es peor.

De pronto sentí caer, cerca de mí, un trapo mojado. Pero resultó ser una gran hoja de plátano cargada de humedad. Al poco rato ella volvió a preguntar:

—Dígame la verdad, ¿cómo es ella?

Al principio a mí me hizo gracia. Después me vino a la memoria una novia que yo había tenido. Cuando yo no la quería acompañar a caminar por la orilla de un arroyo—donde ella se había paseado con el padre cuando él vivía—esa novia mía lloraba silenciosamente. Entonces, aunque yo estaba aburrido de ir siempre por el mismo lado, condescendía. Y pensando en esto se me ocurrió decir a la mujer que ahora tenía al lado:

nose and eyes to see if any tears would come, but then I thought I shouldn't try to bring on tears the way you'd wring out a dishrag. I'd have to give myself over to it with more sincerity. So I put my hands over my face. That position had something serious to it; I was unexpectedly moved, felt a certain pity for myself, and the tears began to flow.

I'd been crying for a while when I saw two feminine legs wearing semibrilliant *Illusion* stockings descending the wall opposite me. Right after that, I caught sight of a green skirt that blended in with the ivy. I hadn't heard the ladder being put in place. The woman was on the bottom step, and I quickly dried my tears. But I lowered my head again, as if I were pensive. The woman slowly walked over and sat down next to me. She had come down the ladder with her back toward me, so I didn't know what her face looked like. Finally she said: "What's wrong? You can talk to me..."

A few seconds passed. I furrowed my brow as if to hide and go on waiting. I'd never made a face like that, and my brows were trembling. Then I waved my hand, as if I were about to begin speaking, but I still hadn't thought of anything to say to her. Again, she spoke to me: "Go on and talk. I've had children, so I know what sorrow is."

I'd imagined a face for that woman and that green skirt. But when she mentioned children and sorrow, I imagined a different one. At the same time, I said: "I have to think for a moment."

To which she said: "With things like this, the more you think, the worse it is."

Just then, I felt a wet rag fall near me. But it turned out to be a big leaf, covered with dew, from a plane tree. A short time later, she again asked: "Tell me the truth, what's she like?"

At first I found it amusing. Then I remembered a girl friend I'd once had. When I didn't want to walk with her along a stream— where she'd walked with her father when he was alive—she would silently weep. Then, even if I was annoyed about always having to take the same walk, I would give in. As I thought about that, it occurred to me to say to the woman: "She was a woman who often wept."

—Ella era una mujer que lloraba a menudo.

Esta mujer puso sus manos grandes y un poco coloradas encima de la pollera verde y se rió mientras me decía:

—Ustedes siempre creen en las lágrimas de las mujeres.

Yo pensé en las mías; me sentí un poco desconcertado, me levanté del banco y le dije:

—Creo que usted está equivocada. Pero igual le agradezco el consuelo.

Y me fui sin mirarla.

Al otro día cuando ya estaba bastante adelantada la mañana, entré a una de las tiendas más importantes. El dueño extendió mis medias en el mostrador y las estuvo acariciando con sus dedos cuadrados un buen rato. Parecía que no oía mis palabras. Tenía las patillas canosas comosi se hubiera dejado en ellas el jabón de afeitar. En esos instantes entraron varias mujeres; y el, antes de irse, me hizo señas de que no me compraría, con uno de aquellos dedos que habían acariciado las medias. Yo me quedé quieto y pensé en insistir; tal vez pudiera entrar en conversación con él, más tarde, cuando no hubiera gente; entonces le hablaría de un yuyo que disuelto en agua le teñiría las patillas. La gente no se iba y yo tenía una impaciencia desacostumbrada; hubiera querido salir de aquella tienda, de aquella ciudad y de aquella vida. Pensé en mi país y en muchas cosas más. Y de pronto, cuando ya me estaba tranquilizando, tuve una idea: "¿Qué ocurriría si yo me pusiera a llorar aquí, delante de toda esta gente?" Aquello me pareció muy violento; pero yo tenía deseos, desde hacía algún tiempo, de tantear el mundo con algún hecho desa-costumbrado; además yo debía demostrarme a mí mismo que era capaz de una gran violencia. Y antes de arrepentirme me senté en una sillita que estaba recostada al mostrador; y rodeado de gente, me puse las manos en la cara y empecé a hacer ruido de sollozos. Casi simultáneamente una mujer soltó un grito y dijo: "Un hombre está llorando." Y después oí el alboroto y pedazos de conversación: "Nena, no te acerques."... "Puede haber recibido alguna mala noticia."... "Recién llegó el tren y la correspondencia no ha tenido tiempo."... "Puede haber recibido la noticia por telegrama."... Por entre los dedos vi una gorda que decía: "Hay que ver cómo está el mundo. ¡Si a mí no me vieran mis hijos, yo también lloraría!" Al principio yo estaba desesperado porque no me salían lágrimas; y hasta pensé que lo tomarían como una burla y me llevarían preso.

This woman rested her big, slightly red hands on the green skirt and laughed: "You men always believe in female tears."

I thought about my own. I was slightly disconcerted, so I got up and said: "I think you're mistaken. But in any case, I thank you for consoling me."

I went off without looking at her.

The next day, rather late in the morning, I walked into one of the most important stores. The owner spread out my stockings on the counter and caressed them with his square fingers a good while. He didn't seem to hear what I was saying. His sideburns were gray, as if he'd left shaving cream in them. Just then, several women came in, and before walking off, he signaled to me with one of the fingers which had been caressing the stockings that he wouldn't be buying. I remained calm and considered insisting. Perhaps I could strike up a conversation with him later when no one else was there. I could mention a weed that would dye his sideburns when dissolved in water. The people didn't leave, and an unusual wave of impatience came over me. I wished I could leave that store, that city, and that life.

I thought about my country and many other things. And suddenly, when I was almost completely calm, I had an idea: What would happen if I started crying here, in front of all these people? The very idea seemed bizarre, but for a long time I'd had a desire to challenge the world by doing something unusual. Besides, I had to prove to myself that I really could do something very bizarre. Before I could change my mind, I sat down in a low chair next to the counter: surrounded by people, I put my hands over my face and began to make a sobbing noise.

Almost simultaneously, a woman gasped and said: "A man is crying." Then I heard the hubbub and bits of conversation: "Sweetheart, don't go near him..." "Maybe he just heard some bad news..." "But the train just pulled in, so the mail hasn't been delivered yet..." "Maybe he got a telegram..." Through my fingers I saw a fat woman who was saying, "Just look at the world nowadays. If it weren't that my children would see me, I'd be crying too!" At first I was desperate because no tears would flow, and I even thought they'd think I was playing a trick and have me arrested. But my

Pero la angustia y la tremenda fuerza que hice me congestionaron y fueron posibles las primeras lágrimas. Sentí posarse en mi hombro una mano pesada y al oír la voz del dueño reconocí los dedos que habían acariciado las medias. Él decía:

—Pero compañero, un hombre tiene que tener más ánimo...

Entonces yo me levanté como por un resorte, saqué las dos manos de la cara, la tercera que tenía en el hombro, y dije con la cara todavía mojada:

—¡Pero sí me va bien! ¡Y tengo mucho ánimo! Lo que pasa es que a veces me viene esto; es como un recuerdo...

A pesar de la expectativa y del silencio que hicieron para mis palabras, oí que una mujer decía:

—¡Ay! Llora por un recuerdo...

Después el dueño anunció:

—Señoras, ya pasó todo.

Yo me sonreía y me limpiaba la cara. En seguida se removió el montón de gente y apareció una mujer chiquita, con ojos de loca, que me dijo:

—Yo lo conozco a usted. Me parece que lo vi en otra parte y que usted estaba agitado.

Pensé que ella me habría visto en un concierto sacudiéndome en un final de programa; pero me callé la boca. Estalló la conversación de todas las mujeres y algunas empezaron a irse. Se quedó conmigo la que me conocía. Y se me acercó otra que me dijo:

—Ya sé que usted vende medias. Casualmente yo y algunas amigas mías...

Intervino el dueño:

—No se preocupe, señora (y dirigiéndose a mí): Venga esta tarde.

—Me voy después del almuerzo. ¿Quiere dos docenas?

—No, con media docena...

—La casa no vende por menos de una...

Saqué la libreta de ventas y empecé a llenar la hoja del pedido, escribiendo contra el vidrio de una puerta y sin acercarme al dueño. Me rodeaban mujeres conversando alto. Yo tenía miedo que el dueño se arrepintiera. Por fin firmó el pedido y yo salí entre las demás personas.

anguish and the tremendous effort I made caused me to flush, making the first tears possible. I felt a heavy hand on my shoulder, and when I heard the voice of the owner, I recognized the fingers that had caressed the stockings.

He was saying: "Come on now, pal, a man's got to have more courage..."

I raised my head as if he'd pushed a button, removed my two hands from my face and the third resting on my shoulder and said, with my face still streaming: "But things are going fine! And I have lots of courage! It's just that sometimes it comes over me, like a memory..."

Despite the expectations around me and the silence that fell, I heard a woman say: "Oh! He's crying because of a memory..."

Then the owner announced; "Ladies, everything's all right now."

I was smiling and wiping my face. The crowd quickly dispersed, and a short woman with insane eyes appeared, saying: "I know you. I think I saw you somewhere else when you were upset."

I thought she might have seen me at a concert, bowing at the end of the program. But I said nothing. All the women burst into conversation, and some began to leave. The one who knew me stayed behind; then another woman came over, saying: "I know you sell stockings. It just so happens that I and some of my friends here..."

The owner stepped in: "Don't worry, madam." Then, turning to me: "Come back this afternoon."

"I'm leaving town after lunch. Did you want two dozen?"

"No, half a dozen would be..."

"The minimum order the company allows is a dozen..."

I took out my order book and began to fill in the page using a glass door as a writing surface, without going near the owner. Women speaking in loud voices surrounded me. I was afraid the owner would change his mind. Finally he signed the order, and I left with everyone else.

Pronto se supo que a mí me venía "aquello" que al principio era como un recuerdo. Yo lloré en otras tiendas y vendí más medias que de costumbre. Cuando ya había llorado en varias ciudades mis ventas eran como las de cualquier otro vendedor.

Una vez me llamaron de la casa central—yo ya había llorado por todo el norte de aquel país, esperaba turno para hablar con el gerente y oí desde la habitación próxima lo que decía otro corredor:

—Yo hago todo lo que puedo; ¡pero no me voy a poner a llorar para que me compren!

Y la voz enferma del gerente le respondió:

—Hay que hacer cualquier cosa; y también llorarles...

El corredor interrumpió:

—¡Pero a mí no me salen lágrimas!

Y después de un silencio, el gerente:

—¿Cómo, y quién le ha dicho?

—¡Sí! Hay uno que llora a chorros...

La voz enferma empezó a reírse con esfuerzo y haciendo intervalos de tos. Después oí chistidos y pasos que se alejaron.

Al rato me llamaron y me hicieron llorar ante el gerente, los jefes de sección y otros empleados. Al principio, cuando el gerente me hizo pasar y las cosas se aclararon, él se reía dolorosamente y le salían lágrimas. Me pidió, con muy buenas maneras, una demostración; y apenas accedí entraron unos cuantos empleados que estaban detrás de la puerta. Se hizo mucho alboroto y me pidieron que no llorara todavía. Detrás de una mampara, oí decir:

—Apúrate, que uno de los corredores va a llorar.

—¿Y por qué?

—¡Yo qué sé!

Yo estaba sentado al lado del gerente, en su gran escritorio; habían llamado a uno de los dueños, pero el no podía venir. Los muchachos no se callaban y uno había gritado: "Que piense en la mamita, así llora más pronto." Entonces yo le dije al gerente:

—Cuando ellos hagan silencio, lloraré yo.

Él, con su voz enferma, los amenazó y después de algunos instantes de relativo silencio yo miré por una ventana la copa de un árbol—estábamos en un primer piso—, me puse las manos en la cara y traté de llorar. Tenía cierto disgusto. Siempre que yo había llorado los demás ignoraban mis sentimientos; pero aquellas personas sabían que yo lloraría y eso me inhibía. Cuando por fin

Soon word got around that "that thing," which at first was like a memory, would come over me. I cried in other stores and sold more stockings than I usually did. By the time I'd cried in several cities, my sales were as good as those of any other salesman.

"I do what I can, but I'm not going to cry so people will buy from me!"

To which the sickly voice of the supervisor would say: "You've got to be ready to do anything, even to cry..."

The salesman interrupted: "But I don't get any tears!"

After a silence, the supervisor asked, "What do you mean? Who told you that?"

"It's the truth! There's one guy who cries buckets..."

The sickly voice began to laugh, with difficulty and bouts of coughing. Then I heard whistles and footsteps going away.

Then I was called in and made to cry in front of the supervisor, the section managers, and other employees. At first, when the supervisor called me in and things were cleared up, he laughed painfully, his own tears flowing. In the politest fashion, he asked me for a demonstration. No sooner did I agree than some other employees, who were behind the door, came in. There was quite a racket, and they asked me to hold off crying for a bit. Behind a screen, a voice said: "Hurry up, one of the salesmen is going to cry."

"Why?"

"What do I know?"

I was sitting next to the supervisor, at a large desk. One of the owners had been called, but he couldn't come. The boys wouldn't keep quiet, and one shouted out: "He should think about mommy; that way he'll cry sooner." Then I said to the supervisor: "When they shut up, I'll cry."

In his sick voice, he threatened them, and after a few seconds of relative silence, I saw the top of a tree through a window—we were on the second floor. I put my hands over my face and tried to cry. It was awful. When I'd cried before, those around me didn't know what my feelings were. But these people knew I would cry, and that inhibited me. When the tears finally came, I took one hand away

me salieron lágrimas, saqué una mano de la cara para tomar el pañuelo y para que me vieran la cara mojada. Unos se reían y otros se quedaban serios; entonces yo sacudí la cara violentamente y se rieron todos. Pero en seguida hicieron silencio y empezaron a reírse. Yo me secaba las lágrimas mientras la voz enferma repetía: "Muy bien, muy bien." Tal vez todos estuvieron desilusionados. Y yo me sentía como una botella vacía y chorreada; quería reaccionar, tenía mal humor y ganas de ser malo. Entonces alcancé al gerente y le dije:

—No quisiera que ninguno de ellos utilizara el mismo procedimiento para la venta de medias, y desearía que la casa reconociera mi...iniciativa y que me diera exclusividad por algún tiempo.

—Venga mañana y hablaremos de eso.

Al otro día el secretario ya había preparado el documento y leía: "La casa se compromete a no utilizar y a hacer respetar el sistema de propaganda consistente en llorar..." Aquí los dos se rieron y el gerente dijo que aquello estaba mal. Mientras redactaban el documento, yo fui paseándome hasta el mostrador. Detrás de él había una muchacha que me habló mirándome y los ojos parecían pintados por dentro.

—¿Así que usted llora por gusto?

—Es verdad.

—Entonces yo sé más que usted. Usted mismo no sabe que tiene una pena.

Al principio yo me quedé pensativo; y después le dije:

—Mire: no es que yo sea de los más felices; pero sé arreglarme con mi desgracia y soy casi dichoso.

Mientras me iba—el gerente me llamaba—alcancé a ver la mirada de ella: la había puesto encima de mí como si me hubiera dejado una mano en el hombro.

Cuando reanudé las ventas, yo estaba en una pequeña ciudad. Era un día triste y yo no tenía ganas de llorar. Hubiera querido estar solo, en mi pieza, oyendo la lluvia y pensando que el agua me separaba de todo el mundo. Yo viajaba escondido detrás de una careta con lágrimas; pero yo tenía la cara cansada.

De pronto sentí que alguien se había acercado preguntándome:

—¿Qué le pasa?

from my face to get my handkerchief and so they'd see my wet face. Some laughed, and others became serious. Then I shook my face violently, and they all laughed. Then they fell silent for an instant, only to start laughing again. I dried my tears while the sick voice went on: "Very well, very well." Perhaps they were disappointed. I felt like an empty, poured-out bottle. I wanted to do something, I was angry, and wanted to do something bad. Then I turned to the supervisors and said: "I wouldn't want anyone else using the same technique to sell stockings, and wish the company would recognize my...initiative and grant me exclusive rights for a while."

"Come see me tomorrow, and we'll talk about it."

When I got there the next day, the secretary had already prepared the document and read it out: "The Company commits itself to not using and to respect the system of advertising that consists in crying..." At that point, both laughed, and the supervisor said that just didn't sound right. While the document was being typed out, I walked toward the counter. Behind it was a girl who spoke looking at me, and her eyes looked as if they were painted on the inside.

"So you cry because you like it?"

"That's the truth."

"Well in that case, I know more than you. You yourself don't know you have a sorrow."

At first, I was pensive. Then I said, "Look, I may not be one of the happiest people, but I know how to deal with my misfortune, so in that sense I'm almost lucky."

As I was walking away from her—the supervisor was calling me—I caught sight of her eyes: she'd fixed them on me as if she'd left a hand on my shoulder.

When I went back to selling, I was in a small city. It was a sad day, and I just didn't feel like crying. I wished I could be alone in my room listening to the rain and thinking that the water was separating me from the world. I traveled hidden behind a mask with tears on it, but my own face was tired.

Suddenly, I felt the presence of someone next to me saying, "What's the trouble?"

Entonces yo, como un empleado sorprendido sin trabajar, quise reanudar mi tarea y poniéndome las manos en la cara empecé a hacer los sollozos.

Ese año yo lloré hasta diciembre, dejé de llorar en enero y parte de febrero, empecé a llorar de nuevo después de carnaval. Aquel descanso me hizo bien y volví a llorar con ganas. Mientras tanto yo había extrañado el éxito de mis lágrimas y me había nacido como cierto orgullo de llorar. Eran muchos más los vendedores; pero un actor que representara algo sin previo aviso y convenciera al público con llantos...

Aquel nuevo año yo empecé a llorar por el oeste y llegué a una ciudad donde mis conciertos habían tenido éxito; la segunda vez que estuve allí, el público me había recibido con una ovación cariñosa y prolongada; yo agradecía parado junto al piano y no me dejaban sentar para iniciar el concierto. Seguramente que ahora daría, por lo menos, una audición. Yo lloré allí por primera vez, en el hotel más lujoso; fue a la hora del almuerzo y en un día radiante. Ya había comido y tomado café, cuando de codos en la mesa, me cubrí la cara con las manos. A los pocos instantes se acercaron algunos amigos que yo había saludado; los dejé parados algún tiempo y mientras tanto, una pobre vieja—que no sé de dónde había salido—se sentó a mi mesa y yo la miraba por entre los dedos ya mojados. Ella bajaba la cabeza y no decía nada; pero tenía una cara tan triste que daban ganas de ponerse a llorar...

El día en que yo di mi primer concierto tenía cierta nerviosidad que me venía del cansancio; estaba en la última obra de la primera parte del programa y tomé uno de los movimientos con demasiada velocidad; ya había intentado detenerme; pero me volví torpe y no tenía bastante equilibrio ni fuerza; no me quedó otro recurso que seguir; pero las manos se me cansaban, perdía nitidez, y me di cuenta de que no llegaría al final. Entonces, antes de pensarlo, ya había sacado las manos del teclado y las tenía en la cara; era la primera vez que lloraba en escena.

Al principio hubo murmullos de sorpresa y no sé por qué alguien intentó aplaudir; pero otros chistaron y yo me levanté. Con una mano me tapaba los ojos y con la otra tanteaba el piano y trataba de salir del escenario. Algunas mujeres gritaron porque creyeron que me caería en la platea; y ya iba a franquear una puerta del decorado, cuando alguien, desde el paraíso me gritó:

Like an employee caught not doing his job, I tried to get back to my work. Putting my hands over my face, I began to sob.

That year, I cried until December. I stopped in January and part of February. I began again after carnival. That vacation was good for me, and I went back to crying with enthusiasm. I'd missed the success of my tears, and a kind of pride in crying was born in me. There were many other salesmen, but an actor who takes a role without prior warning and convinces the audience with sobs...

With the new year I began to cry in the west and went to a city where my concerts had been successful. The second time I was there, the public had received me with a heartfelt, prolonged ovation. I thanked them standing next to the piano, and they wouldn't let me sit down to start the concert. This time, I would certainly give at least a performance. I cried there—the first time—in the most luxurious hotel. It was lunchtime on a radiant day. I'd already eaten and had coffee when, elbows on the table, I covered my face with my hands. A few seconds later, some friends I'd just said hello to came to my table. I let them stand there for a time, but in the meanwhile a poor old lady—where she came from I have no idea—sat at my table. I looked at her through my already wet fingers. She lowered her head and said nothing, but her face was so sad it would have made anyone cry...

The day I gave my first concert I suffered a nervousness that came from fatigue. I'd reached the last piece in the first part of the program and played one of the movements too quickly. I tried to slow down, but instead became awkward, without enough balance or strength. There was nothing for me to do but go on, but my hands became tired, lost clarity, and I realized that I'd never reach the end. So, even before thinking it, I removed my hands from the keyboard and put them over my face. It was the first time I'd ever cried on stage.

At first there were whispers of surprise, and for some reason someone tried to applaud. But others silenced whoever it was, and I stood up. With one hand, I covered my eyes and with the other, I felt my way along the piano, trying to get off stage. Some women screamed because they thought I was going to fall into the orchestra pit. I was about to go through a door in the stage set, when someone sitting in the highest balcony shouted: "Crooooocccooooodiiiile!"

—¡¡Cocodriiilooooo!!

Oí risas; pero fui al camarín, me lavé la cara y aparecí en seguida, y con las manos frescas terminé la primera parte. Al final vinieron a saludarme muchas personas y se comentó lo de "cocodrilo". Yo les decía:

—A mí me parece que él que me gritó eso tiene razón: en realidad yo no sé por qué lloro; me viene el llanto y no lo puedo remediar, a lo mejor me es tan natural como lo es para el cocodrilo. En fin, yo no sé tampoco por qué llora el cocodrilo.

Una de las personas que me habían presentado tenía la cabeza alargada; y como se peinaba dejándose el pelo parado, la cabeza hacía pensar en un cepillo. Otro de la rueda lo señaló y me dijo:

—Aquí, el amigo es médico. ¿Qué dice usted, doctor?

Yo me quedé pálido. Él me miró con ojos de investigador policial y me preguntó:

—Dígame una cosa: ¿cuándo llora más usted, de día o de noche?

Yo recordé que nunca lloraba en la noche porque a esa hora no vendía, y le respondí:

—Lloro únicamente de día.

No recuerdo las otras preguntas. Pero al final me aconsejó:

—No coma carne. Usted tiene una vieja intoxicación.

A los pocos días me dieron una fiesta en el club principal. Alquilé un frac con chaleco blanco impecable y en el momento de mirarme al espejo pensaba: "No dirán que este cocodrilo no tiene la barriga blanca. ¡Caramba! Creo que ese animal tiene papada como la mía. Y es voraz..."

Al llegar al Club encontré poca gente. Entonces me di cuenta que había llegado demasiado temprano. Vi a un señor de la comisión y le dije que deseaba trabajar un poco en el piano. De esa manera disimularía el madrugón. Cruzamos una cortina verde y me encontré en una gran sala vacía y preparada para el baile. Frente a la cortina y al otro extremo de la sala estaba el piano. Me acompañaron hasta allí el señor de la comisión y el conserje; mientras abrían el piano, el señor—tenía cejas negras y pelo blanco—me decía que la fiesta tendría mucho éxito, que el director del liceo—amigo mío—diría un discurso muy lindo y que él ya lo había oído; trató de recordar algunas frases, pero después decidió que sería mejor no decirme nada. Yo puse las manos en el piano y

I heard laughter, but I went to my dressing room, washed my face, and went right back out. With fresh hands, I finished the first part of the program. Afterwards, lots of people came to say hello and comment about the "crocodile" business.

This is what I told them: "It seems to me that the person who shouted that is right. Actually, I don't know why I cry. The tears come, and I can't do anything about it. Maybe it's just as natural in me as it is in a crocodile. In any case, I don't know why crocodiles cry either."

One of the people who had introduced me had a long face, and since he had a crew cut, his head made me think of a brush. Another man in the circle around me pointed to him and said: "Our friend here is a doctor. What do think, doctor?"

I turned pale. He looked at me with the eyes of a police detective and asked: "Tell me one thing: when do you cry most, at night or during the day?"

I remembered that I never cried at night because I never sold stockings at night, so I answered: "I only cry during the day."

I don't remember his other questions, but at the end he advised me: "Stop eating meat. Your system was poisoned a long time ago."

A few days later, a party was given in my honor in the best club. I rented evening clothes with an impeccable white vest, and when the moment came for me to look at myself in the mirror, I thought: "No one's going to say this crocodile doesn't have a white belly. Wow! I think that animal's got a double chin just like mine. And does he love to eat..."

When I got to the Club, I found few people there. I realized I'd come too early. I saw a gentleman who was a member of the commission and told him I wanted to practice a while on the piano. That way I could cover up for my early arrival. We went through a green curtain, and I found myself in a large empty hall set up for the ball. Opposite the curtain, on the other end of the hall, was the piano. The gentleman from the commission and the porter accompanied me. While they were opening the piano, the gentleman—he had black eyebrows and white hair—told me the party would be a great success, that the director of the society (a friend of mine) would give a fine speech and that he'd already heard it. He tried to recall a few sentences, but decided it would be better not to tell me anything. I put my hands on the keys, and they left.

ellos se fueron. Mientras tocaba pensé: "Esta noche no lloraré...
quedaría muy feo...el director del liceo es capaz de desear que yo
llore para demostrar el éxito de su discurso. Pero yo no lloraré por
nada del mundo."

Hacía rato que veía mover la cortina verde; y de pronto salió de
entre sus pliegues una muchacha alta y de cabellera suelta; cerró los
ojos como para ver lejos; me miraba y se dirigía a mí trayendo algo
en una mano; detrás de ella apareció una sirvienta que la alcanzó y
le empezó a hablar de cerca. Yo aproveché para mirarle las piernas y
me di cuenta que tenía puesta una sola media; a cada instante hacía
movimientos que indicaban el fin de la conversación; pero la
sirvienta seguía hablándole y las dos volvían al asunto como a una
golosina. Yo seguí tocando el piano y mientras ellas conversaban
tuve tiempo de pensar: "¿Qué querrá con la media?... ¿Le habrá
salido mala y sabiendo que yo soy corredor...? ¡Y tan luego en esta
fiesta!"

Por fin vino y me dijo:

—Perdone, señor, quisiera que me firmara una media.

Al principio me reí; y en seguida traté de hablarle como si ya
me hubieran hecho ese pedido otras veces. Empecé a explicarle
cómo era que la media no resistía la pluma; yo ya había solucionado
eso firmando una etiqueta y después la interesada la pegaba en la
media. Pero mientras daba estas explicaciones mostraba la
experiencia de un antiguo comerciante que después se hubiera
hecho pianista. Ya me empezaba a invadir la angustia, cuando ella
se sentó en la silla del piano, y al ponerse la media me decía:

—Es una pena que usted me haya resultado tan mentiroso...
debía haberme agradecido la idea.

Yo había puesto los ojos en sus piernas; después los saqué y se
me trabaron las ideas. Se hizo un silencio de disgusto. Ella, con la
cabeza inclinada, dejaba caer el pelo; y debajo de aquella cortina
rubia, las manos se movían como si huyeran. Yo seguía callado y
ella no terminaba nunca. Al fin, la pierna hizo un movimiento de
danza, y el pie, en punta, calzó el zapato en el momento de
levantarse, las manos le recogieron el pelo y ella me hizo un saludo
silencioso y se fue.

Cuando empezó a entrar gente fui al bar. Se me ocurrió pedir

As I played, I thought: "Tonight I won't cry...it just wouldn't be right...the director of the society is the kind who'd want me to cry to prove the success of his speech. But I wouldn't cry for anything in the world."

I'd been watching the green curtain move for quite a while, when suddenly from between its folds there emerged a tall girl with loose hair. She closed her eyes as if she were trying to see something far away. She looked at me and came over, carrying something in her hand. Behind her appeared a waitress, who caught up to her and whispered something. I took the opportunity to look at her legs, and I realized she was only wearing one stocking. She constantly motioned that the conversation was over, but the waitress went on talking, and the two of them went back to the subject as if it were candy. I went on playing, and while they talked, I had time to think: "What is this business with the stocking? Did she get a bad one and then, knowing I'm a salesman... And right here at the party!"

Finally, she came over to me and said: "Excuse me, sir, but I wonder if you'd sign a stocking."

At first I laughed, but then I tried to make her think I'd been asked to do that before. I began to explain that the stocking couldn't stand up under the pen, that I'd solved that problem signing a label which the lady in question had stuck onto her stocking. But that explanation only revealed the experience of a veteran business man who had become a pianist. I was just about overwhelmed by anguish when she sat down on the piano bench, and as she put on the stocking, she said: "It's a shame you've turned out to be such a liar...you should have thanked me for the idea."

I fixed my eyes on her legs; then I removed them, and my ideas got all tangled up. An unpleasant silence ensued. With her head bent forward, she let her hair fall down. And under that blond curtain, her hands moved around as if they were running away. I remained silent, and she never stopped talking. Finally, her leg took a dance step, and her foot, on tiptoe, slipped on its shoe just when her hands pulled back her hair. She bade me a silent farewell and left.

When people began coming in, I went to the bar. For some

whisky. El mozo me nombró muchas marcas y como yo no conocía ninguna le dije:

—Deme de esa última.

Trepé a un banco del mostrador y traté de no arrugarme la cola del frac. En vez de cocodrilo debía parecer un loro negro. Estaba callado, pensaba en la muchacha de la media y me trastornaba el recuerdo de sus manos apuradas.

Me sentí llevado al salón por el director del liceo. Se suspendió un momento el baile y él dijo su discurso. Pronunció varias veces las palabras "avatares" y "menester". Cuando aplaudieron yo levanté los brazos como un director de orquesta antes de "atacar" y apenas hicieron silencio dije:

—Ahora que debía llorar no puedo. Tampoco puedo hablar y no quiero dejar por más tiempo separados los que han de juntarse para bailar. Y terminé haciendo una cortesía.

Después de mi vuelta, abracé al director del liceo y por encima de su hombro vi la muchacha de la media. Ella me sonrió y levantó su pollera del lado izquierdo y me mostró el lugar de la media donde había pegado un pequeño retrato mío recortado de un programa. Yo me sonreí lleno de alegría pero dije una idiotez que todo el mundo repitió:

—Muy bien, muy bien, la pierna del corazón.

Sin embargo yo me sentí dichoso y fui al bar. Subí de nuevo a un banco y el mozo me preguntó:

—¿Whisky Caballo Blanco?

Y yo, con el ademán de un mosquetero sacando una espada:

—Caballo Blanco o Loro Negro.

Al poco rato vino un muchacho con una mano escondida en la espalda:

—El Pocho me dijo que a usted no le hace mala impresión que le digan "Cocodrilo".

—Es verdad, me gusta.

Entonces él sacó la mano de la espalda y me mostró una caricatura. Era un gran cocodrilo muy parecido a mí; tenía una pequeña mano en la boca, donde los dientes eran un teclado; y de la otra mano le colgaba una media con ella se enjugaba las lágrimas.

Cuando los amigos me llevaron a mi hotel yo pensaba en todo lo que había llorado en aquel país y sentía un placer maligno en haberlos engañado; me consideraba como un burgués de la angustia.

reason, I ordered a whiskey. The barman recited a list of brands, and since I knew none of them, I said, "Give me the last one you mentioned."

I sat on a barstool and tried not to wrinkle the tails of my evening clothes. Instead of a crocodile, I must have looked like a black parrot. I was silent; I was thinking about the girl with the stocking and the memory of her hasty hands upset me.

I felt myself taken to the ballroom by the director of the society. Dancing stopped for a moment, and he gave his speech. Several times, he pronounced the words "avatars" and "necessity." When everyone applauded, I raised my arms like an orchestra director before he starts the program, and as soon as people were silent I said: "Now, when I should be crying, I can't. Nor can I speak, and I don't want to keep separated all those who wish to join together to dance." I ended with a bow. ·

Then I turned around, embraced the director of the society, and, over his shoulder, saw the girl with the stocking. She smiled at me, lifted her skirt on the left side, and showed me the place on her stocking where she'd stuck on a small picture of me cut out of a program. I smiled, filled with joy, but I said something stupid everyone repeated:

"Wonderful, wonderful, the leg of the heart."

Even so, I felt blessed and went to the bar. Again I sat at the bar, and the bartender asked: "White Horse?"

I pretended to be a musketeer pulling out his sword: "White Horse or Black Parrot."

Shortly thereafter, a boy with his hand hidden behind his back came over: "Pocho told me that it doesn't bother you to be called Crocodile."

"That's true. I like it."

Then he revealed his hidden hand and showed me a caricature. It was a huge crocodile that looked just like me. It held a small hand to its mouth, where the teeth were a piano keyboard. From the other hand hung a stocking, which he used to dry his tears.

When my friends brought me to my hotel, I thought about all the crying I'd done in that country and felt a malignant pleasure for having tricked all those people. I considered myself a bourgeois of

Pero cuando estuve solo en mi pieza, me ocurrió algo inesperado: primero me miré en el espejo; tenía la caricatura en la mano y alternativamente miraba al cocodrilo y a mi cara. De pronto y sin haberme propuesto imitar al cocodrilo, mi cara, por su cuenta, se echó a llorar. Yo la miraba como a una hermana de quien ignoraba su desgracia. Tenía arrugas nuevas y por entre ellas corrían las lágrimas. Apagué la luz y me acosté. Mi cara seguía llorando; las lágrimas resbalaban por la nariz y caían por la almohada. Y así me dormí. Cuando me desperté sentí el escozor de las lágrimas que se habían secado. Quise levantarme y lavarme los ojos; pero tuve miedo que la cara se pusiera a llorar de nuevo. Me quedé quieto y hacía girar los ojos en la oscuridad, como aquel ciego que tocaba el arpa.

anguish. But when I was alone in my room, something unexpected happened to me. First, I looked at myself in the mirror. I held the caricature in my hand and alternately looked at the crocodile and my own face. Suddenly, and without my having thought of imitating the crocodile, my face, on its own, began to cry. I looked at it as if it were a sister whose misfortune I knew nothing of. It had new wrinkles, and down them ran the tears. I put out the light and got into bed. My face went on crying; the tears slipped down my nose and fell onto the pillow. That's how I fell asleep. When I woke up, I felt the burn of the tears that had dried. I tried to get up and wash out my eyes, but I was afraid my face would start crying again. I remained calm and tried to move my eyes around in the dark, like that blind man who played the harp.

LOS CAMALOTES

THE WATER-HYACINTHS

Toby Talbot, translator of José Carmona Blanco

Toby Talbot teaches at New York University. She is the author of the memoir *A Book About My Mother* and numerous children's books. She has translated Luisa Valenzuela's *Black Novel With Argentines* and Jacobo Timerman's *Prisoner Without a Name, Cell Without a Number*, among other works. Talbot's first translation was Benito Pérez Galdós's *Misericordia,* which intrigued her for its various "modalities of speech: the jargon of the beggars, the pretension of Benita's impoverished middle-class mistress, the hybrid *castellano* of the Moorish Almudena and, finally, the author's own nineteenth century voice."

Talbot's haunting translation of "The Water-Hyacinths" evokes the grievous political crisis of the *desaparecidos*. Still totally unknown north of the Rio Grande, its author, José Carmona Blanco, was born in Barcelona in 1926 and has lived in Uruguay since 1951. He practiced journalism in France and lectured on literature at the Spanish Institute of the Sorbonne. His books include *Ciudad caída, De tres mundos, El reencuentro,* and *Los de arriba*.

Having translated Argentine journalist Jacobo Timerman's *Prisoner Without A Name, Cell Without a Number* led Talbot to identify with Carmona Blanco's story about the Argentine "dirty war" of the seventies and the plight of victims and their families. A text, according to Talbot, must satisfy one of three requirements for her to take it on: she must "relish" it, find it challenging, or consider it otherwise important. She says that translation is literary symbiosis with either the author or the text itself. Working with living authors like Humberto Constantini and Luisa Valenzuela has helped her resolve issues that fall in the grey area between English and Spanish, but such a relationship can also become a bilingual tug-of-war. "Constantini fought over every epical *y* and we negotiated fiercely for inclusion or deletion," she wryly remembers. "Nevertheless," she adds in her questionnaire, "dead authors seem to be the ones looking most fixedly over my shoulder."

José Carmona Blanco
LOS CAMALOTES

"Pero no moriremos. Fue tan cálidamente
consumada la vida como el sol, su mirada.
No es posible perdernos. Somos plena simiente.
Y la muerte ha quedado, con los dos, fecundada."
Miguel Hernández
("Muerte Nupcial")

"Déjame que te hable también con tu silencio
claro como una lámpara, simple como un anillo."
Pablo Neruda
("15° Poema de amor")

Al igual que en otras oportunidades todos presenciamos, corriente
abajo, la llegada de los bancos de camalotes cargados de alimañas.
Una vez más los desbordes del Paraná, Paraguay y también de
nuestro litoraleño Uruguay nos obsequiaban con su flora y fauna,
mas en esta ocasión en proporciones que nunca jamás viéramos.
Verdaderos montes flotantes invadieron primero nuestras aguas,
luego la marea los depositó sobre todas las playas de nuestra costa.
Acabaron por cubrir no sólo las vertientes de arena, sino incluso los
médanos.

Este fenómeno fluvial volvió a constituir para no pocos un
hecho en cierto modo entretenido. Los habitantes de las zonas
playeras se divirtieron escarbando entre las plantas varadas,
utilizando estacas y bastones, en busca de víboras, alacranes,
tarántulas, bichos raros procedentes de otras latitudes para
despanzurrarlos a palazos. Muchos buscaban seguramente también,
algo que no sabían con exactitud en qué consistía, pero que
imaginaban como objeto misterioso y exótico, con valor positivo.
Antiguas leyendas han grabado en nuestras mentes la idea de que
los tesoros nos los traen desde muy lejos los mares y los ríos,
entreverados con la resaca, las algas y las plantas acuáticas. Tal vez

José Carmona Blanco
THE WATER-HYACINTHS

Translated by Toby Talbot

But we shall not die. Life
was consumed with ardor,
like the sun by your gaze.
We will not vanish, death itself
has been fertilized by your seed.
Miguel Hernández
("Wedding Death")

Let me talk to you with your silence
clear as a light, simple as a ring.
Pablo Neruda
(15th Love Poem)

As on other occasions, we sighted great clumps of infested water-hyacinths coming downstream. Once again, we were regaled by flora and fauna cast off by the Paraná River, Paraguay and our own Uruguayan coast, but in unprecedented quantities. Veritable floating mounds invaded our waters and then were deposited by the tide on all our coastal beaches, eventually covering the sandy slopes and even the dunes.

This fluvial phenomenon provided a kind of diversionary event for many people. Those who lived along the beach amused themselves by poking around with poles and canes amongst the plants that had been washed ashore, looking for snakes, scorpions, tarantulas, strange creatures from other latitudes whose entrails they smashed apart. Many, no doubt, were seeking something else, exactly what they didn't know—some imaginary, mysterious object of indisputable value. Ancient legends have imprinted our minds with the notion of treasures brought by seas and rivers afar, entwined with surf, algae and aquatic vegetation. This pervasive

sea a causa de este obsesivo pensamiento que cuando paseamos solitarios por la orilla del mar, lo hacemos con la mirada rasante, atentos a cualquier cosa que brille entre los guijarros o restos de crustáceos.

Por lo que a mí respecta el espectáculo de los camalotes, tantas veces visto aunque no con tal magnitud, no me produjo gran curiosidad. Pese a todo también terminé por acercarme a las plantas desde el umbral de mi rancho en Ramírez, casi oculto entre los tamarises que crecen junto a la muralla y que constituye desde hace mucho tiempo mi hogar. Me fui a vivir en él después que quedé solo y decidí deshacerme de una casa que me resultaba vacía.

Las alimañas, venenosas o no, no me interesaban. Tampoco me propuse hallar, como muchos ilusos, alguna pepita de oro decantada por algún lejano e hipotético afluente aurífero. Si me acerqué a los camalotes fue porque sé muy bien que a veces cargan desde su origen, o recogen a lo largo de su descendente trayectoria, objetos que pasan desapercibidos a todo el mundo. Y así ocurrió que al poco de dedicarme a remover con un pedazo de tacuara los tallos de las plantas recogí mi primer y extraño hallazgo. Al pronto no supe de qué se trataba, aunque, por supuesto, no era algo común. En primera instancia creí reconocer en el objeto un alargado crustáceo que me es familiar, aunque no aquí en el estuario, sino en zonas marítimas. Lo observé con atención sorprendido de que pudiese darse también en agua dulce, no oceánica. Mi meticulosa mirada determinó que de pronto se me produjese un violento e irresistible sacudón en todo el cuerpo. Sentí que me erizaba. El objeto casi se me cayó de la mano. Por no decir que estuve a punto de lanzarlo lo más lejos posible de mí. Mas otro sentimiento más fuerte que mi horror me contuvo. Volví a observar la cosa para cerciorarme de que no me estaba confundiendo y ya no me cupo duda. Lo que yo tenía en mi mano era un dedo. Un dedo humano. Para mayor precisión, el anular de una mano derecha. En la base de su primera falange pude contemplar la huella inconfundible que deja un anillo enhebrado durante mucho tiempo.

Al fin, sin saber muy bien por qué, guardé el dedo amoratado, estriado, empalidecido por la humedad, en el bolsillo de mi saco de dril azul. Y seguí buscando. Ahora algo concreto. Despreocupado de la alimaña que, desenbierta sin intención, huía veloz hacia una muerte segura que no faltaba quien le diera, separaba con mi tacuara

notion accounts perhaps for our scanning gaze as we stroll in solitude along the shore, alert to anything that glistens amidst pebbles and crustacean shards.

But as for myself, the spectacle of water-hyacinths, so often seen though in lesser quantity, failed to arouse undue curiosity. And yet, I too, drawn by the plants, wound up leaving the doorway of my hut, which is virtually concealed by the tamarisks growing along the wall. This spot in Ramírez has been my home for a long while. I came here after I was left alone, having decided to dispose of a house that now felt empty. A cot, a table, some pots and fishing gear suffice for my present way of life.

Vermin, whether poisonous or not, held scant interest for me. Nor was I in pursuit, like many dreamers, of a golden nugget deposited by some remote, hypothetical gilded tributary. I approached the water-hyacinths simply because I knew that sometimes, from the very outset of their downstream path, they carry certain objects unperceived by others. And, as it happened, soon after I began rummaging with a bamboo pole among the stems of the plants, I came upon my first strange find. I didn't realize, at first, what it was, though it was obviously something uncommon. I seemed to recognize it as a familiar elongated crustacean not found here on the estuary, but by the sea. I examined it carefully, surprised to find it in sweet rather than salty water. My close scrutiny elicited a violent, irrepressible shudder which ran up and down my body. I felt my flesh crawling. The object nearly fell from my hand. In fact, I was about to fling it as far away as possible; and yet felt constrained by another overpowering sensation. I inspected the object again to make sure I wasn't confused, whereupon any lingering doubt vanished. What I held in my hand was a finger. A human finger. To be more precise, the ring finger of a right hand. At the base of the first joint, I detected the unmistakable trace of a ring that had been left on for a long while.

Finally, not knowing exactly why, I took the bluish, indented finger, which had grown limp from moisture, and put it in the pocket of my blue twill jacket. And then kept looking. For something concrete now. Unconcerned about the random creature, unintentionally exposed, fleeing swiftly toward the death someone was sure to deal it.

las amplias hojas y hurgaba con minucioso cuidado entre los tallos, observando con atención las sinuosidades de sus recovecos. Por fin, entre la horquilla que formaban dos raíces encontré el segundo dedo. Un dedo mayor sin lugar a dudas y que, sin embargo, me pareció de menor tamaño que el anular que encontré primero. Saqué este último de mi bolsillo y los comparé. Efectivamente, el dedo mayor recién hallado era más corto y bastante más delgado que el anular. Los lavé en la lengua ya casi inmóvil de una ola. Los restregué con mis propios dedos e hice saltar el cieno que en parte los cubría. Una vez limpios, las respectivas uñas me dieron la certeza de lo que ya estaba adivinando: Cada uno de los dedos llegados entre los camalotes pertenecía a una persona distinta. A dos personas de distinto sexo.

Mientras los contemplaba escuché la voz del hombre que se me había acercado sin que yo, abstraído en mi investigación, me diese cuenta:

—¿Encontró algún tesoro, compañero?

No respondí a su alegre pregunta pero lo mostré mis hallazgos.

—¿Qué son?—me preguntó el hombre observándolos con extrañeza.

—Percebes—le contesté. Y añadí:—¿No los conoce?

—¡Ah, sí!—exclamó. Y luego me explicó:—Una variedad de crustáceos. Los comí en Chile una vez que fui en excursión. Con jugo de limón son exquisitos. Y vino blanco, por supuesto. Vino blanco chileno—precisó al tiempo que juntaba las yemas de sus dedos y se las besaba.

Yo, a mi vez, siguiendo con mi juego, apoyé el pulgar sobre el índice derechos e hice el gesto de retorcerme un colmillo.

El hombre quedó un rato mirando lo que yo le estaba mostrando sobre la palma de mi mano, como tratando de reconocer en aquellos dos apéndices los percebes que comiera en Chile. Al fin me preguntó:

—¿Es eso lo que busca?

—Sólo por curiosidad—le respondí.

—Parecen estar en mal estado—me observó el hombre.

—Lo están—confirmé.

—Lleve cuidado—me aconsejó.—Los mariscos pasados son un veneno.

With my bamboo pole I parted the broad leaves and probed amongst the stems, meticulously exploring the crannies between the twists and turns. At last, within the notch where two roots met, I came upon the second finger. Unquestionably a middle finger, yet smaller than the ring finger that I first found. I took that one out of my pocket and compared the two. Indeed, the middle finger that had just turned up was shorter and considerably thinner than the ring finger. I washed them both in the ripple of a wave, and rubbed them with my own fingers to remove the patches of silt. The nails, when cleaned, confirmed my suspicion: Each of the fingers found amongst the water-hyacinths belonged to a different person. Two individuals of opposite sex.

As I stood there gazing at them, raptly absorbed, I heard the voice of a man who had approached unnoticed.

"Did you find a treasure, my friend?"

Without replying to his cheerful query, I held up my finds.

"What are they?" the man asked, gazing at them in surprise.

"Goose barnacles," I answered, and added: "Don't you recognize them?"

"Ah, yes!" he exclaimed, and proceeded to elaborate. "A variety of shellfish. I ate them once in Chile when I was there on a trip. They're delicious with lemon. And white wine, of course. Chilean white wine," he specified, bringing two fingertips together and kissing them.

I, in turn, went along with the game, raising thumb to index finger for the gesture of flicking at my eyetooth.

The man gazed a while at what was shown in the palm of my hand, as if trying to correlate those two appendages with the barnacles he had consumed in Chile. At last he asked:

"Is that what you're looking for?"

"Just out of curiosity."

"Looks like they're in pretty bad shape."

"They are" I agreed.

"Be careful" he advised. "Shellfish that have gone bad are poisonous."

—No pienso comerlos. Los colecciono solamente—dije para tranquilizarlo.

El hombre pareció dudar antes de hablar y por fin me explicó:

—Yo tuve más suerte. Vea lo que encontré—y me mostró dos anillos de distinto tamaño, sucios de barro y musgo.

No puedo explicar la causa, pero lo cierto es que sentí como si el corazón me diese un vuelco. De inmediato deseé poseer aquellos dos aros. No se me ocurría nada para conseguirlo. Fue el propio hombre quien se dio la iniciativa al preguntarme:

—¿Le parece que puedan ser de oro?

—¿Vio alguna vez oro que se oxide?—lo interrogué a mi vez, sonriendo y procurando que mi sonrisa poseyera una ligera torcedura despreciativa.

—Eso mismo pensé yo—me contestó. Y luego aseveró con desilusión:—Deben ser de fierro.

—De bronce tal vez—lo corregí, tratando de darle la impresión de que no me importaba cotizar alto sus hallazgos.

De pronto se me ocurrió la idea. Del otro bolsillo de mi saco extraje una caracola la cual había hallado hacía ya varios días y que esperaba vender, como tantas otras, a algún coleccionista. Se trataba de una caracola grande y hermosa, erizada en abundancia por fuera y con una boca nacarada como las tapas de un libro antiguo de comunión. El hombre la miró extasiado, con indisimulada codicia.

—¿La encontró aquí?—me preguntó.

—Sí—respondí. Aquí en la orilla. El mar suele traerlas cuando empuja hacia adentro del estuario. Y es de las maravillosas—añadí.—Pruebe. Tómela. Arrímesela a la oreja y escuche el mar.

El hombre me arrebató prácticamente la caracola de la mano y se la pegó al oído. En su boca se fue acentuando una sonrisa y en sus ojos el deseo de posesión. Dudó, pero, como yo esperaba, se tiró el lance:

—La quiere para usted, ¿no es cierto?

—Bueno...—dije.—Yo encuentro caracolas como esa casi todos los días. Si le interesa le propongo un trato. Se la cambio por sus dos argollas de bronce. A mí pueden servirme para enhebrar tanzas.

—Trato hecho—se apresuró a aceptar el hombre. más enseguida se corrigió:—O, mejor dicho, gracias por su obsequio. Mi esposa se va a volver loca de alegría con esta caracola. Le encantan. Tiene muchas, pero ninguna tan hermosa como ésta.

"I'm not planning to eat them. I only collect them," I reassured him.

The man seemed to hesitate before speaking. "I was luckier. Look what I found," he said, displaying two rings of different sizes, encrusted with mud and seaweed.

At that moment, though I can't explain why, I felt my heart spinning, and was seized by an overwhelming desire to possess those two bands. How to get them was another matter. It was the man himself who took the initiative with his next question:

"Do you think they're gold?"

"Have you ever known gold to rust?" I rejoined with a smile, trying to lend a disparaging twist to my smile.

"That's what I was thinking myself," he answered, then added in disappointment: "They must be iron."

"Maybe brass," I corrected him, trying to give the impression of not caring about enhancing his finds.

Suddenly an idea struck me. From the other pocket in my jacket, I took out a conch shell I'd found several days ago and was planning to sell to a collector, as I'd done with others in the past. This one was a large, beautiful specimen with many exterior whorls and a nacrous aperture like the covers of an old prayer book. The man gazed at it in rapture, with undisguised greed.

"Did you find it here?" he asked.

"Yes," I answered. "Here on the shore. They get washed into the estuary by the incoming tide. And this one's a gem. Look, take it," I added. "Hold it up to your ear and listen to the ocean."

The man virtually snatched the shell from my hands and held it up to his ear. A smile formed at his mouth and his eyes gleamed with the lust for possession. He hesitated but, as I anticipated, fell for the ploy.

"You want to keep it for yourself, don't you?"

"Well..." I said, "I find shells like this every day. If you're interested, let me propose a deal. I'll trade it for your two brass rings. I can use them for winding cord."

"It's a deal," the man was quick to accept, but corrected himself instantly. "That is, thanks for the gift. My wife will go wild with joy when she sees this conch shell. She just loves them. And has many of them, but none as pretty as this one."

El hombre se fue contento y apurado, sin dejar de escuchar junto a su oreja el rumor oceánico. Yo me metí en el bolsillo los dos anillos junto a los dos dedos.

Anocheció y me encontré solo en la playa desierta. De pronto adquirí consciencia de mi inquietud y de mi extraña angustia. Corrí hacia el rancho. Encendí el farol a querosene y volví apresurado hacia los montículos de camalotes. Pasé toda la noche escartando y buscando entre ellos, como quien dice a la encandilada. Rastreé de punta a punta la playa, pero no encontré más nada. De madrugada regresé de nuevo al rancho dispuesto a dormir un rato. Lo precisaba. Antes de acostarme limpié con el querosene del farol los dos anillos. Resultaban ser de oro como yo estaba seguro. Busqué en la superficie lisa interior de ellos un nombre, una fecha, cualquier signo identificativo, mas nada tenían grabado. Calcé uno en el dedo anular y el otro en el meñique de mi mano derecha. De inmediato sentí en cada uno de mis dedos una inexplicable tibieza. Me quedé dormido.

Desperté y el sol estaba ya casi en el zenit. Desenterré la lata y me metí toda la plata en el bolsillo. Llené la bolsa de pesca con los comestibles y me la colgué del hombro. Agarré el farol con una mano. Con la otra el trozo de tacuara a modo de báculo. Emprendí la marcha. Me hallaba seguro de que transcurrirían muchos días antes de que me decidiera a regresar al rancho.

En Pocitos no encontré nada. La playa estaba inusitadamente limpia. La arena blanqueaba y las partículas de mica centellaban bajo el sol. Ni resaca había. Alcancé a ver alejarse por la rambla las palas mecánicas junto con los últimos camiones cargados de residuos. Las malditas esqueriquias en voga, seguramente apresuraron al Municipio a proceder de inmediato a la limpieza de la más copetuda playa urbana.

Maldije mi sueño. Lo maldije inútilmente, ya que pocas horas después, en el Buceo, encontré el segundo anular, el de la mujer. Este también tenía la hendidura producido por el anillo. y fue en aquel instante que se me ocurrió realizar la elemental comprobación. Extraje los anillos de mis dedos y los introduje en los dos anulares hallados. Pese a las deformaciones que estos sufrieran, cada aro se asentó con justeza sobre su propia marca.

Terminé mi búsqueda en el Buceo y la proseguí en Malvín. Después en Carrasco. Día tras día rastreé toda la costa. Playa tras playa. Camalote por camalote.

The man hurried off, contentedly holding the shell up to his ear for the sound of the sea. I took both rings and placed them in my pocket next to the two fingers.

Night fell and I found myself alone on the deserted beach. Suddenly I became conscious of my restlessness, and a strange anxiety. I ran towards the hut, lit the kerosene lamp and hurried back to the clumps of water-hyacinths. I spent the entire night scratching and poking around amongst them, as if stirring up embers. I combed the beach from one end to the other, but found nothing else. At dawn I returned once again to the hut, prepared to sleep awhile. I needed it. Before retiring, I cleaned both of the rings with kerosene from the lamp and examined their smooth inner surface, looking for a name, a date, any identifying sign but found nothing engraved inside. I took one of the rings and placed it on my ring finger and the other on the pinky of my right hand. Then I fell asleep.

When I awoke, the sun was almost at its peak. I dug up a can of silver coins and put them in my pocket, then filled the fishing bag with food and hoisted it on my shoulder. In one hand, I held the lantern and in the other the bamboo pole as a walking stick. I set forth, certain that many days would elapse before my return to the hut.

In Pocitos I found nothing. The beach was remarkably clean. The white sand glistened and bits of mica flashed in the sun. There was not even a surf. I could see power-shovels with truckloads of trash being hauled away on the promenade. Those infernal *escherichia* bacteria, polluting the area nowadays, had undoubtedly forced the municipality to act quickly to clean up this poshest of all the city beaches.

I cursed myself for having slept. No need to have cursed, for a few hours later, in Buceo, I found the second finger, the woman's. This one, too, had the indenture produced by the ring, and it was at that instant that I had definite proof. I took the rings off my fingers and put them on the found fingers. Despite the deformations the fingers had undergone, each ring fit perfectly on its respective imprint.

I concluded my search at Buceo Beach, resumed it at Malvín, and then in Carrasco. Day after day I raked the coast. Beach after beach. Water-hyacinth by water-hyacinth.

Un día comprendí que mi semblante, barbudo y ojeroso, debía parecerse al de un loco. La gente que continuaba matando alimañas a palazos en las playas de todos los balnearios del Este, me miraba con extrañeza y se alejaba de mí. La actitud de la gente no me importaba. Mas yo mismo llegué a pensar si de verdad no habría enloquecido. De todos modos razoné con claridad. Me dije a mí mismo que de estar loco no podría ni siquiera pensar en lo que estaba. Me tranquilicé. Recordé a Descartes e imaginé que también él, cuando al cabo de tanto barruntar dio con su famosa definición ontológica, al igual que yo debió tranquilizarse. Me reí de mí mismo y de Descartes.

Encontré dedos en Solymar, Parque del Plata y Punta Colorada. En Solana del mar completé los diez. Es decir, cinco y cinco. Estuve a punto de dar por finalizada mi tarea. Una tarea sin sentido. Como todas aquellas que Dios encomienda a los hombres. Me lo impidió una especie de chispazo que se produjo en mi mente. Una pregunta que hasta aquel instante no me había planteado: ¿Por qué sólo los dedos?

Desparramé mis hallazgos sobre una roca plana. Los observé uno por uno con mucha atención. Comprobé que mi sospecha era en verdad un acierto: Los dedos no había sido seccionados. Ninguno de ellos mostraba la particularidad de un corte limpio. Simplemente se desprendieron, desgajaron de sus respectivas manos, a causa de la incipiente descomposición y por efecto de la turbulencia delas aguas. No tomé, pues, el camino de regreso. Proseguí buscando en cada camalote. Costa adelante.

Transcurría ya el mes de abril. Por lo tanto, lo que llamamos temporada turística había terminado. En la Playa Brava de Punta del Este no se veía a un alma. Únicamente la resaca y los vegetales procedentes del Paraná se secaban al sol. Mas cuando yo llegué allí era, porque Dios quiso, fin de semana. En la Rambla, entre Gorlero y el Edificio Estrella, se hallaban más de cincuenta automóviles con matrícula argentina estacionados. Persona ninguna. Me dije que iba a poder trabajar tranquilo. Me puse a hacerlo.

Sin prisa y con meticulosidad comencé a revisar los camalotes ayudándome, como hasta entonces, con mi pedazo de tacuara. A las dos horas encontré la primera mano desprovista de dedos. La chica. Una hora más tarde la otra, la del hombre. Ambas parecían so pequeñas bolsas de pergamino, abultadas por los huesos

One day I realized that my face, all grizzled and darkly-circled under my eyes, must look like that of a madman. People flailing away at vermin on all the beach at El Este were giving me odd looks and shying away from me. I didn't care what they thought, though I myself was beginning to wonder if I hadn't in fact lost my mind. My reasoning, however, seemed intact. And if I were crazy, as I told myself, I couldn't even speculate on whether I actually was or not. This had a calming effect. I recalled Descartes and imagined that he too, having hit after much conjecture on his famous ontological definition, must have, like myself, felt reassured. I laughed at myself and at Descartes.

I discovered fingers in Solymar, Mar de Plata and Punta Colorada. Their number reached ten in Solana del Mar. That is, five and five. My task, as I saw it, was almost complete. A senseless task: like all those delegated by God to man. A question then arose which hadn't come up until that moment: Why only fingers?

I spread my finds on a flat rock and examined them carefully, one by one. It confirmed what I had suspected: The fingers had not been chopped off in sections. None showed any sign of a clean cut. They had simply dropped off, broken away from their respective hands due to gradual disintegration and the turbulent waters. Thus I didn't head homeward. But kept looking inside every water-hyacinth up and down the coast.

It was April by now. Our so-called tourist season had come to an end. Not a soul to be seen at Brava Beach in Punta del Este. Only the tide and vegetation from the Paraná drying in the sun. But on the day of my arrival it was, as God foreordained, a weekend. Over fifty automobiles with Argentine license plates were parked on the Rambla between Calle Gorlero and the Estrella building. Not a single person. I'd be able to work in peace, I told myself, and proceeded to do so.

Unhurried, I meticulously began combing through the water-hyacinths, aided as before by my bamboo pole. After two hours, I found the first hand, stripped of its fingers: the girl's. An hour later, the other, that of the man. Both hands looked like parchment bags, enlarged by the metacarpal bones contained inside. The extremities,

metacarpianos que contenían. Las extremidades que alguna vez se unieron a las muñecas mostraban la marca inconfundible de un tajo limpio, exprofeso, casi quirúrgico. Sin conciencia de ello me eché a llorar. No en silencio como tal vez hubiese preferido, sino como un chiquilín, dejando que mis entrecortados gemidos vibraran en el aire salobre y con olor a mar.

Después que la congoja quiso abandonarme, saqué del bolsillo todo mi botín. Con la palma de mi mano alisé un espacio en la arena. Sobre él reconstruí las dos manos, entrelazando los dedos de una con los de la otra. Finalmente introduje en cada anular su correspondiente anillo. Encima de aquella piel negruzca, el oro refulgía al igual que dos pequeñas llamas, rescoldo de una hoguera que hubiese carbonizado las dos manos, las cuales parecían estrecharse en un adiós.

Volví a llorar. Pero esta vez mis gemidos no se perdieron entre el rumor del mar, sino que obtuvieron eco de voces a mis espaldas. Me di vuelta asustado. Desde la baranda de la rambla más de cien personas me observaban y gritaban. Me alcé del suelo y me alejé caminando con lentitud por la orilla del agua. No corrí, mas es verdad que en cierto modo huía. Antes de perder de vista aquel lugar, pude observar a la gente amontonándose en torno a las manos que dejé descansando allí.

Regresado a mi rancho de Ramírez me hallé un atardecer sentado entre los tamarizes, observando como de entre los ya resecos y despreciados camalotes surgían de a miles pequeñas mariposas blancas. Perforaban los pequeños capullos de baba e iniciaban primero un vuelo rasante, entreverándose, buscándose afanosamente entre sí. Después permanecían por un rato pegadas de a dos, sobre la arena, sexo contra sexo. Luego que la hembra desovaba en las pequeñas grietas de la arena, creyendo asegurar en aquel medio hostil el futuro de la especie, recomensar un proceso que, como tantos otros, resultaría estéril por desarraigo, iniciaban un torpe vuelo que las estrellaba en un suicidio colectivo contra las lámparas de mercurio de la rambla. Aquel espectáculo me hizo pensar en si mi demente aventura de casi dos meses, no habría constituido, al fin y al cabo, una especie de metamorfosis a la inversa, si partiendo de la mariposa no habría yo llegado a la mismísima baba del gusano.

once joined to their wrists, revealed the unmistakable mark of a clean, deliberate incision. Involuntarily, I burst into tears. Not silently as I would have preferred, but like a little child, allowing my broken sobs to vibrate in the briny, sea-scented air.

With anguish spent, I took all the booty from my pocket, and with the palm of my hand, leveled a clearing on the sand. And on it, reconstructed the two hands, linking the fingers of one with those of the other. Finally I inserted each finger into its corresponding ring. The gold flashed on that darkened skin like two small flames, blazing embers charring the two hands, which seemed joined in a parting handshake.

Again I began to weep. But this time, my sobs didn't fade away into the murmuring sea, but resounded in noises in back of me. I turned around. Over one hundred people were standing at the railing on the promenade looking at me and shouting. I rose from the ground and slowly walked off along the shore. Not running, though, in a way, actually fleeing. Before that spot vanished from sight, I noticed clusters of people milling around the hands that I'd left resting there.

One afternoon, back in Ramírez, I sat amongst the tamarisks, watching hordes of little white butterflies flutter forth from the shriveled water-hyacinths cast ashore. The creatures broke through the sticky little buds and began flying, skimming the ground at first, intermingling, avidly searching amongst themselves. Then they paired off, clinging to each other above the sand, one sex cleaving to the opposite. The female deposited her eggs in the sandy little crevices, believing that thus she would perpetuate the future of the species in that hostile environment, recommencing a process which, like many others, would ultimately prove sterile, due to the uprooting. And then the creatures wended upward in clumsy flight, only to crash in a collective suicide against the mercury lights on the promenade. That spectacle made me wonder if my crazy adventure of almost two months had not become, in the end, a sort of metamorphosis in reverse—if having been a butterfly I had not turned into larval spittle.

Lo que sucedió después de mi peregrinación hacia el Este lo supe porque salió impreso en todos los diarios de Montevideo: Varios ciudadanos argentinos, con propiedades en la península, denunciaron que un hombre de aspecto insano había abandonado restos humanos en la Playa Brava de Punta del Este. Ningún diario hizo referencia a los dos anillos de oro.

No me importó. Ni una cosa ni la otra. Mi mente ya no estaba en aquel asunto. Precisamente ese día me dio por recordar a mi hijo y a su mujer. Hace ya mucho tiempo que se fueron y todavía no he recibido ninguna noticia de ellos.

What happened following my pilgrimage to El Este, I learned from all the Montevideo newspapers. Several Argentines with property on the peninsula reported an insane looking man discarding human remains on Brava Beach at Punta del Este. In no newspaper was there was any mention of two gold rings.

I didn't care, about either item. My mind was no longer occupied with that subject. It was precisely on that day that I happened to remember my son and his wife. They've been gone a long time, and I haven't had any news of them yet.

EPILOGUE
Margaret Sayers Peden

What a novel idea. (Should I say, What a short story idea?) A collection shaped by translators. All books that make their way into English from a different language are necessarily "shaped," like it or not, by the writers who effect their passage from one tongue to another. These stories, however, give the distinguished translators gathered here an opportunity to reveal personal choices, allow us insights into the kinds of literature that intrigue and please them, the pages that challenge and tease them, as well as brief glimpses of their philosophical approaches to their craft.

Who would have expected Rick Francis to choose the delightful, but far from stylistically radical, Reyes tale, when we know him best for having taken on the intricate and convoluted creations of Severo Sarduy and Julián Ríos? Contrast that departure to Suzanne Jill Levine's ultimately logical choice of a piece by Silvina Ocampo, given that Ocampo "makes her laugh." What would we expect from Levine but a writer who resonates with the wit and inventive sense of humor evidenced in her classic translations of Manuel Puig and Guillermo Cabrera Infante? And is it not appropriate that Donald Yates, the earliest of Borges's translators, should contribute a mystery from the author of "The Man Who Stole from Borges?" One would like to know even more about how these authors and translators found one another, what the reasons that these specific stories now exist in English while others from the same writers wait in a book or on a desk to spark interest from someone who will give them life in a language not their own.

How does a text make that voyage to a new life? Apparently by hook and by crook. These translators' comments prove that there is no "correct" or uniform approach to the way a translator performs his or her craft (and I shall return to the question of that word "perform"). Several very experienced translators tell us that they do not feel the need or desire to communicate with the original author. Alberto Manguel, for example, says that "the less you know about a writer, the better." And Hardie St. Martin writes, "I need no relationship with the prose writer to come up with a decent

321

translation," though he adds that "it can sometimes make it easier for me if I follow his work closely." Edith Grossman, in contrast, believes that "it is very helpful to consult with the author," and the doyenne of U.S. translators (senior in prestige and accomplishment, not age!), Helen Lane, even divides her perception of her work into "early" and "late" periods based on when she did and did not consult the original author.

But while there is no cookie-cutter pattern for rolling out a translator, any more than there is uniformity among the writing habits of biographers or poets or novelists, despite the fact that some translators work in the morning, some in the evening, some start blind, some assiduously study the text before beginning, some write their own prose or poetry and others write translations only, perhaps we can venture one area of accord. Surely all of us feel an empathy for Dick Gerdes's statement that by contributing his translation of a story by Ana María Schúa, he will enable "wider audiences to discover a new generation of 'exhilarating writers from Latin America.'" While Gerdes is referring to showcasing the work of younger and lesser known writers from Latin America, that general motivation is likely what drives all translators: the pleasure of acting as a conduit between cultures; the satisfaction of making significant literature available to readers unable to read it in its original form.

A significant amount of attention has been paid recently to what constitutes a translation, and symposia sponsored by national and international translation associations, investigation at respected translation centers, the papers and books of distinguished scholars, are producing an imposing body of research on the subject. (As an example, we find Ilan Stavans's magnificent introductory essay, so convincingly placing translation in Mexico in its historical context, as well as illustrating the timeless need to erase barriers of language if we are to understand our heritage.) But far less has been written on the subject of the writers who produce translations. Where are the biographies of world class translators like Ralph Mannheim? Or, closer to home, the scholarly monographs on the writing of a Gregory Rabassa or Helen Lane?

To some degree that absence can be attributed to the general disregard in which translation is held. Only last week a poet friend of mine reported that he had about had his fill of translating

Verlaine and was going back to "real" writing. Aza Zatz addresses that issue directly in his comment stating that he suffers from "a creativity-gene defect" that "disabled" him from writing his "own stuff." I don't know how serious Zatz may have been (I know he has a good sense of humor), but would ask him to check the table of contents of any recent book review and weigh the ratio of "creative" writing to that of all other prose genres. In truth of fact, translators are a hybrid breed, the last generalists—linguists, critics, scholars, cryptographers, sociologists, historians, and, yes, creative writers.

And one thing more. Translators are performers. One reason that translation may be difficult to assess is that it spills over from writing into interpretation. When Olivier played Hamlet, it was taken for granted that his performance would be judged on its own merits. That appraisal did not diminish Shakespeare's play; it merely meant that reviewers were evaluating Olivier's individual translation-to-the-stage of an established text. So, too, the translators who offer us their interpretation of the stories of so many talented and varied authors.

Hats off to a first-rate performance!

CURBSTONE PRESS, INC.

is a non-profit publishing house dedicated to literature that reflects a commitment to social change, with an emphasis on contemporary writing from Latin America and Latino communities in the United States. Curbstone presents writers who give voice to the unheard in a language that goes beyond denunciation to celebrate, honor and teach. Curbstone builds bridges between its writers and the public - from inner-city to rural areas, colleges to community centers, children to adults. Curbstone seeks out the highest aesthetic expression of the dedication to human rights and intercultural understanding: poetry, testimonies, novels, stories, children's books.

This mission requires more than just producing books. It requires ensuring that as many people as possible know about these books and read them. To achieve this, a large portion of Curbstone's schedule is dedicated to arranging tours and programs for its authors, working with public school and university teachers to enrich curricula, reaching out to underserved audiences by donating books and conducting readings and community programs, and promoting discussion in the media. It is only through these combined efforts that literature can truly make a difference.

Curbstone Press, like all non-profit presses, depends on the support of individuals, foundations, and government agencies to bring you, the reader, works of literary merit and social significance which might not find a place in profit-driven publishing channels, and to bring the authors and their literature into communities across the country. Our sincere thanks to the many individuals who support this endeavor and to the following organizations, foundations and government agencies: Josef & Anni Albers Foundation, Connecticut Commission on the Arts, Connecticut Arts Endowment Fund, Connecticut Humanities Council, Lawson Valentine Foundation, LEF Foundation, Lila Wallace-Reader's Digest Fund, Andrew W. Mellon Foundation, National Endowment for the Arts, the Open Society Institute, Puffin Foundation, Samuel Rubin Foundation and the Witter Bynner Foundation for Poetry.

Please support Curbstone's efforts to present the diverse voices and views that make our culture richer. Tax-deductible donations can be made by check or credit card to Curbstone Press, 321 Jackson Street, Willimantic, CT 06226, ph: (860) 423-5110, fax: (860) 423-9242.